I0763424

WAR AND COLD WAR

A HISTORICAL NOVEL BY

JACK R. WILLIAMS

2nd Printing

ISBN: 978-1-60414-947-0

For information, please contact
Fideli Publishing, Inc.:
info@fidelipublishing.com

www.FideliPublishing.com

TABLE OF CONTENTS

PART 4

THEORY OF WAR

This book follows the Lees, a military family group, and those in the Lee orbit as they made their way through the wars and upheavals of the 20th century. I am Charlie Chiavo, pulled into that orbit by friendship and later by marriage to Charlotte Lee. I was an Army pilot warrior from 1941 through 1945, the WWII period. Jackson Lee, her younger brother, was only 17 years old at war's end so he was not a veteran. This caused considerable enmity between Jackson and me. I was a veteran with many adventures and he was only a 'wannabe' hero. Jackson joined the Navy in 1947 and was an air crew member for almost five years.

Then it happened! The Soviets shot down an unarmed American Navy four-engined aircraft in 1950. All ten-man of the crew perished. The Soviets had continued nipping at the ankles of the West from the end of WWII to this shoot-down. This was a brazen challenge. During this post-war time, the Russians had occupied Eastern Europe and forced numerous other countries into the Soviet sphere. They were complicit in ending the Chinese Civil War whose government remains Communist to this day, in the Korean Civil War that has yet to be resolved, in the Vietnam War and in numerous lesser wars. They had imposed the Berlin blockade that was countered with the Berlin Airlift. The shoot-down sent a message to America and the world, one of military confrontation.

By this time, Jackson Lee had reached the age of 17. He joined the Navy and was a crewman on a PB4Y2, the same airplane type as the plane that had been shot down. Prior to that incidence, his squadron patrolled the East Coast from Greenland, Labrador, and Iceland to Cuba and Porto Rico. Because of the incident, his squadron was reassigned to the Mahgreb or North Africa. His squadron's aircraft were then armed and patrolled across North Africa, the Middle East, Turkey, and Europe.

In the next dozen years, the Soviets shot down numerous aircraft — mostly reconnaissance craft — that usually were unarmed and flying over international waters. Their crews and often their innocent passengers were the victims. This and other recon-flights were largely responsible for keeping the U.S. informed and preventing wars based on false or misinterpreted information.

A truncated description of the Theory of War might help to explain some of the horrendous conflicts of that period.

War is a conflict between two or more entities, usually sovereign states for continental armies such as Germany according to Clausewitz's book, *On War*. Throughout history there was little constraint on the weapons used, until the introduction of Atomic weapons by the Americans at the end of World War II. Whatever man could conceive and implement was reluctantly tolerated or accepted up to that point. These were all bizarre experiments. If the objective was not achieved, the experiment — such as a gas attack — was abandoned or replaced.

After 1945, Weapons of Mass Destruction (WMD) were defined. WMDs included atomic weapons as used on Japan, all-out war carpet bombing as applied to Europe in WWII, concentrated incendiary bombings as used on Japan's thatched construction and both gas and biological warfare, though the last two have had limited tactical success. Great efforts were made by the United Nations and elsewhere to outlaw these WMDs, but these efforts met with little success.

At the height of the Cold War, there were more than 40,000 atomic weapons in America's inventory. A modern American bomber typically holds four bombs containing one million tons of TNT-equivalent explosive power each. Thus, one Cold War bomb is greater by a factor of 50 times than the bomb dropped on Hiroshima. Several nations now have these weapons in quantity, and the ballistic missiles to deliver them. Each missile has been proven to deliver multiple hydrogen warheads (Multiple Independently-targetable Re-entry Vehicles (MIRV).) With sufficient accuracy, such a missile could deliver even conventional warheads effectively and a GPS-targeted cruise missile or drone could do the same. Warheads became larger and more precise.

Conventional wars continue to occur, but they now exist under a nuclear umbrella and the retaliatory threat of other weapons, either conventional or WMD. Because of this, there is a constraint on the weapons used. The general effect of nuclear war on society is still unknown but it is expected by many to be mankind's Armageddon.

Fundamentally, conventional state wars such as WWII have the objective of forcing one state to bend to the will of the opposing state. In the end, the objective is manifested as unconditional surrender as was recognized by Japan and Germany at the end of World War II. A lesser conclusion is a stalemate where both belligerent parties negotiate a tolerable peace, as happened with the Korean War.

General wars are fought with little restraint on weapons and practices. The states throw it all in until their resources — men and equipment — are exhausted. The social system often pits soldiers with little enthusiasm against those with courage and wild passions. One intuitively knows that motivated soldiers will win battles and usually prevail even against relative larger numbers. Large military material and equipment advantages also favor an army, as seen with the Americans in WWII.

Military victories are often achieved with the above considerations. Yet, victories are dependent on drama in the final stages of battle. Those that control the drama are at a great advantage over the slogging grunt soldiers. Some in the Japanese War Cabinet favored a continuation of the war, even after the nation had been brought to the edge of starvation and the first Atomic bomb had been dropped. The Emperor intervened after the second atomic bomb was used on Nagasaki. These events provided the necessary drama according to the recent book by Herbert Bix, *Hirohito and the Making of Modern Japan*. The devastation from these bombs appeared to justify surrender to both participants, the vanquished and the victors.

Contrary to one's dedication to the nation concept, civil wars are prevalent where an entity breaks apart into two or more splinters. These wars often cause great bloodshed in the civilian population. Eventually, one side prevails, as in the American Civil War.

The splintered group often reverts to a pirate, guerilla or a terrorist war as seen in present-day Syria, South Sudan, Somalia and numerous others. The disintegration into terrorism is a form of anarchy. The one unifying objective for terrorists is to cause the population to lose faith in the government or elite control group. Then, each individual or small group feels compelled to make a mark by carrying on poorly coordinated attacks on mankind.

The group or government under attack appears impotent and unable to perform the necessary functions of the state. The participants, bomb-makers or shooters in this endeavor, believe the government, being impotent, will fall and a new one will be established. This is often a utopian government that means well but is fatally flawed. Finally, anarchy is reached. Many call this anarchy a Failed State. An example is Somalia on the Horn of Africa and many more countries racked by terror, particularly in Africa and the Middle East.

Wars have a consistency, as defined above, ranging from the use of atomic weapons to anarchy. WMDs currently invoke a new division of warfare. These weapons create forbidden zones, and the costs of warfare using nuclear and WMD weapons in these zones are unimaginable.

No-fly and other such zones are often advocated to limit the destruction potentially caused by nuclear weapons, yet the soldiers, aircraft and refugees keep coming. Flight-Free zones are only effective after achieving decisive air superiority. It is but a false hope that participants can agree to Queensbury rules of conduct when waging wars.

Another such false hope is the constriction against harming civilians. For instance, the Western nations in WWII agreed that carpet-bombing was a way to destroy war production *and* the workers. It was soon recognized that no distinction could be enforced between military and non-military workers. Such bombing made a shambles of Europe, invalidating the concept of free zones in warfare.

The conditions after WWII were dubbed the "Cold War." That is, the Soviet Union and her subsidiaries paired off against America and her allies, forming a bipolar world that lasted five decades. Multiple nations joined each side in a consortium expected to last for a long time. There was seldom a direct confrontation but many hostile situations and proxy wars were fought, including Korea and Vietnam. It is reasonable to expect a future emulating the Cold War, as nations continue to engage in similar hostile divisions.

Urban warfare is noted for its ruthlessness and high civilian casualty rates. Rugged terrain with caves and tunnels almost always favor the defense. Combatants often use civilians as shields. The defending enemy must be rooted out, room by room. The rules of engagement work against the friendly troops since they often require visual identification, etc., which makes them excessively vulnerable.

America and Britain developed a counter to these vulnerabilities in WWII — the carpet bomb. The Rules of Engagement restricted bombing to military targets, however, that was indecisive. When carpet-bombing was instituted, this removed the restrictions and allowed the allies to massively bomb Germany and Japan and huge numbers of civilians perished.

Another similar project during WWII was to test the limits of incendiary bombs. For this, a large number of B-29 bombers were used in a single raid on Tokyo. A giant firestorm resulted from these incendiary bombs. Japanese housing, typically made of wood, was vulnerable. Use of these bombs killed 100,000 people in one raid on Tokyo, mostly civilians. This rivaled the atomic bombs as people-killers. Again, it was a war against civilians. These did, however, help to provide the drama that brought the war to an end.

After an admixture of theory and history above, the world prior to WWI and WWII was essentially divided into empires whereby several European nations developed notions of control, economics and exploitation. Clausewitz developed the issues of the continental army or those resident and operating on large land masses such as Germany, Russia and France. He recognized the prohibitive issues facing the army when it reached the sea. An alternative was the Navy. A unique set of issues then faced the Naval force, as developed by Admiral Mahan in *The Influence of Sea Power upon History*. The naval forces depend on total national commitment, just as did Clausewitz's continental army. During WWII, surface ships and submarines restricted Japanese shipping until the country's food supply approached starvation level, yielding to maritime and naval dictates. The German army could stand on the shore of France and see the British Army but an invasion was not to be. Fear of the German Navy and Mahan's naval dictates prevented it. Clausewitz developed theories defining continental army warfare while Mahan and British Admiral John Fisher did similarly for naval warfare.

British imperialists were the ones that successfully understood and developed the concept of empire consisting of both a vast continental army and a powerful Navy. The Royal Navy even set up coaling stations across the world as the fuel supply for the British Navy. Or, Britain could cut off fuel supplies to others in times of crisis, thereby controlling the seas. The sun never set on this empire, they boasted, and it ruled the world for close to five centuries. Although Clausewitz and Mahan did not invent the concept of empire, they explained it and sold it, allowing the British to rule India through deals with its colonies and dominions while draining only 100,000 British functionaries to the sub-continent to rule 300,000,000 subjects for hundreds of years. Notions of empire drove the rulers of the world. Even the Americans succumbed to this at the turn of the 19th century as they leapt into the race for the Pacific and Atlantic islands. Is there any wander that these two theorists were feted on the Kaiser's yacht, that of the Russian Czar and the British fleet? Admiral Mahan was chosen to lead the Naval Academy where his theories could be aggressively propagated. America profited from these imperial adventures in Hawaii, the Philippines, the Panama Canal and islands around the globe. The world was set up and orchestrated by treaties and empire ambitions. Clausewitz and Mahan made the world ready for WWI and WWII.

At the turn of the century, battleships were considered the rulers of the seas and guarantors of the empires. These ships, however, were prohibitively expensive to build and to operate. Only a few nations could afford them, mostly Britain, Japan, Germany and America. Japan attacked the battleships in Pearl Harbor. However, this was a mistake on many levels. The most serious, was in failing to recognize that aircraft now ruled the world. Further, the power at sea had shifted to aircraft carriers. We could show battleships but we fought WWII with aircraft and aircraft carriers augmented with submarines.

The world had pivoted, had turned a corner in conventional armaments. Aircraft carriers with their advanced airplanes became the primary fighting ships or capital ships of the Navy. They remain to this day the most complex and powerful machines in the world.

Intelligence is a central function of the armed services. They develop and deploy their own satellites, aircraft and other resources. The military must continually develop more and more sophisticated systems and incorporate them into the aircraft vehicles. All vehicles are candidates for this procedure.

One of the most important missions of intelligence is to intercept and break other countries' codes.

General Eisenhower called the intelligence services "decisive" in WWII. Although that might be an exaggeration, it does emphasize the importance of intelligence. These operations are a critical function that must be continuously attended to by all combatants. It is a fundamental requirement of all who aspire to statehood. The requirement is also no less binding for the infrequent periods of peace. Both military and civilian segments must continually monitor their environment and be cognizant of potential threats and their own vulnerabilities.

As an example of war planning and tactics, in WWII the Navy chose an island-hopping strategy that employed amphibious techniques. Specialized landing craft and carriers were developed to attack from the sea, supported by our intelligence operations. This tactic was what won the war in the Pacific.

We Americans read the Japanese naval codes. The Japanese set up ambushes and then coordinated their ship movements to implement them. The Americans could thus direct their fleets to positions for ambushing the Japanese ambushes. This yielded many victories for the Americans such as the Battle of the Coral Sea.

The last great Japanese battle was that of Midway, in July 1942, one month after the Coral Sea Battle and only seven months after Pearl Harbor. Again, the Americans followed the preparations for an attack and knew a great deal about the Japanese planning for the attack. The Japanese were repulsed. The Americans then had the initiative for the rest of the Japanese war. The Battle of Midway was the turning point of the war. Intelligence did the trick. It converted a losing to a winning war for the Allies. The rest of the war was a slaughterhouse for the Imperial forces, not to mention the suffering of the American forces. Yet, the Japanese forces did not suspect their codes nor their communication methods had been compromised. They never implemented a coordinated intelligence defense.

Once more, the gathering and analysis of intelligence must be continuous and in-depth. There must also be research to support this requirement. Active and strenuous defenses to protect your own methods must be implemented.

This war theory gives a phenomenally condensed universe for such a complex subject; but you get the general idea.

INTRODUCTION

In a brief synopsis, this story surveys a broad horizon of modern warfare as it develops a theory of war and chronicles examples from the last century. It follows Clausewitz's development in his book on continental armies and Mahan similarly on naval forces. It combines the army and navy theories and implementation of wars that killed more than 70 million people in the last century and put to risk hundreds of millions more from nuclear arms. This tale brings together the theories and examples of periodic wars. It develops military intelligence gathering as a continuum requirement and an imperative for nations. Both theorists here advocated the development of empires through military actions and these notions drove world political divisions for centuries.

By the beginning of WWII, battleships had been supplanted by aircraft and aircraft carriers. We paraded battleships but we fought with aircraft and carriers. The characters here are aviators in love with flight, in the flights of big birds, in airplanes, in drones, in space flight and in all those vehicles used for electronic intelligence. I am Charlie Chiavo, an Army Air Corps pilot. The service was later renamed as the Air Force.

Jackson was five years younger than me so he did not participate in WWII. Both protagonists here became intelligence officers and flyers. I participated in many of the Wars and the Cold War. I was a veteran throughout WWII while Jackson was not old enough to join the service.

A metaphor is drawn here with the Rime of the Ancient Mariner. The Mariner and Jackson both participated in disasters that left only a single survivor in each case. This lead to curses, magic spells, gambling for souls and zombie dice rolls that appear as the main character sinks into madness. This follows Jackson's over-flight into China as a crewman. War here is addressed across a wide horizon but it is finally winnowed down to Jackson, a single character, a mad man in a mad world.

The Ancient Mariner was part of a large crew as his ship sailed from England down through the South Atlantic and around Cape Horn. This is the southernmost headland of the Tierra del Fuego archipelago of southern Chile. The ice and extreme conditions around the cape caused dire circumstances. The Mariner killed a trailing albatross and the crew blamed the Mariner as having put a curse on them all. Zombie Woman, that some called Zombie Death, had won the curse playing dice. They hung an albatross around the Mariner's neck as part of the curse. Soon, all the crew died except the Mariner. The Mariner thought the crew watched him with a glassy eye. By mysterious happenings, the ship returned to its home port but by this time the Mariner had gone completely mad. He spent his time wandering from place to place in his home port telling anyone who would listen of his crazed voyage and his cursed situation.

The Rime is a long poem decrying the Mariner's fate. It recounts the bizarre story and the crazed actions that had befallen the Mariner.

The pitiful situation suggests an apt metaphor with Jackson's cold war. Both Jackson and the Mariner are faced with perilous voyages, both are cursed by big birds and mysterious fates befall them. Jackson is a lone survivor facing the crazed situation and narrative.

Of course, the details of the situations are different. The modern curse is greatly different from that of the Mariner's wooden ships and canvas sails. The ships and sails give way here to aircraft sweeping into the target area seeking existential information.

The inter-war period during the '20s and '30s saw jockeying back and forth diplomatically and the development of diabolical arms. Mobile warfare was developed and led to awesome military performances dependent on the machine gun, artillery, aircraft, tanks and amphibious vehicles. These mechanisms incorporated the miracles of engines, electricity and electronics including radar and other marvels.

WWI did not end with a definitive conclusion — as negotiation at the end of WWI. This allowed the leaders to lay down their arms and walk away — it set the pot to boil and 23 years later we were fighting WWII. This was a hot shooting war waged from 1941–1945, causing over 70 million deaths. This was the greatest and most consequential event in human history thus far. America called fifteen million people to the armed service during WWII.

The Cold War, following WWII, was a completely different animal — it was contained. During this time, many nations built and maintained large stockpiles of nuclear weapons and had the ability to deliver them at a moment's notice. This provided a nuclear umbrella under which conventional wars could be, and were, fought — including Korea and Vietnam. Armageddon was avoided but not by much. History as a subject connects these events and the milieu that defines them.

The Lee family lived in Larchmont, New York after moving there when Jackson was 15 years old. His father was appointed as Argentina Ambassador. That was the luck of the draw. He had been offered the job by Franklin Roosevelt after Roosevelt's first choice had refused it. His first choice considered it a backwater post to a backward country. It was beneath him. The name of James Lee lacked prominence in the Democratic Party but he had worked on Roosevelt's election campaign. This was sufficient to get him to be known at a relatively low level. He was enthusiastic over the appointment and he proved to be completely loyal to Roosevelt and to the Democratic Party.

James Lee, Jackson's father, moved to Buenos Aires with his daughter, Charlotte, and Jackson's mother. Jackson and his brother remained In Larchmont and his father kept the Larchmont house, which was central to their lifestyles. After all, his mother and Charlotte were more or less free to move from one house to the other, depending on their moods. A housekeeper kept the boys on the straight and narrow. It all worked out.

The choice of what country they were destined to live in was more or less random; they developed strong roots to the Bruno family and to all things Italian. Bianca Bruno grew close to Charlotte and they both got degrees from Colombia University. They took their time in working at this but they both eventually graduated.

This close relationship lasted for all their lives although it was pure chance that they became loyal to Argentina and to Italy from which the Bruno's owed allegiance. The Bruno's were immigrants from Italy that was now one generation removed.

Jackson visited Argentina only once or twice but preferred the freedom the Larchmont house provided. His sailboat gave him great pleasure and it also attracted many friends while he was in high school. He would have graduated from high school in 1943 but the state changed from an 11-grade requirement to 12 grades. This added a year to his school. As much as he tried, he could not get a path to avoid the extra year although he tried. Even his father tried but to no avail. He always thought his father did not try with enough conviction but what could he do? Jackson served his time, so to speak, and graduated in 1947 when he was 17 years old.

"Son," his father said. "I did my best."

Jackson also used the boat when he was in the service when he could get enough time. He was stationed in the Washington area and his crew flew out from there so he kept his boat in a marina in that area. He could trailer the boat but It was too big to be easily moved from Washington to New York. He was also able to use the boat after the service while he was in college and even later.

During this time when the Cold War was at its height, the American Strategic Air Command (SAC) continuously flew nuclear bombs that would be launched in response to any Soviet attack. B-52 and B-47 aircraft patrolled for Soviet threats 24 hours a day, and could respond to a nuclear strike with at least 12 bombers within 10 minutes. Each bomb these planes carried was the equivalent of a megaton — one million tons — of TNT.

These efforts were denoted as project Chrome Dome. This resulted in a nuclear standoff, and lasted from 1960 until 1968. Numerous crashes and nuclear accidents coincided with pressure from the Allies that broke up these deployments. Even so, similar missions were implemented until SAC was disbanded in 1992. Meanwhile, the Air Force faced enormous risks of nuclear war from both assigned missions and accidents within the program.

This book chronicles the story about me, Charlie Chiavo, and Jackson Lee. I am Charlie Chiavo, the chronicler of this story while Jackson Lee is the metaphorical Mariner. I was 17 years old at war start in 1941, while Jackson Lee was 12 years old or 6 years younger. The age difference between him and I brought about a supreme rivalry. Jackson was hypersensitive about it. He was always jealous that I was a veteran of WWII and he was not.

Jackson spent several years as an air crewman in the Intel Wars. He was driven to get out of the service when his time expired and finish college. He completed his term In the Navy in 1951 after about five years. He had worked as a technologist in several Cold War locations.

During the Korean War, his term ended and he got out of the Navy. He then entered a university and got an engineering degree. He opened opportunities for himself by joining the ROTC, the Reserve Officer's Training Corps. He then became a flyer, traveled with the military and worked in the defense industry as his career unfolded.

During the time of the Cold War, America made reconnaissance flights on the edges of dangerous locations. In this, the intercept aircraft usually flew just outside the edge of international waters. That is usually about 12 miles offshore but is determined by treaties. It was often 3 miles at that time. The higher an Interceptor flies, the better it is since microwave propagation is line-of-sight or constricted by mountains and the earth's curvature. However, higher altitude exposes you and an alert defense system gets target practice or worse. These are edge-flights and are legal but not always wise.

These distance restrictions often require over-flights. The public is aware of these after the Soviets shot down the over-flight aircraft of Gary Powers. It is public knowledge that there are over-flights of Russia, China, Cuba and other hotspots. These over-flights were largely responsible for keeping the U.S. informed and preventing wars based on false or misinterpreted information.

Part of this story reflects personal experiences suggesting a memoir. The rest is true to history in the most part and recounts the story mostly with historical facts. The experiences here are usually true to historical details but the people are usually fictitious. In this sense, this story has the definitions of being part novel (or fiction) and part memoir (or personal participation) that follows the historical settings. I often call it a historical novel.

Thus, this book is often murky in trying to interpret events and put them into the proper slots. For instance, the story of the Flying Tigers in China is murky. This is true for events in the U.S., China, Southeast Asia and other countries. It is especially true for over-flights and other similar challenges to sovereignty.

Then the Soviets shot down an unarmed American Navy aircraft in 1950. This was a brazen challenge. During this time, the Russians had occupied Eastern Europe and forced numerous other countries into the Soviet sphere. They had implemented the Berlin blockade. The Allies countered the blockade with the 'Berlin Airlift' but that required heroic measures. The shoot-down sent a message to America and to the Soviets, one of military confrontation.

This was an important occurrence in Jackson's life because he would become directly involved or was to be a part of this military confrontation.

In the next dozen years, the Soviets shot down numerous aircraft — mostly reconnaissance craft — that usually were unarmed and flying over international waters. Their crews and often their innocent passengers were victims. This and other recon-flights were largely responsible for keeping the U.S. informed and preventing wars based on false or ambiguous information.

Jackson's aircrew experience in the Navy was from 1947 until the early 1950s. He then received a technical degree. Afterwards. He was a technologist in Taiwan and other Cold War locations until the Soviet's demise in 1991.

Jackson flew several edge-flights and at least one over-flight while he was in Taiwan. The over-flight proved to be disastrous for Jackson and the crew.

PART 1

CHAPTER 1

CHARLIE'S EARLY ATLANTIC WAR

I had many of the characteristics of Jackson. I had met him through Charlotte, his sister. A mutual friend had introduced us. She had a friend, Bianca Bruno. Charlotte, Bianca and I were of the same age group. They both were beautiful and had animated personalities. That made for a powerful attraction so I often found myself at their home visiting them. I guess I had spent enough time on Jackson's sailboat that I swaggered down the pier, as did he. Many people remarked about this. Although I did a lot of sailing then, I didn't do nearly as much as Jackson. I think it helped my poise but it could have been improved further.

It was a fiery hot day on Jones Beach in New York. I was posted in New York temporarily. The sands scorched the bottom of my feet. Even so, a slight breeze reminded me that I was in hot, summer weather. Sometimes we would go to a movie house and sit there because they had air conditioning where none were in homes. Here, the summer always weighted everyone down and slowed their movements. It called for a cool drink. I did not have one. The best I could do now was to trot along the beach as the waves exhausted themselves and periodically covered my feet.

That gave a wonderful relief. Splash! Splash! Splash! My feet splashed on. Each step reverberated through my body and shook my whole frame. My brain played with ideas and searched for simple mind-games to occupy it and keep it busy. Splash! I thought. I could visualize the surf splattering as my foot stepped on the sun-splashed shore. My brain clutched the idea. I played with each splash as an onomatopoeia, as a word mimicking the sound it makes. The word here is *splash*, an onomatopoeia describing my footsteps. It might also be *clutched* or make the implied sound of a transmission engaging. It is the sound of a sudden connection of a thought to the brain itself. These were but word games. My trot ran on while the mind games continued.

I saw Bianca on the beach and I sat down to talk with her. She was a hot, fun-loving Italian girl whose family had emigrated from Italy to Argentina.

Italian Bianca Bruno of Argentina

Once when we were at a small park near Larchmont, I asked Bianca a question that had been on my mind. By this time, Bianca had been in the U.S. for a long time and was in her second year at Columbia.

"Bianca, how did you get here?" I asked.

"It was simple enough," she answered. "I came here on a student's visa to attend Columbia."

I asked, "Did the submarine threat not bother you?"

"Sure it did. Our steamer hugged the coast pretty closely. The Germans don't waste torpedoes on small ships. It is a long way from Argentina to Germany for repairs and replenishment. The submarines seem to operate mostly down the coast of Africa and across the North Atlantic. All those make my chances along the American coast pretty good," she said.

"Anyway, I am here," Bianca said. "I am in the University. I have made friends with Charlotte and others. I am happy."

Sensing that she enjoyed the conversation, I asked her, "How do you compare life in the U.S. to Buenos Aires?"

"That's a difficult question," she declared. "First, the Latin social life is very different than the English-based way of doing things here. However, most of us are not really Latinos. We are Italians once removed. There is similarity, though. We are much more family oriented. You usually see us in a group like that in my school. That is because of these family ties. Americans tend to go around without that. Americans are looser in social ties. I have heard it said by several people that when you meet an American on the beach, for instance, after a few minutes you know their whole life story. Europeans and Argentines are not like that. You may know someone for a long time and still only know a part of them.

"In the end, the Americans tend to be English-oriented while we tend to be Italian-based. The Americans are freer in their outlooks and in their social activities while we are more restrained and even allow chaperones to dictate to us.

She declared, "I am not like that, though. I am free. I demand it. I consider myself to be a modern woman. If I return to Argentina, I wonder what my attitudes will be?"

She asked, "How do you think of me? Do I look like a modern woman to you?"

I thought about that. "Well, you do have all the characteristics of a modern woman but you are a work in progress. You are far more amenable in giving in than those flag-burners on campus here."

She said, "I do see a great similarity between Charlotte and me. I really like her. She is my model."

"Well," I said. "Age has a lot to do with how we feel about things. I went directly from high school to the army so there was a shock wave that went through my whole body."

As time went on, I missed my opportunity. On one of my lengthy trips, Bianca's affections moved elsewhere. She lost interest in me. Of course, I will never know what really happened and what conversations took place between Bianca and Charlotte.

A romance soon developed between Charlotte and me. Bianca had moved elsewhere romantically.

This had been a circuitous route for Bianca. At any rate, I thought that Charlotte was making a play for me. It must have been pretty obvious. I even arranged a short trip to Buenos Aries. I tried to hide the real reason. However, her father noted it too. Bianca noted it. And Charlotte noted it. I thought I was a cool customer but I must have been pretty naïve. At any rate, they all thought Charlotte was my girl after that. I was the only one that didn't seem to notice that. Even so, it was a wonderful trip and Buenos Aries was beautiful.

She remembered the discussions with her family in the late 1930s as they considered a school for her education. The family was moderately successful and had made a good name for themselves.

Roberto Bruno, her father, had been in the Argentine military. He had been offered a big bank job and he took it. This was in partial payment for his loyalty to Juan Peron, the general that rose through the political ranks from the Army to become the president of Argentina. He led a coup of military officers. He was elected three times from June 1946 to September 1955.

Roberto had worked in Peron's party before that. His role continued to increase until he was fairly well known by campaign workers. Most of Bianca's relatives and friends were from Italian immigrants. Most of the men's surnames were Italian, reflecting this.

Roberto was not just a worker in the party. He believed in Peron. He believed in the party. The war, or rather the aggressive stances in Europe and at sea, put Argentina on a wartime economy and the Bruno family had prospered. Beef was in worldwide demand as well as machine shop labor and other activities that were favorable to Roberto's income. It went beyond that, however. Roberto continued to grow politically. Even Peron knew his name and sensed his loyalty to the cause.

Eva Perón was a success and a powerful political figure by this time. She had ingratiated herself to the labor unions and also knew Roberto's name. This was a badge of honor in the political arena. Eva set much of the social patterns in the country. She was born in 1919, the same year as Bianca, and was a powerful influence in the country. She unfortunately died a painful death in 1952. She had become the second wife of President Perón.

She served as the First Lady of Argentina from 1946 until her death. She was born in a rural village. At the age of 15 in 1934, she moved to the nation's capital of Buenos Aires to pursue a career as a stage, radio, and film actress. She met Colonel Peron there in 1944 during a charity event. The two were married the following year. Juan Perón was elected President of Argentina in 1946 and remained so during the next 6 years, Eva Perón became powerful within the pro-Peronist trade unions and founded the nation's first large-scale female political party.

"It is beef," cried Eva. "The Allies want us. They need us. They are hungry all over the world and the answer is beef. We have it. They want it. We must make the most of this opportunity. As always, when there are foreign wars, this presents great opportunities for non-belligerents.

"Look at America!" she yelled. "World War One made America rich. They made steel for ships and canons. J. P. Morgan and Andrew Carnegie got rich and ruled the world. We can do the same with beef." The workers cheered her and waved their hats.

"We can do it!" she exclaimed. They all stamped their feet. The members of the Cattlemen's Cooperative showed their approval. She made hundreds of such speeches around the country. Eva had looked them in the eye and pressed their flesh. She soon was better known than Juan.

In fact, she became a threat to him. He had to decide to join her or oppose her. He chose the path of least resistance, which was to join her. They made a formidable pair.

Unfortunately, her reach was too ambitious. After her wartime successes and with a growing economy just after the war, she arranged a grand sweep through Europe. The one ambition was to meet the Queen of England and present herself as belonging on the same pedestal. At the last moment, the queen and the British snubbed her. There was no meeting. She had to return to Buenos Aires a scorned woman. The star was beyond her reach.

Argentines stewed that their quasi-queen should be snubbed in this manner. Who did that English queen think she was? After all, she was only a throwback to earlier times.

Charlie had sort of a flash-forward in the 1980s about the Falkland War. By this time, he was reeling off his career. It had come a long way from when he was a college student. It only makes sense to address the Falkland War as a flash-forward for him. After all, it only affected about 3,000 people that lived on the island and was really just a sideshow to history and only became a gripping story to those directly involved. Charlie's partnership had provided some financing during the war. That accounts for his being In England at that particular time.

Argentina became an international issue in 1982 during the Cold War. The Argentinians always held that the Falkland Islands belonged to Argentina. These are in the south Atlantic, only 950 miles from the capitol of Argentina or about 300 miles to the nearest point on the mainland. The distance from the Falklands to the southern tip of Cape Horn where Chile and Argentina meet is similar. A war erupted in the Falklands between the Argentine government in April 1982 and the British government. This was surprising since only about 3,000 people inhabited the islands. Argentina backed the sovereignty of the Islands while Britain represented the defunct empire. This was a serious matter, lasting about three months. Almost a thousand lives were lost. England won the conflict but the hostility remains there to this day. As said, Charlie was in London during this altercation. He was staying with English friends. They went to a pub. The British typically go as a family to the neighborhood pub in the early evening. The conversation in the pub was resentful for they thought the U.S. should pitch in with fighting ships, commerce haulers, electronic systems and other war material. All the families including children were very vocal in this.

"Don't worry," Charlie said. "The U.S. will come in before it is over." He had many opportunities to make this point before their dinners were cold. He had stubbornly held his ground on this until the evenings were over.

The British won the war. One imagines the U.S. provided war material and assistance but this was not publicized if they did. By this time, I was somewhere else so I didn't have to eat crow.

Returning to the story, in 1951, Eva Perón announced her candidacy for the office of Vice President of Argentina, However, opposition from the nation's military and bourgeoisie, coupled with her declining health, ultimately forced her to withdraw her candidacy. She was given a state funeral upon her death, although this is generally reserved for heads of state.

Eva Perón has become a part of international popular culture, most famously as the subject of the Broadway musical *Evita* in 1976. That is a diminutive for the name Eva. It is regarded by many as one of the best musicals ever presented on Broadway. Actually, the lack of dialog makes it a candidate for an opera, a folk opera.

Roberto Chiavo, Bianca's father, wanted his two children to be educated in the U.S.

The family talked a lot about Bianca getting into Columbia University; this would be after taking a ship to New York. Transport was still relatively safe from German submarines before 1940 or so. However, the threat was real enough for her family to talk about it, and worry.

"But, Dad," she pleaded, "I don't know anyone there so it will be so lonely."

"Lonely?" he responded. "Don't you know you will make friends there? Do you think Buenos Aires is the only place in the world?"

Meanwhile, in the late 1930s she took courses at the University of Buenos Aires, arguably the most prestigious university in Argentina. Finally, she left for New York in the spring of 1940 when wartime concerns were reaching a high plateau.

During this time, Charlotte's father had similarly worked for the election of Woodrow Wilson, the U.S. president from 1913 until 1921. Her father had shown a political bent and impressed others with his diplomatic ability and grasp. He had even authored a pamphlet explaining the WWI issues that impressed Wilson although her father was far to the right of Wilson. The pamphlet was used to good effect and many defensive Democrats used it to bolster their positions.

The president needed diplomatic representatives loyal to him. He reviewed her father in 1937 and thought Mr. Lee would be a good candidate. There was a lot of infighting by this time so the party was not as stable as Wilson wanted. His first two candidates to replace the ambassador to Argentina rebuffed Wilson, seeing that as a poor posting in a backward country. Mr. Lee was anxious to receive the posting. Wilson obliged him as the ambassador in 1937.

Charlotte moves to Argentina

Charlotte talked her father into letting her join him in Buenos Aires in 1939. She did so and remained there until the spring of 1940. Charlotte had met Bianca. They were both considering entering Columbia during this time. Both were headstrong young girls just passing from their teens. Charlotte loved the posting. Her brother, Jackson, was also in Buenos Aires but only for a short time. He was constrained by his youth and schooling requirements.

The girls became close friends. They both were aggressive for young ladies but Bianca was far more restrained due to the Italian and Latin cultures. They did, however, meet here and there including dance spots. Bianca paid what amounted to bribes for the chaperone that followed her around. Charlotte avoided this outrage. Her father tried to restrain her with positive counseling but that was whistling in the breeze. Charlotte was Charlotte and Bianca was Bianca.

They formed a bond that would stay with them as they both went to Columbia. They did this in the fall of 1940. Charlotte confided in her, "I'm so glad to be out from under my father's wing. I cannot stand much of that."

Bianca was less open, but there was no doubt that she felt the same way. Her restraints were tighter but from where she stood in Italian encumbrances, she suffered much more from her tighter restraints.

"You don't understand," Bianca said. "They think they have control of me but I can't handle their little tea parties. I want to let go and fly," she said. "I want to fly." She did a pretty good job of doing just that.

Italian immigration to Argentina began in earnest in the 19th century, just after Argentina won its independence from Spain. Argentine culture has significant connections to Italian culture in terms of language, customs and traditions. The principal causes for the large immigration were that Italy was enduring economic problems caused mainly by the unification of the Italian states into one nation at that time. The country was impoverished; unemployment was rampant. Further, some areas were overpopulated, and Italy was subject to significant political turmoil. Italians saw in Argentina a chance to build a brand new life for themselves.

The country's growth was significant with a change in population from 12 million in 1930 to 15.4 million in 1945. Italians began arriving in Argentina in great numbers from 1857 to 1940, totaling 44.9% of the entire immigrant population; more than from any other country.

To Charlotte, Buenos Aires was a playground as she frolicked from museum to museum, from restaurant to restaurant and other places that suited her. Even shows and opera were available. As the daughter of the American Ambassador, she was invited to all the official Argentine functions. Or, she was 'on the list' as they say.

Afternoon Refresher

"So, how do you characterize the Argentines?" Charlotte's father, the ambassador, asked as they lounged on the screened balcony with tall rum drinks. She was caught off-guard with this question and had to think about it for a while.

"I really like them," she said. "Of course, we are not talking about Hispanics here, but generally about Italian immigrants. This is opposed to talking of Latinos which are those of Spanish-speaking culture."

"Whoa," he said. "You are going deeper than I anticipated. So go ahead. What do you think of Italians, or of Italian-Argentines, if you will? I know you have thought about that since your mother and I sent you to Italy for a vacation a couple of years ago."

"Okay," she said. "I find the Italians are fun people. They live a relaxed life style. The get to work at 10 am or so and leave for lunch near 2 p.m. They go to a restaurant late, by 9 p.m. or later. They tend to eat from 10 p.m. to midnight.

"They take wine. They tell jokes. They laugh. They horse around. Even the language is fun. They are always in motion. Their arms are always flying while they talk with their hands. I love their families that are close. I wish I had been born an Italian.

"Now," she said. "Don't take me literally. I know they don't all drink wine into midnight. I just speak hyperbolically to emphasize my point."

The News

The news headlines from Europe kept the wires hot and were the continuing topic of conversation in the chic coffee shops on the main boulevards. Hitler's shenanigans were watched with great interest. In fact, there was a great deal of entertainment associated with the news. It was hard to tell the difference between serious concerns and entertainment.

Up until about 1939, Europe was in the 'phony war.' Hitler had been appointed Chancellor of Germany but these lesser titles did not express the actual status; this was corrected by 1940 or so after the annexation of Austria-Hungry and by Hitler and Stalin dividing Poland between themselves. By this time, all Germans were paying homage to their ultimate leader. They did so by swearing allegiance to him, by arm salutes, by shoulder patches and by all-consuming obeisance.

Even Japan continued to make moves in Asia after the rape of Nanking in 1937. The bombing of Pearl Harbor in December 1941 and consequent declarations of war caused that to be recognized as the war's start. On the other hand, the war actually started well before Pearl Harbor. There is no doubt, however, that the declarations of war caused death and violence to explode after Pearl Harbor.

Charlotte did minor tasks for the American embassy in Buenos Aires. She happened to be there in December 1939 when the pocket battleship, *Admiral Graf Spee*, met its fate. The world press could not get enough of this. Reporters and the general population hungered for glimpses of the drama. They wanted to witness a great event. Both flocked in from every direction. They would not be disappointed as such an event unfolded.

Germany had built a strong navy. Many people believed the role of large surface ships during the war would be as surface commerce raiders. The

Graf Spee was a class of miniature battle ships. The German Navy had built a number of these. The *Graf Spee* and her oiler support ship were dispatched to the South Atlantic as a raider before Pearl Harbor. She had been moderately successful by December, having sunk 9 commercial ships with cargo totaling about 50,000 tons. As a benchmark, the average prize for submarines in WWII was about 3,000 tons. When war was declared by Germany 11 December 1939, the *Graf Spee* was already at sea just outside the Buenos Aires estuary. Hitler immediately ordered the *Graf Spee* to attack all surface shipping. The British knew the *Graf Spee* was in the South Atlantic and had dispatched a hunter group of warships to find and engage her. The Battle of River Plate ensued.

The British fleet was heavily damaged during the battle and the *Graf Spee* experienced some damage, although light. The *Graph Spee* made port in Uruguay for repairs. International law at the time limited a fighting ship's stay to 24 hours at neutral ports. This was extended to 72 hours after British intelligence maneuvering. The intelligence crowd and the government people worked hard to convince the German Captain that a large British fleet waited outside the estuary to attack the partially crippled *Graf Spee* when she put to sea and the *Graf Spee* bought this story. The captain imagined this imagined fleet would have outgunned the *Graf Spee.*

Going into Montevideo was a mistake. The Uruguayans were neutral and tended to play by the book. The neighboring Argentines were much more favorable to the Germans. Many considered Argentina as more hostile to the Allies and favorable to Germany. This might have allowed more time for *Graf Spee* repairs and the sorting out of intelligence. The Uruguayans provided a little time relief but drove the ship away after 72 hours.

An estuary is a partially enclosed coastal body of brackish water with one or more rivers or streams flowing into it, and with a free connection to the open sea. They can have many different names, such as bays, harbors, lagoons, inlets, or sounds. Buenos Aries is on the south bank of the Plate River and is much further up-river than Montevideo, the capital on the north bank. The distance between the two is a little less than 100 miles or a three-hour ferry ride. Of course, buses also connect the two points but are slightly slower.

Charlotte, in the embassy, was privy to some of the information as the British jockeyed for position. She relayed some of this to Bianca so they each could follow the story. The world press also jockeyed for position. Some reporter estimated the crowd of 20,000 people gathered to watch the proceedings, a scuttling or a fight to the death.

Maneuvering by British intelligence operatives, by diplomats and further pressure applied by several governments orchestrated pressure on Uruguay to drive the ship to the ocean. An early return to sea had to be the least preferable option.

Both Charlotte and Bianca experienced the traffic jams in Montevideo as they all watched in wonderment. The ferries from Buenos Aires to Montevideo normally took 3 hours. They were now swamped by people headed to Montevideo, causing massive traffic jams of people. There was a carnival atmosphere. Those who made it lined the shore as the *Graph Spee* moved along the estuary. Based on faulty information, Captain Langsdorff, in communications and consultation with Berlin, scuttled his ship in the estuary where some of the superstructure remained above the surface. It became a tourist destination, similar to the USS Arizona in Pearl Harbor to commemorate her sinking. Ferry boats soon hauled visitors to the memorial constructed around the sunken superstructure. The Argentine memorial was mostly removed only decades later.

At about 09:00 p.m., the first scuttle charge went off. The next three hours were the perfect time for evening entertainment. The crowds were pleased.

The crew had distributed their ammunition explosives along the whole ship for scuttling. Boom! The first was a massive explosion, Parts of the ship, a huge plume of smoke and then a growing smoke cloud rose skyward. Then, other lesser explosives took place. The great ship settled in the shallow water of the estuary.

The captain committed suicide three days after the scuttling.

Only a skeleton crew scuttled her. About a thousand crewmen had been offloaded to the *Graph Spee's* tender or supply ship, *Altmark*. Those as well as a few other vessels took the crew aboard.

The carnival-like, playful atmosphere lasted for days. It never did totally disappear. Somewhat like Pearl Harbor, the tourists streamed to the site for decades to come.

The destruction of the *Graf Spee* was treated as a great triumph in Britain. It was the first real Allied success of the war. This was stated as the defeat of Poland and then the start of the 'phony war.' Hitler was predictably furious with Langsdorff's decision to destroy his own ship. The fate of the *Graf Spee* put the entire concept of commerce raiding by warships in doubt. New orders to the navy stated that, "The German warship and her crew are to fight with all their strength to the last shell; until they win or go down with their flag flying."

The two girls as well as the American Ambassador had witnessed the first surface ship battle of WWII. Many more were to come.

After WWII, Argentina had one of the largest economies in the world. She had one of the most stable economies and one of the largest growth rates.

Starting with Peron, they flirted with dictatorship and controlled economies. Somewhere, she lost the driving force of their economy. No longer could the romance of the Gauchos on the pampas hold their fondest dreams. The Gauchos on the pampas faded into history much as the American cowboys did on the western plains.

Eventually, only a few Argentines could afford their own private planes to haul teams of polo ponies all over the world for international matches. Alternatively, the best players in future decades hired themselves out to foreign teams as 'hired assassins' or 'gunslingers', again reminiscent of the western plains. Nevertheless, the Argentina love affair with polo ponies and horse flesh continued unabated.

Charlie of the Bronx

I joined the military in 1941, just as WWII was beginning. I served through the war and later supported the Cold War until my retirement in 1970. I supported technical intelligence flights and other activities in one way or another throughout the Cold War.

I had met Charlotte and Bianca through friends. Both made me proud to be with them and both were beautiful. I dated them whenever I could but this was not often.

By this time, Jackson's close friend, Malinda Lane, was maturing. She had developed a one-sided romance for Jackson and waited for him through thick and thin. He was ambivalent about this romance. Sometimes he tried to stop it and sometimes he was proud of Malinda and reveled in her personality and good looks. It is funny how things eventually work out.

The U.S. and others flew intelligence flights during the war and afterwards. After the war, black reconnaissance missions were flown. The U.S. flew such missions. Our allies flew such missions. The Chinese Nationalists and others flew such missions. It would be naïve to think that Intel flights only occur during moments of international crisis. Such flights occur all the time. Some are by the Americans, some by Chinese, some by Russians and others. They are occurring more-or-less simultaneously. It does not make sense, therefore, to treat them as a point in time to be described and then dismissed. They are always rubbing against one country after another. There is friction between countries over these and always the threat of war. It's tale must be treated as a continuum. An example tale is told here, then the story moves on.

I am Charlie and I remember passing through Taiwan just after the war. Only later did I pilot Cold War aircraft on all kinds of flights. I performed analysis of information from electronic intercepts and photoreconnaissance data.

During the Cold War, flights continued their assessment of adversarial troop dispositions, radar order-of-battle and other aspects of a nation's capabilities and intentions. The closed countries had policies that demanded it. Over-flights are tied with the concept of sovereignty and nation states. Think of it! Sovereignty expresses the nation's right to maintain impenetrable borders where anything the nation wants is allowable. Sovereignty says the state may abuse their own people, uproot them, favor them or what-have-you. Germany even interpreted this as their right to stick people into ovens as in the holocaust.

Utopian concepts of nation building run directly opposite to the sovereignty imperatives. One's concepts say they can implement progressive policies within their country but one cannot interfere with other countries that have sovereignty. Does one choose sides during civil wars by neighbors? There is no right to interfere with the neighbor's internal affairs, so we vacillate. The conservatives want closed borders while the progressives and liberals want porous borders.

If one chooses to act, whose side will one be on? It is crucial then to pick the right side. Unfortunately, there are usually several splinter groups to choose from and the choices must be wisely made. It modifies the neighbor's actions or violates sovereignty. This is an area requiring Solomon's wisdom to be successful.

Life is a contest between Utopia and sovereignty. Utopia seduces us with good things, but we can't have them. We are shown how wonderful things can be. However, if we seek them, we bump head-on with sovereignty. Utopian governments are liberalism taken to the extreme. They encourage experimentation in the social arena.

Sovereignty tells everyone that there is a limit to where they can go. Utopia cannot interfere with those nations because they have complete stricture from interference from any quarter. Utopia promises our remaking the global social structure for everyone's benefit, but sovereignty denies that. Liberalism stops at a nation's border.

Nowhere do we run up against this conflict as in "The United Nations Convention on the Law of the Sea (UNCLOS)." This defines the boundaries of countries and islands. These borders are unique to a given territory and are based on sovereignty. They are generally 12 miles seaward from the 'coast' having been 3 miles in the past. The Chinese on Taiwan flew both non-penetration and penetration flights deep into Communist territory to monitor capabilities and intentions, according to Taipei newspapers. We know the U.S. flew such flights over Russia based on numerous newspaper accounts of the Francis Gary Powers incident and his shoot-down in 1960.

The Chinese and Americans paid special attention to Communist Chinese nuclear facilities. President Nixon claimed such monitoring was necessary and sometimes provided information from the flights to the Russians to convince them of Chinese policies. Nixon then had the Nationalist Chinese and American flights discontinued around 1976, according to accounts in Taipei newspapers.

Thus, Nixon and Kissinger dealt the coup de grace to the Taiwan Nationalists, our ally during WWII. The U.S. policy had biased the outcome of WWII based mostly on incompetence until the final blow. The coup de grace made Taiwan a pariah state without representation in the U.N. and other trappings of statehood. Taiwan then acted as a client state under continued threats by China and by others. Meanwhile, its population grew from about 10 million to 25 million people.

The Chinese themselves in an over-flight museum now give credit to these flights and say they were largely responsible for keeping the U.S. informed and preventing wars based on false or misinterpreted information.

But at what price? The abandoning of allies is always a costly thing. But there we have it. This tale has the appearance of a start and a finish but that is illusory. It slides from a slippery opening to a time mirage that disappears beyond the horizon. It is a continuum and that will not be denied.

CHAPTER 2

AVIATION REVOLUTION AND WAR PREPARATION

The Great Ships

Transportation across the Atlantic has always been by ships. There was an increasing call for more and larger ships. The demand that fueled it all was the flow of lower class passengers at the turn of the century. This continued until immigration to the US was cut to a trickle in about 1920. The lower classes generated the demand but this was interpreted in the 1930s as a popular demand for luxury ocean liners for wealthy passengers as well. On top of that was the necessity for transporting millions of soldiers in WWII to Europe.

The governments of the leading ocean liner shipping companies were operating their most recent ships when war cries were the loudest. This caused demands that the biggest and fastest ships be modified and rigged for military transport. This caused the luxury amenities to be discontinued so the ships tended to be pedestrian in appointments. The ocean liners were big enough to haul masses of men and fast enough to run on the outside of convoys that were constricted to slow convoys of 9 knots or fast convoys of 12 knots. The great ships could outrun these convoys avoiding the great speed disadvantage. Their speed advantage let these great ships avoid and outrun the submarines.

The primary nations serving the ocean liner trade before WWII were Great Britain with the *Queen Elizabeth* and *Queen Mary*, France with the *Normandie* and America with the *United States*. The maiden voyage of each was 1940, 1936, 1935 and 1952 respectively. The lengths of all were about 1000 feet or 300 yards, the length of 3 football fields. The tonnage was about 53 thousand tons to 83 thousand tons. The speed of each was 28.5 to 33 knots and each carried about 2000 passengers plus the crew of about a thousand. America launched the *United States* in 1950 so their great ship was too late to participate in the war.

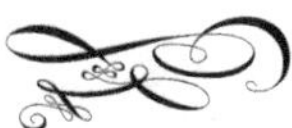

In this ocean liner race, there was also a separate competition of ships versus aircraft. Ships finally lost this market decisively by the introduction of the Boeing 707 jet aircraft in about 1960. Each aircraft could carry heavy loads and they could scurry across the Atlantic numerous times while the great ships took a week or so. Ocean liners after the war were reduced to sponsoring tourist cruises and tourist attractions. Serious transport, both cargo and passengers, were often allocated to aircraft. This was to the detriment of the ships.

The British *Queen Elizabeth* and *Queen Mary* had stellar records during WWII. They both were outfitted as troop carriers and served well.

In the late 1930s, a proposed ship, the *Queen Elizabeth*, improved upon the design of the older *Queen Mary*. She was to be eleven feet longer and of 4,000 tons greater. The plan was for the ship to be launched in September 1938, with fitting out intended to be complete for the ship to enter service in the spring of 1940. Due to the outbreak of World War II, these two events were postponed. The *Queen Elizabeth* was sent with a minimum crew to New York as a haven on 13 November 1940. She later left for Singapore to receive her troopship conversion.

As a troopship, the *Queen Elizabeth* left Singapore on 11 February, and initially she carried Australian troops to operating theaters in Asia and Africa. After 1942, the two Queens were relocated to the North Atlantic for the transportation of American troops to Europe. The *Queen Elizabeth* and the *Queen Mary* were both used as troop transports during the war. During her war service as a troopship the *Queen Elizabeth* carried more than 750,000 troops, and she also sailed some 500,000 miles.

From May to September 1943, the average number of troops ferried by each ship on every voyage exceeded 15,000, and during the winter of 1943-44, despite adverse weather conditions, the average number of troops aboard rarely fell below 13,000 for the *Queen Elizabeth* and 12,000 for the *Queen Mary.* These figures increased with the coming of summer. By the end of 1944, they could claim to have ferried, since their war service began, a total of 944,000 troops, of whom over 80 per cent had travelled eastwards from New York.

Like the *Queen Elizabeth, Queen Mary* had been based for a large part of the war in Sydney, during which time the two ships had steamed some 339,000 miles and carried 105,000 troops.

Following the end of World War II, the *Queen Mary* remained in her wartime role. She was used for returning troops to the United States. The *Queen Elizabeth*, meanwhile, was refitted and furnished as an ocean liner. The two queens dominated the transatlantic passenger trade until their fortunes began to decline with the advent of the faster and more economical jet airliner in the late 1950s. Cunard retired both ships by 1969.

Near the completion of a conversion in Hong Kong harbor for a new purpose, the Mary caught fire on January 1972. There is some suspicion that the fires were set deliberately. The ship was completely destroyed. The water sprayed on her by fireboats caused the burnt wreck to capsize and sink.

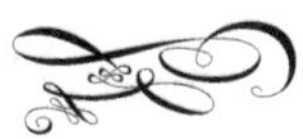

France's *Normandie* entered service in 1935 as the largest and fastest passenger ship afloat. Her novel design and lavish interiors led many to consider her the greatest of ocean liners. Despite this, she was never a financial success. WWII found *Normandie* in New York harbor. The US government had interned her in September 1939, two days after Germany and Russia invaded Poland. The *Normandie* had Art Deco interiors but a conservative hull design. The designer for the great ship was Vladimir Yourkevitch. He was a Russian designer and architect for the Imperial Russian Navy. The French intended their new superliner to be similar to earlier rakish French Line ships. He had immigrated to France after the Russian Revolution. His ideas included a slanting clipper-like bow and a bulbous nose beneath the waterline, in combination with a slim hydrodynamic hull. Yourkevitch's concepts worked wonderfully in scale models, confirming his design's performance advantages. The French engineers were impressed and asked Yourkevitch to join their project. Reportedly, he also approached Cunard with the ideas, but was rejected because the bow was deemed too radical.

The ship reached a top speed in a braking test and performed an emergency stop from that speed in less than 5,600 ft., an unprecedented distance. His design included a novel hull, which let her attain speeds at far less power than other big liners. *Normandie* was filled with technical advancements. She had turbo-electric transmission, with turbo-generators and electric propulsion motors. The turbo-electric transmission provided the ability to use full power in reverse. This accounted for the short stop distance. According to officials, the design was quieter and more easily controlled and maintained than similar ships. The engine installation was heavier than conventional turbines and slightly less efficient at high speed but allowed each propeller to operate even if its driving engine was not running. An early form of radar was installed to prevent collisions.

The war found *Normandie* havened in New York harbor. The US government interned her in September 1939. In May 1940, she was taken in by the Coast Guard and then later by the US Navy.

On February 1942, sparks from a welding torch set off a fire that burned her out. This was caused by the stress of accelerating all schedules because of the war. The ship had a very efficient fire protection system, but it had been disconnected during the conversion and its internal pumping system was deactivated. The New York City fire department's hoses, unfortunately, did not fit the ship's French inlets. After several hours, the ship rolled over and sank on its side in the mud of the Hudson River at Pier 88, NYC. This was one of many factors keeping the Normandie from being recoverable. As firefighters on shore and in fire boats poured water on the blaze, the ship developed a dangerous list to port. Water was being pumped into both the lee side and the seaward side by fireboats. The ship's Russian designer, Vladimir Yourkevitch, who happened to be in New York, arrived at the scene to offer expertise, but he was soon barred from the site by harbor police. His suggestion was to enter the vessel and open the sea-cocks. This would flood the lower decks and make her settle the few feet to the bottom on her keel. With the ship thus stabilized, water could be pumped into burning areas without the risk of capsizing. The suggestion was rejected by the commander of the 3rd Naval District, Rear Admiral Adolphus Andrews, who had the designer barred from the cite.

The ship lay on its side at Pier 88 for more than a year. The dramatic fruits of war were not hard to imagine when a prime example was on the doorstep of so many people, although only one person had perished in this debacle.

Charlotte and Bianca loved to go to midtown. There was so much to see and do. It was only a short ride on the New Haven railroad so they hankered for going there often. They were taking courses at Columbia. Although Columbia had a fine library, it could not compete with the NY City Library. There was always an excuse to go to the mid-town library. That was always an interesting experience.

The NY library was located at 41st Street and 5th Avenue. It had great marble steps going up to the entrance that reminded one of the Supreme Court building In Washington. At the top of these, there are giant columns. Two giant stone lions named 'patience' and 'fortitude' stand on either side. They appear aggressive and fierce regardless of the passive names. Inside, there is the smell of books and newsprint in the giant well-lit reading rooms. The 53 million Items there assure the data is available even if you may not be able to find it. This number of items is only surpassed by the Library of Congress and the British Library. It was always a soothing experience to relax after identifying one's requirements and then going to work in the reading rooms.

Both the girls loved to lounge on the park behind the library on a spring day. There is nothing quite as satisfying as bringing sandwiches and a blanket and then lying on the green grass with a multitude of other people. It gives one the sense of belonging in this giant metropolis.

Bianca was nostalgic. She confessed that she missed Argentina and her family and friends in Buenos Aires. She began to cry. It was a soft moaning sound. Charlotte hated that.

"Come on," she said. "Keep a stiff upper lip." Of course, that was easy for Charlotte to say. Her life was in NY and she had no strains pulling her to a different continent.

"I know, I know," she said. Bianca acknowledged her reliance on her aunt in Brooklyn that held her all together. "If it weren't for her and your family, Charlotte, I could not stand it." However, she continued to sniffle and wallow in her misery.

Charlotte got up, began to fold the blanket and pack their basket. "Come on," she commanded. We are going to have an ice cream and then walk down to Pier 88 or 49th Street and 12th Avenue. That's where the *Normandie* lies in the mud.

They walked behind the library and park. It was a tawdry area with parolees spilling into the street and always seemed threatening. A police department horse stable was nearby and sent a foul odor behind the library and park. Nevertheless, they found a small ice cream parlor and enjoyed It. Bianca had recovered her composure and no more tears flowed. "I get so lonely," she confessed.

"Okay," they said. "Let's take a look at the *Normandie* lying on her side." They didn't know the distances and addresses exactly, but approximately. It was about 17 blocks or more than a mile down to the 49th Street Pier and 12th Avenue. They decided to take a cab.

Their long slender legs were beginning to feel all the walking and strain. They were not the only ones at the pier, or the only cabs arriving. Lying down below the piers was the great ship. She lay between a pair of piers but was askance. She was rolled on her side, too heavy to be raised. There were attempts after her sinking but there seemed to be more attempts to pilfer the ship and relieve her of her priceless fixtures. These attempts continued until the war was over.

"Look," cried Bianca. "The hull has the sleek lines of a great ship even when she lies crippled. It does not take an artist to appreciate the great beauty of her lines." The hull below the waterline was painted black while her upper decks were painted white. She was about 1,000 feet in length, which meant that every part of the ship appeared streamlined with racing stripes along every deck. The bottom or the keel was painted a dull red color, probably anticipating the marine attachments and corrosion that were already attacking the great ship. Of course, the huge black clouds of smoke from the fire that brought her down had discolored parts of the superstructure. Even this did not hide the discolorations. The artistic experience from the architecture controlled the emotions, not the blemishes.

Charlotte then said, "The French know how to do it. How can one not love the French?"

After this, they taxied back to the Grand Central station and caught the New Haven line back to Larchmont. Their car was in the small parking lot. They were exhausted. They were glad to get home again.

Aviation Revolution

We say that aviation started with the Wright brothers but that fails to recognize history. When the Wrights launched their rickety craft from the sand hills of the outer banks, there were numerous cells in most every country that were pursuing aircraft theory, building prototype aircraft and generally furthering aviation ambitions. Several countries had enthusiasts on the edge of flight while technology was ripening their enthusiasm. It could not be long before some of them put it all together and took to the air.

During the war, I was a pilot, an intelligence officer, and would soon be an aeronautical engineer. I decided to stay in the Air Force after the war. I was then assigned to Wright Air Force Base in Dayton Ohio. I had fallen in love with Charlotte Lee near the end of the war. We were married soon after war's end. Naturally, Charlotte, now my wife, moved with me to Dayton where we established a home. This satisfied her. My work was demanding and required a great deal of travel. On the other hand, Charlotte was a city girl and the military life did not exactly suit her.

"Charlie," she said. "I love our life and I am happy. Yet, there are times that I miss my family and my friends. This is total isolation for me. Look at me. I have nothing to do all day but entertain myself. This is no life for me."

Yet, she did not attend to her distress. Time passed. She had children. She became involved in the military families around her. The families of military officers formed a close relationship or clique and this resolved many of her concerns and longings.

Even New York and Larchmont were not that far from Dayton so they visited often.

Charlotte missed the excitement of the subway to midtown. She missed the shopping and big city delights. My work consumed me. She had to accommodate me and did so. This arrangement left her free to satisfy herself. She did this. Further, her family was near the New Haven railroad and its stations so she could have both: a direct line to Manhattan, a loving family and a peripatetic husband that was good to her. We had an arrangement. We had two children, a boy and a girl. Afterwards, our lives became much more stable and was generally loving. Both our ages accommodated a concurrency with the major events of the war. For this, we were thankful.

I was a serious person. The Air Force moved me to Dayton where I applied my formal education and practical experience in aircraft. It was natural for me to pursue all kinds of technical things after the end of WWII. I particularly wanted to know the technical performance of aircraft, their production numbers and those of the other combatants. I tried to characterize the most important aircraft and determine these things.

In some respects, it was like technical engineering talk while on a date with a lovely woman. I talked numbers while she imagined flowers and honeybees. As surprising as this was, we both found something to admire. We gave solace to one another when needed and I was a loving father.

The explosive growth of aviation was witnessed by the number of aircraft being produced. There was a huge spike during WWI and later in WWII. By modern times, there were about 35,000 passenger planes over the U.S. every day. I enjoyed researching the number of planes being produced.

During the course of WWI, German aircraft losses accounted to 27,637 by all causes, while the Allied losses numbered over 88,613 lost (including 52,640 by France and 35,973 by Great Britain). Thus, all told, production during WW1 was greater than 116,250 aircraft. Aviation growth was explosive but at that time no one could foresee what a developmental and manufacturing explosion could occur as we experienced in WWII. As seen, aircraft had a profound effect on the war since so many machines were built. This interest and effectiveness was extrapolated to the machines of WWII and that amounted to a revolution.

The little WWI airplanes were not fast but fast enough to give a thrill. Even most schoolyards were adequate for landings and takeoffs of these flimsy machines. Millions of people therefore braved the dusty, windy air shows that blew a storm of dirt, grass and dust into the crowd as the aircraft maneuvered in the crowds to get airborne with passengers. Boys loved it. They seemed heroic. Even grown men puffed out their chests and recognized a new dimension was being added to our lives. Girls and women chased after the planes or tried to stay out of their way. They, too, were a part of this aircraft movement although they were more restrained than the men. One could see women hanging around aviation facilities or running around on the dusty, makeshift fields. Women hung onto the ropes while in flight holding them down on the wing tops. They helped put the show into show business.

Men were heroic in flying the aircraft and showing them at air shows. They lived dangerous lives. Their skills displayed miraculous exhibitions. Yet, the women often showed similar skills and their heroism was as good as the men. They thought it was sometimes better.

After WWI, there was a plethora of excess aircraft and flyers that could keep the pot boiling. After the hiatus between the two world wars, every nation built aircraft by the tens of thousands and trained an army of flyers. These capabilities guaranteed a bright future for the industry.

Of course, this was nothing compared to WWII and aircraft production there.

I said, "Get ready, Charlotte. Here comes a barrage of numbers."

"I love it," she said, but her mind was off in the stars.

During WWII, the Allies built a total of 637,248 airplanes, while the Axis built 229,331. WWII here is assumed as the years 1939 through 1945. Of these, the U.S. built 324,000 units while the British Empire built 177,025 and the USSR built 136,226 units for a total of 637,021 units.

Meanwhile, Germany produced 133,387 aircraft, the Italian Empire built 13,402 and the Japanese Empire built 71,580 for a total of 218,369 craft ignoring the few round off units. Technology advanced and shoved the world forward into modern times. There is said to be over 35,000 commercial flights by 2015 over the U.S. on any day.

The bureaucrats were right. Governments have invested trillions of dollars in the aviation industry over the years, in runway and terminal and other construction, and to a large extent made the world what it is.

In 1958, jet passenger aircraft were introduced across the world. Several aircraft companies built jets that were introduced at almost the same time — some succeeded and some failed. None were as successful as the Boeing 707. This could only be described as an aircraft revolution.

There was a further serious limitation that could not be solved. At sea, wind makes waves. As the wind increases nearby and at far fetches, the nearby seas roll with ever-higher waves. This imperils the craft similarly. The planes required low sea states to land and take off. This greatly restricted their operations on the open ocean. Juan Trippe of PanAm passenger service, Oleg Sikorsky, Charles Lindberg and others made designs that had the seaplanes competing with landplanes in performance. The industry turned out some beautiful designs but it was difficult or impossible to make money from operating the planes, although they all tried.

"Something that became clear was the competition between seaplanes and landplanes. Clearly, since there were 4,000 PBY or seaplanes produced, this is a very significant number.

Ranges and speeds are given here in statute miles and statute miles per hour, or mph, as opposed to nautical miles, or nm, and nautical miles per hour, or knots. Expressing these in nautical dimensions rather than statute dimensions would lower the nautical conversion values by 13%.

The PBY Catalina seaplane first flight was March 1935. It was produced by Consolidated Aircraft Company of San Diego and had a speed of 125 mph (statute miles per hour or 109 kts), a range of 2,500 miles, (statute miles) an altitude of 15,800 feet, and a lift of 2,000 pounds The number produced reached 4,000 seaplanes. This number was beyond belief but the war changed everything.

The China Clipper was the ultimate seaplane. It was a thing of beauty. However, like most commercial romances, it was expensive and not very satisfying. As a technology, the seaplane time window collapsed at the end of the war.

In summary, the M-130 *China Clipper's* first flight was March 1935. Built by Glenn L. Martin Company of Baltimore, it had a cruise speed of 141 knots or 162 smph, a range of 3,200 statute miles, an altitude of 17,000 feet, and a lift of 47 passengers. A one-way ticket to Manila, including overnight stays at PanAm hotels in Honolulu, Midway, Wake and Guam, cost $950 — the equivalent of $14,650 in 2014 dollars today. The average wage based on the hourly rate for manufacturing was $ 416 per year at that time. So, the ticket price was 2.3 times an average man's salary for a year. This got you from Hawaii to Manila in luxury, but only the rich and famous and government bureaucrats could afford it.

After WWII the use of flying boats rapidly declined for several reasons. The ability to land on water became less of an advantage owing to the considerable increase in the number and length of land-based runways during the war that consisted of concrete, macadam or other materials. As the reliability, speed, and range of land-based aircraft increased, the commercial competitiveness of flying boats diminished; their design compromised aerodynamic efficiency and speed to accomplish the feat of waterborne takeoff and landing. Landing 'channels' had to be surveyed and marked with anchored channel buoys. The 'water runways' had to be 'swept' before each takeoff or any debris had to be removed. Salt water and spray caused rapid deterioration of metal skin and parts. Transfer of passengers from small boats to seaplanes was a very unwieldy operation, even if mooring piers were built.

These doomed the flying boats.

The aviation revolution could have been characterized by one plane, the DC-3 by Douglas. The aircraft that put the flying boats out of commission was the landplane DC-3 Skytrain. This also appeared in 1936.

The DC-3 was the most influential aircraft ever built. A total of 16,000 were assembled around the world. Introduced in 1936, it was a two-engine craft with a cruise speed of 207 mph (or 180 kts) and a range of 1,500 miles. Every conceivable use of the plane was tried including pulling gliders for combat troops, as the author witnessed at Fort Bragg in WWII. They even put a harness on a man on the ground and jerked him into the air while the DC-3 stuttered but did it. In fact, he witnessed them do the same thing with a 12 piece band aboard a glider.

The DC-3 first flight was December 1935. It was built by Boeing Aircraft of Seattle and had a cruise speed of 129 mph (112 kts) that changed as the air craft was updated), a cruise range of 1,500 statute miles, a ceiling of 20,800 feet, and a lift of 28 passengers. The number produced reached 16,000 landplanes.

The top of the window for landplanes was the DC-4 (or C-54 by Douglas) followed by the DC-6 and DC-7 as logical redesigns. These were variations on the same aircraft. The DC-4 first flight was December 1938. It was built by Douglas Aircraft Company in Long Beach. It had a cruise speed of 227 mph (197 kts), a range of 4,250 statute miles, a ceiling of 22,300 feet, and a lift of 20,000 pounds. The number produced reached 4,000 planes. This had been beyond belief but the war changed everything.

Thus, the comparison has been made with the benchmark aircraft where the top of the class was the PBY early seaplane. The DC-3 early landplane and the DC-4 later landplane. This does not imply that they are the aviation industry, only that they characterize the planes. They probably define the overall aviation landscape at that time.

In summary, the 4-engine Stratocruiser first flight was July 1947. It had piston engines. The aircraft was built by Douglas Aircraft Company, Long Beach, CA. It had a speed of 192 mph (167 kts), a range of 4,200 miles, a ceiling of 32,000 feet, and a lift of 20,000 pounds or up to 100 seats in many configurations. The number produced reached 76 units. This was a herculean effort but technology had passed them by.

Then, a tsunami hit the aircraft business. The jet engine revolution changed everything. It was a surprise to the aircraft community but the jets were reliable beyond anyone's expectation. The maintenance costs across whole fleets of these new aircraft ushered in performances that changed everything in the designs. What had not been economically feasible now became well within budgets.

The Boeing 707's first flight was in December of 1957. It had a cruise speed of 525 mph (456 kts), a range of 6,620 statute miles, a ceiling of 32,000 feet, and a lift of 20,000 pounds or up to 219 seats with many seating variations. The number produced reached 1,011 planes.

In the time frame of 1958 or so, the jet airliner drew upon the B-29 bomber design to produce a revolutionary landplane, the Boeing 707 jet. The whole world within 2-3 years changed to this airplane's basic design for passenger service. Meanwhile, all aircraft from high performance fighters to mammoth freighters and everything in between redrew all their designs. A new era was entered.

The next major change was wide-bodied jets. Aircraft have revolutionized the world. Needless to say, they have also revolutionized the intelligence business.

Amidst this fog of numbers, the world's future was wrapped up in the new jet aircraft. These swept through the world's transportation capabilities. Within a period of a little less than a couple of years, jet aircraft became workhorses. They took over passenger and cargo functions. Needless to say, Intel functions and intercept aircraft soon yielded to the superiority of the jet engine. This occurred only after WWII (abut 1958) but the conversion to jet passenger planes was almost universal. Many jet aircraft were produced after WWII (some even during the war). Some even reached a production stage.

The world was set on its present course primarily by the West and Russia. The way we understand this is through the extrapolation of WWII events. This story describes many of these most important events during WWI, through the interwar period, during WWII and then during the Cold War period. After all, the extrapolation of these events from point to point determines our place in the cosmos, or rather, it guides us and has a profound effect on things defining us today.

Treaty of Rapallo (1922-1933)

The interbellum or interwar period was 22 years long, lasting from 1918 until 1941. It defined an extremely productive period between wars. Not only did manufacturing excel but research produced awesome machines. This period set up the war and its aftermath.

Russia had fallen apart during WWI. It's revolution kept the Russians in turmoil and chaos until the rise of Lenin and the Bolsheviks in 1917. They were anxious to sign a peace treaty with the Allies, mostly Britain, the U.S. and France. Basically, it was an unconditional surrender by the Russian forces. Then, the Red Army and Lenin's government approached stability in the early 1920's. Russia had simply stopped fighting and her army mostly dissolved and disappeared into the hinterlands.

The Germans were also in disarray with debased currency and political anarchy. No one during WWI had prepared the Germans for surrender. The population therefore believed their leaders had sold them out; it was a vast conspiracy. The soldiers often believed that their Army was strong and ready to keep fighting, as Hitler's *Mein Kampf* illustrates. Both Germany and Russia were pariahs after WWI. This was an opportune time for cooperation between the two. However, the true agreement had to be done in secrecy. Therefore, the Treaty of Rapallo was negotiated as part public and part secret codicils. The treaty lasted from 1922 until 1933. Hitler then came to national power. The Russians were nominally accommodating to the Bolsheviks as they settled into the seats of power.

Part of the common interest between the Allies and the Axis was the Allies pressuring Germany for huge war reparations after the war. They needed each other as recognized in 1922, with Lenin's Treaty of Rapallo, the name of a colorful town near Genoa on the main road to Portofino on the coast. Jackson had even visited the town on one of his trips through Italy. Most importantly, secret protocols to the treaty provided mutual assistance in military preparations. The Soviets needed German military help, and Germany wanted to evade the disarmament clauses of the Versailles Treaty. Under these secret protocols, Germany immediately sent military personnel to Russia to rejuvenate the Red Army. Germany sent personnel to Russia as the quid-pro-quo. These groups initiated the joint manufacture of tanks, submarines, poison gas, and other war materials, in cooperation with Russian technicians. This gave the Germans a place for manufacturing their war machine and Russia technical assistance in manufacturing modern arms. The Germans could also develop strategies for implementing their ideas on mobile warfare. Joint military training and exercises were conducted on Russian soil.

The Soviets and Germans partitioned Poland in starting WWII. Adolph Hitler had made it clear in *Mein Kampf* that he expected to acquire new territory for Germany, primarily from Russia and her vassal states. Stalin read the book, but was not alarmed.

Hitler gained power by 1933, and revoked the Treaty of Rapallo in 1934, although it is not exactly clear why.

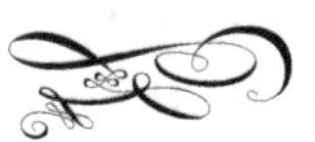

Molotov-Ribbentrop Pact (23 Aug. 1939)

Germany had profited from the Treaty of Rapallo. By 1934, Germany was becoming militarily strong and did not have to skulk. Stalin started various negotiations with Britain and France during their 1936 until 1939 appeasement period. Hitler occupied the Rhineland in 1936, but he and Stalin supported opposite sides during the Spanish Civil War, from 1936 to 1939. Hitler annexed Austria in March 1938 and annexed the Sudetenland in November, completing the partitioning of Czechoslovakia.

By 1939, Stalin had soured on British and French resolve. He admired and feared Hitler's successes. On August 2, 1939, Germany and the Soviets announced the Molotov-Ribbentrop Pact, signed in Moscow on August 23. In a secret protocol, they agreed to partition East Europe between themselves. Poland east of the Vistula River was to be taken by the Soviets. So were Estonia, Latvia, and Bessarabia. Lithuania and the rest of Poland were to be taken by Germany. The agreement was signed August 23. Germany attacked Poland and the others on September 1, seven days later. The Soviets attacked Poland on September 17. Remember, Germany partitioned Poland 1 September while the Russians stumbled before partitioning their part of Poland 17 September. There was a Soviet delay of only 17 days while they digested their victory over Japan in Khalkhin Gol.

Battle of Khalkhin Gol (16 Sept. 1939)

This little-known battle was extremely important since it set the Soviets and the Japanese on different courses. In turn, these changed the world.

While Japanese leaders squabbled over their commitment of forces in Mongolia, General Zhukov and others began to focus on overcoming the daunting logistical challenges of maintaining a sizable defensive force in the region. In an impressive effort that would provide valuable lessons for future operations, Russian truck convoys drove day and night over desert tracks, a grueling round trip of 868 miles. The Soviets employed 3,800 trucks and

1,375 fuel tankers in their supply organization. Those trucks transported 18,000 tons of artillery shells, 6,500 tons of bombs and 15,000 tons of liquid fuel, as well as troops and weapons.

General Zhukov, now commanding the First Army Group, planned to launch an offensive of his own. He would use the 57,000 men, 542 artillery pieces, 498 tanks and 515 aircraft of his army group in a double envelopment of the Japanese.

To secure operational surprise, Zhukov employed many varied deceptive measures. Radios broadcast false information and transmitted soundtracks of construction noise. Trucks and aircraft operated day and night to muffle the sound of unit deployment. Such measures convinced the Japanese that the Soviets were digging in for the winter.

The Khalkhin Gol battle had a profound effect on WWII. Not only did it greatly reduce Japan's military power in the region, it also convinced many in Tokyo headquarters that they should reduce their emphasis on capturing the interior of China but should concentrate on the Navy-based Greater East Asia Co-Prosperity Sphere. This was implemented immediately. So relieved, the Soviet Red Army in Asia was reposted to Europe for the joint dismemberment of Poland in Hitler's Barbarossa campaign initiating WWII as some would define it.

To discourage any Soviet move into Manchukuo and to prepare for renewed ground action, the Japanese mounted an intense air campaign in September. For that purpose, six fighter squadrons were transferred from China. By September 13, the Japanese army air force had arrayed 255 warplanes, including 158 fighters along the front. Air battles swirled in Mongolian skies in the first and second weeks of September and climaxed on the 15th, as 200 Japanese warplanes struck Soviet air bases in Mongolia. Fierce aerial combat ensued as 120 Japanese fighter planes fought 207 Russian adversaries. All combat came to an end, however, when a cease-fire agreement was signed on September 16.

The Battle of Khalkhin Gol was over with a sound defeat of the Japanese.

The Japanese conceded the loss of 8,717 soldiers and airmen killed and missing, and 10,997 wounded and killed during their incursion into Mongolia. Soviet sources report 8,931 killed and missing, and 15,952 wounded and sick. But both sides' losses may well have exceeded those figures.

The Soviet Union provided a large number of aircraft and pilots throughout this period. Their war was primarily with the Japanese but the battleground was generally China. The scope and results of this battle were not widely known at the time. Mortified by defeat in battle, the Japanese sought to conceal their disgrace. For its part, the Soviet Union was preoccupied with seizing territory in the West with the division of Poland and the occupation of the Baltic States. The Soviets also did little to trumpet its victories.

In addition, having killed most of his military leaders in his purges, Stalin was unwilling to promote Zhukov's victory and see the general emerge as a popular hero. Even so, later actions during the war would ensure that Zhukov would become justly famous as the leading Soviet commander of WWII. Many of the characteristic features of the Russian way of war can be seen in his leadership at Khalkhin Gol: massive firepower; tight integration of infantry, artillery, tanks and warplanes; elaborate deception measures that exploited electronic means; and ruthless sacrifice of lives.

Stalin remembered the fierce fighting in Mongolia. Even as he summoned 1,000 tanks and 1,200 warplanes from Soviet Far Eastern forces to battle the German invaders who were making spectacular gains, 19 reserve divisions nearing 15,000 soldiers each, 1,200 tanks and some 1,000 aircraft remained in Mongolia to confront the Japanese.

Although small by the standards of later WWII battles, the fighting between Soviet and Japanese forces at Khalkhin Gol cast a long shadow over subsequent events in the Pacific theater and on the Russian front. Further, the Soviets had provided a great deal of air power, both pilots and aircraft, although it was mostly restricted to Chinese Communist interests. It was clear, however, that air superiority was critical to either offense or defense. This caused the Chinese to look for a means to replace the Soviet aircraft as early as possible. When Germany attacked Russia, the Soviet military and their aircraft in China was ordered home. This included aircraft and pilots.

Dunkirk Fiasco; May 27, 1940 – June 4, 1940

Thus, the Dragons of War were unleashed. They were un-tethered first by Japan in 1937, and they were set upon the world in all their fury by the concerted joint action of Russia and Germany in 1939.

Hitler and Stalin set loose the war in Europe by their annexation of Poland. Britain and France recognized this by immediately declaring war against the Germans, only days after the invasion. The Soviets attacked eastern Poland only seventeen days after the Germans. It is curious that Britain and France did not act against the Soviets as they did Germany. Their response was to try every way to get the Americans involved. Eventually they succeeded.

Many Americans were not particularly fans of Winston Churchill. They thought he was jerking the U.S. around. Churchill was calling many of the shots of the war and most of these were for the advantage of Britain and the Empire. Many were ambivalent about the British and they believed Churchill was protecting the interests of the empire. Who knew how it would all shake out after the war? But, they did not believe the Empire would survive, certainly not in its form at that time.

In many respects, it was Churchill and Roosevelt plotting the war as masters of the joint Anglo-American team. Sometimes one forgot that Roosevelt was representing America although he himself seemed at times to lose that perspective. Meanwhile, they courted Stalin. He did not join the fight against the Japanese and held out until five days before Japan's surrender before declaring himself. Many argue that Stalin and Germany played their own game and often put America in a box where they had no alternative but to play the foil to the continental powers. Britain certainly saved itself and had their chance of saving the empire. Stalin meanwhile changed China to a communist stronghold and played his game in Asia and the world.

Everything would have changed had the Soviets declared war on Japan in December 1941. This was abundantly clear. *Had they done so at that time, Eastern Siberia and the Aleutians would probably have been used as a launching area for air, sea and probably land attacks against Japan by America,* I thought. *The fight that would have been launched across Russia and the Aleutians. These would probably have been used as a launching area for air, sea and probably land attacks against Japan by America.*

Charlotte worried herself sick at how things were turning out for her friend, Bianca, during the early part of the war. I was God-knows-where when I would go away. I did not tell her anything in my infrequent letters and besides, the heavy black ink of the censor made her imagination run wild. She did not yet worry about her brother, Jackson. He was too young for the military or draft and she could not imagine the war lasting long enough to reach him.

It did not take long for the next moves. Surprisingly, Germany grabbed most of Europe. The ultimate surprise was that Hitler then invaded Soviet Russia. Both the moves and the timing were unforeseen. The war clouded the whole world.

Charlotte knew I was somewhere in England from casual slips in the censor's ink. That did not give her too much comfort since the real hazard was in the Pacific and he was sure to go there before long. The newspapers in Japan blared every day how the U.S. was losing the war as island after island fell to the Japanese. If it were not islands, it was fleets at sea.

The real danger to Japan did not occur until the Americans captured the Mariana Islands in mid-1944 with Guam, Saipan and Tinian. This was over two years from the war start. Long-range B-29 bombers used these bases for the bulk of their bombing campaign against the home islands of Japan. This led to the capture of Okinawa, Iwo Jima and similar forward bases, mostly in early 1945.

The war culminated in streams of heavy B-29 bombers attacking the Japanese homeland.

In the end, they were decisive.

CHAPTER 3

WWII, ATLANTIC—GERMANY INVADES RUSSIA (22 JUNE 1941)

The Ukraine schism came in 22 June 1941 when Germany occupied Denmark, Norway, Holland, France, and Belgium. The war was on in every way

Hitler and Stalin had bickered for a year over the spoils of war and new acquisitions, and at the same time jockeyed for tactical and strategic positioning. Operation Barbarossa was the code name for Nazi Germany's invasion of Russia. The operation was driven by Adolf Hitler's ideological desire to conquer the Soviet territories as outlined in his 1925 manifesto *Mein Kampf*. Over the course of the operation, about four million soldiers of the Axis powers invaded the Soviet Union along an 1,800 mile front, from the Black Sea to the Baltic Sea.

The Axis was composed of Germany, Italy and Japan while the Allies were composed of Britain, America, China and Russia. The Soviets were ambivalent and did not declare a war with Japan until five days before the Japanese surrender in the fall of 1945.

Operationally, the Germans won resounding victories and occupied some of the most important economic areas of the Soviet Union, mainly in the Ukraine, both inflicting and sustaining heavy casualties. Despite their successes, the German offensive stalled on the outskirts of Moscow and was subsequently pushed back by a Soviet counteroffensive. The Red Army repelled the Wehrmacht's strongest blows and forced Germany into a war of attrition for which it was unprepared. Further, that winter was the coldest of record for which they were similarly unprepared. The failure of Operation Barbarossa was a pivot point in the fortunes of the Third Reich. The Eastern Front became the site of some of the largest battles, most horrific atrocities, and highest casualties for Soviets and Germans alike, all of which influenced the subsequent history of the 20th century.

The causes of the final schisms are still cloudy. With this, the two war-makers would throw most of their strength and venom against each other. Germany had annexed Europe and mobilized the armies and police of conquered countries to control their own populations, and to comply with the onerous policies laid down by the Nazis. The Germans mobilized their industries for the German war machine and their agriculture to feed the Germans and their armies. Germany drafted millions of civilians for slave labor battalions; and brought a black civil night to the whole continent of Europe.

Hitler looked at the granaries of Russia and the millions of peasant workers described in *Mein Kampf.* The German appetite and greed had not been sated. Soon they were hauling most of Russia's grain to Germany to feed their own citizens, while the Russians were left to starve. Russian peasants saw little difference between the Germans and Soviets, but the Germans showed a sadistic delight in murder and oppression that even the Soviets lacked, and they were foreigners. The Russian countryside turned against the Germans.

Shortly after this, I pulled the trigger by signing up to join the Army Air Corps. This organization was renamed the Air Force just after the war. I then threw my whole being into learning all I could about the Air Force. During the early stages of the war, I was commissioned and earned pilot wings. I met and became friends with George Grayburn who traveled a parallel path in the Air Force. He became my sidekick. Both of us transitioned into an intelligence career.

The Russo-German annexation of Eastern Europe appalled Britain and the U.S. The military situation deteriorated so rapidly that hard positions against Russia were not taken; near-by Germany was a far more pressing problem to the West. Soon, England was fighting for its life in the Battle of Britain and the submarine Battle of the Atlantic, after Germany's occupation of Europe.

Immediately after Germany launched its attack against Russia, Churchill ignored Stalin's history of criminal collaboration with Germany and his joint annexation of Eastern Europe with Hitler. He cynically viewed the Soviet Union, as "an enemy of mine enemy is my friend." Churchill announced unconditional aid to the Soviet Union in a June 22, 1941 radio address. He was totally dependent on U.S. aid for his own survival at that time, and for most transport to Britain, and thereby committed the British and, by proxy, the Americans, to accept the Soviets into the camp of the Allies. He foretold, or ostensibly committed, American Lend-Lease to Stalin. Stalin never saw himself as an ally of Britain or the U.S., but as an accomplice of Hitler who had been betrayed. Soon, in their zeal to mobilize public opinion, Churchill and the English found only good things to say about Stalin and the Soviets as Allies in a great cause. Roosevelt and the Americans practically lionized Uncle Joe Stalin and the Soviets in the Allies' cause to save democracy. The West had bought into the Soviet lie, at least in public statements. Stalin and the Soviets were the beneficiaries.

It was noteworthy that Russia remained neutral toward Japan to the war's end.

Hitler and Stalin agreed to and did partition Eastern Europe by open warfare. England declared war on Germany; Britain's reaction to the Soviet partition is not clear, but it was stillborn in any event. Then, Hitler attacked the Soviet Union. Hitler soon attacked England, preparing for an invasion. The U.S. and Britain became extremely close allies. The U.S. supplied a besieged Britain through Lend-Lease. Britain obligated itself to supply the Soviets with war material the British did not have, committing to the Soviets as allies. The participants in the war in Europe, by this means, were clear except for the details.

In this manner, Britain also committed the U.S. to the Soviets as allies. This masterstroke by Churchill committed the U.S. to fight Japan that was threatening a war to an area vital to American interests. The Japanese war was a fight primarily between the U.S. and Japan where Britain's interests were not vital. Further, those interests were lost in any event as the empire dissolved shortly after the war.

The Soviet Union and Nazi Germany invaded Poland in September 1939, marking this as the beginning the Second World War in Europe. The partitioning of Poland was brief with the Poles often on horseback defending against German tanks. The British, French and Americans declared war on Germany within days.

The British Expeditionary Force, BEF, went to aid in the defense of France. The eight months with little belligerent activity became denoted as the 'Phony War'.

Germany invaded Belgium and the Netherlands on 10 May 1940, and three of their Panzer corps attacked France through the Ardennes and rapidly drove to the English Channel. By 21 May, the German forces had trapped the BEF, the remains of the Belgian forces, and three French armies in an area along the northern coast of France. The British Commander of the BEF saw that evacuation across the Channel was the only reasonable course of action, and began planning a withdrawal to Dunkirk, the closest location with good port facilities and the longest sand beach in France.

The German soldiers were given a halt order by Hitler as one of the most puzzling orders of the war. This order gave the trapped Allied forces time to construct defensive works and pull back large numbers of troops toward Dunkirk.

The Dunkirk evacuation denotes the retreat of Allied soldiers from the beaches and harbor of Dunkirk between 27 May and 4 June 1940. The operation became necessary when large numbers of British, French, and Belgian troops were cut off and surrounded. In a speech to the House of Commons, British Prime Minister Winston Churchill called the events in France 'a colossal military disaster'.

Both George and I wanted to help in the evacuation from Dunkirk. Our solution always depended on the use of aircraft. The war office would have none of it. Aircraft had their place, we were told, but this is beyond that.

"We need ships and crew," he said. "We have small boats with no crew and large boats with partial crews. You have been assigned to a small boat to go to Dunkirk and return with as many soldiers as it can handle. You both are sailboat captains, I was told. In this assignment, you will have a powerboat. So do your duty."

We had both gone to England as support for some weapon system lend-leased to the Brits under Roosevelt's clandestine agreements.

The man from the War Office told us, "I know there's a great deal of difference between a sailboat and a powerboat. I also know you blokes know a lot about sailing, so we expect you to make several trips and help us in this emergency." As it turned out, we both did know a lot about sailing. We managed to get to Dunkirk in heavy seas. Soldiers appeared on the beaches of Dunkirk by the thousands. We had to push many off our deck so they would not capsize our boat and drown us all. Our freeboard was high and the swimmers were weak so this was not much of a problem. We made several trips. We were thankful for the men we saved but we would never be free of our conscience for the events. This included those that we could not bring aboard and those we pushed to their almost certain death as they gasped for air off the beaches.

After the operation, I had been informed of the numbers evacuated. On the first day of the evacuation, only 7,669 men were evacuated, but by the ninth day, a hastily assembled fleet of over 800 boats had rescued 338,226 soldiers. Many of the troops were able to embark from the harbor's protective mole onto 39 British destroyers and other large ships, while others had to wade out from the beaches, waiting for hours in the shoulder-deep water. Some were ferried from the beaches to the larger ships by the famous little ships of Dunkirk, a flotilla of hundreds of merchant marine boats, fishing boats, pleasure craft, and lifeboats called into service for the emergency. The British Expeditionary Force lost 68,000 soldiers during the French campaign and had to abandon nearly all of their tanks, vehicles, and other equipment. In his speech to the House of Commons on 4 June, Churchill reminded the country, "We must be very careful not to assign to this deliverance the attributes of a victory. Wars are not won by evacuations."

The retreat was undertaken amid chaotic conditions, with abandoned vehicles blocking the roads and a flood of refugees heading in the opposite direction. Due to wartime censorship and the desire to keep up British morale, the full extent of the unfolding disaster at Dunkirk was not initially publicized.

The British Expeditionary Forces let themselves become trapped at Dunkirk between land on three sides and the sea. They became literally 'driven into the sea'.

Hitler then made the most daffy decision of WWII. He posted the famous "Halt Order" to his army at Dunkirk. He ordered his soldiers to stop fighting. This saved well over 300,000 soldiers of the British Expeditionary Forces. This organized and trained army was used to replicate itself for the ongoing war and to derail Hitler's agenda.

On 22 June 1941 the Germans began Operation Barbarossa with the intention of defeating the Soviets in a Blitzkrieg lasting only months. The offensive met with initial success before the Germans were stopped at Moscow. The Germans captured vast areas of land and important industrial centers and they remained in the war. In the winter of 1941–1942, the Soviets struck back in a series of counteroffensives, repelling the German threat to Moscow, and making it clear the campaign against the Soviets would become a long battle of attrition.

Both George and I performed well in the evacuation from the beaches of Dunkirk. Our sailing knowledge had been put to good use. For that, the war office was thankful. We were to receive commendations for our good work and for the many soldiers we had saved.

Pearl Harbor

The Japanese attack on Pearl Harbor occurred 7 December 1941. The Allies and Axis were all in at this juncture. For these, there was no quibbling over the date when the war started.

The date, 7 December 1941, was the start of WWII. This ignores Operation Barborossa and various other serious altercations and preparations for the war. One then treats the period of 1937 with the rape of Nanking until

7 December 1941 as pre-war preparations. There were also other military clashes before this.

Germany declared war against the U.S. four days after the attack on Pearl Harbor. This solidified the two world camps. The Axis consisted of Germany, Italy and Japan. The major Allies were the U. S., the U. K., and China. The USSR was an ally against Germany and Italy, but neutral against Japan. (This neutrality lasted until 5 days before the Japanese surrender to the allies. Then, the Soviets declared war against Japan.) The Russians therefore hung around for a better deal. Many think that was confirmed when the USSR declared war on Japan, 5 days after Japanese capitulation to the Allies. They believe the 'loss of China' to Communism in 1949 was a result of this.

Why did Germany attack Russia?

Well, there is no doubt that was her long-range plan as related by Hitler in *Mein Kampf*. He wanted Russian oil, her vast grain harvests and expanded German living space.

The Japanese effectively occupied the whole Co-Prosperity area within a few weeks of Pearl Harbor. Further, this was a long time after the catastrophe of Dunkirk."

It was now March 1942 in Tokyo. The chill of winter still blanketed the grimy city. Everyone had a serious countenance and rapid step as they went purposefully about their business.

The war against America was continuing. The newspapers disseminated the news, but otherwise there was little evidence in neighborhoods that the war was on them. There were more uniforms. The Japanese were uniformed people, anyway. Japan had become a garrison state since the Pearl Harbor news. The radio sang the praises of the Japanese Samurai; the warriors. There was almost continuous martial music. Shinto prayers were often read for the brave warriors. All over Tokyo, trucks would drive to street corners and stop while their loudspeakers played martial music. Then a message would blare out in all directions exhorting everyone to work, work, work hard and produce for the fatherland; provide food and materials for the brave fighting men in the outposts of empire. A series of victory bulletins would be read. Victory will be ours! Fight on! An article would be read about some Japanese hero who had just sunk two American destroyers, and so forth. Generally, several very stiff Japanese officials sat in chairs on the truck bed. They usually wore long black morning coats, stiff upward collars, white shirts and dark top hats. The loudspeakers then blared "Banzai," there was a long pause for the people to respond, and then "Banzai," a pause, "Banzai." The martial music resumed and the truck would speed away.

In such performances, both on the radio and in the newspapers, the news was always good, the battles always ended in victory, Japan always succeeded. Even so, there was no doubt in anyone's mind that Japan was having its way. They were occupying vast numbers of Pacific islands, the Philippines, Java, Samatra, Timor, New Guinea, Borneo, Sarawak, Singapore, French Indo-China, and Burma. On and on it went. There were no bad stories circulating word-of-mouth, nothing to discount the official stories. The official stories were mostly true. The Japanese people rejoiced as they reflected the success of the Japanese army and navy. They began to haul the petroleum products from the East Indies on the long journey to Japan.

George and I discussed the Japanese war all the time. The North African campaign was winding down. In fact, the bulk of the troops and military might had been used to invade Sicily and then the Italian mainland.

The war moved up the Italian peninsula until the invasion of Europe finally led to the defeat of the Germans. The Italian army, hunkering down in the mountainous crevices, did not complete their northern thrust until the German army surrendered all of Europe.

The losses of the Japanese Army to Zhukov and the Soviets in KhalKhan Gol in August 1939 had caused a turn in Japanese strategy. Suddenly, the Army's continental policies for taking Chinese territory were in disarray and the Navy's Co-Prosperity concepts of taking Pacific islands and Southeast Asian maritime territory were favored. This policy change was fateful for the Americans because of America's Southwestern Pacific interests. Those included the Philippines, Australia, the British around Malaya and Burma, the Dutch colonies around the East Indies, the friendship and interests still maintained with China and its government, and the islands in the Southwest Pacific that were strategically critical to all their interests.

The Japanese struck the battleships tied up to the quays or concrete pillars alongside Pearl Harbor's Ford Island. Unfortunately for them, battleships were losing their effectiveness in the naval battles of the world. They mattered less and less. Further, two American aircraft carriers were at sea that morning and could not be attacked at all; one was at sea and one was on the West Coast for repairs. The planes also flew over the American submarine facilities as they were attacking battleships and those submarines proved to be extremely effective in bringing the war to the Japanese immediately. Japan also ignored the fuel storage tanks on the hill beyond Pearl Harbor, thereby foregoing the ability to starve the fleet for immediate retaliation, particularly starving the aircraft carriers. Lastly, the repair facilities and workshops for ships were not attacked leaving the ability for quick repair of the fighting fleet.

One must accept the fact that the great Japanese victory at Pearl Harbor was mostly illusory.

George and I continued to discuss Japan and its likelihood of success. In the end, it did not look promising.

"The land empire," I told George, "was not providing the raw materials and markets that Japan desperately wanted, but it was causing an enormous drain. It certainly was not opening Japan to the sources of oil, to rubber, tin, aluminum, iron, chemicals, world-shipping lanes, and the other necessities of a major world power. Mostly, she knew that she must have an easy, assured access to major oil fields. As she well knew, and the navy enthusiasts continually pointed out in their advocacy, these things abound in Southeast Asia. The Dutch oil fields in the Netherlands East Indies (Indonesia) and Borneo (Brunei), the rubber plantations and tin mines in French Indo-China, the shipping lanes of the Straits of Malacca by Singapore, British Hong Kong harbor, and other resources and shipping facilities of Southeast Asia were mighty attractions.

"However, the naval might of the Americans, Dutch, French, and British had held them back. They reasoned before the war that since the European colonial powers were engaged in Europe, how could they deny a mighty Japanese Navy with relatively short supply lines to the homeland? France was occupied by this time, and what remained of its fleet was in Vichy hands or in the hands of the Free French in Africa, the exile government. The Dutch Government was in exile in England. The British were fighting for their survival, trying to defeat the aircraft of the German Luftwaffe and prevent an invasion of the home islands. Britain was deeply engaged in the crucial submarine wars where her shipping lifeline hung in the balance. She was in no condition to pay too much attention to Asia.

"Only the Americans stood between the Japanese Navy and the Navy's ambitions. America's only big possession west of Hawaii was the Philippines. Hadn't America declared the Philippines would be given independence in 1947? It certainly could not be considered a vital interest for America, Japan reasoned. Clearly, America would not risk a full-scale Pacific war with Japan when she had no critical possessions or critical interests in the Southwest Pacific. She was getting more and more involved in the European war. She was supplying war material, having naval engagements with German submarines, essentially patrolling for submarines as part of the British fleet, and taking other warlike actions. She was clearly destined to come to the aid of England if the war lasted. With these European engagements, surely the Americans would not engage in a two-ocean war for the sake of friendship and when they had no compelling national interest there."

I was often conflicted in my attitudes and beliefs. This applied to the Japanese and their questionable policies toward America and by the Communists that preached dissension. I was not driven by politics and policies like many of my fellow officers. I was a stable, restraining influence on all my mates. I think I exhibited leadership when it was required. I believe I also showed a large amount of charisma. As my friends and I walked to the Officer's Club or elsewhere, more often than not, I was leading the way. The group clung to me but not one could tell you why. That is part of charisma and leadership. These indicated character, all right, where this was substantial and did not swing on trivial matters.

They reasoned that if the Japanese strike dramatically and cripples the American Pacific fleet and bases, America will not have any credible power in the Pacific. Surely, she will not deplete the critical Atlantic forces where she does have critical possessions and interests, to reconstitute a new Pacific force.

Japan was wrong. My friends and I laughed in some kind of bizarre amusement. We slapped our sides at the prospect of these little guys thinking they could best the great American fleet. She staked it all on the strike at Pearl Harbor. And now look where Japan is. We laughed even harder.

They didn't sink any aircraft carriers. They didn't report any. Don't you understand? They didn't get the aircraft carriers. Do you know what happened in December of last year, in the very same month as Pearl Harbor? The British lost the battleship Prince of Wales and the battle cruiser Repulse that was really a disguising designation for another battleship. This occurred off the coast of Indo-China. Japanese land-based airplanes sank both battleships before taking Singapore and the Malay Peninsula. Then look at Europe where a bunch of Italians riding torpedoes with saddles, for goodness sake, sank two more British battleships in Egypt's Alexandria harbor! Don't you get it? We rolled in merriment on how the joke was on the Japanese.

We all continued our skepticism. Battleships don't matter anymore, we said. They're outdated. Horse cavalry! They savored the prospect. Horse cavalry, indeed!

With my friends, I said and believed that. I thought that *it had now been shown that battleships can't survive aircraft attacks. And, the world is filled with aircraft. The end of battleships is at hand. Aircraft carriers are now the capitol ships of the fleet!*

The battleship is not totally dead, however. It has provided bombardment near beaches in many wars beyond WWII. It generally has 16-inch guns and that makes an impression in bombardment if the target is near the beach and ocean waters are deep enough to support a battleship. Unfortunately, it serves as a poor gun platform so the accuracy is not great. At best, it is a rocking mortar. There is presently not one battleship in the world but there are many aircraft carriers.

Many feel it is very unlikely that the United States Pacific Fleet would have challenged the Japanese if Japanese aggression had been limited to the British and Dutch colonies, which possessed the oil, rubber, and other resources coveted by Japan. There are three important reasons for this. First, there were isolation and neglect of the military. Second, the U.S. focused on Europe. Third, the U.S was committed to Rainplan-5 war plans, again focusing on Europe and the Atlantic.

These many feel that had Japan been more astute, the Co-Prosperity Sphere policy might have survived.

"The Japanese know they made a mistake," I said. "They talk a big game but their goose is cooked."

Many responded from conviction. "Japan doesn't understand what a real industrial power can do. Look at the Great War. American industry overwhelmed Europe. She'll do the same thing to Japan. Japan is filled with a bunch of hotheads now, but they'll all regret it. America can build a thousand ships and ten thousand airplanes. In the end, it won't matter if there's both Europe and Japan."

If the Axis had declared war, Roosevelt and the anti-war factions would have been in a real quandary, but the Germans, for no apparent reason, declared war on the U.S. four days later. My group in the Officer's Club laughed. We raised both hands. "Why would Japan do such a dumb thing?" we asked. We then laughed hopelessly. All the aircraft carrier enthusiasts laughed at the joke, this time on the Germans.

The daffy thesis struck again. Japan's actions were daffy. Even much of her war-provoking against America and the Allies was daffy. Her deep cruelty in China, such as the rape of Nanking and everywhere she went, was irrational, illogical and daffy. Retribution was inevitable.

Lewis Carroll's Alice found little humor at the Mad Hatter's tea party. It was a daffy tea party.

Dieppe Raid (16 August 1942)

There were pressures to make a strike as soon as possible to reassure Stalin and the British military. I joined the services in early 1941. I had an excellent background for general knowledge. I made high scores in the service's aptitude tests. This was a kind of intelligence or IQ test. I was assigned to a ranger group in preparation for special assignments.

The Dieppe Raid was an Allied attack on the German-occupied port of Dieppe. The raid took place on the northern coast of France on 19 August 1942. The assault began at 5:00 a.m., and by 10:50 a.m., the Allied commanders called a retreat. Over 6,000 infantrymen, predominantly Canadians were supported by a Canadian Armored regiment and a strong force of Royal Navy plus smaller Royal Air Force landing contingents. It involved 5,000 Canadians, 1,000 British troops, and 50 United States Rangers.

Virtually none of these objectives were met. Allied fire support was grossly inadequate and the raiding force was largely trapped on the beach by obstacles and German fire. With only 6 hours action on an enemy beachhead before calling for a retreat, this was a sorry use of soldiers and equipment. The Allies were on the beach only 10 hours. This was indeed a disastrous effort conceived at the upper level of government.

After less than 10 hours since the first landings, the last Allied troops had all been killed, evacuated, or left behind to be captured by the Germans. Instead of a demonstration of resolve, the bloody fiasco showed the world that the Allies could not hope to invade France for a long time. Nevertheless, some intelligence successes were achieved, including electronic intelligence.

Pre-strike Intelligence on the area was sparse: there were dug-in German gun positions on or in the cliffs, where these had not been detected or spotted by air reconnaissance photographers. The planners had assessed the beach gradient and its suitability for tanks only by scanning holiday snapshots, which led to an underestimation of the German strength and of the terrain. The Allied tanks crossing the beach lost their treads or traction on the hard paving tile of the beaches.

I was an American intelligence officer for the strike; I was eighteen at the time. I received special training in Britain. This was my first combat assignment. I was aware that no one knows how they will hold up in battle. Fortunately, I acted with honor. I had, nonetheless suffered two separate wounds. I was dragged out over the beach by an unknown angel. They were never able to identify the soldier that saved me.

The wounds were not life threatening. I suffered a shrapnel wound in my right leg. Afterwards, I received a wound across my chest. I was later awarded a medal for my participation in the raid.

In my mind, it was worth it. I had stood up under fire. I was a soldier that could take combat. I then offered the plea, "Please God, let me be normal."

This was answered.

By far the most fundamental plea of all was, "Please, God. Don't let me fuck up."

This was also answered.

For the Allies, 3,623 of the 6,086 men (almost 60%) who made it ashore at Dieppe were killed, wounded, or captured. The Royal Air Force failed to lure the Luftwaffe into open battle and lost 96 aircraft (at least 32 to flak or accidents), compared to 48 lost by the Luftwaffe. The Royal Navy lost 33 landing craft and 1 destroyer. The lessons at Dieppe helped preparations for both the North African and *Normandie* landings, which were to come in time.

Allied tragedies were occurring everywhere in 1942.

The Dieppe Raid was a daffy catastrophe. The objectives were beyond reason. The intelligence was missing or muddled. There were too many objectives. The whole thing was a fiasco.

The Caucasus and Germany's Winter Campaign

The Axis suffered setbacks, but the Germans still required the rich oil resources and grain of the Caucasus. They planned a campaign to get them and to capture Leningrad, which was in the region

The Caucasus is on the western edge of the Sea of Azov that also holds Baku, the oil center. This and Rumania held most of the oil available to the Germans. This area in southern Russia holds the Ukraine and the Crimea. It also holds most of the oil and foodstuff of Russia. Thus, it is the primary oil source and the breadbasket of Russia. This is not to mention that much of the machinery and industrialization are there. It was unthinkable that the Germans could prevail in the war without the resources of the Ukraine, especially since the German losses had been so enormous during the cold winter of 1941. This they were not prepared for.

The immense Caucasus region is bounded by the Black Sea to the west and the Caspian Sea to the east. The region north of the mountains was a production center for grain, cotton and heavy farm machinery while its two main oil fields, south of the mountains lay the densely populated region of Transcaucasia, comprising Georgia, Azerbaijan and Armenia. This heavily industrialized area, had a greater population density than New York State, contained some of the largest oil fields in the world. Baku, the capital of Azerbaijan, was one of the richest, producing 80 percent of the Soviet Union's oil.

The Germans expected a quick victory in the USSR but they were simply not ready for the bitterly cold Moscow winter where the weather was the biggest reason for their not winning the Battle of Moscow. The Germans had sent huge numbers of tanks and artillery to this front but they were always low on oil. Many of the soldiers died from the cold temperatures that were often below 14°F.

During the winter of 1941, The German Army lacked necessary supplies to cope with the Russian winter, such as uniforms. Operation Barbarossa miscarried before the onset of severe winter weather. The Germans were so confident of a quick victory that they had not prepared for even the possibility of winter warfare in Russia. Yet, the German army suffered more than 734,000 casualties (about 23% of its average strength of 3,200,000) during the first five months of the invasion.

From the start of Operation Barbarossa, 22 June 1941, until the end of 1942, the gains and losses of the Allies were reported primarily from the Russian front. Military action during this time was primarily in Russia while America was preparing for offensive action starting with Operation Torch, the invasion of North Africa, 8 November 1942.

The Soviets accurately saw how the situation was developing and began attacking the freezing Germans who were finally driven away from the Moscow area on 7 January 1942.

The Germans suffered an enormous defeat in the last months of the winter of 1941 with close to a million dead. They never recovered from this. Meanwhile, the Soviets built tanks and more tanks and war materials of all kinds beyond the Urals and out of sight of the Nazis. They were also buttressed by large quantities of Lend-Lease war materials. These facts only became known as Russians ploughed across the landscape toward the German Army in a massive counter-attack.

George and I were both in Britain getting ready for Operation Torch against North Africa. Like most of the American military, we were waiting for the build-up of our forces. The Eastern front was located in deep Russia and it was the dead of winter. Americans were therefore spared the horrors befalling the Soviets. Further, the German army on the Eastern front was encountering the terrible winter, the harshest in many years. Thus, both the Soviet and German armies were draining each other's blood while America stood free of this.

Churchill's Soft Underbelly Strategy

Churchill had a plan of attacking the soft underbelly of Europe. The plan was accepted as Operation Torch, the mass landings in North Africa. The Italian campaign then received a lower-priority reflecting Roosevelt's desire to keep U.S. troops active in the European theater during 1943 and his attraction to the idea of eliminating Italy from the war.

The Allied plan was to occupy North Africa, then invade Sicily and the Italian mainland. The Allies would then fight along the spine of Italy until Germany was defeated. The Americans were defeated at the Kasserine Pass, in Tunisia. As it turned out, both the Germans and the Americans fought ferociously up the Italian spine until reaching Germany at war's end.

Even as the Allies were preparing to invade Sicily, the Italian people and their government increasingly turned against the war. After the loss of North Africa, the invasion of Sicily, and the first bombing of Rome, the Italian king forced Mussolini to resign as head of the government. The Italians wanted to pull out of the war, but they were virtual prisoners of German forces in Italy.

I was in an operational flight squadron in Italy at that time. My participation consisted of ground support for the army as the Americans fought northward. This was thought to be an assignment lasting for a few months. The Germans had other plans.

The southernmost German defensive line, which was a series of military fortifications in Italy, ran east-west across the country. Called the Winter Line, it was the strongest German defensive line south of Rome, and was fortified with gun pits, concrete bunkers, machine-gun emplacements, and mine fields. The western part of the line, which was centered on the historic Monte Cassino monastery, was called the Gustav Line. Those defensive lines proved to be major obstacles to the Allies.

The German Army stuck like glue. The Italians provided huge numbers of soldiers but that was only part of the story. The Italian army was not very effective so the Germans operated such that the Italians were virtual German prisoners. The Germans gave the marching orders for operations along the Gustov Line until the end of the war. The Apennine Mountain Range facilitated the defense of Italy all the way to the northern border with Germany.

Meanwhile, the long slog up the Italian peninsula continued until the invasion of Europe finally defeated the Germans.

The Air Force was not very effective in these mountainous areas against German fortifications, fog, rain and a continuous assortment of weather limitations. This was not to mention the massive German army behind the defensive lines thrown across this mountainous spine of Italy running all the way from the toe in the south to the northern border of the Italian boot.

The Air Force had no choice but to wait on the ground while the army was chewed up in the mountainous crevices. Finally, the Air Force was given respite. I was transferred back to operational duty in the intelligence game. As the fighting armies of Germany fell back further and further toward the German airfields of northern Italy and the German border, my intelligence activity was of considerably greater importance than the tactical flying I was doing.

The Battle of Monte Cassino was a series of four battles that began on January 4, 1944. Monte Cassino fell in May 1944, which allowed the British and American divisions to begin their advance on Rome. They overcame Rome just two days before the Normandy invasion.

I participated in the battle for Rome. The mountainous terrain that defined the Gustav Line assured that Allied air power would be curtailed. Mountainous defenses restrict air operations and favor the defense. The fight here was particularly intense. Monte Cassino became a famous name into the far future.

In the spring of 1945 Allied forces penetrated the final German defensive line to enter the fertile plains of the Po River valley. On May 2, the Germans in Italy surrendered.

Less generally acclaimed than other phases of WWII, the campaign in Italy nevertheless played a vital role in the overall conduct of the war. The Italian campaign involved some of the hardest fighting in the war and cost the United States forces some 114,000 casualties.

I had been reassigned to the Pacific theater in late 1943 as an intelligence officer. This was well appreciated since it gave me a couple of weeks in New York as part of my travel orders.

I was lucky in that I avoided the killing machine that rode the Italian spine all the way to the German border. Unfortunately, the killing machine in the Japanese islands was even worse than that in Italy.

By this time, I sometimes flew in a ground support role. My main role, however, was in intelligence.

When In an intelligence roll, it was not unusual for me to get away to London now and then. When standing in a plush bar or rolling dice with mates, I sometimes felt a pang of conscience. Charlotte would be In Larchmont with her studies while I was enjoying myself. What could I do? It was the roll of the dice. I liked Charlotte and I could tell that she liked me too. I didn't want to transfer my troubles to her so I kept all my letters jovial and humorous. You would have thought we were a couple at Yankee Stadium watching a ball game. She played along with this and also did a lot of joking.

I suspected she knew better and was just stringing me along. By this time, it was clear to both of us that she was my girl although I only saw her on very infrequent leaves or furloughs.

She once told me that she knew better than to believe the stories about how everything was safe and she had no reason to worry. She knew I was in danger. There had been occasional periods that I was in real danger. As before, I could only do my best. At other times, I was in plush surroundings and enjoyed my situation. I felt bad about that but again, what could I do? Charlotte sensed these anomalous periods from the few stories I told her. She knew I was participating in the fight.

However, she was not like Bianca. Bianca confessed loneliness a lot. To Charlotte, this was a weakness that her schoolmate transferred to her companions. Charlotte could not understand this. She was more self-sufficient. She was a stronger personality. Nevertheless, the two girls had many features in common.

It was not like I could confide to someone. The military had strict rules against that for good reason. 'Loose Lips Sink Ships', it was said.

CHAPTER 4

TO NORTH AFRICA, 1942-1943

Regardless of my antipathy toward war after my experiences as a combat soldier in the Dieppe raid, I did return to the war. I still had all the élan and enthusiasm that could be expected of me. I had become attached to the Air Force and steadily improved my flying skills. This was especially valuable since it reinforced my intelligence background. When George got the word on this operation, he wanted to be included.

"Charlie," George explained to me as his friend. "This operation will be across all of North Africa. We will land in the West corner of North Africa and send forces from Casablanca on the east coast of Africa to meet the German army in Libya and Egypt. Rommel was recovering from being sick in Germany. Hitler put him in charge of the African army. "

The young Jackson would treat the Air Force almost as incidental when he joined years later but I took it almost as a religion. I took the intelligence job as a way to keep flying. Jackson would later take the intelligence job for itself. On these common goals, these never coalesced but remained a difference in our approach to the world.

George said, "I got this from a briefing I was at the other day. That's one thing that worries me. Everyone is too open about the secret invasion. They are bound to give it away. Furthermore, they have Americans, French, Brits, Italians, Vichy French and god knows what else involved in the planning. I got this from the briefing.

"The invasion force will consist of three convoys; two will sail from Britain and one from the U.S.

"The one from the U.S. will stage out of Solomon Islands, Maryland, in the Chesapeake."

Although somewhat rude, I interrupted him. "I have sailed that area and know something about it," I said "It is the first river north of the Potomac. The amphibious training school is about a mile or two upriver, beyond a sharp bend in the river called Point Patience. There is a basin there with the Navy's amphibious school. It does training, develops landing craft and various strategies for amphibious landings."

The American forces will train there and then form a convoy to sail out of the Chesapeake at Norfolk and across the Atlantic to Morocco. Extraordinary effort will be made to divert German submarines from discovering it. Radio silence will be maintained with diversionary tactics and false radio networks sending false messages.

"Charlie," his friend, George, said. "I'm sure you would like to know something about Port Lyautey since that is where we are going."

George said, "The allies will land in Port Lyautey, Rabat and Casablanca. Afterwards, the intelligence service will be centered in Port Lyautey. That is because they have a port, a military airfield and facilities right on the ocean."

Port Lyautey is a French village that contains a port and airbase. An entrance from the ocean is into the Sebou River that wraps around the air base on three sides. The air base sits atop a plateau of perhaps several hundred feet.

Italian Campaign

All combatants in the North African Maghreb knew the power of intelligence but none of them used it to the fullest extent. Early code machines were developed in Poland but copies were bought or fell into the possession of France, Britain. Italy, and Germany. All these and the rest worked on similar machines. These all copied one another to the extent possible, they all dashed across the desert under the influence of intelligence, all tried to steal one another's secrets, often with success, and all these caused the technology to advance.

There were interesting developments in military coding that were to profoundly influence military intelligence. The back and forth British and Italian effort in intelligence and breaking codes was critical to that campaign and it later established the pivot of the war in the Pacific. The North African Campaign included Germany's Africa Korps. It took place 10 June 1940 to 13 May 1943. It included campaigns fought in the Libyan and Egyptian deserts, and in Morocco, and Tunisia. The campaign was fought between the Allies and Axis powers, many of which had colonial interests in Africa dating from the late 19th century. The Allied war effort was dominated by the British Commonwealth and exiles from German-occupied Europe. The United States entered the war in December 1941 as part of the Pearl Harbor realignment and began direct military assistance to troops in North Africa on 11 May 1942.

Italy had declared war on Great Britain in June. At that time, Italian General Rodolfo Graziani had almost 10 times the number of men in Libya that the British forces in Egypt had. These were primarily to protect the North African approaches to the Suez Canal. A vast western desert stretched between the antagonists, who sat for months without confrontation. In the meantime, Italian forces had passed into Egypt — but Britain had also reinforced its own numbers. British cryptographers were also able to break the Italian military code, enabling British commanders to anticipate Italian troop movements, size, and points of vulnerability.

On 7 December 1939, British armored car patrols surreptitiously set out to determine gaps in the minefield the Italians had laid. In the chain of forts the Italians had established, the British 7th Armored Division swept along the western coast to cut off any hope of an Italian retreat. Within three days, 40,000 Italian prisoners were taken. The end of the Italian occupation of North Africa had begun.

At the beginning of WWII, Italy remained neutral with the consent of Hitler, but it declared war on France and Britain on June 10, 1940, when the

French defeat was apparent. Mussolini believed that Britain would beg for peace, and wanted some casualties 'in order to get a seat at the peace table', but that proved a huge miscalculation. With the exception of the Navy, the Italian armed forces were a major disappointment for Mussolini and Hitler. The Italians constantly needed German help in Greece and North Africa. After the German army defeated Poland, Denmark, Norway, the Netherlands, Belgium, Luxembourg and France, a jealous Mussolini decided to use Albania as a springboard to invade Greece. The Italians launched their attack on October 28, 1940, and at a meeting of the two fascist dictators in Florence, Mussolini stunned Hitler with his announcement of the Italian invasion.

After the invasion of the Soviet Union by Germany failed (1941–42), and the United States entered the war, the situation for the Axis started to deteriorate. In May 1943, the Anglo-Americans completely defeated the Italians and the Germans in North Africa, and in July, they landed in Sicily. King Victor Emmanuel III reacted by arresting Mussolini and appointing a new Prime Minister.

While Allied troops slowly pushed the German resistance to the north, Rome was finally liberated in June 1944, in the Battle of Monte Cassino and Milan in April 1945. The monarchic government finally declared war on Germany, and an anti-fascist popular resistance movement grew, harassing German forces before the Anglo-American forces drove them out in April 1945.

The new government officially continued the war against the Allies, but started secret negotiations with them. Hitler did not trust the Italians, and moved a large German force into Italy, on the pretext of fighting the Allied invasion. The Germans also liberated Mussolini, who then formed the fascist Italian Social Republic, in the German-controlled areas.

The German Afrika Korps, to be commanded by Erwin Rommel, was dispatched to North Africa. This was to reinforce Italian forces in order to prevent a complete Axis rout.

A seesaw series of battles for control of Libya and parts of Egypt followed. Information gleaned via British Ultra code-breaking intelligence proved critical to Allied success in North Africa. Victory for the Allies in this campaign immediately led to the Italian Campaign, which culminated in the downfall of the fascist government in Italy and the elimination of a German ally.

Italy had been a liability from the beginning.

It lusted after Ethiopia, Egypt, Libya, Greece and other parts of Europe and the Middle East. They were eager to announce the trappings of an empire builder but lacked the top echelons, wealth and industrial capacity to pull it off. At last, their African chickens came home to roost. Its army was ineffective but posed a powerful military in the region, finally erupting in the joke that she was.

The Italian Campaign lasted from September 1943 to the end of the war in May 1945. During this time, some 60,000 Allied, and 50,000 German soldiers died in Italy. Overall Allied casualties during the campaign totaled about 320,000 and the corresponding Axis figure (excluding those involved in the final surrender) was about 336,650. No campaign in the West, including the Mediterranean, Middle East and Western Fronts, cost more than the Italian campaign in terms of lives lost and wounds suffered by infantry forces.

Even prior to victory in the North African Campaign, there was disagreement between the Allies on the best strategy to defeat the Axis.

Operation Torch

In 1942, having been persuaded of the impracticality of launching an invasion of France as a second front, American commanders agreed to conduct landings in northwest Africa with the goal of clearing the continent of Axis troops, particularly Rommel's Africa Corps, and preparing the way for a future attack on southern Europe. To aid in assessing local conditions for Operation Torch, the American consul in Algiers was instructed to gather intelligence and try to attract sympathetic members of the Vichy French government. Meanwhile, planning for the landings moved forward under the overall command of General Dwight Eisenhower. It was named Operation Torch. The operation called for three main landings to take place at Casablanca, Oran, and Algiers.

America had gathered information that the sentiment for the Allies was stronger in the Port Lyautey area than any other section of Morocco. This was soon to be contested as the local French went to war against the Americans.

The prevailing atmosphere at the French headquarters in Port Lyautey was one of sympathy toward the Allied cause and distaste for the current fighting. What was lacking was an authorization to stop fighting. Pending receipt of such authorization, the French at Port Lyautey continued to fight.

Finally, on the third day, 10 November, the fortress was overrun and captured, leading to the final success of capturing the local airfield. These victories led to a truce being established on 11 November.

After the battle, most units remained in the area. In January, President Roosevelt visited the area, as a surprise to the troops. He toured the Kasba, and saw the area where the troops had come ashore. In a small cemetery of American dead, he placed a wreath to commemorate their sacrifice.

General George Patton proclaimed the Battle of Port Lyautey as being very serious and important to the Allies cause. Beach conditions were bad, many boats were lost in the landing, and it took more than two days to capture the fort. The French, he diplomatically proclaimed, had put up a gallant fight. However, the Americans had performed badly across all of North Africa. They would later be overwhelmed by the seasoned German army.

America's first major confrontation with the German army had been in The Kasserine Pass near Tunis, Capitol of Tunisia. After taking several months to regroup, Rommel decided on a bold move. He set his sights on Tunis, the capitol and a key strategic goal for both Allied and Axis forces. Rommel determined that the weakest point in the Allied defensive line was at the Kasserine Pass, a 2-mile-wide gap in Tunisia's Dorsal Mountains, which was defended by American troops. His first strike was repulsed, but with tank reinforcements, Rommel broke through on February 20, inflicting devastating casualties on the U.S. forces. The Americans withdrew from their position, leaving behind most of their equipment. Hundreds of American soldiers were killed by Rommel's offensive, and hundreds were taken prisoner. The United States had finally tasted defeat in a ground battle. It was questioned whether the U.S. had the capacity to fight winningly against the Germans.

Now, was this Daffy? We had allies fighting allies with major naval warships. Soldiers were at war and naval battles were engaged. This was a fine how-do-you-do to start the invasion of North Africa and Europe.

Operation Torch cost the Allies around 480 killed and 720 wounded. French losses totaled around 1,346 killed and 1,997 wounded. As a result of Operation Torch, Adolf Hitler ordered German troops to occupy Vichy France. In North Africa, the French Armée d'Afrique joined with the Allies, as did several French warships. Building up their strength, Allied troops advanced east into Tunisia with the goal of trapping Axis forces. American forces encountered German troops for the first time in February when the U.S. was defeated at Kasserine Pass. Fighting through the spring, the Allies finally drove the Axis from North Africa in May 1943.

Rommel had counseled Hitler to allow a full retreat to a defensible line but Hitler thought otherwise. On 9 March, Rommel being sick left Africa for Germany and was replaced.

I had sweet satisfaction in the final defeat of Rommel in North Africa. Rommel was reposted to be responsible for fortress Europe.

I, Charlie, had earned my commission and wings early in the war. Both George Brayburn and I in 1942 were assigned to England in anticipation of the North Africa campaign. Our first assignment was as intelligence officers during the invasion.

Following that campaign, we both were sent to the Pacific and served together again as intelligence officers, first on Guadalcanal, and then we followed the Navy and Air Force as they hopped from island to island on their way to Japan.

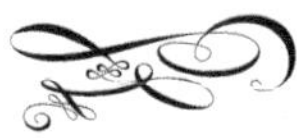

Germany Under Siege

This campaign illustrates a state-versus-state war. Powerful continental armies clashed with thousands of tanks, a greater number of airplanes and millions of soldiers.

Media reports and discussions said that most of the action occurred on the Western Front. This is opposite from the truth. Actually, one might take the position that Russia won the war while America was almost a sideshow!

According to Max Hastings in *Armageddon: The Battle for Germany, 1944-1945,* Americans wildly overrated their battlefield contribution to WWII victory in Europe, and grossly underestimated their decisive industrial output. The Russians barely acknowledged that the western allies had participated in the war at all.

Today, people are often surprised to learn that U.S. and British troops on the battlefield killed only 200,000 German soldiers, contrasted to the Russians who killed over 3,000,000. Some feel the Soviet Union did most of the fighting necessary to defeat the Wehrmacht, whereas the United States did provide a critical portion of the weapons and tools necessary to do so. In Russia, objectivity remains elusive. The western contribution to the war is regarded by Red Army veterans and by many historians even today with something close to contempt. They remain skeptical of British and American contributions. There is little doubt, however, that the U.S. did defeat the Japanese.

Remember that the Russians were neutral against the Japanese, only joining the Allies a few days before Japan surrendered. The Russians played their own game toward Japan. They took the Japanese surrender in Manchuria, getting about 750,000 troops and their weapons. These were used as the beginning of the Chinese Civil War, ending with a Communist China. The Communists maintain control in China to this day, 70 years later.

The Soviet game further won them East Germany and all east Europe after WWII. The Soviets then controlled a huge area for half a century, until the collapse of the Soviet empire.

They had apparently out-maneuvered the Allies in the peace process dating from Yalta.

The German army was victorious from the time of the invasion through the winter of 1941–1942. This resulted in an almost unbroken chain of battlefield successes until the winter of 1942. All Europe lay under German domination. After a successful German advance in the summer of 1942, the battle for the city of Stalingrad in late 1942 proved a turning point. Soviet forces halted the German advance at Stalingrad on the Volga River and in the Caucasus.

Charlotte was 22 years old during the black times. Newspapers reported a great deal of information about the specifics of Germany's plight. However, she had no knowledge of these far-off places.

"Charlotte," Bianca said to her friend, who was the American Ambassador's daughter in Buenos Aires. "I have no understanding of this war in Russia, where cities and battlefields are. The Ukraine and other battlefields present a huge fog to me; I have no knowledge of those places."

"I know," responded Charlotte. Yet, Bianca was from an immigrant Italian family so she had far more interest in Italy and Europe than Charlotte. Those that have interest look at maps and follow newspaper articles, so Bianca had far more knowledge of the Russo-German Theater than she confessed to Charlotte. She wanted to be agreeable.

"Those boys are off fighting and maybe dying and we don't even know anything about it," Bianca allowed.

"Don't worry about it," said Charlotte. "They are in no danger as far as we know."

Bianca did not know much but she, at least, knew it was a long way to Russia from England where George and I were located awaiting the North African campaign.

They both knew the papers were reflecting the enormous defeat for both armies in the cold. She worried. American women hung their little banners on their windows to show how many soldiers came from this or that home. Gold or dark blue stars also indicated if he or she were dead or alive. Increasingly, more and more stars were turning gold as America faced the reality of war. Of course, there was no such banner at the Lee family address.

After the winter defeat, German troops were forced on the defensive, beginning the long retreat westward in what was to end with Nazi Germany's surrender in May 1945, some three years later. Soviet forces launched a counteroffensive in the Ukraine against the Germans arrayed at Stalingrad in mid-November 1942. They quickly encircled an entire German army, more than 220,000 soldiers. In February 1943, after months of fierce fighting and heavy casualties, the surviving German forces of about 91,000 soldiers surrendered. After Stalingrad, Soviet forces remained on the offensive for the remainder of the war, despite some temporary setbacks.

A last German offensive at Kursk and the Oral salient failed in the summer of 1943. The Soviets pushed the Germans back to the banks of the Dnieper River in 1943 and then, by the summer of 1944, to the borders of East Prussia. In January 1945, a new offensive brought Soviet forces to the banks of the Oder, in eastern Germany.

From their bridgehead across the Oder River, Soviet forces launched a massive final offensive toward Berlin in mid-April 1945. The German capital was encircled on April 25. That same day, Soviet forces linked up with their American counterparts attacking from the west at Torgau, on the Elbe River in central Germany. In Berlin itself, heavy fighting took place in the northern and southern suburbs of the city.

As Soviet forces neared his command bunker in central Berlin on April 30, 1945, Adolf Hitler committed suicide. Within days, Berlin fell to the Soviets. The German armed forces surrendered unconditionally in the west on May 7, 1945.

The battles on the Eastern Front constituted the largest military confrontation in history. They were characterized by unprecedented ferocity, wholesale destruction, mass deportations, and immense loss of life due to combat, starvation, exposure, disease, famine and massacres. This again demonstrates a state-versus-state war with the Red continental army as the winner, at least, with the military part of the war.

The Eastern Front, as the site of nearly all extermination camps, death marches, ghettos, and the majority of pogroms, was central to the Holocaust. Of the estimated 70 million deaths attributed to WWII, over 30 million, many of them civilian, occurred on the Eastern Front. The Eastern Front was decisive in determining the outcome of World War II. It resulted in the destruction of the Third Reich, the partition of Germany for nearly half a century and the rise of the Soviet Union as a military and industrial superpower.

Between June 1941 and May 1945, Nazi Germany and the Soviet Union engaged in a cataclysmic struggle. The resulting war was one of the largest and deadliest military duels in all of human history, and ultimately turned the tables on the Nazi conquest of Europe. It was also a conflict marked by strategic blunders, mass atrocities and human suffering on a previously unimaginable scale

Joseph Stalin disregarded early warnings of the German attack. Adolf Hitler had designs on attacking the Russians — whom he viewed as an inferior race — as soon as the time was right. Nevertheless, Stalin appeared blind to the Nazi leader's true intentions. In the months before the German advance, he brushed off dozens of reports from Soviet spies warning that an invasion was imminent. Stalin's puzzling trust in the Third Reich was finally dashed on June 22, 1941, when the Germans launched Operation Barbarossa and invaded the Soviet Union with more than three million men.

Most people believed Germany would quickly crush the Soviet Union. Operation Barbarossa was intended to deal a total defeat to the Soviets in only three to six months, but in the early days of the invasion, many thought the fall might come even sooner. German troops killed or wounded 150,000 Soviets in the first week of the campaign, while the Luftwaffe—the Nazi air force—destroyed over 2,000 Russian planes in just the first two days. As German tanks and troops swarmed through Soviet territory in a three-pronged attack, most outside analysts began predicting that a Russian defeat was only weeks or even days away. Despite these early setbacks, the Soviets' seemingly inexhaustible supply of troops ultimately proved too much for the Germans to overcome. While the invaders succeeded in knocking several million Russian soldiers out of the war by November 1941, they had also suffered more than 700,000 casualties of their own. Following a series of ferocious counterattacks by the Soviets, the Nazis were forced to abandon all hope of a swift victory. The war would drag on for another three and a half years.

Extreme weather conditions played a crucial role in the Soviet victory.

In addition to the might of the Red Army, German troops were also worn down by winter itself. Adolf Hitler's invasion plans called for the Germans to conquer the Soviet Union before the legendary cold could set in, but supply issues and an unexpectedly spirited resistance combined to stall the advance at Moscow's doorstep in late-1941. Still clad in their summer uniforms, the German Wehrmacht had to resort to using newspaper and straw to insulate themselves against subzero temperatures. They soon faced frostbite in epidemic proportions. Some 100,000 cases were reported by the end of 1941, resulting in the amputation of nearly 15,000 limbs.

Russian women served in front line combat roles. Soviet-era Communism tended to embrace the equality of the sexes, and perhaps nowhere was this more apparent than in the Russian attitude toward female soldiers. Nearly one million Soviet women took up arms and served on the front lines of WWII as anti-aircraft gunners, snipers, partisan guerillas and even fighter pilots. More than simply providing the Red Army with an unanticipated boost in numbers, female troops eventually earned a reputation as some of the fiercest fighters on the Eastern Front. Anxious to prove their worth in combat, women regularly signed up for some of the most hazardous combat positions.

Stalin ordered Soviet forces to fight to the last man. After seeing millions of Soviet troops captured in the early days of the German blitzkrieg, Joseph Stalin issued August 1941's "Order," which proclaimed that any troops who surrendered or allowed themselves to be captured were traitors in the eyes of the law and would be executed if they ever returned to Russia. The dictator later upped the ante with July 1942's famous "Order," better known as the "Not One Step Backward!" rule, which decreed that cowards were to be "liquidated on the spot." Under this order, any troops who retreated were to be shelled or gunned down by so-called "blocking detachments"—special units who were positioned behind their own lines and charged with shooting any soldier who tried to flee. Stalin's draconian orders were designed to increase the Red Army's fighting spirit, but they weren't empty threats. According to some estimates, Soviet barrier troops may have killed as many as 150,000 of their own men over the course of the war, including some 15,000 during the Battle of Stalingrad.

This included the largest tank battle in military history. The Eastern Front is best known for the multi-year Siege of Leningrad and the bloody Battle of Stalingrad, but it was also the site of the largest armored confrontation of all time. During July 1943's Battle of Kursk, some 6,000 tanks, 2 million men and 5,000 aircraft clashed in one of the most strategically important engagements of World War II. The campaign began when the Germans set their sights on a 70-mile-long salient, or defensive bulge, in the

Soviet lines in western Russia. Hitler delayed the attack by several weeks to allow the Nazis' new Tiger tanks to reach the front, which gave the Soviets time to fortify the entire region.

Finally, the orders came. Thousands of engines roared as they belched clouds of black diesel smoke above them.

When the German offensive finally commenced, it was met by artillery fire that eventually destroyed hundreds of tanks and left a total of some 350,000 men dead on both sides. Unable to match the Soviets in a contest of attrition, the Germans reluctantly withdrew from the region on July 13. The retreat marked the last gasp of Nazi offensive operations in the East.

Both sides engaged in large-scale atrocities and war crimes. The struggle for the Eastern Front was bigger and costlier than the fighting in the West. It was also significantly more brutal. The Red army practiced institutionalized acts of cruelty against enemy troops, prisoners and civilians. The Germans wiped out scores of villages during their advance through Russia. Jews and other minorities were regularly rounded up and shot or poisoned in mobile gassing vans. Other cities were looted or starved into submission, most famously, Leningrad, where as many as one million civilians may have perished during a 28-month siege. The Red Army responded by giving no quarter during the Soviet push to Berlin in 1945, when hundreds of thousands of German civilians were shot, burned alive in buildings, crushed by tanks and even crucified. According to some studies, Soviet troops may have also been responsible for the rape of some two million German women during the last days of the war. Many think this was state policy at the time.

The last German POWs weren't released from the Soviet Union until 1956. Many Russian POWs were kept under lock and key for several more years. Most were used as slave labor in copper or coal mines, and anywhere between 400,000 and one million eventually died while in Russian custody. Some 20,000 former soldiers were still in Soviet hands at the time of Stalin's death in 1953, and the last 10,000 didn't get their freedom until 1956—a decade after the war had ended.

The Germans had raised the murder of civilians to a formal state policy. These oven policies reached about 6 million Jews and another 6 million non-Jews. This is often miss-stated as 5 million but that accounts only for Jews.

The numbers are contested. It is only fitting that approved military operations be considered as legitimate state policies. Mass murder by state policy is a new innovation of statehood that requires special condemnation.

Most victorious armies behave miserably in their jubilation but we like to think this is a failure of the government. In truth, we suspect it was Red Army policy and Nazi intentions that resulted in millions of murders and deaths. Clausewitz and Mahan, as theorists, were meanwhile high above this fray.

CHAPTER 5

WWII — PACIFIC

When the Allies won the North African Campaign in May 1943, a quarter-million German and Italian troops surrendered in Tunisia, on the north coast of Africa. The Allies began the Italian Campaign that inaugurated the invasion of Sicily.

I had been very fortunate since I had been transferred to the Pacific before the Italian Campaign began. Both George and I had been transferred and assigned to the Solomon Islands at Guadalcanal in late 1943. Our careers in intelligence continued.

After being transferred, George and I remembered discussions we had even as far back as our stay in England before the invasion of North Africa. Both of us were discussing Japan and its culture while in England in early 1942. The Allies' focus then had been on Africa but we still worried about Japan. Both George and I tried to upgrade our knowledge of Japan and how their culture would affect the Pacific war.

"George," I stated, "a major question occurs about the war in the Pacific and it is germane to all aspects of this Pacific War. Was the Emperor complicit in starting and prosecuting the war?" Some believe the military was guilty of this while others believe the Emperor was the real power but exercised it behind screens of secrecy. As the lord of all lords developed, they founded the Shinto religion to anoint the Emperor as the descendent of the Sun God.

"I don't know," responded George. "All spiritual and secular power resides in him, they say. However, as opposed to the Russians, he was spiritually constrained; he and his warlords had mutual spiritual duties and constraints, ritual constraints and responsibilities. The system works by ritualism, and all the people have been forged into this one family over centuries and centuries. They try to reach a consensus in that the weights of the votes rise exponentially up the ladder, and if there is even one dissent, they deal with it heavily and summarily. But it is a democracy where the lords vote and the Emperor counts. All others ratify."

Japan fielded a maritime army and naval force in the state-versus-state struggle of WWII. This was true to the theories of continental armies and naval forces as advocated by Clausewitz and Mahan.

This was in line with the thinking long after the war with the modern book, *Hirohito and the making of modern Japan,* by Herbert Bix. This was written and widely circulated.

George said to me, "There is a lot of talk in Tokyo newspapers and radio about a 'Co-Prosperity Sphere,' which means they want a major expansion into Southeast Asia. This would mean an empire built on islands in the Pacific down the coast all the way to the Netherlands East Indies. What's that going to do?"

"That is crazy," I said. "I know about it, but they will not be able to do it. The British, Americans, and everyone else would jerk them out of those crazy notions.

"The Japanese Army is opposed to it, but the Japanese Navy and part of the government are pushing that notion. That's why they were so upset at the Washington conference in 1922 and the Kellogg Naval Conference in New York in 1928. The Japanese battleships were restricted to a 5-3-5 ratio with the U.S. and Britain at five each, but Japan had to take hind tit at three. They are still incensed about that, because it denied the Japanese naval policy and treated Japan as inferior."

"The strategy of empire was best formulated and advocated by Admiral Alfred Thayer Mahan as part of an overarching naval theory. He published a number of books on the strategy of sea power around the turn of the century. His strategy of empire was so intriguing and compelling; it was influential in the American acquisition of the Philippines, Cuba, and other islands during the Spanish-American War, the Annexation of Hawaii, and the building of the Panama Canal.

"This occurred as America began to implement an empire, emulating Britain. Mahan explained the role of sea power in building ocean empires. The empire-builders in the early part of this century loved him, especially the Russian Czar, the German Kaiser, and the Japanese Navy. He was feted on the Czar's yacht, on Kaiser Wilhelm's yacht, and the Japanese put him on a pedestal. He lectured, authored articles, taught, spoke at government functions, and his advocacy squared exactly with the developing Japanese notions of sea power and colonies and empire. It particularly squared with the Japanese Navy's embryonic concepts of a Southeast Asia Co-Prosperity Sphere."

I stopped my oration long enough to get a glass of water.

"My God!" exclaimed George. "Will this never stop?"

"Be patient," I retorted.

"Japan had another taste of the forbidden fruits from the earlier Chinese and Russian wars, and didn't Mahan's theories and acquaintances at the highest levels of the American government, particularly with President Teddy Roosevelt himself, and the European heads of state, give such methods an aura of respectability? The pursuit of empire has driven the Japanese for the last half century!

"Yeah," said George. "I love it. All these countries fighting in the Great War were drinking from the same fountain. They all wanted a piece of empire, their place in the sun. They all wanted to be Britain." He laughed at the irony.

George said that it was amazing. England is an island off the continental coast, just like Japan. Now they're both continuing to drive for an ocean empire. Mahan lives on!

"Nevertheless, Mahan didn't set the Japanese on their course," said George. "He was just singing their song. He was resonating with them. He was articulating and intellectualizing what their geography drove them to do. Their genes drove them in their decisions, in their environment and in their neighborhoods. Who knows?

"And the continental powers such as Germany and Russia also kept at their empire work. It is the continental empires versus the ocean empires, the continental armies versus the naval forces. Who will win and who will lose?

"Well, I'll tell you something, George."

"I am not sure any of this business about concessions matters now. The Japanese Army occupies large areas of the Chinese mainland, especially around the treaty ports, and they aren't concerned about treaties.

"Most people know that. But it always helps to keep a legal pretense," I told George.

"Japan later made its famous twenty-one demands, that China was able to reject in 1915. If accepted, this would effectively have made China a ward of the Japanese state.

I then continued. "In January 1932 another dangerous incident exploded in Shanghai between Chinese Nationalist forces and the Japanese Special Naval Landing Party, a euphemism for a large, armed Japanese Marine force which had become a permanent unit in the Shanghai international settlement. Because of fighting that ended in May 1932, the Japanese greatly reinforced their garrison in Hongkow Park. A permanent barracks was erected, which was faced in granite and covered two city blocks. It could, and did, house 2,000 soldiers as well as tanks and armored cars. From these fortifications, it dominated the international settlement from then on.

"After Marco Polo Bridge, I thought the Japanese should withdraw their communities from all their concessions in South China and the Yangtze Valley. They would then dispatch large military forces to Shanghai, Tientsin, and Hangkow. In mid-August, they launched their full-scale military attack, which is now a full-scale war all along the Chinese seaboard.

"You knew it had to come, though," I stated. "How do the Chinese people feel? You know feelings were running high. After all, one could see Japanese ships deep in the interior running up and down the Yangtze and Yellow Rivers with the Rising Sun flags flying on the fantails. The Chinese seemed infuriated. They always considered the Japanese little monkeys, anyway! They couldn't do anything. Japanese army units were stationed on Chinese soil, and marched aggressively any time they wanted to, which was often."

"The Westerners did the same thing." George said.

"The Japanese appeared as Martians to the Chinese. The Chinese always considered themselves superior to other people," I told George. "They never quite accepted Westerners as other people. We Da Bitsu, or Big Noses might as well have come from Mars, as far as the Chinese were concerned. The Chinese could live with us white Europeans to some extent, since we Big Noses did not represent the real world. But the Japanese were a different matter. They were real people to the Chinese, even as the Chinese defined it; even if they were nothing more than supplicants and tributaries! The Chinese thought, this is too much."

We both laughed at these truisms; at the rank indictments, and at such notions.

As one passed through this heightened naval and military activity, they could not know. No living person could know then. This war would soon affect every man, woman and child on the planet. It would cause the premature deaths of tens of millions of people who now loved life dearly, and would suffer terribly.

The two men stood in the ship's wardroom. They had been assigned to this ship on a message-delivering service for some admiral. The sun was falling low toward the horizon in the west. It made a long, brilliant streak from the horizon toward the ship, a silver streak across the water.

Both men looked out over their ship's shadow on the water as they slid northward. They saw their ghosts and images sweeping across the watery space. They saw their own perception of themselves. Their cerebral images silently galloped across their screen, even as their shadows slid across the watery plains before them.

In the early evening, they heard all kinds of sounds from the sonar room. The sailors laughed and clapped their hands.

"What's the matter with you?" I asked. "I heard all kinds of yelling from the ship's interior. Have you all gone mad?" They waved back.

"You just wait." they said, "You will see the strangest thing. Go outside and look for the porpoises."

We did that and saw a very odd thing. The ocean was a mirror. The ocean had almost no waves and there were hardly any breezes. The bow waves of the ship peeled out across the mirror. They made a perfect 'V', each side stretching in a straight line to the horizon. Riding the bow wave were perhaps a thousand porpoises. They were about six feet apart and skimmed the breaking water. When they got close, they were audibly screaming. That was generally not audible from a single porpoise but with this many, their sounds were clearly audible. They stayed lined up and kept pace with us for at least half an hour. Then they started drifting away. They had surely made a wonderful sight for a long time.

Doolittle Raid

The morale for America and her Allies could not be lower. The strike at Pearl Harbor appeared devastating; though it could have been much worse had the Japanese struck the aircraft carriers there. Furthermore, The Japanese had struck a multitude of targets in Southeast Asia. All the news was bad as the Japanese occupied the Philippines, Indo-China, Malaya, and numerous islands. America desperately needed a morale boost.

In response to this, the Doolittle Raid was launched on Saturday, April 18, 1942. This was an American air raid primarily against Tokyo. This was the first strike on the Japanese home islands. It demonstrated that Japan itself was vulnerable to American air attack, served as retaliation for the Japanese attack on Pearl Harbor and provided an important boost to American morale. Lieutenant Colonel James Doolittle led the raid. As an indication of his drive beyond his military exploits and education, he had earned a masters degree and a PhD from MIT. The raid had a devastating affect on the Japanese military leaders.

Sixteen B-25 Mitchell medium bombers were launched beyond fighter escort range from the U.S. Navy's aircraft carrier USS Hornet, where each had a crew of five men. The plan called for them to bomb military targets in Japan, and to continue westward to land in China. After the bombing, fifteen aircraft reached China, but all crashed, while the 16th landed at Vladivostok in the Soviet Union. All but three of the 80 crew members initially survived the mission. The Japanese Army in captured eight soldiers in China; three of those were later executed.

After the raid, the Japanese Army conducted a massive sweep through the eastern coastal provinces of China. This was a search for the surviving Americans and was to inflict retribution on the Chinese who aided them. The Army wanted to prevent this part of China from being used again for an attack on Japan.

The raid caused negligible material damage to Japan, but it achieved its goal of raising American morale and casting doubt in Japan on the ability of its military leaders to defend their home islands. It also contributed to the Japanese decision to attack Midway Island in the Central Pacific that might be used in the future for such attacks

Doolittle's first report on the plan suggested the bombers might land in Vladivostok, shortening the flight by 600 nautical miles on the pretext of turning over the B-25s to the Soviets as Lend-Lease equipment. The Soviets denied permission to use Vladivostok. The project continued with the China coast as the landing objective.

Potential crews were offered the opportunity to volunteer for an "extremely hazardous", but unspecified mission. This appeared to be grossly understated considering what was to occur after the bombing.

Battle of Coral Sea and Port Morseby

The Battle of Coral Sea was fought during 4–8 May 1942, about 3 weeks after the Doolittle raid. It was a major naval battle. The battle was the first action in which aircraft carriers engaged each other. Japanese forces decided to invade and occupy Port Moresby on the south coast of New Guinea, near the most northern point of Australia and Tulagi, across from Florida Island in the Solomons. The plan to accomplish this involved several major units of Japan's Combined Fleet, including two fleet carriers and a light carrier to provide air cover for the invasion fleets, under the overall command of Japanese Admiral Inoue. The U.S. learned of the Japanese plan through Elint or electronic intelligence. The Americans decided to respond with two United States Navy carrier task forces and a joint Australian-American cruiser force, under the overall command of American Admiral Fletcher.

On 3–4 May, Japanese forces successfully invaded and occupied Tulagi, although several of their supporting warships were surprised and sunk or damaged by aircraft from the U.S. fleet carrier Yorktown. Although a tactical victory for the Japanese in terms of ships sunk, the battle would prove to be a strategic victory for the Allies because two Japanese carriers, one damaged and the other with a depleted aircraft complement, were unable to participate in the Battle of Midway, which took place the following month. This ensured a rough parity in aircraft between the two adversaries and this contributed significantly to the U.S. victory in that battle. The severe losses in carriers at Midway prevented the Japanese from reattempting to invade Port Moresby from the ocean. Two months later, the Allies took advantage of Japan's resulting strategic vulnerability in the South Pacific and launched the Guadalcanal Campaign that, along with the New Guinea Campaign, eventually broke Japanese defenses in the South Pacific and was a significant contributing factor to Japan's ultimate defeat in World War II.

Unknown to the Japanese, the U.S. Navy had for several years enjoyed some success with penetrating Japanese communication ciphers and codes. By the end of April the Americans were reading up to 85% of the Japanese signals broadcast.

In March 1942, the U.S. first noticed mention of the MO operation in intercepted messages. On 5 April, the Americans intercepted a Japanese message directing a carrier and other large warships to proceed to Admiral Inoue's area of operations. On 13 April, the British deciphered a Japanese message informing Inoue that two fleet carriers were en route to his command from Formosa via the main Japanese base at Truk. The British passed the message to the Americans, along with their conclusion that Port Moresby was the likely target.

Admiral Nimitz, the new commander of Allied forces in the Pacific at Pearl Harbor, and his staff discussed the deciphered messages and agreed that the Japanese were likely initiating a major operation in the Southwest Pacific in early May with Port Moresby, New Guinea as the probable target. The Allies regarded Port Moresby as a key base for a planned counteroffensive, under Douglas MacArthur, against Japanese forces in the southwest Pacific area. Nimitz's staff also concluded that the Japanese operation might include carrier raids on Allied bases in Samoa and at Suva. Nimitz, after consultation with Admiral Ernest King, Commander in Chief of the United States Fleet, decided to contest the Japanese operation by sending all four of the Pacific fleet's available aircraft carriers to the Coral Sea. By 27 April, further signals intelligence confirmed most of the details.

On 29 April, Nimitz issued orders that sent his four carriers and their supporting warships towards the Coral Sea as commanded by Rear Admiral Fletcher and consisting of the carrier Yorktown, escorted by three cruisers and four destroyers and supported by a replenishment group of two oilers and two destroyers. These were already in the South Pacific, having departed Tongatabu on 27 April en-route to the Coral Sea. It was commanded by Rear Admiral Fitch and consisted of the carrier Lexington with two cruisers and five destroyers, was between Fiji and New Caledonia, commanded by Vice Admiral Halsey and including the carriers Enterprise and Hornet. They had just returned to Pearl Harbor from the Doolittle Raid in the central Pacific. The Task Force immediately departed but would not reach the South Pacific in time to participate in the battle. Nimitz placed Fletcher in command of Allied naval forces in the South Pacific area until Halsey arrived. Although the Coral Sea area was under MacArthur's command, Fletcher and Halsey were directed to continue to report to Nimitz while in the Coral Sea area, not to MacArthur.

Battle of Midway

Midway Island is located roughly half way between Hawaii and Japan. The battle began on June 3, 1942, when U.S. bombers from Midway Island struck ineffectively at the Japanese carrier strike force about 220 mi southwest of the U.S. fleet. Early the next morning, Japanese planes from the strike force attacked and bombed Midway heavily, while the Japanese carriers again escaped damage from U.S. land-based planes. But as the morning progressed, the Japanese carriers were soon overwhelmed by the logistics of almost simultaneously sending a second wave of bombers to finish off the Midway runways, zigzagging to avoid the bombs of attacking U.S. aircraft, and trying to launch more planes to sink the now-sighted U.S. naval forces. A wave of U.S. torpedo bombers was almost completely destroyed during their attack on the Japanese carriers at 9:20 a.m., but at about 10:30 a.m. 36 carrier-launched U.S. dive-bombers caught the Japanese carriers while their decks were cluttered with armed aircraft and fuel. The U.S. planes quickly sank three of the heavy Japanese carriers and one heavy cruiser. In the late afternoon U.S. planes disabled the fourth heavy carrier (scuttled the next morning), but its aircraft had badly damaged the U.S. carrier *Yorktown*. On June 6, a Japanese submarine fatally torpedoed the *Yorktown* and an escorting American destroyer; that day a Japanese heavy cruiser was sunk. The Japanese, however, appalled by the loss of their carriers, had already begun a general retirement on the night of June 4–5 without attempting to land on Midway.

The Battle of Midway was fought almost entirely with aircraft, and the United States destroyed Japan's first-line carrier strength and most of its best-trained naval pilots during that fight. Together with the Battle of Guadalcanal, the Battle of Midway ended the threat of further Japanese invasion in the Pacific.

Despite a setback in May 1942 in the indecisive Battle of the Coral Sea, the Japanese had continued with plans to seize Midway Island and bases in the Aleutians. Seeking a naval showdown with the numerically inferior U.S. Pacific Fleet, Adm. Isoroku sent out the bulk of the Japanese fleet, including four heavy and three light aircraft carriers, with orders to engage and destroy the American fleet and invade Midway. U.S. intelligence had divined Japanese intentions after breaking the Japanese naval code, however, and the Americans were ready: three heavy aircraft carriers of the U.S. Pacific Fleet were mustered. These ships were stationed 350 miles northeast of Midway and awaited the westward advance of Yamamoto's armada. Whereas the Japanese had no land-based air support, the Americans from Midway and from Hawaii could commit about 115 land-based planes.

What helped the Navy gain the upper hand in the Pacific more than anything else was its ability to know what its enemy was planning to do before they did it. The Combat Intelligence Unit in Pearl Harbor was responsible for this. They were on a quest to crack the complex Japanese code, which carried the Japanese' most secure communications. Messages were routinely intercepted and exhaustively analyzed with mathematical, technical and creative skill. And by March of 1942, the code was finally broken — essentially giving access to the Japanese playbook of planned operations. Having secretly taken away the Japanese element of surprise, the Navy was able to shift to the offensive and, at Midway, turn a planned ambush by the enemy into one of its own.

Located approximately 1300 miles northwest of Pearl Harbor, Midway was already the site of a Navy base with an airport. Fittingly, it would be the focal point of a calculated Japanese plan. The Japanese goal was to attack it, capture it and use it as an advance base that would establish control for its own Pacific operations. They knew the U.S. would defend it with all available resources and hoped to lure the Navy carriers and fleet into a trap. But the U.S. knew of the plan ahead of time and would be ready to deploy its three aircraft carriers and supporting force of ships, submarines and aircraft accordingly.

The Battle of Midway marked a turning point of the war in the Pacific.

Battle of Guadalcanal

The Guadalcanal Campaign originally applied only to an operation to take the island of Tulagi. It was a military campaign fought between 7 August 1942 and 9 February 1943 on and around the island of Guadalcanal. It was the first major land offensive by Allied forces against the Empire of Japan.

On 7 August 1942, United States Marines landed on the islands of Guadalcanal, Tulagi, and Florida, all in the southern Solomon Islands, with the objective of denying their use by the Japanese to threaten Allied supply and communication routes between the U.S., Australia, and New Zealand. The Allies also intended to use Guadalcanal and Tulagi as bases to support a campaign to eventually capture or neutralize the major Japanese stronghold at Rabaul on New Britain. The Allies overwhelmed the outnumbered Japanese defenders, who had occupied the islands since May 1942, and captured Tulagi and Florida, as well as an airfield — Henderson — that was under construction on Guadalcanal. Powerful U.S. naval forces supported the landings.

Surprised by the Allied offensive, the Japanese made several attempts between August and November to retake Henderson Field. Three major land battles, seven large naval battles (five nighttime surface actions and two carrier battles), and continual, almost daily, aerial battles culminated in the decisive Naval Battle of Guadalcanal in early November, in which the last Japanese attempt to bombard Henderson Field from the sea, and land with enough troops to retake it, was defeated. In December, the Japanese abandoned their efforts to retake Guadalcanal and evacuated their remaining forces by 7 February 1943.

The Guadalcanal campaign was a significant strategic combined arms victory by Allied forces over the Japanese in the Pacific theater. The Japanese had reached the peak of their conquests in the Pacific. The victories at Milne Bay, Buna-Gona, and Guadalcanal marked the Allied transition from defensive operations to the strategic initiative in that theater, leading to offensive operations, such as the Solomon Islands, New Guinea, and Central Pacific campaigns that resulted in Japan's eventual surrender.

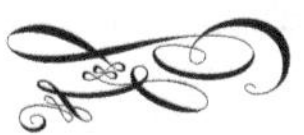

Battle of the Philippine Sea and Tinian

The springtime offensive of fleet against fleet became known as the Battle of the Philippine Sea. This merged with the Battle of Saipan. The invasions of Guam and Tinian occurred a month after Saipan so this led to confusion all around.

The Japanese naval strategy was to have a major naval battle that would decide the issue for all Japan. They knew they could not win a sustained conflict. Thus, their actions often made sense from that perspective although it looked bazaar in the long run.

I had been assigned to Guadalcanal in the Solomon Islands a short while after arriving in the Pacific. There were rumors around the headquarters compound that the Japanese were preparing for a great naval battle to decide WWII. In early 1943, I was reassigned to the flag carrier intelligence unit. I served on the Admiral's flagship until after the Americans took the Marianas. I loved being in the center of the action. The intelligence unit was always in the dark in that they never knew enough, but they did know more than anybody else. The Southwest Pacific was a giant chessboard. The queen was often in check. However, the Japanese played a different game and their checkmate was usually mortal.

I was loyal to my admiral and this made a wonderful, professional relationship. He saw the potential of aircraft and the carrier. I had a great influence through my admiral on the war and its conduct. Never would he again have as great an influence on the war or his surroundings.

I believed in Intel, or electronic intelligence, and he believed in aircraft carriers as the future of warfare. The carriers built before the war such as the Yorktown had a complement of 90 aircraft and a speed of 37.4 mph. The last commissioned carrier in WWII carried 137 aircraft and had a speed of 38 mph. This made an awesome projection of power. My admiral sided more and more with me. To a large extent, the admiral became an advocate of airpower. The carrier ruled the sea and those who ruled the sea, ruled the world.

I was also steadfast in my beliefs. The admiral could trust me.

By mid-1944, the Mitsubishi "Zero" aircraft was no longer on the cutting edge among fighter designs. Ignoring the fact that by this time the United States was out-producing the Axis in war machinery, the new F6F Hellcat was better armored and better suited for dogfights than their Japanese counterparts. Meanwhile, the Japanese Navy's pilot pool was running dangerously short. It was becoming common to see combat pilots with less than 50 hours of flight training.

On 18 June, as the American Marines secured the beachhead at Saipan for an Army landing, search planes from Admiral Ozawa's fleet discovered the American fleet. Ozawa decided to forgo the opportunity for a surprise attack, and wait until the beginning of the next day before launching an attack, despite the fact that he had numerical advantage, or he had more planes available to him than the Americans, and range advantage in that his Zeros had longer range than the American counterparts. He was concerned that his fighter pilots were not capable of making safe night landings on carrier flight decks. This decision proved to be fatal in hindsight; by the time he launched his fighter attacks, the Americans were already alerted to Ozawa's presence, and prepared for such an assault. Spruance, knowing very well of Ozawa's timetable at this time, launched a strike against Guam to pin down the Japanese aircraft there. This damaged the airfields there so that the eventual Ozawa attack was unable to utilize Guam to augment the attack. Admiral Mitscher, at the same time, launched his aircraft against the small island of Rota while sending a few to reinforce Admiral Spruance.

During the day of 19 June 1944, between Ozawa's attacks on the American fleet and the attacks on Guam and Rota, 429 Japanese planes were shot down. The Americans lost 29. This battle was commonly referred to among the U.S. Navy men as the 'Great Marianas Turkey Shoot'. Many historians agree that this event marked the end of Japanese naval air power. Coming events would force Japan to rely on the guns of its battleships and cruisers, driving the Japanese to believe even more deeply in seeking a decisive battle with the U.S. fleet.

A submarine, among others in a wolf pack, found their way to the Japanese carriers during the confusion of battle. One launched torpedoes that struck squarely on the carrier Taiho's starboard side. The Taiho was filled with leaked fuel vapor and a spark somewhere triggered an explosion that sunk the ship. Another submarine, USS Cavalla, fired six torpedoes into the group, sinking the Shokaku. Three of the torpedoes hit the Pearl Harbor veteran and caused a tremendous explosion. Ozawa escaped his burning flagship, the Taiho, after 3:30 p.m., and ordered the ships to withdraw from the heavily damaged cruiser Haguro. After losing over 400 pilots and then two precious carriers, Ozawa would finally get his small bit of luck that day as what was left of his fleet escaped American detection for two days, allowing him to regroup his ships.

From the start, the Imperial Japanese Navy sought to engage the American fleet in a single decisive battle in early 1944. From early in the conflict, the Japanese war plan had been to discourage America by inflicting such severe and painful losses on her military that the American public would become war weary and the Americans would allow Japan to keep her conquests in east and Southeast Asia. The Japanese still clung to this pre-war strategy and did so throughout the war and preparations for it. America was a paper tiger, they reasoned, so one great Japanese onslaught would sour them on the idea of a prolonged war.

It took nearly a year for the Japanese to reconstitute their air groups following the Solomon's campaign. The decisive battle necessarily had to be delayed. Meanwhile, American material production capacity, aircrew training and technological advances made a Japanese victory increasingly difficult to achieve. By the end of 1942, the Allied navies had overcome most of the technological edges Japan's ships and planes had held at the start of the war. Furthermore, by mid-1943 America's mass production of ships and improved aircraft began to tip the balance of forces in the favor of the Allies.

On 20 June 1944, the Japanese naval forces were decisively defeated with heavy and irreplaceable losses of their carrier-borne and land-based aircraft.

Thereafter, U.S. forces executed landings on Guam and Tinian in July 1944. After heavy fighting, Saipan was secured in July and Guam and Tinian in August 1944. The U.S. then constructed airfields on Saipan and Tinian where B-29s were based to conduct strategic bombing missions against the Japanese mainland until the end of World War II, including the nuclear attacks on Hiroshima and Nagasaki.

When Saipan was invaded, the resistance as reported by American intelligence, was to be greater than they had experienced. Fortunately, as the Americans would later find out, most of the supplies the garrison badly needed were taken away, thanks to the American submarine campaign and air superiority. The transport ships simply could not reach the Marianas in one piece. Regardless, the commander, as well as Tokyo, knew the importance of the Marianas. From there, 1,100 miles south of Tokyo, the new American B-29 "Super Fortress" bombers could reach the Japanese home islands and would have enough fuel for the return trip. The pre-landing preparations came like a thunderclap for the Japanese garrison.

Since Guam had been delayed, Saipan became the first in the Marianas to be attacked. D-Day for Saipan was 16 June 1944.

By 5 July, despite the bitter political battles that ensued, the remaining Japanese troops were driven to the northern tip of the island. With their backs to the cliff, the largest banzai charge took place. Three thousand Japanese troops valiantly charged the advancing American line, and broke through the western flank, but American Marines ultimately stopped them. While the banzai charge was breaking through American front lines, Lieutenant General Saito and Vice Admiral Nagumo, after giving orders for such a suicide charge, committed suicide in their respective command bunkers.

When the Americans declared the island secured four days later, Holland Smith's men counted over 23,000 Japanese troops killed. Holland Smith lost 3,426 Americans in comparison. Unfortunately, that was not the end of major bloodshed on Saipan. Encouraged by Tokyo, thousands of Japanese civilians on Saipan committed mass suicide to avoid the shame of being ruled by the conquering Americans. Many men dived off cliffs into shark-ridden waters and mothers threw their babies against rock walls before jumping into the water to join their husbands and brothers. Even children committed suicide, holding on to grenades before they jumped off the cliffs. Nearly 8,000 civilians of Saipan died in this mass suicide. Americans watched in absolute horror, but were able to finally stop the madness by convincing the Japanese of fair treatment over loudspeakers. After the battle, the two sites where the mass suicide took place were named Banzai Cliff and Suicide Cliff as memorial to these fallen civilians.

Americans were horrified by these suicides.

"There are instances in history where suicide was the result of defeat in battle," I said to George. "However, there are not many and they usually consisted of relatively few victims." Generals command armies and as the commander goes, often the army follows.

George and I were shocked with the news of the suicides on Okinawa. This was especially traumatic to me who had so recently been on Saipan and Tinian. Charlie's Caper required him to go to both these sites. He was emotional about the battles on Saipan and Tinian. As often said, "War is Hell."

Across the islands of Asia, there were often suicides by losing commanders.

The Okinawa campaign saw suicides similar to that on Saipan.

Adolph Hitler committed suicide at the end of the war in Europe. Later, Hermann Goring committed suicide while in prison for his war crimes, as did many German commanders and common soldiers.

Many think war is a noble endeavor. Therefore, suicide is a noble act when the soldiers don't measure up.

The girls found the headlines to be confusing. "How could they commit suicide?" they asked. Bianca was deeply affected since she was a witness to the suicide drama on the scuttling of the *Graf Spee* in Montevideo. Charlotte was a similar witness as the American Ambassador's daughter.

I talked to the girls a lot about these suicide pacts. There was a certain fascination in soldiers paying the ultimate price, but even that was often thought to be a cowardly act.

Watson had earned a reputation at Saipan as a hard-charging leader. When the division stalled fighting its way up Mount Topatchau, he was unimpressed. The historian Ronald Spector wrote of Watson in the midst of that effort.

General Watson vented his anger at the stalled troops. He was heard shouting over a field telephone, *'There's not a goddamn thing up on that hill but some Japs with machine guns and mortars. Now get the hell up there and get them!'"*

On 20 June 1944, the Japanese naval forces were decisively defeated with heavy and irreplaceable losses of their carrier-borne and land-based aircraft.

Thereafter, U.S. forces executed landings on Guam and Tinian in July 1944. After heavy fighting, Saipan was secured in July and Guam and Tinian in August 1944. The U.S. then constructed airfields on Saipan and Tinian where B-29s were based to conduct strategic bombing missions against the Japanese mainland until the end of the war, including the nuclear attacks on Hiroshima and Nagasaki.

After the American invasion and when under American control, a massive construction project was begun on the north end of Tinian. Operating for over 45 days and nights, often while under fire, the Seabees initially repaired and extended the existing 4,380 ft. runway and then added an additional two runways, each 8,000 ft. long and lying in an East-West direction. Nearly the entire northern end of the island was occupied by runways, the airfield area, and various support facilities and containment areas.

The Ushi Point Airfield was expanded with three 8000-foot runways involving the movement of nearly 1,000,000 cubic yards of earth. A fourth runway was constructed in May 1945 and hardstands built for 265 B-29 bombers. The four parallel 8,000 ft. runways are oriented nearly East-West. Upon completion, North Field was the largest airfield in the world.

Once in place, The 313th Bomb Wing with 4 groups began flying missions, initially against Iwo Jima, the Truk Islands, and other Japanese held areas. Later, they flew low-level night incendiary raids on area targets in Japan; participated in mining operations in the Shimonoseki Strait, and contributed to the blockade of the Japanese Empire by mining harbors in Japan and Korea. In April 1945 the 313th assisted the invasion of Okinawa by bombing Japanese airfields used by kamikaze pilots.

The 509th was preparing to drop nuclear weapons on Japan. The 509th was given a base area near the airfield on the north tip of the island, several miles from the main installations in the center part of the island where the other groups were assigned. The 509th aircraft group almost always used runway "A" and the aircraft were parked away from the other groups on the north side of the runway for security purposes. When Jackson was on Taiwan, he befriended a mechanic on one of the B-29's that operated from Tinian during WWII. The man's name was Jerry Stankowsky. After the war, Jerry was transferred to Taiwan. Jerry told me later that he had passed through the 509th Composite Group once on business. He was on the flight crew of a regular B-29 flying from Tinian.

Jerry was a very bright person. He knew not only the mechanisms of the B-29 but he was remarkably knowledgeable of what was going on in the headquarters buildings and the general attitudes of the colonels and generals there. Steve infrequently confided in what special information he had known during WWII and his time on Tinian. The regular B-29 crews would look at the frantic 509th activity occurring on the operational airfield and wander about it but there was no general knowledge of what was going on. No one seemed to know anything about the 509th. Jerry's friends could see the big planes taxiing with take offs and landings but they had no idea as to the purpose of it all. There was a beehive of activity. At night, the place was lit like daylight. All this activity prompted questions by the standard crews and supporters. The 509th people stayed by themselves and no one was allowed into the 509th area except for exceptional circumstances. The non-509th people were resentful and discussed this among themselves in whispers. They were cautioned to keep their mouths shut. "Who the hell do they think they are?" Jerry's friends asked in hushed tones. "We're winning the war and all they do is sit there."

After it was announced that a new bomb, the atomic bomb, had been dropped on Hiroshima by the 509th, their attitudes changed totally. "Well! I'll be damned," Jerry said. "We are working ourselves to the bone and they end the war with one bomb. I'll be damned." Jerry always confessed he and his friends were stumped by the fortunes of war.

After the Japanese surrender in August 1945, some units dropped food and supplies to Allied prisoners and participated in show-of-force flights over Japan. Units were either reassigned or inactivated within a few months after the end of the Pacific War. The last Air Force unit left North Field on June 30, 1946, ending its use as an operational airfield. The wing moved to Clark Field, Philippines on 1 February 1946.

The base was placed in a standby status until being closed on 30 March 1947.

Seeing no official use after 1947, North Field was completely abandoned. Immediately after the war, the natives didn't have to farm or do work of any kind for the first two years because the military left entire warehouses full of everything imaginable from food, brand new uniforms, and even ice cream makers. Anybody who wanted a vehicle could just go pick one up and drive it until it fell apart, than go and get another one.

The airfield has been being abandoned and is steadily becoming overgrown and reclaimed by the Tinian jungle. It is easily accessible by traveling a few miles north of San Jose on the main north-south road, 'Broadway'. The crushed coral runways are grayish and weathered-looking, but Runways 'A' and 'B' and some of the taxiways remain drivable in an ordinary car, with only some weedy growth crawling out onto it here and there. Some abandoned B-29 hulks were left at the airfield after the war, but were melted down for scrap in the 1950s. Tinian played a significant role in the war and afterwards.

Other than the runways, remains of former Japanese buildings and the preserved pits used to load the atomic bombs into their aircraft, nothing is left of the old facilities. The jungle has grown right up to the edges of the runways and taxiways.

In 2013, 'B' runway was partially refurbished by the United States Marine Corps for an exercise. A Marine Corps KC-130J Super Hercules landed on the runway 5 December 2013, being only the second aircraft to use North Field since 1947.

Taiwan had been ceded to the Japanese in 1895. The island then became a province of Japan. It became a food-producer for the Japanese and life must have been relatively blissful. One draws that conclusion because the Japanese and their culture are looked on with great fondness by the Taiwanese. This is striking because in most places ruled by the Japanese, they are hated. There must have been enough time for assimilation in the 50 years after the Japanese occupation while they were only on their occupied islands for a few years.

CHAPTER 6

CHARLIE'S CAPER

I had been pulling my weight until mid-1943 in North Africa. However, that campaign was over. In fact, the whole campaign had moved to the invasion of Sicily at first, then to the south of Rome. It then moved towards the north of Italy and began to threaten the airfields in the south of Germany by the end of the war. Italy had proved a very costly slog, both to the Allies and to the German defenders. The Apennine Mountains along the spine of Italy was a nightmare for attackers. The mountains of the north are the Alps, reaching toward Austria and France; again these greatly favored the defenders. The Americans, British and their Commonwealth soldiers continued their battles for Italy until the end of the European war. It cost them dearly. I transferred to the Pacific in late 1943. I became attached to a headquarters staff in Guadalcanal. I remained in the intelligence game. The strategy at that time was an island-hopping campaign under its chief proponent, Admiral Nimitz, in his headquarters in Honolulu. The U.S. was to take various islands heading toward Japan from which they would be used for a massive bombing campaign of the Japanese home islands.

This strategy necessitated an early capture of the Mariana Island group consisting of 3 principal islands: Guam, Saipan and Tinian. Planning was underway at the fleet headquarters when I arrived.

I was immediately assigned to Tinian as the admiral's special planning responsibility. It was generally thought that the Marianas would be taken sometime in mid to late 1944.

The Marianas are a line of islands running roughly south to north.

Tinian, with its sister island, Saipan, of the Marianas group, had passed through Spanish and German hands prior to becoming a Protectorate of Japan following World War I. Under Japanese administration, Tinian was largely a sugar plantation with fields and fields of sugar cane. There were buildings and machinery to convert the cane stalks into sugar. In 1939, large-scale military construction began on Tinian by the Japanese Military. 1,200 prisoners were sent to the island from Japan for the construction of airfields as part of the defense of the Mariana Islands. By 1944, the island had three military airfields with a fourth under construction. What would become Tinian's North Field was a Japanese airstrip 4,380 feet in length; it was home to Japanese reconnaissance aircraft. Until the spring of 1944, the base remained largely out of major action.

The Marianas consist of Guam, the southernmost Island of about 400 square miles, and two large islands, Saipan and Tinian, lying about 130 miles to the north. These are about 5 miles apart. Rota and others serve as lesser ports of the Marianas.

I jumped into the planning with fervor. I was clearly conscious of how my work would affect the lives of the marines that depended on it. I thought the plan was not too binding but having a plan was critical. I knew I had to have excellent data on the geography and terrain as well as the Japanese defenses. I knew we could depend on reconnaissance and the normal channels to satisfy most of my requirements but certainly not all.

The invasion would be on Saipan, while Guam and Tinian would occur almost simultaneously about a month later. The Saipan landing and occupation were expected to be over by the time of the Tinian landing. The Navy was to cover the landing by field artillery on Saipan and by naval bombardment from the sea.

Saipan is a twin of Tinian. Saipan is about 12 miles in length by 5 miles in width covering 44 square miles. Its highest elevation is Mount Tapochau at 1560 feet.

Tinian is, like Saipan, an island about 12 miles long and 4 miles wide for an area of 38 square miles. It is hot and wet. It is dense jungle mostly starting from the sand beaches along the shore. Coconut palm trees provide a palm forest along much of the shore. Heavy forestation is encountered as one falls back from the beaches. The ground is not volcanic but is formed by limestone and characterized by cliffs and caves. Of course, there are patches of ground that are scrub sand. The general terrain is hills and mountains up to 560 feet high. This terrain makes moving around difficult and it would be hazardous in any military situation.

It soon became clear; however, that I did not have enough information to satisfy the requirement and to prevent a disastrous situation under certain circumstances. The jungle terrain was bad enough but limestone cliffs, tunnels and caves greatly favor any defenders. This situation actually occurred with the Japanese on Saipan and only a vitriolic enmity between the Army and Navy commands kept the casualties relatively small, compared to what they could have been.

Seeing this situation and mindful of the number of marines that would probably be killed for lack of information in the planning, I worked on a plan that could improve the chances to be effective. Later, this was to be called, "Charlie's Caper."

My plan called for the Navy to place me on Tinian 2 months before the invasion and I would work with an Australian resident Coast Watcher to obtain the information. The Coast Watcher had a primary responsibility to watch for attacking Japanese planes heading to islands south of the Marianas and report them to the headquarters. He also must watch for any important information and report it.

The Watcher usually must stay in a single place to impart his information since his equipment alone weighs several hundred pounds. This requires natives to help move the ponderous equipment. This includes the receiver and transmitter for communications and it includes car batteries and a manual generator to provide power for the communications gear. This severely limits ones mobility, the length of time to get the message out and restricts communications relays among the Coast Watchers.

I learned that Allan Whitsmith was the Watcher that would take care of me. Whitsmith was an old hand Australian in the Coast Watcher organization. Although everyone believed that Watchers worked alone, their positions evolved during the war and by this time they were in the army, somewhat subject to military orders. Whitsmith had been a planter on a lesser Mariana island before the war. He had given that up pending the end of the war. He had now established relationships with the natives and other Watchers that allowed him to operate on Tinian and Saipan. At first, he was mobile. He could move around himself collecting data and watching for aircraft formations. He would then hurry back to his cave on Tinian where his gear was hidden. Only he had discovered this cave so he was relatively safe.

The Japanese had treated the natives of Guam very badly with incarceration, slave labor, torture, beatings and public beheadings. There was no reason for the Guam natives to cooperate with the Japanese and they did not. The Northern Marianas natives had not endured such mistreatment but they had received enough to embitter them and drive them to cooperate with the Americans on Saipan, Tinian, and many of the numerous small islands. Many of the smaller islands were inhabited now and then with a few natives communicating with outrigger canoes.

I proposed my scheme based on the extreme importance of the Saipan and Tinian targets and the expected casualties that would be incurred when we were attacked. Mine was a life-saving act in general.

I soon received orders that my plan had been approved and I was given a departure date and time. A submarine would pick me up on Guadalcanal, transport me to Tinian and drop me off at a rendezvous just off the island. Signaling instructions and codes were given. Allan Whitsmith, the Coast Watcher, would meet me. I was also given a backup plan in case the first plan could not be followed.

I had made plans based on the Navy's knowledge of the Marianas. I was to get all the information I could on the Japanese army dispositions, on their routines and capabilities. They had emplaced defensive positions and these needed to be known. It was known that they had prepared caves and tunnels to repulse invading troops along the beaches and shoreline. It was critical to understand these dispositions. Whitsmith was to continue his previous responsibilities while we both would help each other.

Whitsmith then led me off the beach and into the jungle. The rendezvous was about 3 miles from Whitsmith's hideout. The hideout was a particularly treacherous and dense jungle area. Whitsmith pulled and pushed me through. The entry cover was nondescript and I had avoided greens that wilted. Further, he never used the same trail or path to get there, as that would leave broken jungle plants to give away the cave. He had placed radio equipment in the cave. The most burdensome by far was the batteries necessary to operate the radio and generator. These were very heavy and burdensome.

He had also hidden a small electrical generator that could be used to charge the batteries. This was dangerous since it made noise when running; yet, these realities had to be faced. The radio antenna had to be strung. This consisted of a single small wire wrapped around treetops. This was also dangerous since it exposed the cave's presence. Just my presence further endangered Whitsmith since he doubled the necessities of life that had to be accommodated.

This is saying a lot. Taking a systemic approach, one must have all the feedstock required of a properly operating system. This includes dry food in packages, cans of food where the cans must be disposed of, usually by burying, water that is often in short supply being somewhere else, and fruits, particularly coconuts. The body digests those things and exhausts certain products that must be disposed of. All this must be done continually by burying so that no evidence of it occurs on the surface. The Japanese could detect it by random, roving patrols, by suspicions or by some giveaway that confirms the Coast Watcher is there except the troops don't know exactly where. All are extremely dangerous.

"Allan. How am I to get information from Saipan? That's about five miles away. So, how do I get there?"

"That's no problem mate," he said. One can swim if you can stand the strong currents. Otherwise, you can take a canoe and wait for the correct tide direction. I prefer to have a couple of natives pick me up in an outrigger. They can do that in an hour or so. They can also pose as fishermen if a Japanese patrol boat comes along."

"What is the incentive for the natives doing this," I asked.

"You see, these fellows have been mistreated by the Japanese and this goes a little way toward evening the score. We also make promises to them about how we can square accounts after the war. It all works out. When you have been beaten by the butt of a gun, you get mighty indignant. Also, these native blokes have been drug around or forced into slave labor. In many cases, their kin have been killed. The Japanese often require the girls to become unpaid prostitutes and forced to satisfy huge numbers of soldiers. The Japanese call these 'comfort women'. These cause the natives to hate the Japanese."

"I see," was the weak reply.

"Just think of it," Whitsmith said. "We have checked it out and confirmed that girls on all the islands and in China have been enslaved by the Japanese. Yes, that is what it is. They have been forced into unpaid prostitution of the whole Japanese army."

Whitsmith seemed to spit the words out as if he was disgusted by the thought of such knowledge being harbored in his mouth. All Whitsmith's discussions concerning the Japanese seemed to reflect this terrible knowledge that he wished he did not have. He could only spit out the words as he thought of the hundreds of thousands of respectable girls and women across Asia being forced by bayonet to perform acts they loathed. Furthermore, they had to repeat it hundreds of times a day, one could only imagine. This was an unimaginable fate, and it was expected to last for years. Even today, there are millions of women across Asia still embittered by such a history forced on them.

This was in mid February, I thought afterwards. I expected to be on the island for about 2 months. This would be enough time for gathering the data well before the invasion.

Our first excursion was along the hill line so that we could see the general disposition of the troops, their boats and artillery. They had also placed anti-tank and boat-landing spikes along the beaches and in the surf. From the dispositions, we could tell where the Japanese thought the Americans would attack. The long beaches caused their defenses to be really spread out. This was helpful to our marines. However, the Japanese had about 20,000 troops on Saipan and Tinian that didn't leave too many weak spots.

This routine was followed for three nights or so, until we had confidence that we could move with some ease. Of course, Whitsmith had this confidence from the beginning but he was concerned about me, and when I would be ready.

Several nights later, we crossed the Saipan Channel to Saipan itself. The Japanese had larger outlays of defense on this island than on Tinian. We later learned that Guam would be attacked first and then Saipan and Tinian. These two northern islands would be attacked at about the same time a month later. It would be assumed that Saipan would be secured before attacking Tinian so bombardment from the air and the sea would support the Tinian invasion.

We came to a small cove on the north point of Tinian. There we met several natives who were expected to row us to Saipan. The natives had taken two boats using one as a reserve. They had hidden their reserve boat in the cove and covered it with jungle growth. The four of us got in the outriggers and used the current to guide us to the south Saipan shore. They did not speak English but the Watcher was able to communicate with them in a kind of pigeon English. After an hour or two, we came to the Saipan shore and hid our boat on the jungle edge. Allan guided us to a point that we could observe the troops and their disposition. We also used a cave known to the Watcher. I thought he had arranged it beforehand for this purpose. We were in a great hurry on Saipan since our radio equipment was in Tinian and observed Japanese aircraft squadrons could not be reported until we got back there. This was usually too late for the defenses on islands to our south. Thus, our visit to Saipan left bomber squadrons heading south unreported until we returned to Tinian.

By some time I had become quite adept at getting the information needed and in observing their defenses. After all, I now had a lot of practice. We stayed there three nights. Then, the outrigger canoes were waiting for us with the native crew for our return to Tinian.

We loved those natives. They had faced danger on our behalf and returned us safely. I could not have been more profuse in thanking them for all they did. The reconnoitering had been extremely successful.

Australia was a wonderful place during the war, I thought to myself. *The Aussies had disproportionately called on the Commonwealth to fight their wars. This meant that Australia provided a great many soldiers to fight and die in some far-off land while the continent was crawling with unattached women. These were not the ordinary unattached women but often it was the crème-de-la-crème of femininity. They were just desperately short of everything that men provide.*

This was also true of much of the empire: the New Zealanders, South Africans, Indians, Canadians and others.

The Japanese wanted to attack northeastern Australia in the worst way. There were huge coal supplies and all the riches one can dig from the ground, all the things the Japanese needed and wanted. The Americans stood in their way and eventually repulsed them. Meanwhile, the Australian men were in Europe, North Africa and in the skies above Germany fighting the wars. The Australian women have always been grateful for this and especially appreciated the Americans in WWII.

When we returned, it was clear that no one had entered our cave. Everything was in place, just as we had left it. Allan restrung his antenna, his wires, and connected the batteries. He made his contact to Guadalcanal and provided them his information.

I was then given the radio. Whitesmith made his contacts and sent his information. We waited for a few hours before I sent his since they worried about being on the air for so long. The contacts were happy to get the data and congratulated us for the data and on still being alive. That was a bit disconcerting.

This was in March 1944. My contacts accepted my data but did not send me any messages that didn't pertain directly to the work. However, one could surmise that a big battle was brewing out at sea. This was a huge American fleet that prowled the Philippine Sea. There were often attacks on Tinian from the sea and from aircraft. We assumed this was part of the softening up process leading to an invasion. The timing did not seem right, however. We believed the invasion would occur in the mid-to-late summer. These bombardments seemed too early to be part of that imagined process.

We could only stay out of the way and away from the beaches when these attacks occurred. Our best bet was to stay up in the mountains. This contrasted to our duty to observe the Japanese defenses during these times and the dispositions of their weapons. We also kept close count of their defense strength as best we could. We worried that Japanese reinforcements would be sent to the islands, to Saipan and Tinian, but we did not discern any. That puzzled us. We thought they would be reinforcing their strongholds there since an invasion of these seemed obvious to us and it must to the Japanese.

A few days later, he and I were hunkered down watching the troops go through some kind of drill. There was the cry of aircraft engines. Then we heard shooting as tens of aircraft fought above our heads. This dogfight produced a number of aircraft spinning into the earth while they were afire with flames shooting out of them. They made a huge bang when they hit the jungle. All the crashing planes had Rising Sun markings on their wings so we could tell we Americans were winning.

The next day, we were sitting close to the same place doing the same thing. We were especially alert this day because we knew the Japanese would be out looking for downed planes. Nothing seemed out of the ordinary but at about 3:00 p.m. we heard mumbling from just down the hill. We threw ourselves into the dense jungle foliage so we would not be detected. The mumbling and cursing continued until they were quite close to us. There was a pause and we assumed that a rest period had been ordered. They were using machetes so it was really hard work. They all collapsed right where they were.

We were genuinely frightened since they were practically on top of us. They stayed there for about 10 minutes and then moved on. We never figured out if they were a normal security patrol or a patrol out looking for a downed aircraft.

We began to see a lot of naval aircraft activity on both Saipan and Tinian. Of course, we could not see anything associated with Guam since it was 130 miles or so to the south.

It was clear that invasion activity was getting cranked up on Saipan and Tinian. Further, I had seen some plans before and knew those islands were directly in the invasion plans in midsummer.

"Allan," I queried. "One thing puzzles me. I know we are going to strike the Marianas sometime in mid-summer. Nevertheless, I don't really see any build-up for defense or the supplies necessary to maintain a strong defense. Where are the supporting ships? Where is the extra ammunition? Why do I not see any growth in support troops?"

"I don't know," he answered. "Are you sure the invasion will be as planned?"

"No. But it only makes sense. The U.S. is building up supplies every day. The Marianas are on the hit list. The B-29s from the Marianas can hit Japan and that is where we are going with the war. What is happening here?"

There was a reason for these observations. Allan and I could not know it then but there was a poisonous major war going on between the Japanese Army General and the Navy Admiral where both commanded a fleet or an army. This proved fatal to any coordinated action.

In March 1944, the Commander of the Combined Fleet, Admiral Mineichi Koga, was killed when his aircraft flew into a typhoon and crashed. A new Commander-in-Chief of the Combined Fleet, Admiral Soemu Toyoda, was appointed. He continued his current work, finalizing the Japanese war plans known as "Plan A-Go." The plan was adopted in early June 1944, then within weeks quickly put into place to engage the American fleet now detected heading for Saipan.

Most of the Japanese activity was near the shoreline; even their barracks and outbuildings were there. They huddled their forces mainly in the encampment. They did not patrol the jungle area too much; it was difficult at best.

I was moving one morning without Allan. He and I often worked separately after I had been there a few weeks and got my bearings. Something caught my eye. I don't know if it was the reflection off a weapon or belt buckle or something. It was gone as fast as it appeared. I sat down and waited. Nothing happened for a few minutes. I again started creeping along my trail. I did not see movement where the glint had occurred but something did not feel just right. I sank further back into the jungle, where it is much deeper. I decided to wait for some time there. I would outwait whoever it was if there was someone.

Perhaps the tall weeds and grass and jungle foliage near me did not separate just right or it did not react just right to the winds that were softly blowing. It just seemed like someone was there. Someone was stalking me. If I was being stalked, he could certainly bring in a large group to search me out. In that case, I'd be lost for sure. My best strategy was to put distance between me and the tracker.

By this time, my heart was in my throat. I knew I was being tracked because I could see the rush of the leaves. I thought I heard the whisper of a voice as speaking into a microphone. I was not long before I heard the rattle of several people coming toward me and they were moving fast enough that it did not bother them if they were heard. The whole patrol was now upon me. They were sticking bayonets into the undergrowth. They were now standing up and in the open as they sought after me. Then, someone behind me stuck the point of a bayonet into my back deep enough to draw blood and sufficient to put me out of commission. He yelled something in a guttural kind of language. He then sucked through his teeth and yelled it again.

It was no use. I knew I was caught. I was suddenly a prisoner of the Imperial Japanese Army. My fate was sealed.

He yelled again. You don't have to speak a language when someone is yelling and cursing. You just know you are in trouble. Then he hit me in the jaw with the butt of his rifle. Damn! That hurts. Blood began to run from my nose and mouth. He then cursed and hit me again. I fell to my knees. That was a mistake since he kicked me real hard in the pit of my stomach. I could see by his neat tunic and insignia that he was an officer.

The other soldiers came up and gathered around us. They wanted to bash me also with the butt of their guns but he yelled at them. They quieted down. The officer then spoke a couple of words to me in a pigeon English. 'Up, up", he commanded. Meanwhile, he pulled me and jerked me through the underbrush. I was dragged into captivity. He searched for any weapons on me. He had ambushed me — saw me first — and now gloried in his acquisition. He barked an order and the others snapped to attention. He then smacked me behind the head to indicate we should go and the smack indicated the direction. We marched down the hill and through the jungle to their compound that I had been watching for so long. Unfortunately, I could not watch them all. Somehow, he had slipped into the jungle and got on my path, got the better of me. What a fool I was.

At first, there was some dismay of what to do with me. First, they apparently wanted to interrogate me and get whatever information they could. They then sent a messenger out that must have been to find a translator, someone who knew English. I was a mess. I had on non-descript jungle rags and must have looked like one of the natives, but one who had been injured. Blood had run down the left side of my face and was clotted. Jungle trash had set in the cold blood. My left eye had swollen and I was beginning to feel the pain.

My arresting officer stood at attention also. He must have been really pissed off at this because he kept mumbling things that sounded like he was venting his frustration. Finally, the messenger returned with another officer, that I assume was a translator. The patrol and the other officer then marched me to the headquarters building. The officers saluted the commander very stiffly. Then they stood at attention. The commander asked and answered several questions from the translator. That was the first time they let me talk. My mouth was so badly injured that I could hardly answer the translator's questions.

"Why you here?"

"I am reconnoitering the island." I answered.

"Why?" The interview lasted for an hour or so. It was relatively civil, considering the situation. He was not happy with any of my answers about my help, what my job was and how I got there.

He looked at me disapprovingly. "You look like a civilian to me. You certainly don't have on a military uniform. You are dressed in civilian clothes so you are a spy."

"You know you are a spy and you know what happens to spies," he said. "We shoot them," he answered his own question.

Finally, two heavy, strong men appeared. They took me to another building and began asking me question. The interrogators and I were the only ones in the room. Instead of registering disapproval at many of my answers, they whacked me across the face with a swagger stick. This stick instead of a rifle butt assured that the beatings would become more severe and would last longer.

The men took pleasure in their work. One could just see the joy on their faces as they brought the swagger stick down. They had seen the blood thirst in their commander's eyes so knew their work was honorable and for the emperor. Jackson had to be strong and hold up. He could not reveal Whitsmith and his mission. Jackson gave them answers but he conjured up a fictitious world, a parallel world with its own requirements, purposes, and assumed realities. They seemed to think this was a game. When they didn't like the outcome, they blasted him with the swagger stick. It soon felt like not just a stick but a log that they could somehow swing and they hit him with a mighty log blows.

After a while, I don't think they really cared about my answers. They were just in love with the game, the sharp sting across the face so they could see the blood gushing. They would ask another, then smack with another, and then this would be repeated. By the time a session was over, my face was a bloody mess. They had also focused now and then on my rump, on my legs and ankles. My back looked like the slashes administered by the Royal Navy back when ships were ships and men were men. That's when the navy was made up of wooden ships and canvas sails.

By this time I was hanging by my wrists from the ceiling. I think these interrogators realized they had gone too far. At this rate, their quarry would escape them by dying. They must not have wanted that, just enough pain that I could stand it so they could repeat this show for a long time. At any rate, they stopped. I was unstrung and dragged to my stall, just a little box area that looked like a storage bin. Later that night, they dragged me to a 'hot box'. That is what they called it and it consisted of a vertical coffin with little air, no light, no hygiene facilities and nothing to support life. My only respite from this hot box was the interrogation sessions that lasted a couple of hours. This routine continued as long as I was there.

I believe this was an anomalous period for the Japanese on Tinian. The commander surely knew his island was in the crosshairs of the might of the U.S. Navy. He had more of his share of things to think about. He must defend his island the best he could. He surely knew the commander of Saipan and the vitriolic hatred between him and this commander of Tinian. The Tinian commander must have known the Saipan commander well enough to know that he would order mass suicides after losing the battle. However, there was no honor when thousands commit suicide after losing a battle. My captor, an admiral, must have known what was ahead of him and coming fast. His thoughts were certainly not on some junior spy running around in the jungle. That would take care of itself.

As to the junior officer that had tracked me down and captured me, he had gained all the glory associated with that. Leave it alone since there is little more to be gained.

The interrogators were perfunctory in their job. They loved to inflict pain and they were certainly having joy in that. Their reward may be in the pain and blood and not in the revelations they cause, if any.

At any rate, they certainly did not react in ways that I understood so they must have had reasons. I was not the prisoner celebrity that one would have expected but just another problem to be filed away for a more opportune time.

How did the Japanese get this way? How did a whole nation of people become savages and animals? The Japanese behavior was beastly through the whole war. They were unique in this respect. It is difficult to understand how total cruelty during all of their occupations was to benefit them. Why did they conclude that was helpful in instituting their Co-Prosperity Sphere? We will never know. This seemed to be a matter of state policy from the beginning.

The Rape of Nanking is described in the following from *The History Place, Genocide in the 20th century.* I often talk to my psyche in trying to understand the world and the way it works. While standing or slumping in the hotbox coffin, I reviewed this as part of my regimen to stay alive and remain sane. The rape of Nanking is certainly near the nadir of civilization's long march.

What had happened to these extraordinary people to cause them to react in this manner? The world had never seen anything like this. First, the army ordered the bloody killings. These were not random acts of violence and mass murder but they had institutional structure where the culture not only condoned mass murder but also organized it and gave orders that structurally caused it. How can that be?

In December of 1937, the Japanese Imperial Army marched into China's capital city of Nanking and proceeded to murder 300,000 out of 600,000 civilians and soldiers in the city. The six weeks of carnage would become known as the Rape of Nanking and in some ways represented the single worst atrocity during the war era in either the European or Pacific theaters of war.

The actual military invasion of Nanking was preceded by a tough battle at Shanghai that began in the summer of 1937. Chinese forces there put up surprisingly stiff resistance against the Japanese Army, which had expected an easy victory in China. The Japanese had even bragged they would conquer all of China in just three months. The stubborn resistance by the Chinese troops upset that timetable, with the battle dragging on through the summer into late fall. This infuriated the Japanese and whetted their appetite for the revenge that was to follow at Nanking.

After finally defeating the Chinese at Shanghai in November, 50,000 Japanese soldiers then marched on toward Nanking. Unlike the troops at Shanghai, Chinese soldiers at Nanking were poorly led and loosely organized. Although they greatly outnumbered the Japanese and had plenty of ammunition, they withered under the ferocity of the Japanese attack, then engaged in a chaotic retreat. After just four days of fighting, Japanese troops smashed into the city on December 13, 1937, with orders issued to 'kill all captives.'

Their first concern was to eliminate any threat from the 90,000 Chinese soldiers who surrendered. To the Japanese, surrender was an unthinkable act of cowardice and the ultimate violation of the rigid code of military honor drilled into them from childhood onward. Thus they looked upon Chinese POWs with utter contempt, viewing them as less than human, unworthy of life.

The elimination of the Chinese POWs began after they were transported by trucks to remote locations on the outskirts of Nanking. As soon as they were assembled, the savagery began, with young Japanese soldiers encouraged by their superiors to inflict maximum pain and suffering upon individual POWs as a way of toughening themselves up for future battles, and also to eradicate any civilized notions of mercy. Filmed footage and still photographs taken by the Japanese themselves document the brutality. Smiling soldiers can be seen conducting bayonet practice on live prisoners, decapitating them and displaying severed heads as souvenirs, and proudly standing among mutilated corpses. Some of the Chinese POWs were simply mowed down by machine-gun fire while others were tied-up, soaked with gasoline and burned alive.

After the destruction of the POWs, the soldiers turned their attention to the women of Nanking and an outright animalistic hunt ensued. Old women over the age of 70 as well as little girls under the age of eight were dragged off to be sexually abused and molested. More than 20,000 females (with some estimates as high as 80,000) were gang-raped by Japanese soldiers, then stabbed to death with bayonets or shot so they could never bear witness.

Pregnant women were not spared. In several instances, they were raped, then had their bellies slit open and the fetuses torn out. Sometimes, after storming into a house and encountering a whole family, the Japanese forced Chinese men to rape their own daughters, sons to rape their mothers, and brothers their sisters, while the rest of the family was made to watch.

Throughout the city of Nanking, random acts of murder occurred as soldiers frequently fired their rifles into panicked crowds of civilians, killing indiscriminately. Other soldiers killed shopkeepers, looted their stores, then set the buildings on fire after locking people of all ages inside. They took pleasure in the extraordinary suffering that ensued as the people desperately tried to escape the flames by climbing onto rooftops or leaping down onto the street.

The incredible carnage — citywide burnings, stabbings, drownings, strangulations, rapes, thefts, and massive property destruction—continued unabated for about six weeks, from mid-December 1937 through the beginning of February 1938. Young or old, male or female, anyone could be shot on a whim by any Japanese soldier for any reason. Corpses could be seen everywhere throughout the city. The streets of Nanking were said to literally have run red with blood.

Those who were not killed on the spot were taken to the outskirts of the city and forced to dig their own graves, large rectangular pits that would be filled with decapitated corpses resulting from killing contests the Japanese held among themselves. Other times, the Japanese forced the Chinese to bury each other alive in the dirt.

After this period of unprecedented violence, the Japanese eased off somewhat and settled in for the duration of the war. To pacify the population during the long occupation, highly addictive narcotics, including opium and heroin, were distributed to all people of Nanking, by Japanese soldiers. An estimated 50,000 persons became addicted to heroin, while many others lost themselves in the city's opium dens.

In addition, the notorious Comfort Women system was introduced which forced young Chinese women to become slave-prostitutes, existing solely for the sexual pleasure of Japanese soldiers.

News reports of the happenings in Nanking appeared in the official Japanese press and also in the West, as page-one reports in newspapers such as the New York Times. Japanese news reports reflected the militaristic mood of the country in which any victory by the Imperial Army resulting in further expansion of the Japanese empire was celebrated. Eyewitness reports by Japanese military correspondents concerning the sufferings of the people of Nanking also appeared. They reflected a mentality in which the brutal dominance of subjugated or so-called inferior peoples was considered just. Incredibly, one paper, the Japan Advertiser, actually published a running count of the heads severed by two officers involved in a decapitation contest, as if it was some kind of a sporting match.

In the United States, reports published in the New York Times, Reader's Digest and Time Magazine, were greeted with skepticism from the American public. The stories smuggled out of Nanking seemed almost too fantastic to be believed.

I had more than I could handle in alternating between hot boxes. I certainly did not have reserve mental or emotional capacity to worry too much about past terrorism. My only hope was to transform my mental existence onto another planet, another cosmic place in the universe.

"How could I possibly survive?"

"I knew the first sub pick-up rendezvous was to be at the end of April and the second a month later. However, there is no likelihood that I could be near one of those. There is no doubt, I am a dead man."

Nevertheless, fate is a sometime thing. It is nothing if not a bag full of surprises.

The 15th of April 1944 was a fateful day for me. The day would begin in total darkness but a slow leakage of light through the hot box cracks revealed a beautiful Philippine sunrise. One knew that a colorful day would be rising on the horizon in this natural paradise. Battles had been raging in the Philippine Sea, the guns of the multiple ships would be banging away soon at Saipan and Tinian, aircraft had been launched and the world awaited the God-awful din of explosives.

This day in mid-April was different. All the guns, missiles, and aircraft of the world seemed to be pointing at Tinian. The ordinance all wanted to congregate in one point, it seemed. And that one point was me. Boom! Boom! Boom! The Japanese could be heard running and screaming. They, too, could not escape but they had the freedom of space to run. They ran and yelled. Then, the human cries ceased. I assumed all the Japanese ran into the forest, as far away as they could run. When it seemed no further increase in the bedlam could be made or endured, the hot box just disintegrated. The sides flew up into the air. I thought that I would disintegrate myself. My head exploded. I felt intense pain in every pore of my body. Could this be hell?

I began to run as fast as I could toward the jungle while the bombs kept falling. Japanese bodies were everywhere. Some showed signs of life with movement but most did not. After my sprint, I fell down exhausted in a jungle space. I had escaped death, I thought, from the bombs. I just laid there.

After what seemed like a very long time, I began to get my wits. First, was I all in one piece? The answer seemed to be yes but I was so smashed up from the beatings that I could not make a full inventory or a reliable one, anyway. The second thought I had was how to get out of there. How do I rid myself of the tortures I have been enduring from the inquisitors? I managed to run and crawl further into the jungle. There were several soldiers that I passed but they were as concerned as I was to merely get away. None took an interest in me with my rags as clothes and looking like death walking. They merely struggled onward up the hill. I did the same but I was more focused on where I was going.

After an eternity, I slid myself through the jungle to the hideout. With gargantuan effort, I finally managed to pull the growths off the cave entry and pull myself inside. Whitsmith was not there. He had been somewhere in the jungle observing the carnage. I did not care and it did not seem important. I then fell asleep from exhaustion or maybe I just passed out. I was gone in this stupor for most of the day.

I had been phenomenally lucky in his hotbox coffin. Apparently, a shell demolished the hot box coffin but the forces aligned themselves just right for me to escape mortal injuries. The Japanese around me were not so lucky and suffered the consequences of a massive bombardment.

Even the infrastructure was dealt a heavy blow. Water that was normally brought up from springs by pipe and pumps to distribution buildings looked barren and inoperative. The same could be said for their electrical generators. A crowd of soldiers stood around these sites scratching their heads. In the days that followed, there was a lot of activity around the mouths of numerous caves. Much of their daily activities seemed to be moving underground. Their infrastructure was being reconstituted. The whole compound began to look like a huge construction site. Much of their activity seemed to be rebuilding the infrastructure but they were building it underground, in caves.

About all I could do was hide and watch. My body had taken about all it could take. However, I was soon recuperating fast. A few more days and I would be mobile again and could continue working.

Much later, I said to Whitworth, "I'm very uncomfortable that you are staying on Tinian. We could get the orders changed so you could get off this island with me. Why not?"

"That's not my job."

At the appropriate time, we saw the sub. It was ballasted deep in the water to reduce the silhouette. She was a thing of beauty. Allan used the signal light. He pointed it out to sea past the sub and sent dash-dot light messages in Morse code. The natives were adept with their outrigger canoes taking him to the submarine.

My planning information proved to be critical to the whole operation in Saipan and Tinian. Alan and I had provided not only personal observations about defense dispositions but also on exact topography. The staff during the Saipan invasion was a little skeptical but during the Tinian campaign, there was confirmation of my data. Then my data was accepted without reservation and the results show this.

None of my military associates think of me as being vain. I do my duty. I do my job. Beyond that, I am like everyone else trying to do my part of the war. Yet, I knew my role in the fight was of great importance. This was true of Whitsmith and numerous more. Yet, I burst to tell someone, to make my heroic actions known. It was little of me but I needed space too. I longed to describe my exploit, to polish my image.

The girls were proud of me, even so. To them, I was a hero more or less. They treated me as a hero. That was gratifying. But somehow, I wanted more. After all, I had pulled off an important assignment. I particularly wanted to tell Charlotte. I wanted to impress her. Of what value is heroism when no one knows? I wanted to bypass the censors somehow, but that was way beyond my character.

Charlotte understood those things. She was always an adult when a question of that kind came along. We all acceded to her judgment. But I always played by the rules. Sooner of later, I would find the occasion. Unfortunately, it would most likely be after the war. But then, the value of heroic actions would be faded.

I learned something there. Charlotte was the only one I wanted to impress or I wanted to share the victory with. She really had become "my girl" and I loved her.

I dreaded those long times that I could not see her of even receive a letter from her. I fantasized and invented situations that made me look good in her eyes. I longed for her. This bloom of youth could not be controlled. The result was toxic. It was a chemical reaction that glowed in the breast and captured the essence of love's object.

This was not all there was to be of it, however. Bianca was less understanding. "Why don't they write? She asked. We are at wit's end waiting for a tiny word and they can't even do that." She railed against them but she would soon have a change of heart.

"Okay," Charlotte would say, "that's enough of that. They are busy, don't you understand? Don't show so little understanding." But, even Charlotte would soon start taking sides with Bianca. Then they would both have a good cry. At least, they could console one another. There was no military constriction against that.

Life went on but it was only half a life. A major part of living was missing, it was put on hold while they all waited for an unknowable future.

There was one unifying activity. Everyone rushed to get the newspapers. This gave the names of servicemen who had been killed. It was a daily ritual. This even happened when no relative was a candidate to appear on the list. Most everyone might know someone on the list. The casualty list brought grief or joy depending on the newspaper report. Further, the list often took up pages in small print. One thought the length of the list Indicated the intensity of the war and their mood changed with It

People sought out the casualty list. People also kept vigil on how many stars hung in the window and if the color of the stars was blue or gold. A blue star indicated a family member was in the service while a gold star meant one killed in action. A gold star usually meant the family had great patriotic fervor and neighbors showed sympathy to them. The fortunes of battle had overtaken their lives and they would see their family member never again.

CHAPTER 7

GREATER EAST ASIA CO-PROSPERITY SPHERE

T*he Greater East Asia Co-Prosperity Sphere* was an imperial concept created and promulgated for occupied Asian populations. It declared the intention to create a self-sufficient 'bloc of Asian nations led by the Japanese and free of Western powers'. It was announced in a radio address entitled 'The International Situation and Japan's Position' on June 29, 1940.

A secret document completed in 1943 for high-ranking government use, laid out the superior position of Japan in the Greater Asia Co-Prosperity Sphere.

The staggering losses of the Japanese Army to Zhukov at Khalkhin Gol changed everything for the Soviets in August 1939. It also caused a total turn in Japanese strategy. Suddenly, the Army's continental policies for taking Chinese territory were in disarray and the Navy's Co-Prosperity concepts of taking Pacific islands and Southeast Asian maritime territory were favored. This policy change was fateful for the Americans. It now put Japan squarely in confrontation with America, because of America's southeastern Pacific interests. Those interests were the Philippines, Australia, the British colonies around Malaya and Burma, the Dutch colonies around the East Indies, the friendship and interests still maintained with

China and its government, and the islands in the southwest Pacific that were strategically critical to all their interests.

The Japanese Co-Prosperity Sphere was mostly a drive for oil and secondarily for other raw materials and markets. Although some oil was obtained in Manchuria and China, the great oil prizes were Java, Sumatra, Timor and the rest of the Netherlands East Indies. Because of the shift in policy, the Japanese set their aim for a decisive, surprise strike against the U. S. Fleet in Hawaii. This was to be immediately followed by a quick occupation or control by its fleet of the Co-Prosperity Sphere. This was to be an area bound by a line extending from the Aleutians down the international date line to the Gilberts at about 15 degrees latitude below the equator. Then it would go westward below the Solomons in the Pacific, across New Guinea and surrounding the Netherlands East Indies, then north to Burma, French Indo-China, and coastal China to the Soviet border in the north.

The wars, like all life's activities, revealed themselves in those days in the terribly realistic shadows of radio imagination rather than in the colored images of televisions that were far in the future. Each fear, joy, or terror occurred in the ultimate realism of the mind.

On this day, one could not know all these numbers, nor implications, nor what catastrophes waited. It was like Rudyard Kipling's giant sand pit with the sand sides falling toward the bottom; the leaders scrambled upward, but the sand footing gave way, and they all sank faster than they rose. It was of no use. They were all in the sand pit falling toward Armageddon. Nevertheless, they could not know it.

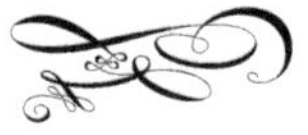

Stalin's War Preparations (1940)

"Good morning, good morning."

They were all participants in this war. Every human being in the world was a participant. The world would change forever. For now, they could not know it.

The atrocities did not follow neatly into a single time line. Nevertheless, they did occur and waited during the 1930s for someone to interpret them properly as history.

China and the Japan wars were in the news. They filled the press. The radio operator tacked news releases on the bulletin board as he read the world press reports in international Morse code. The dash-dots swept out the day-to-day activity of all mankind; all man's activities and opinions condensed to just a series of dots and dashes. Through this, the passengers clung to their magic contact with the rest of the planet.

There was also further news on the show trials in Russia. Stalin maneuvered. The Comintern weaved, bobbled, and made pompous statements about the workingmen of the world. There was a profusion of Soviet words that were highly intellectualized. They continued to redefine language, not to mention logic and reality!

The winds of war swept Europe and Asia. Armies were collecting and marching. Every country was arming itself; but Stalin was decimating the Red Army officer corps. The purges continued and spread.

George Grayburn spoke as they continued the conversation from the previous day, "They say that Lenin only murdered hundreds of thousands, but Stalin has already murdered around six million people. Stalin's collectivization as part of the first five-year plan caused havoc in the country's agriculture. Before the revolution, kulaks were small farmers who owned a small piece of land, had horses, and hired help. Stalin stated the kulaks were to be 'liquidated as a class.' Soon, anyone opposed to collectivization or opposed by the Soviets were denounced as kulaks to be liquidated. In 1929, the state levied a special tax on the kulaks to be paid in 24 hours. On failure to pay, the farm was confiscated, the owner deported, and the farm collectivized.

"The Soviets had deported some 5 million people to the slave labor camps of Siberia by 1934. These were later to be termed the Gulag Archipelago by Alexander Solzhenitsyn; island prisons across the great Siberian landmass. Collectivization caused shortages and famine. Millions starved, partially as Soviet reprisal against kulak resistance, through the first and second 5-year plans from 1928-1938, while Stalin continued to sell Russian grain internationally the whole time. At least 5 million people perished during this collectivization process.

"That was only 5 million dead, and at least that many sent to slave labor camps. Stalin's real Reign of Terror was the Show Trials and Great Purge of 1934 through 1938. These were passion plays and high state theater.

"The Soviets held the first show trial in August 1936 for Zinoviev, Kaneniev, and 14 other leading Communists. All confessed and incriminated the others. The Soviets patiently orchestrated these, usually with the accused making a futile attempt to save their families.

"The Soviets initiated the Purges at the beginning of 1935, after decreeing the entire family would be responsible for certain high crimes, and extended the death penalty down to 12-year-old children. On Dec. 1, 1934, the Secret Police assassinated a Stalin competitor, Kirov, of Leningrad probably on orders from Stalin. The assassin and 49 alleged accomplices were immediately shot. The top Communists, Zinoviev and Kaneniev, were charged with complicity. The Soviets deported around half a million Russians to concentration camps.

"By the time Stalin's great Purge had run its course in 1938, about 8 million people had been arrested, about 1 million executed, and another 8 million were in slave labor camps. Stalin published his Dizzy with Success article, charging the secret police with over-zealousness. The Russian media praised him for his magnanimous concern for the welfare of his people! By this time, 9 of 11 cabinet ministers had been executed, as had 27 drafters of the 1936 constitution and bill of rights. That was an ironic laugh in itself. Also executed were 3 of 4 Marshals, 13 of 15 Army Commanders, and all 8 Admirals in the Navy. The Soviets executed 60 of 67 Corps Commanders, 110 of 195 Division Commanders, 220 of 406 Brigade Commanders, and 75 of 80 members of the Supreme Military Council. Altogether, about 35,000 officers, or 50% of the officer corps, were affected, but not all were shot. Stalin's preparations for the coming war were strange indeed.

"Subsequently, ethnic unrest took additional victims. During his uprooting of Islam and change of Arabic script to Cyrillic, a great deal of resistance occurred. During this time, the population of Kazakh decreased by 1 million Moslems, but the Russians moved in colonists until they were in the majority. Again, 'colonization is the essence of Russian history.'"

CHAPTER 8

UNLEASHING THE PACIFIC DRAGONS

The U. S. Congress declared war on the Japanese Empire on 8 December 1941, the day after the Pearl Harbor strike.

Hitler and Stalin started WWII by partitioning Europe in the Molotov-Ribbentrop Pact. The two were natural enemies. Stalin thought of Hitler as an ally that had betrayed him. Meanwhile, Hitler plotted Stalin's actual betrayal.

After the spring or 10 May 1940, Germany occupied Denmark, Norway, Holland, France, and Belgium. Hitler and Stalin bickered for a year over the spoils of war and new acquisitions, and at the same time jockeyed for tactical and strategic advantage. Then, on June 22, 1941, Hitler attacked Russia across a broad front in Operation Barbarossa.

The military situation deteriorated so rapidly that hard positions against Russia were not taken; near-by Germany was a far more pressing problem to the West. Soon, England was fighting for its life in the Battle of Britain.

The losses of the Japanese Army to Zhukov and the Soviets in August 1939 caused a turn in Japanese strategy. Suddenly, the Army's continental policies for taking Chinese territory were in disarray and the Navy's Co-Prosperity concepts of taking Pacific islands and Southeast Asian maritime territory were favored. This policy change was fateful for the Americans because of America's Southwestern Pacific interests. Those included the Philippines, Australia, the British around Malaya and Burma, the Dutch colonies around the East Indies, the friendship and interests still maintained with China and its government, and the islands in the Southwest Pacific that were strategically critical to all their interests.

In the Pearl Harbor attack, the Japanese struck the battleships tied up to the quays or concrete pillars alongside Ford Island. Unfortunately for them, battleships were losing their effectiveness in the naval battles of the world. They mattered less and less. Further, two American aircraft carriers were at sea that morning and were not harmed; one was at sea and one was on the West Coast for repairs. The planes also flew over the American submarine facilities as they were attacking battleships and those submarines proved to be extremely effective in bringing the war to the Japanese immediately. Japan also ignored the fuel storage tanks on the hill beyond Pearl Harbor, thereby foregoing the ability to starve the fleet for immediate retaliation, particularly starving the aircraft carriers. Lastly, the repair facilities and workshops for ships were not attacked leaving the ability for quick repair of the fighting fleet.

One must accept the fact that the great Japanese victory at Pearl Harbor was mostly illusory. The Japanese had been successful militarily in Manchuria; they had even installed a puppet government, and exercised complete control. Yet massive Japanese resources had been poured in which couldn't repay Japan for years to come. Establishing the land empire was not providing the raw materials and markets she desperately wants, but it caused an enormous drain. It certainly was not opening Japan to the sources of oil, rubber, tin, aluminum, iron, chemicals, world-shipping lanes, and the other necessities of a major world power. Mostly, she knows that she must have an easy, assured access to major oil fields. As she well knows, and the navy enthusiasts continually pointed out in their advocacy, these things abound in Southeast Asia. The Dutch oil fields in the Netherlands East Indies (Indonesia) and Borneo (Brunei), the rubber plantations and tin mines in French Indo-China, the shipping lanes of the Straits of Malacca by Singapore, British Hong Kong harbor, and other resources and shipping facilities of Southeast Asia were mighty attractions.

Only the Americans stood between the Japanese Navy and the nation's ambitions. America's only big possession west of Hawaii was the Philippines. Hadn't America declared the Philippines would be given independence in

1947? It certainly could not be considered a vital interest for America, Japan reasoned. Clearly, America would not risk a full-scale Pacific war with Japan when she had no critical possessions or critical interests in the Southwest Pacific. She was getting more and more involved in the European war. She was supplying war material, having naval engagements with German submarines, essentially patrolling for submarines as part of the British fleet, and taking other warlike actions. She was clearly destined to come to the aid of England if the war lasted. With these European engagements, surely the Americans would not engage in a two-ocean war for the sake of friendship and when they had no compelling national interest there.

So, Japan reasoned, if we strike dramatically and cripple her Pacific fleet and bases, she will not have any credible remaining power in the Pacific. Surely, she will not deplete the critical Atlantic forces where she does have critical possessions and interests, to reconstitute a new Pacific force.

"Japan was wrong," we said to one another. We laughed and joked. The news was some kind of bizarre amusement. We continued the joke by slapped our sides at the prospect of these little guys with bow legs thinking they could best the great American fleet. She staked it all on the strike at Pearl Harbor. "And now look where Japan is." We laughed even harder.

"They didn't sink any aircraft carriers," we said. "They didn't report any. Don't you understand?" I said. "They didn't get the aircraft carriers. Do you know what happened in December of last year, in the very same month as Pearl Harbor? The British lost the battleship Prince of Wales and the battle cruiser Repulse that was really a disguising designation for another battleship. This occurred off the coast of Indo-China. Japanese land-based airplanes sank both battleships before taking Singapore and the Malay Peninsula. Then look at Europe. A bunch of Italians riding torpedoes with saddles, for goodness sake, sank two more British battleships in Egypt's Alexandria harbor! Don't you get it?" They rolled in merriment that their friends did not understand how the joke was on the Japanese.

It was a time for experts. Military people met and each talked about how the war was not being competently fought. If their proposal were just implemented, the war would soon be over. The non-commissioned personnel blamed incompetence on the officers. The officers blamed it on the higher ranks. According to them all, the President was the problem. Henry Hopkins and other consultants were advising him wrongly. Some said it was the British Churchill.

Civilians also believed they were the experts. All the people had been pressed into service but the war just drug along indecisively. If we only did so and so, it would all work out. The disagreements often resulted in fights. Each was convinced he was right; he knew more than all the generals.

People did daffy things and got daffy results.

CHAPTER 9

JAPAN'S PACIFIC WAR

We all continued our skepticism. "Battleships don't matter anymore," we said. "They're outdated. Horse cavalry!" They savored the prospect.

"Horse cavalry, indeed!" they said.

We said and believed that. It's now been shown that battleships can't survive aircraft attacks. And, the world is filled with aircraft. The end of battleships is at hand. Aircraft carriers are now the capital ships of the fleet!

The battleship is not totally dead, however. It has provided bombardment near beaches in many wars beyond WWII. It generally has 16-inch guns and that makes an impression in bombardment if the target is near the beach and ocean waters are deep enough to support a battleship. Unfortunately, it serves as a poor gun platform so the accuracy is not great. At best, it is a rocking mortar. There are presently no battleships in the twenty-first century world, but there are many aircraft carriers.

The failure to destroy these vital assets of the Pacific Fleet would rebound on the Japanese during the first six months of 1942 when the American aircraft carriers Lexington and Enterprise, augmented by the arrival of the carriers Yorktown and Hornet from the Atlantic Ocean, would exact from the Japanese a heavy penalty for Pearl Harbor. Between 1942 and 1945, American submarines and aircraft carriers based at Pearl Harbor would play a key role in defeating Japan by strangling its supply lines to its vastly expanded western Pacific empire.

Many feel that had Japan been more astute, the Co-Prosperity Sphere policy might have survived.

"The Japanese know they made a mistake. They talk a big game but their goose is cooked."

We responded from conviction. "Japan doesn't understand what a real industrial power can do. Look at the Great War. American industry overwhelmed Europe. She'll do the same thing to Japan. Japan is filled with a bunch of hotheads now, but they'll all regret it. America can build a thousand ships and ten thousand airplanes. In the end, it won't matter to America if there's both Europe and Japanese theaters. She will prevail."

Roosevelt would have had a real quandary, but the Germans, for no apparent reason, declared war on the U.S. four days later," he laughed. He raised both hands. "Why would she do such a dumb thing?" they asked. In America, the isolation advocates, that had considerable political strength, collapsed immediately." We then laughed hopelessly. All the aircraft carrier enthusiasts laughed at the joke, this time on the Germans.

The argument is made that the military organization is basically a *government-in-waiting*. In many respects it is a hierarchical structure with an officer corps peaking at the top. There is one man on top and many in this pyramid of authority. In times of peril or war, it is a parallel organization that can be substituted for civil authority on a moment's notice.

It is no surprise, therefore, that there are men of the caliber of a Dwight Eisenhower, George Marshall, Douglas MacArthur, Omar Bradley and a total structure to exercise the required functions in the common endeavor of the war. Again, it is a *government-in-waiting*.

MacArthur was a significant problem to the Navy since he wanted to free the Philippines and then launch an American invasion of the Chinese seaboard where bombers could operate against the Japanese homeland. In contrast, the Navy wanted to take critical islands while bypassing others and letting the soldiers on unoccupied islands starve. Island airbases would then be used to pound the Japanese homeland with heavy bombers. The Navy chafed at his strategy since it did not attack Japan directly and immediately. The Navy responded to this by a dual strategy, dividing the forces into MacArthur's Philippine strategy on the one hand and the rest on the other hand to an island-hopping strategy of conquering islands close enough to Japan so that aircraft could attack their homeland directly from these island bomber bases. B-29 bombers executed the strategy by hauling massive amounts of bombs and incendiaries to the Japanese homeland.

The U.S. therefore executed two strategies during the Pacific war since this daffy duality was never resolved. Due to the great preponderance of resources available to America compared to Japan, she could afford a dual strategy. It was MacArthur's Philippine strategy backed by George Marshall and the army in the Pentagon as opposed to a Navy Island-Hopping Strategy backed by Admirals King and Nimitz. MacArthur's strategy was to use bombers from the Philippines with new bases along the Chinese mainland against the Japanese home islands. The Navy was also to make a coordinated campaign for an air war against the Japanese home islands but from islands captured by America. These two strategies pitted the MacArthur Philippines War against the King-Nimitz Island-Hopping War. It ended up that both war strategies were pursued.

As unlikely as it was, Clausiwitz and Mahan were both violated by America undertaking the issues of a continental army and a naval force, exposing themselves across Europe and the Maghreb and simultaneously across the Pacific islands.

The daffy thesis struck again. Japan's actions were unbelievable. Even much of her war-provoking against America and the Allies was similarly illogical. Her deep cruelty in China, such as the rape of Nanking and everywhere she went was irrational, illogical and daffy. Retribution was inevitable.

Lewis Carroll's Alice found little humor at the Mad Hatter's tea party. It was a daffy tea party.

Japan's changing fortunes of war news in 1942 and later continued to be good for Japan, and the Japanese seemed to be ecstatic through mid-summer in 1942. The mood became less jubilant in the late summer. Then the mood became more and more somber until the end of the year. There was no distinct pessimism, but there wasn't the ecstatic jubilation and bonsais heard earlier in the year.

This reflected the great naval battle at Midway Island during June 3-6, 1942. In this, the Americans mortally wounded four Japanese aircraft carriers. This would prove to be the turning point of the war. Never again would the Japanese have cause for celebration. The disastrous loss occurred because the Americans were reading the Japanese Navy code and knew where to find Japan's fleet. The Americans were augmenting this with advanced radar. To make matters even worse, the Americans were reading their shipping codes and knew where to find their cargo ships and oil tankers; American planes and ships and submarines kept finding and destroying them with uncanny insight, thought the Japanese. The Japanese remained blind, while the Americans could see with their radar eyes. The Japanese kept whispering their secrets into the ears of their American enemies throughout the war. Was this daffy, or what?

The war would go increasingly bad for the Japanese. As 1943 wore on, a deeply foreboding mood began setting in. The Japanese asked one another about their kin in whispered tones, as if they were not sure they wanted to know, as if there was some military secret hovering over military personnel, and civilians shouldn't talk about them. More often than not, the questions were deflected, not answered. There was to be more talk of heroes, sacrifice, duty, devotion, and loyalty. All these words and expressions were not to connote joy and military heroics anymore, but were to begin the ring of death, of dismembered relatives, of relatives without legs or arms. More often, vacant stares toward an imagined ocean where vast numbers of fighting ships, troopships, and cargo ships with their sailors and merchant marines and soldiers were to be sucked into the vortex. Disaster would begin to appear.

The Americans were going to be coming up from Australia and staging from New Caledonia and New Hebrides, on to Guadalcanal and Bougainville in the Solomon, New Ireland and New Britain, and into Port Moresby in New Guinea. For two years, an American slaughterhouse was to be developed for dismembering Japanese ships in The Slot, and their crews and their loads of supplies and fighting men; it would slaughter Japanese soldiers and marines on the islands; it would carve up Japanese fighters and bombers and their aircrews in the whole South Pacific region. The slaughterhouse churned and churned, and ground fine. By early 1943, even the masses of Japanese people were to be slowly made aware of this killing machine, the South Pacific, and by the end of 1943, the stench of death would begin to permeate the home islands.

Pilots would begin to return home dismembered, with stories of their comrades who were long dead. There were stories of their squadrons lost long ago; rescued sailors were to make it to the home islands with stories of sinking ships and drowning sailors that they had seen across the whole ocean. There were increasing numbers of survivors who made it home or told their stories to comrades who came home. There were tales of untold numbers of heavily loaded Japanese troopships that plunged to the bottom with their human cargo. Though it was held as a state secret, more and more people would become aware that the revered Admiral Yamamoto, the planner and commander of the Pearl Harbor treachery, had been singled out and killed by the Americans over Bougainville by targeting his airplane after reading his ciphers. They knew where he would be. It was uncanny, so uncanny, the Japanese high command thought.

In China, there would be stiffening resistance against Japanese armies. Around the whole Japanese Sphere, from Guadalcanal, Sumatra, Burma, and China, there would be challenges to their hegemony; walls of blood and steel were to be erected around the Japanese occupying armies, and now these walls would begin to move on all fronts toward the home islands. No longer would Japan feel a sense of victory, as she did when her soldiers raped Nanking by slaughtering a quarter of a million civilians, and as she did with her numerous other outrages. She would begin to sense the terrors of enemies and retribution that were just over the horizon.

By the summer of 1944, America would have its armada in place. She would take the Marianas from which vast fleets of B-29 bombers would devastate the home islands. American submarines and planes would halve the Japanese merchant fleet, and this of a country totally dependent on oceanic supply for food, raw materials, oil, and the maintenance of an ocean empire; and America would emasculate Japan's fighting fleet. The empire and home islands would be naked before America's might. Japan remained defiant, maniacal, and then suicidal.

Within the next year, 1944-1945, most of Japan's Pacific islands would be stripped from her and her naval fleet would be nonexistent; ninety-five percent of her merchant fleet would be destroyed, the home islands would be bombed unmercifully. Her home islands would be on the verge of starvation. Still, she would be defiant. Nuclear weapons were to obliterate Hiroshima and Nagasaki, and only then would there be sufficient drama in the holocaust to prompt the War Council to reach an armistice. This would happen on August 15, 1945.

No one in Japan could know these things in 1942.

In June 1944, the real war came to Japan, with a vengeance.

It was Japan's first traumatic experience on the home islands. Wars in the past had been fights between Samurais and warlords on the islands. Big wars and small wars had been fought like that. There was the fright of Genghis Kahn's armies coming across the sea in a thousand ships. The Kamikaze, Divine Wind, had destroyed his armada and saved Japan. In modern times, war was in foreign places that consumed her sons. Most of her fighting and suffering were in Manchuria, China, or the far-off Pacific islands, but in 1944, war came to Japan. There were no soldiers, no tanks, and no battlefields. War came from silvery planes in the sky. They came in massive numbers, seriously prepared for the business of mass killings and mass destruction.

General LeMay wanted to prove that with incendiaries, the Americans could destroy the Japanese will to fight and the invasion of the homeland might be avoided. Of course, his forte was to bomb into oblivion so he may have only been seeking a more deadly strategy.

LeMay's fire bombing experiment was ready for the test. America was ready for the home island bombing campaign. During the night of 9-10 Mar 1945, the residents of Tokyo really felt the impact of Americans making use of the Marianas for their war effort. 325 B-29 bombers dispatched from the Marianas loaded with E-46 incendiary clusters, magnesium bombs, white phosphorus bombs, and napalm flew over Japan; 279 of them targeted Tokyo. They successively flew over Tokyo during a three-hour window in the early morning of 10 March; their 1,665 tons of bombs destroyed 267,171 buildings.

The result was a *firestorm*, fed by the wooden mat construction, similar to the death toll of even the Hiroshima atomic bomb.

This incendiary attack killed 83,793 civilians, comparable to the killing in Hiroshima.

Malinda Bowman, an Australian nurse who was imprisoned in Totsuka POW camp some distance outside of Tokyo recalled: "Flames were caught in the swirling winds and danced upward, turning into fireballs feverishly feeding upon themselves. Explosions tortured the air and the shocking scene took on the spectacle of a volcano in violent eruption." The destruction was also observed from high above; pilots of latter waves of bombers reported detection of the stench of burning flesh as they flew 4,900 to 9,200 feet over the city. Although it was to be the largest carpet-bombing raid against Japanese cities for the remainder of the war, it was only the start of a bombing program aimed at bombing Japan into submission. Most of these bombing missions were to be launched from the airfields in the Mariana Islands.

LeMay had proved his point. America had the firepower for mass killings.

The heavy-laden, huge, powerful, American bombers lumbered up from Kwajalein, Saipan and Tinian, non-stop. By this time, America had effectively destroyed Japan's air and naval defenses. Most of the planes, pilots, and ships had been sent off and destroyed in battles.

Japan ordered, and prepared herself for a massive suicidal land battle in the home islands.

Instead of launching a bloody invasion, America rained bombs, thousands of tons of explosives on Japanese military installations, on her government facilities, on her cities and on her civilian population. Tokyo was a prime target.

The planes came primarily at night in the beginning. Soon, the population was going to underground air-raid shelters on regular schedules. The people would take their teapots, bedding, and books and go to the shelters. It was a regular journey, part of their routine. The bombs came closer and closer.

One night in the spring of 1945, the Americans rained millions of incendiary bombs on the wood, bamboo, and paper houses across Tokyo. America intended to bring the Japanese government to the realization that the war was lost and further resistance was futile, suicidal.

The Japanese waited and prepared for one mighty battle that would decide the war. They based Pearl Harbor on that strategy. They based the war in the Pacific on that strategy. Under the direction of the Emperor, they prepared the home islands based on that final strategy. The incendiary campaign by the Americans gave notice that the one mighty battle would not occur. America was not to invade the home islands.

Over a hundred thousand Japanese or so in the City of Tokyo died that night! The number approximated those lost in Hiroshima, which was to come.

Many in the Japanese war cabinet felt the war was lost as these incendiaries alone could bring the Japanese population to its knees. In other words, conventional arms with the B-29 aircraft could destroy the Japanese will to fight. There was little evidence to support this argument. War is about drama. If the conventional arms argument had prevailed, there probably would have been a slow build up. Such a build-up would not have provided the drama to force decisive action — particularly sufficient to force surrender.

The Japanese are a unique race of people. They seldom surrendered in the islands campaign; even some civilians joined the soldiers in committing suicide. This provided a stark environment for a decision of invading the home islands. The drama for such a decision was essential and it was missing.

The Japanese high command and people accommodated the slaughter. They accepted it as one more milestone in the ineluctable path toward Japanese destiny.

The Japanese trained young Kamikaze pilots, who had the looks of innocence, to drive their planes, bombs and themselves into the American ships in one last suicidal sacrifice or act of honor for the Emperor, descendent of the Sun God.

On August 15, 1945, the Americans deprived them of their sacrificial offering. A lone B-29 hauled a single bomb to Hiroshima. This bomb demonstrated that the Americans now had unlimited destructive power in both incendiaries and in atomic bombs.

It demonstrated that the Japanese could commit national suicide if they wanted; they could take their ceremonious hari-kari to its ultimate limit by putting the whole people to sacrifice, but America would not send more of her sons to join them on their tatami altar. America would accommodate the Japanese fetishism for suicide-sacrifices, even for its whole people if they insisted; but America would not send a million of her sons to sacrifice themselves.

There would be no invasion of the home islands!

Japan had the choice of surrender or annihilation by these American warriors.

Over a hundred thousand Japanese had died on the night of the incendiary bombs! These were cluster bombs in that as they were falling, the sheet metal holding them together dropped away spewing thousands of tiny bomblets from each bomb container. The number of killed approximated those to be lost in Hiroshima, which was to come. These incendiaries caused the firestorms that destroyed everything in their way.

After the incendiary experiments, one lone B-29 in August 15, 1945 hauled a single bomb to Hiroshima from Tinian. This one atomic bomb demonstrated that the Americans had unlimited destructive power.

There would be no invasion of the home islands!

Japan had the choice of surrender or annihilation. She lay down her arms. The war was over.

CHAPTER 10

WAR'S END

On September 2, 1945 there was a gathering on the battleship USS Missouri in Tokyo Bay. General Douglas MacArthur, as Supreme Allied Commander led the signing of the surrender document.

To this day, the Japanese present to themselves and to the world with this Emperor Hirohito view: The Japanese were victimized by atomic weapons in the hands of the barbaric American war machine that threatened civilization. The Emperor did the only humanitarian thing open to him!

As unlikely as it seems, I managed to be aboard the USS Missouri for the signing. I meshed into the great crowd of soldiers and sailors witnessing the momentous event. By this time, I had been in the military since Pearl Harbor. I had witnessed many of the major events that had occurred across Africa, Italy and the islands as the American fleets hopped from island to island preparatory to an anticipated invasion of the Japanese homeland.

America and the Allies burst into victory celebration. Every town launched parades, celebratory speeches and unorganized rejoicing. The long war was over. It was now a question of governing.

Over a million American deaths were avoided, as the final battle did not have to be fought. There would be no final battle of the Japanese Islands.

Even if incendiary bombs had been depended on for the victory, the American death toll would have been intolerable. The deaths avoided by the use of a single Hiroshima bomb would have been in the vicinity of 100,000 civilians.

There has been considerable controversy since the war of the Emperor's responsibility for starting and conducting the war. Many believe that to this day, and there is no consensus among historians, that the Emperor exercised considerable authority over war decisions that were made. This is researched in the book by Herbert Bix in *Hirohito, and the Making of Modern Japan.*

CHAPTER 11

INTELLIGENCE SAGA AND LAPSES

The tale of intelligence is not compartmentalized such as a battle that has a start and an ending. The intelligence function is spread across all locations and is a continuum in time. It Is treated here as a function following the end of the war. Only in this delay of time can we speak with knowledge; thus, it appears out of place, but is not. WWII had been over for years before the depth and breadth of many of their catastrophes became known. Then, the poor Japanese intelligence became public knowledge. It was a daffy situation with apocalyptic results for the Japanese. It had a profound effect on the war's outcome.

The gathering and analysis of intelligence did not happen in a concentrated form. This must be a continuous function as long as the state continues. It is concentrated here but that is misleading. Like history, intelligence gathering must be a continuum, a woven tapestry with data points everywhere. The dots must be continually positioned to illustrate deeper knowledge being gained.

I often talked with George about the American lapses against Japanese Intel during the war.

"Charlie, one can hardly believe these episodes," George Grayburn said.

He continued. I can understand their not knowing because they never learned somehow but the Japanese Navy was told about the methodology in a book by Herbert O. Yardley in 1931, *America's Black Chamber.* This became something of a best seller in Japan, selling 33,931 copies. This became a bible of cryptology. It also sold 17,931 copies in the U.S. Many in the U.S. thought Yardley should be tried for espionage and selling secrets to foreigners. This never happened.

The Japanese took it seriously enough that they invited Yardley to Japan as a trainer and a lecturer to the Navy. Japan was put on notice.

I answered, "Just as puzzling, Japan is a closed society. They do not readily accept Japanese outsiders as part of their culture. Yet, Richard Sorge was a grand spy. How could they possibly have opened themselves for such perfidy by the Sorge spy ring and for Yardley's espionage where these were in the open literature? For this, they paid the awful price of military defeat. One must have awesome military power but also awesome power in every branch of society."

"I know." George replied.

I then continued. "Code-breaking by Americans was a disaster for the Japanese. Before and during the war, the Japanese had numerous code weaknesses, yet there was no appropriate alarm. They continued their way as if it were not happening. Somehow, strange events befell the Japanese for no apparent reason. It was as if the rules of chance suddenly favored the Americans or they had special knowledge that was catastrophic to Japanese forces. This outcome must be based on knowledge gained just by chance, they reasoned. The dice had just fallen the wrong way. It could never happen again. Fate had just interceded against them, they reasoned. They thereby displayed a phenomenal arrogance where they had reasons to suspect the Americans were controlling the games of chance by manipulating the dice table.

CHAPTER 12

INTEL AND CODE BREAKING SAGA

"The Kellogg Naval Conference in 1921, and sequences thereafter, was to decide the number of battleships allowable for the U.S., Japan and Britain. During the conference the diplomats communicated with their home countries using coded messages sent through commercial wire services. The messages often were composed of 5-character groups such as 'eklzp', etc. The messages were in code. The international communications companies included Western Union International, RCA, Marconi and others. These provided copies of the coded communications to the American intelligence group. This small group was set up during the negotiations to monitor the conference proceedings. Herbert O. Yardley and his staff controlled it. They broke the Japanese diplomatic and naval codes and read them for the duration of the conference. This gave the Americans a great advantage as one might expect. This had a profound effect on the outcome of the conference according to participants. Japan was incensed at the limitation imposed by the Conference. It was humiliating, they thought.

"After WWI, Secretary of State Stimson made his famous and naïve statement that 'gentlemen do not read other gentlemen's mail.' He then cut off the funding and disbanded the code-breaking group. Yardley was incensed. He was an egoist that lived the good life but he suddenly found himself without a job. He then retaliated by publishing a book revealing his role in the Washington Conference. He presented code-breaking examples and methods of breaking codes in the future. The methodology was thereby open to anyone in the open literature. The book, *America's Black Chamber*, became a best seller. America sold some 17,931 copies in the U.S. Others translated it into Japanese, French, Swedish, and Chinese. The Japanese version sold an unprecedented 33,119 copies, far surpassing the U.S. sales.

"Through this work, an estimated 19 nations were soon to learn that their codes were being broken." Means and methods were described in detail.

"Incredibly, the Japanese failed to take precautions against what they had been warned of for all that time. Even with no warnings, they should have taken precautions. The Japanese Navy invited Yardley to lecture their officers on codes and code breaking in the 1930's and he did for a price. The Japanese even hired him as a consultant on the same subject. Many Americans at the time wanted to prosecute him as a traitor while others considered him as the father of crypto-analysis. In this murky world of intelligence and cryptology, no one was quite sure of how to handle code-breakers and intelligence officers that wander off the farm. That problem remains to this day. The most recent is a contractor working for the CIA who has taken millions of files with him and left the country in 2013. The total extent of the damage is unknown. Edward Snowden and his kind do inestimable damage to the nation. The fact that they succeed in walking off with the farm testifies to the difficulty of stopping them. It also shows the stupidity of those setting up ineffective defenses. James Jesus Angleton, chief of the CIA's Counterintelligence staff from 1954 to 1975, was guilty of this in setting up defenses and also of actively being a proven spy using his official position. Israel's Jonathon Pollard and many others have also delivered stolen classified documents to foreigners.

The Japanese had this information early on, but even so, they failed to fix their vulnerabilities. Even after these revelations, the Japanese lost the Battle of Midway where American code breaking was decisive against the Japanese. The Battle of Midway proved to be the turning point of the war. It is ironic that the Americans taught the Japanese; they gave the Japanese the technology; then, code-breaking caused the Japanese loss at Midway; and Midway turned the war.

Spying is as old as man; it reaches back into antiquity. One must prepare for it in detail but somehow the Japanese did not heed the obvious for the duration of what was to come. They put mighty warships across the Pacific, yet America listened to what was transpiring on the bridges of those ships and in the minds of the white-clad naval officers controlling them.

The Japanese did not fix the problem for the remainder of the war and thereafter.

America continued to read the Japanese naval and diplomatic codes. Amazingly, this continued throughout the war. The Japanese obviously saw the importance of codes, as Yardley's book was a best seller. Further, they hired him as a consultant to teach their Naval Officers the craft. In addition, Japan is in some respects a closed society. Their social organization is similar to a citizenry in straightjackets. Nevertheless, their codes were consistently read.

Further, the Japanese hosted Richard Sorge who was probably the master spy of all time. He operated in Japan from the German Embassy, providing information mostly for the Soviet Union.

He was a Soviet military intelligence officer, active before and during WWII, working under the cover of being a German journalist in Nazi Germany, the Soviet Union and the Empire of Japan. Sorge is most famous for his service in Japan in 1940 and 1941, when he provided information about Adolf Hitler's plan to attack the Soviet Union. The Japanese allowed him and the spy ring he controlled to travel in Manchuria, China, the Soviet Union and across Japan. This enabled his spying activity during the war.

In late 1941, he informed the Soviet command that Japan was not going to attack the Soviet Union in the near future, which reportedly allowed the command to transfer 18 divisions, 1,700 tanks, and over 1,500 aircraft from Siberia and the Far East to the Western Front against Nazi Germany during the most dangerous months of the Battle for Moscow, one of the turning points of the whole of World War II.

In 1964, Sorge was posthumously awarded the title of Hero of the Soviet Union.

He was born in 1895 and hanged by the Japanese in 1944.

A number of military and intelligence professionals and historians have described Sorge as one of the greatest intelligence officers of all times, and one of the few who changed the history of a conflict. This makes absolutely no sense and was a daffy situation that defies imagination.

It is ironic that this spy operated in Japan, a country thought to be the most closed society in the world.

There was no time that code breaking was not at the center of activity of military operations. This has been true as long as man has fielded armies. Of course, with time, the Americans perfected different technologies. This puts the whole genre at another level. It is for this reason that one gives great attention to the art.

In WWII, the Americans spent a great deal of time on code machines, typically Ultra and its progressions. These generally had spinning wheels to match an inserted code and were often changed.

Ultra was the designation adopted by British military intelligence in June 1941 for wartime signals intelligence obtained by breaking high-level encrypted enemy radio and telegraphic communications at Bletchley Park. Ultra eventually became the standard designation among the western Allies for all such intelligence. The name arose because the intelligence thus obtained was considered more important than that designated by the highest British security classification then used (Most Secret) and so was regarded as being Ultra secret. The U.S. used the code name Magic for its decrypts from Japanese sources.

Much of the German cipher traffic was encrypted on the Enigma machine. Used properly, the German military Enigma would have been virtually unbreakable. In practice, shortcomings in operation allowed it to be broken. The term 'Ultra' has often been used almost synonymously with 'Enigma Decrypts'. However, Ultra also encompassed other decrypts such as "PURPLE."

The official American intelligence assessment during and after the war was by the *United States Strategic Bombing Survey.* This was a board of experts assembled to produce an assessment of the effects of Anglo-American strategic bombing. After publishing its report, the Survey then turned its attention to the efforts against Imperial Japan during the Pacific War, including a separate section on the recent use of the atomic bombs.

This shows that the Nazis were basically starving at the end of the war. In addition, their war-making capacity had been almost eliminated. The same was true of Japan. The Army Air Corps and Navy had savaged the countries and their ability to make war. Yet, that destruction was a team effort, not the result of a single service. This can be seen in the conclusions of that report. The major points of the report are shown.

TABLE 1. ASSETS BOMBED AND SURVEY RESULTS.

ASSET	RESULTS
Oil Refineries	Catastrophic
Ammunition	Catastrophic
Truck Manufacturing	Catastrophic
Submarine Mfg.	Halted
Aircraft Production	Catastrophic
Armor Production	Catastrophic
Ball Bearings	Bombing Failure
Missiles	Limited Effect
Steel Production	Limited Effect
Consumer Goods	Adequate Production

In total, the reports contained 208 volumes for Europe and another 108 for the Pacific, comprising thousands of pages. The reports' conclusions were generally favorable about the contributions of Allied strategic bombing towards victory, calling it "decisive."

"Decisive?"

Decisive it was, but it surely did not provide a decision of victory or defeat. No man can know this. However, we can know what would surely lead to defeat if that service is totally absent during the war. One questions the finality of the word 'decisive'. There were too many military components that were decisive to allocate finality to one.

Surely, infantry soldiers were decisive in WWII as it is in any victory. Industrial production and logistics are decisive in any victory. And so it goes. We do not buy into the daffy theory that a decisive service of a whole army and theater stands alone in the victory. Normandy needed soldiers like it needed airplanes, and like it needed intelligence. The Navy was decisive. Cutting Solomon's baby into pieces does not yield a decisive piece. It is the whole that matters.

In September 1941, an Italian named Fellers had stolen a codebook, photographed it and returned it to the U.S. embassy in Rome. The Italians shared parts of their intercepts with their German allies. In addition, the Germans were soon able to break the code. Fellers's reports were extremely detailed and played a significant role in informing the Germans of allied strength and intentions

In addition, the Africa Korps had an intelligence service-monitoring-element commanded by Hauptmann Alfred Seeböhm. This Battalion monitored radio communications among British units. Unfortunately for the Allies, the British not only failed to change their codes with any frequency, they were also prone to poor radio discipline in combat. Their officers made frequent open, un-coded transmissions to their commands, allowing the Germans to more easily identify British units and deployments. The situation changed after a counterattack during the Battle of Gazala resulted in the unit being overrun and destroyed, and a number of their documents captured, alerting British intelligence to the problem. The British responded by instituting an improved call signal procedure, introducing radiotelephonic codes, imposing rigid wireless silence on reserve formations, padding out real messages with dummy traffic, tightening up on their radio discipline in combat and creating an entire fake signals network.

Allied code-breakers read the much-enciphered German message traffic, especially that encrypted with the Enigma machine. The Allies' Ultra program was initially of limited value, as it took too long to get the information to the commanders in the field, and at times provided information that was less than helpful. In terms of anticipating the next move the Germans would make, reliance on Ultra sometimes backfired.

The primary benefit of Ultra intercepts to the effort in North Africa was to aid in cutting the Axis supply line to Tunisia. Ultra intercepts provided valuable information about the times and routes of Axis supply shipments across the Mediterranean. This was critical in providing the British with the opportunity to intercept and destroy them. During the time when Malta was under heavy air attack, the ability to act on this information was limited, but as Allied air and naval strength improved, the information became instrumental to Allied success. It is estimated that between 40% to 60% of Axis supply shipping was located and destroyed due to decrypted information.

Recently, Jackson told me he had the opportunity to meet one of the dozen major authors of the Strategic Bombing Survey at a State Department lunch. The author was gracious in response to the introduction and they had a conversation about his young age during the war. He was from a very prominent scholastic, patrician and finance family in the U.S. and this was apparent. He was only 38 years old at war's end, a lofty position for a young man, long considered a graybeard in the post-war world. He became the Secretary. He indicated that hardly anyone recognized his role in the Survey anymore, so he was most happy with their conversation. I later saw that he passed away and the Navy had named a destroyer after him. He also served as Secretary of the Navy for a period.

These code-breaking efforts continued throughout the war, with ever-increasing success.

The story jumps to Jackson as the lead character, with Charlie.

Jackson entered the picture in 1947 by joining the Navy and being assigned to Taiwan. WWII had recently ended and a new world was taking shape. It resembled not the past with the depression nor the future with restoring the economy. The Cold War was thrust upon us with Russia challenging the West at every turn.

By the mid 1950s and after WWII, Jackson had arrived some time ago on the island of Taiwan as a guest of the Chinese Air Force. His function was to install and maintain special equipment in their special reconnaissance airplanes and to provide expertise in the data they collected. He had invented several of the important boxes placed there. Additionally, he was very knowledgeable of the purpose of the missions and had expertise in general analysis. This led to trips by Jackson to other Asian countries where such expertise was needed. Jackson was to stay in Taiwan for several years.

By then, WWII had recently ended. The Soviets had declared war against Japan only a few days before the Japanese surrender to the Allies with the hope of participating in the division of the spoils. This included the Pacific world and the peace treaty to follow. Their strategy was rejected by the Allies but the Soviets handed over sufficient war weapons to equip a 750-thousand man Chinese Communist army. Soviet backing put a huge, well-equipped army into northern China that helped decide the Chinese Civil War, a war between the Chinese Communists under Mao Tse-tung and the Nationalists under Chiang Kai-shek.

The pot continued to boil as Russia blocked pathways between East and West Berlin, prompting the Berlin Airlift in 1948-1949. This airlift effectively defeated the blockade.

The Korean War followed the airlift and after that, the Vietnam War. The Soviet army had rolled over East Europe in the final stages of WWII. The Russians soon incorporated those countries into the Soviet empire.

Since the Allies had essentially disarmed at the end of the war, America's fate and that of Western Europe were not particularly rosy.

The Russians in WWII killed German soldiers by a factor of 15 (3,000,000 vice 200,000) over those killed by the Allies. The United States did provide a critical portion of the weapons and tools necessary to do so. As the Russians saw it, they had won the war and were now justifiably aggressive against the Allies.

After the war, Russia was a closed dictatorial state hiding behind cloaks of secrecy while the U.S. and Britain were open democratic states, voluntarily sharing information with the world. For this, America used both conventional aircraft and developed special aircraft with exotic photographic and electronic sensors. I helped provide this intelligence during the war, as did Jackson afterwards. I did it more conventionally by military over-flights during the war and clandestinely after the Cold War started. Jackson provided over-flight information during the Cold War and other Intel services for years after its onset.

Yet, the Ancient Mariner was a curse on us all. Most events here were a foreshadowing of curses, violence, madness and death.

PART 2

CHAPTER 13

SUNY AND LAX COMPLEX

After several years in the Navy, Jackson had taken many courses and then entered SUNY to get a university degree in a technical field. He was commissioned in the Air Force after this. He had served in the ROTC and taken a degree in aeronautical engineering. He had several years experience as an air crewman so things were not so different in the Air Force.

He was easily able to handle all the Air Force requirements. In fact, as a part of his commissioning, the Air Force had recognized the value of his several years in the Navy as an air crewman. He therefore entered the service as a First Lieutenant, while most became Second Lieutenants. This put him as the leader of most all newly commissioned officers in his outfits and established his level as first among his peers.

Nevertheless, his eager beaver status stayed with him and remained in effect for most of his life. This applied not only to travels but extended to work and to his interests in general.

By the time he got a commission, Jackson had visited all the states (then there were 48), Alaska and Hawaii. He had traveled to most every place between the Caribbean and the North Polar Region, perhaps 20 countries across the Atlantic, Africa, Europe, the Middle East and twenty-to-thirty islands.

Jackson had met Eliot in SUNY and became good friends with him as a fellow student. Eliot had a good feel for technical matters and was enrolled for a technical degree. Eliot was to join the Air Force after graduation. Both he and Jackson also had earned degrees and silver wings.

Another student that Jackson met in SUNY was William Callona. He was generally called by his nickname, Billy. Billy Callona had a fiery disposition. This did not become apparent for most of his encounters but there were times when he could hit the ceiling. The best way of handling this was to just walk away. Otherwise, one would be pulled into the confrontation. Fortunately, Billy's temper never seemed to bother his career.

Billy Callona often joined Jackson for weekend activities. Billy was a few years younger than Jackson so that inhibited their friendship somewhat but not too much.

CHAPTER 14

THE NEW AVIONICS AGE

After his stay in SUNY and getting a degree there, he accepted a job with the government and moved to Los Angeles for a year or two.

The world is such a different place now than it used to be. Jackson had learned to live with the modern world of the new millennium but it was hard. Gone are the moderate-sized airports to be replaced by mammoth city-sized airports where the smaller airports used to be. Gone are the days of sitting in the small waiting rooms and watching the planes take off from a single runway. Gone are the propeller airplanes with slow takeoffs and climbs. Gone are the number of passengers below tens or hundreds per flight. Gone are the female stewardesses that have been screened for their youth, gender, beauty and personality.

Enormous terminals replaced these, with hundreds of aircraft parked in smaller satellite terminals, many having electrified trams for rapid ground transportation between terminals. Gone are the single terminals, to be replaced with many huge satellite terminals, massive waiting rooms, franchised fast foods and other products. Gone are small, propeller airplanes to be replaced by wide-bodied jets where each hauls hundreds of passengers. Gone are the beautiful stewardesses to be replaced with those of longevity. Little or no vetting occurs since that may now be politically incorrect. Catch-all men and women stewards and stewardesses are now used and these are often aged, plain, grumpy and with dull personalities. They bring no passion to the job and no glamour. Meals now consist of crackers and little else.

Los Angeles Airport used to be a place like that. One could sit in the single terminal and watch the few airplanes take off and land. And, one could imagine far places and visit them through National Geographic and the tales of friends. Now, after 2015 or so, the airport is surrounded by 20 to 30-story hotels, aerospace office buildings reaching much higher than this and it spreads in every direction for a mile or so. The old LAX terminal is now replaced with a huge freeway interchange and with buildings, parking structures, streets, satellite terminals and the hubbub of traffic usually associated with the center of a major city like Manhattan.

Jackson lived in an apartment near the airport. This general area is next to the sea and is in the southern part of the city. The whole area of a little less than five square miles or so is dedicated to airport activities, now with four parallel runways of 9,000 to 12,000 feet lengths.

It is very difficult to imagine how the area in 1955 and 2015 are the same place that has been transformed. Some sense of the change is described. When he first arrived, it was apparent that the airport leased out areas away from the runways. Some farmers were even growing vegetables. As an ultimate anachronism, the farmers were using mules to turn the soil. This went on for a couple of years when tractors replaced animal power. Soon, the grass was mowed and those areas became little more than lawns between taxi strips.

The terminal was destroyed during the conversion to a modern airport, passing underneath two of the runways of the Los Angeles International Airport. A whole freeway interchange now replaces the old terminal but construction was going on for years.

Los Angeles was experiencing explosive growth during those years. As stated, this moved on from mules to the jetports of the Jetsons. Every homeowner during this growth used a rotor-tiller or a small handheld tractor. This helped plow the ground so that grassy lawns could be planted. In many cases, this was a hopeless dream. The soil in L.A. is hard, compacted adobe. The rotor-tiller should dig deep, perhaps 4-6 inches. The soil only allowed a few inches and below this, it appeared to be hard concrete. They did the best they could.

When Jackson went to Taiwan, farmers on Taipei used water buffalos to plow their fields and rice paddies, similar to the Americans using mules. Every farmer had a buffalo. Ten years later, a few farmers were rich enough to have a tractor for their rice paddies. The tractors they bought were the little hand rotor-tillers or plows similar to the lawn machines being used in Los Angeles.

Jackson had to find a place to live when he got to Los Angeles. He rented an apartment near the L.A. Airport. The whole area was to satisfy the need for accommodations near the airport. The number of stewardesses needing housing was astonishing.

Jackson thought he had died and gone to heaven.

This whole area, perhaps 20-30 square miles and about five square miles for the airport proper, was to satisfy this need for pilots, stewardesses, and ground crews. They needed apartments. In those days, there was vetting by the airlines for stewardesses. Most were therefore young, 20-30 years old, very attractive, with great personalities. The airlines ran schools on how to behave and radiate class.

The apartments were mostly studio apartments where that described an open area with two daybeds, bathroom, kitchen and open area. This often satisfied the need of transient airline personnel. Naturally, two and three bedroom apartments were also available. These were mostly built around a pool and surrounded the pool on all four sides. The pools and all the area had all the amenities. The apartments filled all the space around the pool including deck chairs, barbeque grills, diving boards, towel service and storage.

Most were two stories high.

Many of the stewardesses were here-today-gone-tomorrow. This was a major aircraft stopover or airlines hub. The girls generally stayed long enough to rest up and get their things in order before hitting the road again. Many were on fixed schedules and rented out their apartments long term. When these owners were away, they often managed to keep the apartments filled by prior arrangements or from short-term agreements.

He did not know the ratio of girls to boys in the apartments but it had to be quite high. If one did not like the crop today, then wait until next weekend when the whole crop usually changed. Of course, many were semi-permanent as the airlines held trainers for future stewardesses. There was a huge crowd of transients but a very large number of permanent girls.

Further, there were a huge number of massive buildings for workers in the aerospace industry in the same area. Aircraft were designed and many were manufactured in the vicinity and that brought in an ever-increasing number of young boys and girls. These generally provided new jobs. Many of these buildings had been built by the government in WWII and were now leased to the aircraft companies. These included North American Aviation, Hughes Aircraft Company, Northrup, Douglas, Lockheed and others.

In these days, Eisenhower was president, the Cold War was well underway and defense spending was at its height. The nation was intent on developing Intercontinental Ballistic Missiles (ICBMs) to deliver nuclear weapons to Russia or elsewhere. There were years of exploding fireballs at the launch cites but in the end, the accidents stopped and we were successful in the development, both from land using missile silos across middle America and from the sea using submarines.

In every waking hour, one could throw on a bathing suit, go outside and lounge on the numerous beach chairs and make acquaintances.

As stated, Jackson knew that he had died and gone to heaven.

CHAPTER 15

MALINDA LANE

Malinda Lane was a beautiful redhead, an airline stewardess. Her hair was scarlet, a brilliant red color with a tinge of orange and plenty of yellows. The color was slightly less orange than vermilion. Scarlet and other bright shades of red are the colors most associated with courage, force, passion, heat, and joy. She certainly met these attributes.

Jackson met her at one of the numerous parties thrown in his apartment. Billy Collona was his roommate there and parties were his specialty. I don't know where he got all the women but there were plenty around that loved dancing and partying.

Malinda was shapely and had a wonderful personality. She was from New England. Somehow, she fell for Jackson. This turned out to be a hit or miss relationship in that she was almost always gone or so it seemed. They became fast friends and saw each other whenever she was in town.

Did we say she was shapely? She was a knockout horse. Her torso was just right in every dimension and her limbs were incomparable. She had beautiful red hair that shone in the sunlight. The passage of the sun caused her hair to radiate differently with each angle of the sun. When she laughed, she lit up the world in reds and scarlet and soft yellows. It was a beautiful sight.

She was tall with slender arms and legs. She grabbed all the attention when she entered a club or restaurant. She had never met a stranger. Soon, she had the whole crowd incorporated into her sphere. They laughed with her, sought her attention, told stories with her. She was a magnet of attraction, the light that drew all the moths.

Malinda Lane was a beacon to us all. Her attachment to Jackson was deep and affectionate. One could tell she was in love and to some extent, so was Jackson.

However, there was a schism or a split in the road. The pull of their relationship competed with the thrill of being a traveler and of his contract for work in Taiwan,

"Jackson, stay with me," she pleaded. "One does not have to do the work. Just forget it."

But it was not so simple. He needed the thrill. He needed the money.

"I know. You've got to sell those anvils," she said in reference to the movie, *Music Man*.

"I do. I do." he said. "Forgive me."

Nothing could dissuade him from preparing for the long airplane trip.

After some time, he left Los Angeles for Taiwan. Unfortunately, He had to leave her but they remained good friends until he left. He then lost track of her. That was too bad but seems to be a characteristic of the young. They lose contact with the only things in life that matter.

We heard later that she was in an airplane crash in Palm Springs. As the stewardess, she was responsible for the passengers. It was a serious accident and several people died. Malinda was credited with helping those aboard get out of the wreckage, which then burned. She apparently saved several lives. Unfortunately, she was injured and that took a year or so for her recovery. She performed heroically during the accident. A friend had told Jackson this and it was also in the papers.

This did give her a sense of trauma and how it could affect one. She became far more empathetic for those that were slightly handicapped.

Jackson and his friend, Billy Callona, liked jazz music. At one time, Billy had roomed in the same apartment so it was convenient. They liked the same things and had common interests. They bought records, electronic equipment and books. Best of all, Los Angeles was host to most everyone with artistic skills. This made concerts imminently available. We liked the Hollywood Bowl and the Greek Theater but best of all were the clubs with small groups playing jazz such as that at Hermosa Beach by the airport or downtown near Rosecrans and Paramount Studios.

These were halcyon years for Billy, Malinda, Jackson, Tom, and for those people Jackson befriended. He especially befriended the airline stewardesses that were so bountiful in the area.

Jackson had a friend that was quite older than he, named Tom Hardy. He had somehow made a legend for himself. He was quite generous and threw a party for all his friends often. He had a reputation for partying and for hosting these events that lasted from early to late night. Jackson began to notice that it was a fun time but people took advantage of his generosity. He kept a running tab at two or three lounges. He seldom went to these lounges but his friends did. They invariably started a party for Tom and there was drinking at his expense.

He had an apartment although he was usually traveling and not there. He would invariably invite everyone for a party, often on work nights. Jackson was puzzled about this, why is he funding everything and how does he drink that much? Jackson soon started peeling the onion on this score. He watched Tom Hardy as he, without fail, rooted for the party to take place. At about 9 pm everyone was getting into the fun.

Tom made his getaway at about 9 p.m. He abandoned the party and crept up the stairs to his apartment and went to bed. Jackson found this to be the general rule.

One was happy with Tom Hardy's function and he was a most generous man. Everyone should have a friend like that.

He continued to carry the bar tabs and pay for them. As said, he was a most generous person.

Everyone assumed Tom was beyond sex since he showed little interest in all those pretty girls. Yet, one wonders. He attracted friends and girls all the time. I still wander if more was taking place than we realized. What was happening after 9 pm, we wandered.

Unfortunately, Tom had a serious accident. A fighter jet in Taiwan where he was temporarily stationed, was trailing a target cable down the runway and Tom did not notice that it was still running on the ground as he started across the runway. The cable wrapped around the jeep, turned it over and made a mess of it. Tom was really in a sorry shape. He had two broken arms, gashes and damage to his internal organs. He was returned to Los Angeles for medical treatment.

Unfortunately, he passed away during the treatments.

American Recovery

In those days, America was recuperating from the war, from low GDP and from sparse products in general. Jackson was a teen-ager when WWII ended. Nevertheless, he longed for the adventure of airplanes.

Americans strutted like members of the British Empire. After all, they had just won the war and the large defense manufacturing industry was setting up for the resupply of Europe and the world. The elite of America was strutting and they liked it.

The Navy had an air base called Opalocka Field, FL. All naval officers wore starched white uniforms, long sox and white shoes. Nothing indicates British Empire as much as white uniforms with long stockings. One had to love that place. There were aircraft, plenty of activity and excitement. There were white sand beaches, golf courses, convenient air travel; the world was an oyster.

After the war, the action was in Miami Beach or in Havana, Cuba. Las Vegas was still a vacant place with blowing sand. As luck would have it, one of our friends, James Bailey, at Opalocka said he wanted to go into town to see his mother. What? What does she do? He revealed she was a cocktail waitress in a new hotel on Miami Beach called the Fontainebleau. We knew this to be an elaborate undertaking for a hotel, the biggest thing in Miami.

Three of us, James, George Grayburn and I, went together to see this extravaganza that was partially open. We took an elevator to the penthouse lounge.

This was the most elaborately dressed clientele we had ever seen. Everyone was in tuxedos or tails. Many were in white ties. The lady's gowns were extraordinary. We thought we had died and gone to Hollywood heaven. James Bailey's mother was a cocktail waitress. Her costume was a lot like that of the Playboy Bunny, but preceded it. She was popular with many of the diners and probably was hired for her fun-loving personality and her general bearing. She looked like she belonged there with all the finery of the lounge. Perhaps it was a private party.

Everyone there insisted on buying us drinks. We were all still in our 'teens' then. They had to do something for us. The carpet and pillows were all plush, and the tables were all full of silverware and candles, waiting for the food to be served. This was as plush a setting as most of us had ever seen. Sometimes it is amazing what a uniform will do. They acted as they loved us and we certainly loved them.

We stayed there an hour or two. We surely had a good time. It was too rich for our blood.

Earlier, we had gone to Guantanamo Bay in Cuba. "Gitmo" had been developed as a defense for the Panama Canal. I don't know if it saved the Canal for the U.S. but Jimmy Carter gave it away much later. The skyline for parts of the Canal Zone now looked like New York City.

The gambling dens in Havana were certainly above the ordinary. However, Havana was nothing compared to Miami. Later, times changed. The casinos in Las Vegas outdid Havana and Miami.

A friend of mine later on was quite wealthy. His friends said, "He never worked a day in his life." This was all said in jest and they had a lot of fun teasing him. After all, he had it and they didn't. Someone asked him, "Ed, what did you do during the war?"

He responded, "I was a naval officer in Puerto Rico during the war."

A friend yelled, "And he did a darned good job, too. You never heard anyone during the war complain about Nazis in Puerto Rico, did you?"

No one knew if he'd ever been in Puerto Rico but it made a good story.

America was recovering.

CHAPTER 16

HAZARDOUS BLOCK ISLAND SAIL

There never was a time that Jackson did not get a thrill from sailing. It was part of his blood. One loved the strong wind while it was blowing in on the side. It caused the boat to roll to a substantial angle and then stayed there. Even when the wind came around toward the bow or the stern, there was great fun in trying to come into it. The fun even continued while the sails luffed. There were times when luffing was not fun. Every day is not bright sunshine with blue skies. One worries that the fog is coming in, mist restricts your sight, small boats get in your way and even large boats and barges tend to run you down. Jackson was a teen-ager for many of his experiences on sail boats. Many of these pre-war adventures sound dangerous but he was a competent sailor with a lot of experience.

All these many thrills and horrors are what the sea is all about.

This was later demonstrated to Jackson one more time on a sail to Block Island.

Franklin knew that Jackson was fond of boats and had owned a sailboat before selling it. Franklin was one of Jackson's friends. He invited Jackson to a cocktail party on his boat that was a large sailboat. As we know, Block Island stands out in the Atlantic beyond Long Island and Rhode Island. The communities that represent these are Montauk Point in New York and Newport in Rhode Island.

There was an old saying in Vaudeville and the comedians that never failed to get a laugh when they used it.

"Once you leave Manhattan, it is all Bridgeport."

Bridgeport always bore the brunt of the humor since it was a working town with manufacturing mills for watches, mechanisms, useful household items, razors and God knows what else. The wrong part of town was a rather tawdry place. Yet, the town on the edge of Westchester County in New York had an upscale section. It had fine boats in its marinas and fine houses overlooking the water of Long Island Sound.

Jackson knew some of the people in the town. They sometimes invited him aboard their boats for a drink.

The boat was quite large and made a fine platform for a reception. About 25 people showed up. They were generally well dressed since it was early afternoon on a Sunday. It turned out to be as one would have wished with cocktail attire.

On this occasion, Jackson invited Malinda Lane to go with him for cocktails. Malinda was still flying as a stewardess. She had continued the attachment to Jackson who had just returned from Taiwan. Her knowledge of his true conditions was only marginally known at this time.

The boat was several decades old and was made of wood. It was a beautiful thing, as she lay quiet in the water alongside the pier. For the cocktail party, the owner motored a couple of miles away from the pier and let the boat drift. However, he kept a watchful eye on the boat and stayed a safe distance from the shore.

It was a chic event and everyone enjoyed the afternoon.

Everything appeared safe and under control. This put many of the people in a positive frame of mind. Thus, they began to discuss a trip on the boat at a later time. Somehow, the idea of going to Block Island for the July-Fourth weekend was talked about. In the end, about ten people of the group agreed this was a splendid idea. It was formalized the next week by planning.

Jackson was not the organizer for this but he did indicate he was favorable to the idea. Ten people agreed to go for the weekend, including my 10-year-old nephew, Kurt, and a twelve-year-old. The rest were adults.

On the appropriate date, only a week after the cocktail party, all gathered on the boat in the marina at Bridgeport. We gathered on the pier and put our bags on the boat. Jackson had a boat on Long Island Sound when in high school. The short cruise to Block Island on the Atlantic Ocean gateway at the head of the Sound was a wonderful trip. He sometimes sailed to the island on weekends.

Franklin had offered a sailing trip to Block Island that included several of Jackson's friends. Franklin was offering it as a sort of nostalgia trip for Jackson. It included Malinda. After all, Jackson had made the trip more than once and this would renew his memories of those trips. It was an excellent and caring suggestion.

This was a hazardous place to be and it keeps demonstrating this to New England sailors. Jackson got the chance to make this sail and he took it. The hostile sea around Block Island got its chance to show its stuff and it took it.

We motored out into the Long Island Sound and began our long haul to Block Island.

Block Island belongs to Rhode Island and lies south of the mainland. The island sits at the mouth formed by the mainland of Rhode Island and the eastern end of Long Island. The mouth here is several tens of miles wide, encompassing the Block Island Sound from the island to the mainland. There is a beautiful bay in Block Island that is totally enclosed except for a narrow channel. This is known as the Great Salt Water Pond.

There is a very narrow channel at the northwest. This was originally closed but a man-made channel to the west was dug out at about the turn of the century. No such luck occurred in the short distance to the ocean on the west side of the pond.

A serious accident occurred 2 July 2008. There was a collision between a coast guard boat and the Block Island Ferry. This latter boat is a relatively serious vessel, being up to 200 feet or so in length and the upper deck is about 30 feet or so high. This was the Block Island Ferry in a similar incident that Jackson and his friends were just beginning. The legal findings give some idea of what Jackson and his friends were facing. The boat and the accident were uncannily similar.

The findings from the legal hearing give you some idea of the conditions then. The Block Island ferry was carrying 257 passengers during the busy Independence Day holiday when it collided with a U.S. Coast Guard cutter in dense fog about three miles north of the island yesterday, but no one was seriously injured, authorities said. The 175-foot ferry was on an hour-long run to Block Island from Point Judith. The 140-foot cutter, a buoy tender, was returning to its home base in New London, Connecticut, when the collision occurred about 12:15 p.m., the Coast Guard said. Visibility at the time was about 200 yards, Petty Officer Etta Smith said. The 1,000-passenger-capacity ferry, named Block Island, always uses radar and was using it at the time of the collision, said William A. McCombe, the ferry company's security officer. It is the primary year-round vessel that services the island, he said.

Situational awareness was unexpectedly a challenge in the 2008 moments leading up to the collision. The Ferry captain testified that fog became extremely dense at the same time that pleasure boats appeared from all directions. "The visibility got very poor that day very quickly, and traffic was very, very dense," said Christian Myers, chief of vessel operations for Interstate Navigation Co., which runs the ferry to Block Island.

They collided at 12:15 on July 2, 2008, about four miles south of Point Judith, R.I. The impact dented both vessels, but they remained seaworthy. Two ferry passengers were slightly injured. These Coast Guard findings document that accident as similar to Jackson's on the same Block Island ferry run.

Block Island is a windswept piece of land 13 miles south of Rhode Island and 14 miles east of Montauk Point, New York. The Block Island land measures about 10 square miles. The pond covers about 1700 acres so is a very substantial anchorage. This is a rough piece of land with few trees; mostly scrub bushes. It forms the last refuge for those heading east toward the great ocean. This applies to men and to the restless winds. Major storms and hurricanes frequently sweep the place. Fog and mist often shrouds the way to the mainland so the Block Island Ferry is often blanketed in cruel weather.

The trip from Bridgeport to Block Island was relatively uneventful. This does excuse one exercise that occurred when the owner could not find how to switch fuel tanks. This was of some concern since there was not enough fuel left in the one operational tank to complete our trip. Jackson did not really get involved in that but he became a little concerned to realize the Captain was not too knowledgeable about his boat. But, we moved on.

The Great Salt Water Pond is the destination of most of the boats on the East Coast during the summer, it seems.

There is no real definition of pond or lake. The dictionary definition is almost circular. A lake is defined as a body of fresh or salt water, of considerable (though not defined) size, surrounded by land. A pond is defined as any body of (usually fresh) water surrounded by land, smaller than a lake. The definitions appear rather arbitrary. Thus, as claimed, there is no real definition of pond or lake.

The estimate of the number of small boats in the pond during July 4 is not much more definitive than the definition of a pond. Jackson hazarded a guess that probably a thousand boats or more were at Block Island, mostly in the Great Salt Water Pond.

One thing that was certain. That number of boats was too many for the harbor. All those boats had to anchor and there was considerable tangling of the anchor line of one boat with that of his neighbor. It took them three or four runs before we got an anchor to stick and one anchor did not foul another.

The first indication that something was wrong occurred the next morning. Most were still in their staterooms and heard a loud yell.

"Get that Goddam outboard out of this water, you crazy Bastard."

This was obviously not a trivial nautical greeting such as, "Ahoy there, Mate."

Jackson was aware that Franklin, the captain, was fiddling around with a small outboard motor on the deck, but he had not paid any attention to whatever Franklin was working on. Jackson did notice that Kurt was powerfully interested in whatever Franklin was doing.

One then heard several sputters as the outboard coughed to life for a moment and then died. So that was what Frank was up to!

We then heard a lot of yelling. We ran topside to see what all the fuss was about. Good God! That fool Franklin had got the outboard running. He then told Kurt to take a spin in the harbor. With that, he pushed Kurt into the boat, put it in full speed and pushed Kurt and his outboard away from our boat.

Of course, Kurt, a ten-year old, had never been in an outboard boat before as far as I knew. How he controlled it, I'll never know. I don't think he was controlling it. It just flew at full speed around the bay. He was a loose cannon set free to hurtle at full speed in that unbelievably crowded bay. The crews everywhere were running to the decks of their boats. They waved their arms and yelled. The cursed and did everything they could do to direct this hurtling canon-ball away from their boat, anywhere except their boat.

Jackson was one of the crowd himself waving his arms to push his trajectory away. "Don't come to this boat, you crazy loon."

"You son of a bitch!" they yelled. Far worse expletives floated across the bay. An irresponsible kid and a lunatic sponsor put those hundreds of expensive boats at risk. I wanted to sit down and cry and I wanted to smash someone. One just had to sit down and wait for the inevitable crash as the outboard missile flew into the side of an expensive yacht, costing a fortune and causing bodily harm.

Then it was over. Kurt pulled alongside and cut the engine. The lunatic ride was over. Jackson, for one, felt a little shame at his performance. He cursed and yelled, just the same. "If that ever happens again!—" On and on it went.

Kurt was happy for himself. He had been a quick learner and not one of the catastrophes expected by everyone came to pass. Then the episode was over. We would keep my eye on Frank.

There was a slight cloud cover and showers were predicted. Yet, we had to get home. So we made our way out from Block Island in late morning. We started a slow return since the wind was not very favorable.

After a couple of hours of sailing, a heavy fog settled in. It was pea soup and very dense. We could hardly see anything.

Then, we begin to hear the low-pitched steam foghorn. It had a low-pitched, throaty voice *"Boooop. Boooop."* The Block Island Ferry was on the same course as we were. What the hell! We had no radar and nothing to identify us to the Ferry. We talked to one another about this. We reached a consensus that the Ferry had radar so he could see us even if we could not see him. Meanwhile, we posted someone to sound our chemical horn periodically.

The ferry horn got louder and louder. My God, This was a scary moment. Finally, the ferry horn seemed to blow us right out of the water. Then we heard the thrashing of the propellers, water washing around the hull and that overpowering horn. They all came thrashing right next to us. The ferry side was perhaps only 10 feet away. We felt like we could reach out and touch it. This ferry was not a small ship, being 100 to 200 feet long and two or three decks. "What are we doing here?" one asked.

God must have been in the wheelhouse that morning.

As luck would have it, we read in the papers a year after this that there was a similar event with the ferry. One occurred on July 2 and one on July 4th, each in different years. A fog suddenly shut down their visibility on the same weekend of the year. The reported collision was between the Block Island Ferry and the Coast Guard Cutter, Morro Bay.

Although the ferry had 305 passengers and a crew of 21, the damage was not serious.

Again, this collision happened a year from our passage and is discussed only to validate the danger in that place and at that time of year.

Of course, we were traveling at several knots when the ferry passed us and he was traveling at 10 or 12 knots probably. So it just slid through the water toward the Rhode Island mainland while we thanked our lucky stars and trudged on.

At about 3 or 4 p.m., Jackson noticed the boat was exhausting water used as a coolant for the engine, but the water had a slick, colorful luster to it. He said to one of the women that this was odd. "Why is there oil in the water being exhausted?"

He then went down to the engine room to investigate. "Lord and behold!" he exclaimed. There was a very serious problem.

He found Franklin, the Captain, and said to him, "We have a serious problem, we think."

"Hold on," he said. "Why do you think that?"

"Well, I don't know, but the engine is three-fourths covered with water and the cooling fan is slinging water all over the engine room. Further, the boat is slowly sitting lower and lower into the water. To some, this means there is a serious problem. We are taking on water and we are sinking. He didn't know much about this boat but he guaranteed we were in serious trouble."

He rushed off to confirm whether the things being said were true. He came back a little later and said, 'My God, what will we do?'

He didn't know what to do and slowly became an ineffective Captain.

Jackson then felt it necessary to take most of the responsibilities of the boat. Jackson called everyone together to tell them what was happening.

"Okay, everyone, we are taking water. If we don't do something, we will sink. That's okay. We can declare an emergency and the Coast Guard will come to our rescue. We don't know that will happen so we have to do what we can for ourselves.

"First, you ladies have jewelry and valuables. The first thing is to put them into the clothes you are wearing." Most of the women said that was the first thing they had done.

"Second, we are taking on water and must stop it. I know this is a big boat but we have to bail her out as best we can. Use any container you can to bail. Dump the bailed water into the sink in the galley. Everyone must give it their all and it will take a long time, so good luck. You'll be happy you did. The Captain has gone below to drive shims into the leak so hopefully we will be able to slow the leak and to bail out the water enough to keep her afloat. I don't know how to fix the shims and leaks, so the Captain had to do that.

"We are northeast of New Haven and we will try to get the Coast Guard." This we did.

After this, everyone did his best. But the Coast Guard did not respond to us. They indicated there were 38 emergencies they were working on at the time and they just had to take it all in turn. By dark, a major storm had blown up and the heavens crackled with thunder that roared through the sound. Lightening blasted the black clouds above the New Haven bay. The sky roared and the lightening crackled. Through it all, we tried to keep bailing, decrease the leak and keep afloat. Everyone complained and sharp words were spoken, but everyone stayed true to the task.

The Captain then worked on the radios since they were cantankerous and no one would answer our calls. We hoped he would succeed with both the radio and leak shims.

After dark set in, there was little to no visibility. Then three drunks paddled up to our boat. They were very drunk. "Here, mate," they said. "Hold on, we'll save you.

"Get away," we insisted. "Get away." We pushed them off with our boat hooks. We managed to discourage them.

Fortunately, they were too drunk to protest much so they drifted into the night.

Later, the Coast Guard came in response to our declared emergency hours earlier. By this time, it was near midnight. The Coast Guard cutter had a crew of three that seemed like they were about 19 or 20 years old. By this time, the seas had grown wondrously large. The waves were smashing things and the winds were unleashed and it appeared that wild things were everywhere.

The Coast Guard jumped to their task. They immediately jumped onto our boat and tried to tie one to the other. "Wait!" there was yelling. "Can't you see your metal boat is destroying us with our wooden boat?" Each wave caused their boat to crash into us and pieces of our boat were flung into the air. The pieces became larger and larger. Further, we were sinking. "Back off."

Jackson saw that things were going hideously wrong, but he didn't know why. The Coast Guard crew was in yellow slickers to weather the storm. Jackson jumped onto the Coast Guard boat that was awash in waves and flying debris from the clashing boats. The two boats bounced into the air separately. It was frightening. Jackson looked at the major pumping hose. He saw that there was a large lever that implied the water would flow forward or backwards.

"Holy Christ!" he sounded off. "What in the hell is this?"

He yelled at a girl that was part of the Coast Guard crew and probably only 20 years old. "You're pumping water into our boat, you damn fools! Can't you see we are sinking? Does this lever change the flow direction?"

"Yes," she said. "Yes."

Now, I don't know about Coast Guard cutters and I don't know if many are able to reverse the pumped water flow but that certainly saved us that night. We survived backward water flow and deep water in the bilge. These were heavenly and even I loved the Coast Guard when they got us into New

Haven Harbor. I made it evident how much we appreciated what they had done this night.

We must wait, however. The night was not over, not by a jug full. The Coast Guard nudged this waterlogged load into the harbor and to the northern rim where there had been mills and work. These were clearly abandoned now and had been for some time. The buildings were in disrepair with windowpanes broken and other evidence that the structures had succumbed to the ravages of time. There was a pier extending from an old warehouse out into the water. This had a wooden walkway down near the water level and a main pier that was perhaps 20 feet or so above the water. If one looked up, he could see the main pier was rotten and there were boards missing.

Someone looked around on shore and found a ladder that allowed us to climb up to the main pier.

"Hold on," we said to the Coast Guard. "What are you doing?" It was clear that they were getting their boat in order and were preparing to leave.

"We are leaving," they said.

"What do you mean, you are leaving? These people can't find their way up the ladder and feel their way along a rotten pier. There are boards missing. Look up there. You can see the sky through the holes where boards belong. Besides, we have kids with us."

"We are sorry," he said. "I know that it is difficult but we have many emergencies we are trying to respond to. You'll have to do the rest yourselves."

Fortunately, one of our passengers had a flashlight. We all huddled together and used the flashlight to find our way through this frightening task. We clung to each other and we made it; all of us. We all helped each other and by the grace of God, we all made it to the ground at the pier base. We thanked our lucky stars that we had survived the ordeal.

We found a pay phone and arrangements were made for someone to come and get us. We got home around noon that day.

CHAPTER 17

GROWING UP CHASING NATIONAL GEOGRAPHIC

The sun came up, aft our wake,
Out of the sea came he!
Mariner's soul, in a quake,
Big bird's flight, a mystery.

Higher and higher, every day,
A guiding compass, by evolution,
It never lost its forward way,
Nor failed the exact solution.

Jackson was a little unusual as he grew up, in that he was a big-bird watcher, a compulsive traveler and a sailboat owner.

He had enjoyed travel from his earliest memory. Jackson and his sister, Charlotte, grew up in a happy family. Both were popular in their groups. Charlotte was a beautiful girl. She was ten years older than Jackson but their interests were similar. She had blonde hair and light skin. Her hair was long and wavy.

Jackson had a dark complexion beneath dark brown hair. Both had playful personalities that shone through their youth.

Jackson's travels indicated the world was a much different place than depicted in the National Geographic. In the real world, there was poverty, most people lived in squalor, places were dirty, some cultures carried exposed corpses through the streets to the funeral pyres. There were different cultures and some of these horrified Jackson. Moslems were everywhere with their mosques and minarets. The religious adherents removed their shoes and then prostrated themselves as they moved inside. Jackson and his friends always caused a stir as they walked and especially if they wanted to go inside the mosque. The locals often refused them entry. This we could not understand. I doubt they ever refused National Geographic. The point was that the magazine reality and the actual reality were quite different. The magazine was selective in what the magazine staff revealed about the cities and locations in their particulars. This was a discrimination of sorts that one would just have to learn to live with.

Nevertheless, Jackson's enthusiasm was unabated He wanted to see it all and he often did.

He had discovered *National Geographic Magazine* in grammar grades and read through every copy in the school library. He was innocent at the time and believed everything he read. The highlights of the magazine were the assignments given to its photographer and writers. Every city was full of optical delights in full color using the best resolution compatible with the magazine dimensions. Every city or visit was glorious. The colors practically jumped off the pages and grabbed you. There were few articles in which the pictures were of poverty; there was no down side to most of the articles. It was a grand and glorious world that only a romantic could appreciate to its fullest.

In those early years, he dedicated himself to traveling. At least, in his mind he did. He dreamed of the day he could reach out to those exotic places, those places described in the magazine and his imagination. As said, he was innocent at this time.

Later, in his teens, he became a naval aviation crewman.

He got himself designated as a combat air crewman and the Navy sent this new recruit to Washington for tests. These were to qualify for this designation. He received it. As it worked out, this was not advantageous in a military during peacetime.

Jackson traveled widely as part of the crew. For years, he traveled mainly in Africa, Europe, the Middle East, North Africa, the U.S., the Arctic and the Caribbean. This traveling was before 1951. It would be too boring to remember all the places he had been.

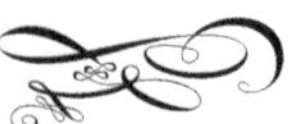

Growing Up; Big Bird Watching

Jackson Lee was among other things a nature lover in those high school days. However, this interest of his stayed with him for all his life. It was a passion that drove his career. He fancied big birds as gateways to flight. Aircraft fueled his ambition for flight. This he satisfied by an Intel career or one based on flight. It was only a step to Intel satellites that drove his later career.

His family consisted of his mother and father, one sister, a brother and Jackson. They lived in eastern North Carolina until he was approaching fifteen years old. The family had a summer house near the beach on Bogue Shores. That sounds rather grand but the summer house was nothing but a small trailer. It was, however, a perfect place to get away from it all and wander along the nearby beaches and sand hills. In truth, the rest of the family seldom used the trailer so Jackson could go there most any time he wished.

He loved lying on the sand beach or sand dunes and watched the sailings of birds. He was particularly interested in big birds. There were plenty of these for him to observe. There were sea gulls, sea eagles or ospreys, hawks, pelicans, ducks, vultures, sea vultures, an occasional eagle and many others. The Atlantic migration path for many species is through this area.

The Wright Brothers brought international fame to Kill Devil Hills in North Carolina because of its favorable winds.

The Wrights used Kitty Hawk to test their flight theories where there was always a brisk and continuous wind. The location was about 60 miles north of Ocracoke and south of the Virginia state line. The outer islands here are known as Cape Hatteras. Jackson watched from Bogue Banks that is part of Cape Lookout. These both have lighthouses in this most hazardous part of the Atlantic with thousands of sunken ships. The distance from Cape Hatteras in the north to Cape Lookout is about 70 miles.

He was thankful for this opportunity to watch so many birds in flight and made use of it.

Jackson found enough books on the subject that he had a fundamental knowledge of flight using wing chords to control attitude, altitude and speed. He knew something of the properties of big birds such as vultures, sea gulls and pelicans. He could watch the birds fishing for hours, using their special techniques. He had a favorite place on the dunes to watch fishing birds. Many of these, for instance, would pick up shellfish or clams from the bottom in shallow water. They would then fly up to about 30 feet and drop them on piers or rocks. The drop crushed the shell and the bird had a tasty morsel. They would do this for hours.

The pelicans flew along the coastline in formations of a dozen or more birds. They miraculously followed their selected leader and continued to account for some birds breaking away and being replaced by other lone flyers. These performed as scouts. Their long necks were pushed back onto their backs with beaks extended. They looked like they were flying in a stuffed living room chair. Most of the time, they just floated along with infrequent flapping of their long wings.

We are told that pelicans use the cyclic wave of the air currents to travel forward. The birds place themselves in the flight path that exploits the rise and fall of the air currents. The first bird in the flight flaps its wings, then the others locate similarly along the air current bunching. This gives a floating in-line squadron that uses this phenomenon to fly with considerable efficiency. A repetitive trail occurs in each end of the cycle that takes some of its flight energy from the air cycles. The air currents from the lead bird roll off his wing flaps. This allows the next in line to fly in an advantageous part of the air cycle where the next bird extracts energy from the cyclic air trail. Thus, he can glide by flapping his wings only occasionally. We see a V-line of birds, or a squadron of a dozen birds or so where most appear to be loafing. This is just another miracle in the animal and insect world.

The existence of flying carpets and curses that can be hurled through the air like Zeus's thunderbolts is attractive but hardly real. Zombie woman is also unreal. Nevertheless, some societies believe in these curses and their magical attributes.

One of the stories in *Aladdin and The Thousand and One Nights* relates how Prince Husain buys a magic carpet. "*Whoever sitteth on this carpet will, in the twinkling of an eye, be borne thither*". The literary traditions of several other cultures also feature magical birds. It is easy to believe that curses abound in this world of magic and flying transport; that Death or Zombies in the form of Living Death can fly on or through the water with slatted hulls without sinking.

Magic spells are conjured up and cast to and fro. In our fantasies, magic carpets are available for casual or instantaneous delivery to one's destination, be it near or far.

We also have suggestions of really big birds in the ancient world. Fossils are found of birds with wingspans double that of today's largest flyers. *Pelagornis sandersi* was truly the big bird of its bygone day. Researchers describing fossil remains of this bird for the first time say the bird had a wingspan of up to 24 feet, qualifying it as the largest flying bird ever to take to earth's skies. Its size exceeded some estimates for the limits of powered flight. Computer models based on the well-preserved skeleton suggest the animal was an excellent glider.

This narrative casually speaks to natural and supernatural beliefs. Jackson had never seen most of the big birds he describes there but he had no doubt that some exist. He dwelt on these big birds that he would probably never see. Yet, he longed to see and study them. He believed he would see them someday, especially if he kept traveling the way he did. Many of those birds roamed the Pacific Ocean, some even ranging as far north as the Aleutian Islands in the north Pacific.

He longed especially to visit and see the birds of Wake and Midway Islands. In fact, there were numerous big birds roving the Pacific Ocean all the time. What was not here today would be tomorrow because of their enormous ranges in search of food. They brought back food for their young in the nesting areas and in their breeding congregations.

Jackson continued to study these big birds and to take notes of special characteristics he expected to see someday. He always kept a small ringed notebook with him and he faithfully recorded these characteristics. Jackson was a serious person. Some might say he was bookish but that would miss the main characteristics of Jackson. That was only one aspect of his multi-faceted surface. Jackson was a puzzlement to his friends but he did keep their interests peaked all the time.

Growing Up; Jackson Sailing

Jackson had worked during summers and with help from his father, he bought a used sailboat. This was a 30-foot Erickson. It was well turned out with a galley, enclosed bathroom and sleeping for four. It had a wheel rather than a tiller. It had a sloop rigging with a foresail. There was an inboard gasoline engine. The lack of a diesel engine bothered him, but there had been thousands of these gasoline engines produced and they had an excellent record for safety. This boat gave him infinite pleasure and he continued to learn as long as he had the boat.

Jackson lived in Larchmont, Westchester County, New York, until he joined the Navy. His family lived there after they moved from Eastern North Carolina. This is a small town just north of The City on the western shore of Long Island Sound, just north of New Rochelle. The county east side is on the shores of Long Island Sound and the west side is on the shore of the Hudson River. The river reaches on up beyond Albany. In fact, New York state years ago dredged an ocean ship turn-around at Albany. This was in the days that cargo was often open. Theft, mostly by stevedores and their outrageously corrupt unions working along the wharfs, was widespread. This made it expensive to use the New York and New Jersey ports around New York City. Shippers began to avoid these ports. One way was to go upriver to Albany. Steel shipping containers are now used that essentially solves that problem.

Westchester County is one of the three or four wealthiest counties in the U.S. and has been for years. Jackson lived near these wealthy communities such as Rye. He attended a city school after moving to Larchmont.

He was not an academic star but was content to sail through schools with adequate but undistinguishing effort. He was not very interested in excelling; his family would always pull him through, he thought.

Jackson was congenial. He was not motivated to excel nor required to by his family. Only when he needed to excel, did he dive in and walk off with an adequate performance.

When growing up, Jackson loved sailing. He loved his 30-foot sailboat. He loved to sail on his weekends. He often sailed on Haverstraw Bay north of Manhattan on the Hudson River and just south of the West Point Military Academy. More often than that, he sailed with his friends on Long Island Sound. Sailing around Manhattan was always a special treat to him and his friends. In this, he sailed from Larchmont down the Sound to the East River separating Manhattan and Queens, then sailed through New York's Upper Bay holding the Statue of Liberty. They then rounded the Battery and proceeded north up the Hudson River past the George Washington Bridge. They sailed southeast through the narrow Harlem River back into the widening East River, under the Whitestone and Throggs Neck Bridges to the Long Island Sound and then to Larchmont.

Rounding Manhattan was always thrilling since it had the most dramatic views of the whole world. Manhattan rose up and surrounded you. It seemed you were right among the towers. Sights came at you too quickly. Although your boat was slow, the views were so close together that one hardly had time to identify that the scenes were changing. One had the perception that the skyscrapers were passing at breakneck speed.

The scenes were changing dramatically which was thrilling. Further, there were added elements of danger and fear since the traffic on the East River posed very serious challenges. The tidal currents actually change directions during a day. Sometimes, the tidal East River current moves north and then south at five knots or more. The waters become turbid and unpredictable. It is easy to run aground or to collide with another boat, barge or structure. Barges or ships often collided during the night and even during the day where the huge barges were under tug control. The tug pilots never see the victims. On the other hand, they do not seem to care much whether they see the victim or not. They just forge ahead. There were just a lot of things going on in the East River and for the rest of the voyage also. You want to stop the movement, go into a memory mode so you can look, take it all in with slow motion, then reel out the next scenes with speed under your control. Unfortunately, real life is not like that.

Jackson was an excellent sailor and captain. He studied the navigational details of his trips and religiously watched the Loran navigation aids. This was before GPS navigation. All sailing captains have emergencies but he handled his with calm and authority. Competent Captains are a different breed. One feels the confidence of the true captain. He wends his way through the world with a slightly different attitude and confidence from others. This is especially true of sailboat captains.

Jackson's sister, Charlotte Lee, was 10 years older than Jackson so they were not destined to be close in any event. That always surprised Jackson. Every time she did go sailing, she handled the boat masterfully and had a great sense of the boat's operation.

Charlotte often asked, "Jackson, why do you waste so much time on that old boat? It gets you nowhere." One is born with a love of sailboats or not.

Even so, Jackson knew that it was always a "to each his own" situation. We are what we are and there are seldom big changes after one's teenaged years.

Popeye, the sailorman expresses that as, "I yam what I yam."

This is a biblical response to "Who am I?" asks Noah of God.

The return is, "I am what I am."

Popeye's vernacular was the speech of the common people and especially of uneducated people.

Charlotte attended Columbia in New York and then worked through graduate school on a leisurely track. *That was too bad*, Jackson thought. *We could have had great times together and fun*. Nevertheless, it was not to be.

I stayed many weekends with Jackson and met Charlotte, his sister, while I was there. I also had met Bianca Bruno earlier. Bianca and I were soon incorporated into the Lee family. At first, they thought I was standoff-ish and rather shy. However, I slowly admitted to myself that I really liked this New York girl, Charlotte. Romance followed slowly between her and me as I strutted with the shiny uniform and silver wings. She and I dated infrequently for some time. She liked sailing with me in Jackson's boat, so we spent many wonderful weekends on Long Island Sound, sometimes with her friend Bianca and sometimes without her.

"Charlie," she said to me. "I like sailing with Bianca. However, I prefer to sail with you alone at times. The boat is then not so crowded." I had to agree with her.

Motorboats are not as demanding of navigation skills as sailboats. If a motorboat heads to a dock at 20 knots, the course will drift little from that intended so the motorboat reaches its target with little correction of course. However, if a sailboat making five or six knots sets a course for the dock, wind and current speeds are significant with respect to the boat speed. Those speeds may even sometimes exceed the wind speed. This will cause serious course drift in reaching the dock so requires continuing tacks. Sailboat Captains are a special breed of men.

Jackson Lee was committed to sailing, sailboats and geography. He had sailed his boat as the captain with another sailor or sometimes with several friends. He had once sailed the boat to Europe and back during his summer vacation. This was a difficult sail. The wind blew heavily to the north most of the time. This caused the boat to heel at a large angle. His friend was the mate with a bunk bed toward the bow, heeling to the left during most of the trip. Rough waves dumped him out of his bunk and onto the deck several times. The bunk was uncomfortable for the whole trip to Europe. It was a rough passage for them and a long one.

Jackson had visited and had sailed through many of the islands of the Caribbean.

He also often invited friends while he was in high school to sail with him to Block Island at the mouth of the Long Island Sound or where it empties into the ocean. It was a wonderful sail and his friends all appreciated it.

He was thrilled by stories of the Suez and Panama Canals. Panama in particular fascinated him. He and two friends sailed his friend's boat all the way from New York to the Canal, passed through to the Pacific and then returned. All these trips were while he was in high school or college. The worst fear was sailing at night since container ships would lose several containers at sea. They would float but mostly they were underwater and could hardly be seen. If anything were to curtail his enthusiasm for sailing, it would be these long voyages at sea with the many emergencies and long, boring watches. However, he thrived on these. His experiences as a captain chiseled a certain bearing and poise in him that always suggested a young sea captain. He thrived on the experiences and this calling of the sea lasted through much of his life.

Jackson had grown up. He then joined the Navy just after the war.

Meanwhile, I had been in the Air Force throughout the war. The 5-year age difference separating us haunted our relationship throughout both our careers. It haunted Jackson because of his unfavorable roll of the dice in life's age game. His roll made him too young to be in WWII. On the other hand, I hardly recognized that my roll of the dice had even taken place.

"Charlie," he sometimes asked me. "What is it like as a pilot to give ground support to soldiers fighting tanks? You know that makes you vulnerable. How does that feel?" Every time I saw him, he had many questions like this. He was like a kid trying to translate his toy tanks and rockets into the reality of war. I don't know why he did this. He seemed to want a change in our roles. He was growing up and would get into this war soon enough. I was weary of the war but he hungered for it. Meanwhile, I, being older, was in the military through the whole war and had seen things that no one should see.

CHAPTER 18

LANDPLANES IN A SEAPLANE HANGAR

Jackson Lee backed into the aviation revolution by joining the Navy just after the end of WWII.

Jackson was barely 17 when he chose aviation. He served as an aircrew member during this tenure. He was still in uniform from the start of the Korean War until a year or so later. In fact, as it turned out, he became a veteran of both wars. This was important to him since it determined eligibility for both the WWII GI Bill of Rights and the Korean bill.

He was legally a veteran of both wars and therefore eligible for both bills. "C'mon! You're not a vet of WWII," his friends sometimes challenged him.

It was curious as to how he was a legal veteran of WWII.

Legally, the Federal Register, FR404.1313, defines a U.S. veteran as follows: *'The WWII period means the time period September 16, 1940, through July 24, 1947. You were a WW II veteran if you were in the active service of the United States during the WWII period'*. Jackson could therefore claim to be a legal veteran of WWII.

There was no question about it for the Korean War.

Jackson was therefore almost last in his WWII GI Bill classes in university. Since he was retained in the service for a year or so after the Korean War started, he was nearly the first Korean War veteran in the school.

The GI Bill was later recognized by economist Professor Peter Drucker as the most fundamental positive change in society of the twentieth century. There is no doubt that it made a historical advance on American society.

Jackson joined the Navy conditionally depending on being designated as a *Combat Air Crewman.* This was a desirable designation during the war but it soon faded with time. He was sent to Bethesda, MD for a series of tests before joining. He was successful in getting the designation. This was a mixed blessing since it limited his assignments sometimes but was helpful in others.

He completed basic training and other service schools. These lasted over a year. Then he was assigned to an aircraft squadron near Washington. This was good enough for his qualifying for the GI Bill. Yet, he did not feel it was good enough to change his status from non-veteran to veteran. He winced whenever his answer was yes to the question and also when his answer was no.

Meanwhile, Jackson had befriended another new member of the squadron named Eliot Carson. Eliot was destined to become a sidekick to Jackson. Their paths crossed often. After Jackson established himself as to housing, sleeping and other arrangements, he and Eliot went to the hangar to which they were attached. What a surprise! The entire squadron and three others had offices and worked at the hangar while their housing arrangements were in the dormitory where they had originally checked in.

As we were riding down to the hangar, Jackson explained what he had read on checking in at the dormitory. It talked about the organizational structure of the squadrons and the hangar.

"Eliot?" Jackson asked. "Did you read the brochure about the squadron and hangars?"

"No. I didn't see one. I don't know anything about it."

"Well, it said we were in a squadron of PB4Y2 aircraft made by Consolidated Aircraft Company in San Diego. It said they were four-engine patrol aircraft. Do you know what that is?"

"Nope."

"Well, I think we are about to find out. I guess they are seaplanes, since they call the space the seaplane hangar." He then added under his breath that *he wished I were there since I would certainly know what these planes were.* Thus, thought Charlie. *However, I was in England at the time as part of the Berlin airlift.*

The hangar was large. The offices for four squadrons were housed there. No one had briefed Jackson and Eliot on where they were being assigned so they were innocent as they walked across the concrete apron of the hangar. There were nine planes assigned to each squadron. There were usually two or three planes per squadron in the hangar being worked on. Further, one or two squadrons were often deployed. Thus, of 36 planes assigned to the squadrons, there were often as many as 16 aircraft parked orderly on the concrete apron outside the hangar.

We looked at the scene and were totally puzzled. What we saw was a dozen or so aircraft parked orderly around the hangar. They looked totally abandoned since there were tarps over the cockpit Plexiglas windshield and another over several gun turrets. This was a weekend so there were only a few people milling around but little real activity.

The airplanes were a Navy version of a B-24. The Navy PB4Y2 had four engines, a stretched nose and a 30-foot high single tail. The most puzzling was the underside of the planes. They had internal bomb bays with corrugated sliding doors that wrapped around the aircraft underside when closed.

"What is this?" Jackson asked Eliot. "Those things can't go into the water!"

Confounding the puzzlement, there were two concrete ramps that went into the water of the river. Clearly, this was a hangar with parking aprons and ramps for seaplanes that one assumes have landed in the broad river and were intended to go up the ramp to the hangar. That assumes that the seaplane had wheels or a wheeled carriage to get up the ramp.

"Darn," said Jackson. "I'm going to keep my mouth shut about this. If I ask someone about it, they will think we are stupid."

"Eliot, you should study this picture. It shows a PB4Y2. It was picked up in the dormitory. We should swear that we will not ask any questions or mention our ignorance in this matter until we figure it out. We don't want to be taken for knuckleheads on our first day in the squadron. We would never live it down."

"I'll sure not tell anyone," Eliot agreed.

Thus, they were mute about this strange observation. It was particularly embarrassing since Jackson thought he knew a lot about airplanes. Yet, he knew practically nothing about seaplanes. They had a lot to learn.

Actually, most all of Jackson's interest and training was of landplanes.

Much later Jackson said, "Eliot, it is good we did not show our ignorance when we first got here and saw the planes were landplanes." They both agreed that keeping one's mouth shut was usually a good policy regardless of the situation.

Jackson as Air Crew Eager Beaver

Jackson Lee was what is called an eager beaver. There was no trip that he would not volunteer for while he was an air crewman in the Navy. There was no place that he did not want to see. He volunteered to go anywhere with anybody.

Each airplane had a crew that stayed together nominally. As part of the crew, he was a radioman. He was usually acceptable as a substitute radar man, a substitute navigator (when not flying over water), an Elint operator or a gunner. He was ready. Are you going to Chicago? I'll take your place. Are you going to Puerto Rico? I'll take your place. Are you going to Newfoundland? I'll take your place. Many in the crew were married so they were more than happy for him to take their place, especially on weekends. Each pilot and crewman had to get their flight time in order to receive flight pay and maintain their flight credentials. Thus, there was always a pool of pilots that wanted to go to an interesting place or an interesting destination. Even when it was not interesting to the pilot, it was interesting in almost every case to Jackson.

However, not everyone was pleased with this. The skipper noticed this and asked to see the crew list for these flights. Lo! Jackson's name led all the rest. It was clear, he was getting most of the training and flight time because many in the crew were intent on avoiding as many training sessions as possible. So a new ruling was made. The regular crew had to do their own flying. The service is adept at always placing new rules.

Nevertheless, the crews are just as adept in finding loopholes, getting around the rules. Anyhow, the new rules soon faded away and Jackson was again up to his old tricks. There was no place he did not want to go.

New Aviation Age

Aircraft and their Intel or intelligence development has fitted well together since the beginning of aviation. Planes offer two unique advantages for gathering intelligence: speed and altitude. Most today cruise about 380 to 600 mph and above 28,000 feet. The payloads are usually unique and define the intelligence performance. Electronic Intelligence is a primary function of many aircraft and there is continuous growth in the technology.

After the war, there were numerous new designs in airplanes. The result was that everything looked new and anything slightly aged looked antiquated.

Jackson remembered a very embarrassing situation his crew had on one of their visits when he was a crew member in the Navy. This was one of several visits to Air Force Bases. An important function was electronic warfare (EW) that allowed the aircraft to intercept signals. The redesigned version was a 20-foot extension of the aircraft nose and a rework of the gun turrets and the tail section. The twin tails of the B-24 were removed and a very high, single tail replaced it.

After the end of the war, it seemed everyone was working on some kind of flier to deliver very heavy loads to the interior of Russia. These nuclear bombs were nominally 10,000 pounds, a heavy load for any allied aircraft. This effort was later recognized as delivery systems for atomic weapons against Russia. Many of these became operational before fading into history. One of these was the North American AJ Savage. It had two piston engines and one jet engine.

The B-29, the original Hiroshima bomb carrier aircraft, was still very much in the news.

When the crew approached the landing on the base, the whole world seemed to be in white marble since everything was so clean, new and spotless. The concrete runways (or was it marble?) appeared brand new and spotless. The hangars appeared new; they gleamed in the sunlight. There were every kind of aircraft imaginable. But these were no ordinary aircraft. They were all of different designs. These were jet propelled and announced the future.

The Movie Screen Battle

After several meetings, there was an important briefing before the crew was free.

This was at the Air Force Research Laboratory, AFRL. Again, there was a senior aircraft investigator that was to brief us. The AFRL had a different mission. Rather than developing operational airplanes directly, their mission was to study all the difficult problems associated with the development of an operational aircraft. They then provided information to the operational designers. Their function was for study and experimentation.

The man briefing them had a very high ranking within the lab. He was one of only several key technologists and technical managers. He had a reputation of being off-centered or the elevator did not always go to the top. He was said to be an odd ball. All those reporting to him were somewhat afraid of him since he was unpredictable and made decisions where no one understood the process but him. They would listen to him but then went off and made decisions by themselves that were rational and logical.

When he entered the conference room, one could see the basis for his off-center reputation. He was ill at ease and tended to stand aloof of those speaking to him. There was a problem with his left eye and it seemed to wander around, sometimes linked to the briefing and sometimes not. His body language was out on the edges somehow. The crew was respectful but ignored the eccentricities. His people sat there as if there was nothing unusual going on. Even when he would make an obvious mistake, they sat silently.

The briefing was to be by this investigator. After the introduction of the material, he indicated the first part of the briefing was to be by a 16 mm movie. Since the screen had not been set up in advance, his people sat up the projector and the screen.

The screen was the folding type around a metal frame where the screen was a plastic material designed to enhance the projections on it.

He got up to adjust the frame since it was slightly sagging on one side. His adjustment made things a little worse. He was not satisfied so he pushed here and there to fix it. It would not be fixed. He left his chair and took a solid hold on the uncooperative screen. The screen sagged far worse with his help. One could see he was becoming totally absorbed by the screen and it was soon becoming a catastrophe.

His people sat as if in stone. No one offered to help or to fix the screen themselves. It was obvious that this was a routine occurrence where no help was needed or wanted. He got down on one knee to get purchase but this only made him fall on the frame. Now he was down on the floor with the screen wrapped around him. It was for all the world like a pair of wrestlers having it out on the floor. He was relentless. He and the screen rolled around but no one offered help. It was as if they were all in the room but no one noticed the wrestling match, as if it was not happening. But it was happening and the screen was obviously winning.

The crew sat in amazement not knowing what to do. Surely, his people would handle the situation but there was no acknowledgment that it was going on. We all wanted to laugh since it was the funniest thing we had ever seen. However, that would have been a violation of the protocol. They all sat there, stone faced, while he was on a different planet. Not a soul looked it the match and no one snickered. It was a mighty effort, however, to sit there while this was going on.

Finally, he got up off the floor. He used brute force to get the frame to stand up as he walked back to his chair. It was certainly not straight since the frame stood there all askew and the screen itself was folded and spindled. One could hardly make out the images that the screen was supposed to portray but at least this got him out of a very awkward wrestling match.

The briefing then went on, just like it was supposed to do. There was a look of triumph on his face as he walked everyone through the annotation. No one mentioned that the film had lost its significance and looked like the trees of a burned forest with charred and tangled trees in every direction.

It was not until the Navy crew had dinner at a restaurant that night that they all broke down in uncontrollable laughter at the wrestling match that afternoon. They were afraid that someone would catch them in this story that conveyed extreme ridicule. They guessed that his people did not show their laughter for the same reasons. After all, he had the power.

Windmill Exit From Dayton

The ultimate embarrassment still awaited Jackson's crew. As if the profile was not enough to identify the aircraft as a WWII relic, it was painted a dark blue. This was the only such plane in Dayton in all likelihood. The crew certainly did not see one like it. Dayton's aircraft were silver and highly polished aluminum.

When we were supposed to leave, the pilot and mechanic tried to start the engine but it was not to be. The battery turned the number one engine over and over again. It made that ghastly spinning noise and the propeller engaged but there was to be no start. Each engine was tried in vain.

The designers had designed the engines to take explosive charges to start an engine as a back-up to a battery start. It looked like a shotgun shell but fit in the engine receptacle designed for this. Naturally, that did not work either.

However, all that shooting on the hangar apron called everyone to come over to see the show, to see what was happening.

Anyway, they were not to worry. The designers of the aircraft foresaw this non-start possibility. So, for the last and desperate attempts, they put in an oversized hand crank and there was a hole in the engine to receive the crank. One spun up the centrifugal weight, then the engine was supposed to engage the propeller and spin it to start. They tried and tried, but that was also not to be. The weight spun but then it wound slower and slower until it stopped. There was no real coughing or gasping as one expected with a start.

This was tried on the number one engine since that had the electrical generator for the whole aircraft. As it turned out, #3 engine blasted away when the hand-crank was tried there. The crank had a long handle so three men could spin it at one time. This further enhanced the show being put on.

Hallelujah! One engine started. There was still a ray of hope for the crew. They would try to windmill the remaining engines.

Did this escape the attention of all the Wright-Patterson people working around the hangar? Not in your life! By the time the cranking was exhausted, there was quite a gathering to see this exercise. You see, the hand-cranking seldom worked, if ever. Even the crew and others like them had never seen this hand-cranking before. It was as a new exercise for the crew as it was for the Dayton crowd.

But, not to give up, there was one more trick in the crew's bag of tricks. The crew got special attention by the aircraft controllers in the tower. The control tower people mercifully cleared the airport for us. The pilot then taxied down to the end of the runway and sped up as if to take off using the one operative engine. The theory was to go as fast as it could. Then the wind on the propellers caused them to spin. They expected the fast-spinning propeller to start the engine.

Glory be, two more engines started during this run. That was phenomenal. All the lookers-on cheered and clapped their hands. Well, since two engines started, they must be on to something. They then got the tower's permission to try a second time. This time, the pilot revved up the three engines at the very end of the runway. He accelerated with the operating three engines as fast as they would go, even into the red zone. Away they went. They raced down the oversized runway with three engines operating properly and one that was spinning, coughing, blasting as clouds of black smoke came from the inoperative engine. Finally, after using most of the runway, the dead engine coughed to life and belched black smoke. The plane stopped and requested permission to take off, this time with four operating engines. The plane and crew then taxied to the runway start, gunned the contrary engines and ran down the runway to a perfect takeoff.

The crew in the air thanked the heavens that the wind-milling had worked. There were congratulations all around. Thank God they had cleared the Dayton area.

The ground people roared their delight. They all clapped their hands, whistled and raised their caps. They had seen a great show. The Astronauts must have had this crew in mind when they offered the *Astranaut's Prayer.* As in, "Please god! Don't let me fuck up."

Although this was definitely a relic aircraft, it would not have mattered to the people working in Dayton. They were the future and we, unfortunately, were relics of the past, whether flying the PB4Y2 or P2V. They would not be impressed about any aircraft we could muster up.

To be sure, we knew the new P2V would not have had the problems we had in starting the engines. In fact, the crew hardly remembered even if that aircraft had a crank or not. This would not have mattered to the Dayton people. They knew they represented the future.

Jackson served as an air crewman until he was aged 21. He then entered the State University of New York, or SUNY University. He received a technical degree and continued to participate in the Cold War.

He joined an aircraft company as an electronic designer. He worked on Radar, Electronic Warfare, Communications, Intelligence and special designs. These covered a broad range of interest. He also worked closely with other aircraft companies in developing equipment and making their installations.

CHAPTER 19

JACKSON'S STREET MEETINGS AND NEW ADVENTURES

Jackson interviewed for a job after graduation and a technical degree. He sought a job associated with the military. He was well qualified for a black job and it was soon arranged. When Jackson accepted the job, he did not realize the extent that they played the game. It was rather cloak and dagger all the way. He was directed to be standing on a street corner in Washington at a certain date and time. He complied and found myself on a corner with little traffic or people. He asked himself, *Is this a hoax?* He had met intermediaries that seemed reasonably O.K., given that they were playing a game where only they knew the full story. But, it was puzzling in this case.

Finally, a car pulled up to the sidewalk. Jackson approached it and looked inside, not willing to be embarrassed if it were the wrong car. Inside were an American civilian and an American army soldier that had lieutenant Colonel's silver maple leafs. Further, there was a civilian Chinese man but Jackson had expected that from the beginning. He was ostensibly to work for the Chinese so it made sense that they would be there.

"Hey," Glen Gable, the civilian said. "Are you the one we are looking for?"

"That depends," Jackson answered.

"Get in," he said without acknowledging that Jackson had spoken.

We made small talk as the civilian who was the driver wheeled the car up Rock Creek Parkway.

They took Jackson to a facility outside Washington. The purpose, he said, was to introduce Jackson to some equipment and they wanted him to bail them out in that they had an equipment failure and no one was there who could fix it.

There was little talk with Jackson and between the other car occupants. They seemed to be strangers and didn't want to give away anything. That desire certainly must have been achieved. Soon, Jackson fell in line with the general game. He didn't ask questions since that would give him away. He did not volunteer any information so it was a very dull ride. Most of the meetings were like this. When someone asked a question, the result was a prevarication. The result was usually an outright prevarication or the truth was avoided by not directly answering the question.

The answers in the car seemed to make sense at a superficial level. That was good enough for the purposes then. Everyone spoke in clipped English with clipped answers.

When they reached their destination, those in the car gave Jackson a briefing that passed for my cover story or narrative. Once this was done, the car people relaxed a bit. Yet, there were still questions that had not been covered. Then, Glen Gable, the heavy-set American civilian took me to an empty room. He then gave me a much deeper briefing. His cover story and narrative prepared me for many more situations.

At best, keep your mouth shut, he advised. Only answer questions addressed directly to you. And, never volunteer anything. This briefing confirmed who was my boss and who paid the bills. The organization was thus revealed to me.

Clearly, Glen Gable was to be my boss, although he was to be more than 8,000 miles away most of the time. Thus, Jackson reported to Glen Gable in Washington, to the company that hired him and loosely, to the Chinese and the local Americans.

This was the beginning of a two-day ordeal where Jackson wrestled with this multi-rack system that he was barely familiar with. At any rate, he repaired the equipment and they came to get him a couple of days later.

Before they left, they hooked Jackson up with a young civilian that stayed with him and drove him when he needed a break such as food and hotel room. Jackson became good friends with him that lasted for some time.

It was clear that Jackson would be working for the Chinese but the Americans would have a large say in how things were to be run. This made Jackson nervous since he had thought that he would be working directly for the Chinese Nationalists. This in many respects had the feeling of the Flying Tigers and their relationship with the Nationalist government in 1941 whereby the Tigers fought almost as soldiers of fortune for the Chinese. In our relationship, the Chinese were to provide housing, transportation and other amenities. In the end, I was to serve both Chinese and American interests. Nonetheless, the final say was with the American civilians.

It is not generally known but the Russian Air Force provided a similar service to the Chinese before the Americans. It was a much larger force. The logistics and personnel had a better record than the Tigers. These Russians received a lot of experience fighting for the Leftists in the Spanish Civil War in the late 1930s. These were all withdrawn to Russia once Hitler invaded the Soviet Union.

CHAPTER 20

DRIVE TO SAN FRANCISCO

It was now time to move on to Asia. Jackson drove his MG-TF to San Francisco where it was delivered to the docks for transport to Taiwan. He took the scenic route of Highway 101 along the coast. This passed the Hearst Castle high up on a cliff from the ocean. His mind was on the airport in San Francisco rather than looking at past glories on the coast. He could not ignore the beautiful Carmel village on Monterey Bay so he made tourist stops there. He then found his hotel in San Francisco after arriving during rush hour in this area unknown to him.

Jackson had always heard about the Mark Hopkins Hotel and the beautiful 360-degree view of the San Francisco Bay. He headed for the hotel in late evening. He then took a shower and headed for the Hopkins. It answered a tourist's prayer. A circular bar was located in the center of the top floor of the hotel. There were no restrictions to viewing in any direction. The Golden Gate Bridge loomed majestically as it reflected a reddish-orange color that could possibly pass as a golden color. This bridge delivered traffic to the north shore where it continued on to northern California. A mountain ridge ran in the northerly direction separating the northern valley from the sea. Turning further clockwise, one encountered Alcatraz Island just offshore from the city. Continuing on, one encountered another engineering marvel, the Oakland Bay Bridge. This jumped from the city to Treasure Island, then to the mainland far to the east and the University of California in Berkeley.

Continuing on, one sees the Bay to the south toward the airport, Stanford University and Silicon Valley.

The bay was alive with ocean-going ships, pleasure craft, sail boats, powerboats and what have you. Jackson could only compare this to Hong Kong, perhaps, and Istanbul. Perhaps he had forgotten some place but one has the idea.

It was majestic and beautiful.

He had an occasion to visit the hotel top floor years and years later. Would you believe it? The whole top had been turned into a quiet, subdued restaurant with heavy drapes and shades. Gone was the circular bar. Gone was the view of San Francisco harbor.

Progress sometimes makes one want to cry. But we must press on!

Fly Hawaii

He left the next day for Hawaii on a Boeing Stratocruiser. This was a large passenger aircraft that was part of a scheduled airliner network across the Pacific and Southeast Asia. The plane had four engines and propellers. Remember, jet aircraft would not arrive in Asia until about 1960.

The Stratocruiser is rather unique in having the relative comfort of Pullman-type sleepers when the seats are converted into beds. This accommodates the very long flights across the Pacific after leaving Hawaii. This Pullman bedding was on the main deck of the airplane.

There was a small cabin on the underside of the airplane. A rounding staircase led to the bar below. The downstairs contained a bar and lounge. It allowed the social life to continue into the wee morning hours. There seemed to always be a small group of holdouts that make use of the bar over much of the Pacific. The lounge in the lower section was a welcome respite.

All the passengers were bright-eyed and bushy tailed as they winged from San Francisco to Hawaii. Jackson started a conversation with the stewardess. She was a good-looking girl of about 23 years of age. Her name was on her uniform but she told him anyway. It was Vicki Morgan.

She lived in San Francisco and this run to Hawaii was a relatively repetitive routine. As they flew along, not only did her looks overtake him but also her engaging personality was also very enticing to Jackson. She was beautiful and desirable. Their conversations on the flight became more frequent and substantive.

My God, he thought. Hawaii is the most romantic and enchanting place in the world. It is a paradise on earth. This was a reflection of reading since he had never been there.

Somewhere on the flight, he fantasized about riding around the island of Oahu in a convertible with the radio turned on and playing Hawaiian music. She was part of the airline crew that was not to fly again until the next day.

He took the opportunity to share his fantasy. He described how he would rent a convertible and they would depart as soon as they were checked into their hotels, actually the same hotel.

They then got a rental convertible and drove north from Honolulu across the mountain spine to the north shore. Passing the airbase there, they then drove on the east to west highway in a leisurely drive. Sure enough, they found a radio station featuring Hawaiian music. Surprisingly, they found only one such station, but that was enough.

To add a touch of paradise, they came across several white sand beaches and shallow lagoons that were too inviting to ignore. There was no one in the stretches. They dressed in the car and played in these virgin sand lagoons. It was easy to see paradise from their vantage points.

They spent the whole day getting to know one another and the island. He pictured himself as suave and poised as he escorted her around. He could do no wrong.

But there was a hole in his plans, and he had big plans for that night.

As they arrived at their hotel in late evening, the valets all seemed to know the plans themselves. They told her she had to go, and it had to be now. Her crew schedule had changed and they were all flying out that evening, back to San Francisco. There had been a scheduling mix-up and she had to leave right now since the rest of the crew had checked out of the hotel and they had left for the airport already. They had packed her things and left her suitcase in the lobby so she was coerced into making haste to the airport.

No one noticed Jackson and the destruction to his plans that they were causing. They had no suspicion that they were wreaking devastation to his plans and he did not fit into the flurry of activity.

Jackson could do nothing but try to talk her into staying. They both considered this but in the end, they were both practical people. They decided it was too disruptive to strike out separately so they did the rational things.

Mark that off as a path not taken by mutual consent.

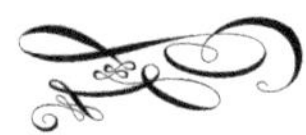

Manila, Years Later

When Jackson left Taiwan to return to the U.S. years later, a coincidence appeared. He was flying from Taiwan to Manila. The stewardess bent over and asked had he not been on the Boeing aircraft years earlier and toured Hawaii in a convertible. I looked at her incredulously. "I think I recognize you but I'm not sure", he bumbled into an inadequate answer.

She was the same stewardess. Yet, the magic had worn off. He doubted that he could rekindle it. Besides, she was going the wrong way for him. They were both going to Singapore but after that she was returning to San Francisco while Jackson was continuing to the Middle East.

They made a date to see each other in Singapore. However, it was half-hearted and she was much more eager than he.

Besides, he had a friend in Singapore that he had not seen for years. He, like Jackson, was a contractor. He got wrapped up in this diversion in Singapore and was unable to make the connection with her. He never saw her again. He often wandered about how she and he had taken different paths. A different path is always the unknown.

Fly Wake Island

Jackson continued the aircraft flight from Hawaii to Japan and then on to Taiwan. PanAm operated the Boeing 377, designed for long range, around-the-world passenger traffic. It was advertised as the greatest luxury liner in the world. It had two decks. The upper or main deck provided the main passenger area while a lower deck bar and lounge provided the luxury they advertised.

The airplane arrived at Wake Island during the middle of the night. Most of the passengers staggered around and tried to see the gist of the Island from the dark airport. They only saw a few aircraft tied down, a few white-washed buildings and a hangar area. Nevertheless, they did receive some refreshment, mostly from coin or canteen containers. They readied themselves for the next jump across the Pacific from Wake to Japan.

Wake Island is about equal distance from Hawaii and Tokyo. This has been used for airline terminals since early days. This competed with Midway Island but Midway was a very small atoll and never supported many buildings and infrastructure.

Yet, who has not heard of the millions of gooney birds on Midway and Wake? These are albatrosses, big birds by most any standard. There are also numerous sea and ground birds on both Wake and Midway Islands.

Jackson's persona appears to have changed as his education progressed. As a youth, he was inquisitive about everything. He particularly liked travel as described by National Geographic, much of his time was spent on a 30-foot sailboat that he owned; and he had something of an obsession with birds or those that migrated down the Outer Bank and other pathways. He became enamored with big sailing birds. He studied aircraft and the general theory of flight. This led particularly to intelligence aircraft. His interest in sailing boats also continued.

Accordingly, a major interest became big sailing birds as these represented a transition between theories of aircraft flight and the flight of birds. There was therefore a straight connection between travel, big bird flight, aircraft flight and intelligence gathering. Although these interests appear diversions down rabbit paths, they are manifestations of his inquisitiveness. They are thereby central to the story.

Jackson's old ways did not abandon him. He could not pass through Wake Island without seeing the famous "Gooney Birds' with their unbelievable characteristics.

Although he was restricted from seeing all the birds in their habitat, he did see enough to satisfy his curiosity. He knew most of the big bird characteristics even without direct observation from his notes. He had faithfully researched many big birds such as the albatross and could easily apply them to what he saw. He could not help dragging out his notebooks and refreshing his memory of what he had written. The narratives here supplement the notes he had taken about big-birds in general.

The aircraft crew kept working on the airplane. It was obvious that they had a problem of some sort. The short stop for refueling stretched on into the night and then the morning. Finally, the officials of the airline and government made an official announcement. There was a problem with the aircraft. There was some kind of mechanical problem. This forced us to stay on the ground and around the hangar for several days. I was thankful for that. It gave me more time to observe the big birds.

While Jackson was in college and before his trip to Taiwan, he made a long tourist trip across Russia and the Middle East. He kept particular alert for big birds across northeastern Europe because he had little experience in those areas.

Storks especially caught his attention. He saw many of these in the fields in Germany and Poland. On the same trip in the fall, he observed storks in migration across Turkey. The flights of storks were the most remarkable thing seen and that is contrasted with the flights of albatrosses, another big bird.

In the first place, storks are large birds. They are heavy, with wide wingspans. The marabou stork, with a wingspan of 10.5 feet or so, weighs up to

18 pounds. They join the Andean condor in having the widest wingspan of all living land birds. Some claim that 14 feet wingspan observations are sometimes made.

Jackson saw many stork nests on tops of houses in Stockholm but no storks. They surprised him because the nests were so large. They were built on the tall chimneys prevalent there. The nests were about nine feet tall and six feet wide. The nests were built with sticks and reeds that ranged in diameter of one-eighth inch to one inch or so. There was also some kind of filling that bound the sticks together. The nests are often used for many years. Many Swedes attribute good luck to the nests. Most hate them and tear them down. They certainly do not get satisfactory chimney drafts with these obstructions.

As they passed through the northern fields of East Germany (at that time), they were startled by suddenly seeing many storks poking around in the ploughed fields.

Storks are large, long-legged, long-necked wading birds with long, stout bills. They dwell in many regions and tend to live in drier habitats than the closely related herons, spoonbills and ibises. Many species are migratory. Most storks eat frogs, fish, insects, earthworms, small birds and small mammals. We assumed they were foraging for food.

Storks tend to use soaring, gliding flight, which conserves energy. Soaring requires thermal air currents. Ottomar Anschütz's famous 1884 album of photographs of storks inspired the design of Otto Lilienthal's experimental aircraft gliders of the late nineteenth century. This was an important waypoint on the way to the Wright Brothers. It illustrates the phalanx of would-be fliers pushing toward manned, powered flight.

Storks have special characteristics of flight that include vortex sailing, exploiting gliding in the vortex or funnels of rotating warm air. This allows storks to sail long periods and great distances. They migrate from northern Europe to the bottom of the Saudi Arabian peninsula by sailing from vertical air vortexes, one after the other. The birds avoid the Mediterranean Sea and other large bodies of water since vortexes do not form over water. The difference between a vortex and a helix is that the vortex rotational axis curves in space while the helix axis is a straight line in space.

On Jackson's many trips to far places, he had observed thousands of storks on their fall migration toward Saudi Arabia and the Persian Gulf. That was a remarkable illustration of vortex sailing while using thermal air currents.

The locals identified to me what they referred to as storks. I had seen many storks in the fields of Germany and Poland. This was powerful evidence that they were right. However, the storks in flight must have been several miles distant so there was some room for identification error.

In migration, there were so many birds in each vortex that the outline of the vortex could be clearly seen. In this, storks enter a rising column of air. This may be a fraction of a mile or two in diameter at the base and then four or five miles in diameter at the top of the vortex, perhaps ten thousand feet or so. Perhaps 30 storks were in each column. When a stork reaches the top, it glides out of this vortex and glides perhaps ten miles to the next vortex. Several scout storks have flown ahead to search out the next suitable vortex. The stork at the top simply sails over to the bottom of the second vortex and begins the climb there, sailing the ten miles or so between vortexes. Perhaps four to ten vortexes of birds could be seen at a time. Remember, there was no effort to measure the characteristics of the phenomenon here, depending only on observations and fallible memories.

There we have the two characteristics of gliding for long distance flying.

One is linear or straight-line sailing and the other is vortex sailing depending on thermals. In linear sailing, the bird simply glides for much of its flight so it is dependent on the glide ratio. Some big birds may have a glide ratio of 32 or so. This means that in static air, it glides 32 feet horizontally for each foot lost vertically. This allows the bird to cover vast distances by linear gliding or by gliding in thermals or vortexes with little expenditure of energy.

A different method is by wave or slope flying where a big bird extracts energy from ocean waves, depending on wave slopes, to achieve speeds greater than the waves. This method is probably used exclusively by albatrosses.

Big Bird Sailers

The methods of flight for all of these big birds is extraordinary. A common sight along most highways in the U.S. is sailing vultures or turkey buzzards. These congregate with one another and sail around and around as they exhibit great hunting prowess using scent to detect their food, usually carrion. This bird has a large wingspread, over ten feet normally but sometime reaching 14 feet. They are sailers in that they sail with infrequent flaps of their wings. They can therefore stay aloft for a long time by conserving energy while they sail.

Even while an air crewman in the Navy, Jackson continued his youthful passion of watching birds and determining how they used flight for their purposes. It was always a surprise that aircraft collided so seldom with birds. However, there were plenty of collisions recorded and they were considered a hazard to flight.

Jackson had heard numerous stories about birds, particularly about big birds such as vultures. These birds are heavy and have large wingspans. Thus, they can bring a plane down easily.

Jackson's Navy aircrew once experienced this. A vulture or a turkey buzzard was on the same course as Jackson and his crew. The pilot only saw this bird for an instant before it was sucked into one of our four piston engines. After we landed at our destination and examined the damage, we found the bird had entered the radial engine tail-first. It was then strained through two of the engine cylinders that knocked that engine out of service. The electrical wires and cables of each piston probably got knocked out or broken and that is probably what caused the engine failure. Fortunately, we could still maintain altitude. We then were always on the lookout for large birds and considered how to avoid them. This was on the east coast.

Pelicans are another big bird that flies in formation and glides through much of his motion cycle. These are usually seen near a large body of water. As one loses airspeed, it flaps its wings to speed up, thereby losing energy. Jackson had seen many of these birds when he was a kid and even until the present. They often skim the water waves feeding by dipping their beaks as they sail along. They are probably using the ground effect for flight to further increase their efficiency.

Pelicans usually fly in a V-formation of a dozen or so birds with 20 feet or so separation. It has been shown that each bird in the formation except the leader flies with a minimum of energy due to the bird's minimum number of wing flaps. It is hypothesized that the lead bird is followed by all the others at a repetitive distance. The air probably has a cycler motion or each air disturbance repeats in distance. All but the lead bird profits by this repetition along each straight line. The lead bird often changes position. The birds all profit by saving energy that allows long flights.

Albatrosses

Since they were on Wake Island, their primary interest was on the albatross, naturally. However, I will first discuss big bird 'sailers.' We encountered an even larger bird, the albatross of Wake Island. The more we learned about the albatross, and about big birds in general, the more respect we had for them.

The albatross breeds on isolated islands in the central Pacific Ocean, but is found throughout the northern oceans during all times of the year. They are most commonly seen in the Bering Sea north of Europe and Aleutian Islands flying low over the waves searching for food. Laysan albatrosses, often called '*Gooney Birds*' are among the largest of all flying birds, that being the Andean Condor.

Early Aleut and Eskimo hunters apparently preferred albatrosses for their meals because archeologists find hundreds of albatross bones in the remains of old houses and villages along the Bering Sea coast. Laysan albatrosses are specialized feeders on schooling fish but they, too, often become prey. Fish or killer whales snatch unwary individuals from just under the surface. Once hatched, albatrosses will return to land only to breed, the rest of their life is spent at sea. They sometimes are seen asleep on the water, but this makes them easy targets for killer whales and stealthy hunters in kayaks; most albatrosses apparently sleep while gliding in the air or resting on the waves.

The Laysan albatross breeds on isolated islands in the central Pacific, but is found throughout the northern oceans. Laysan albatrosses eat mainly squid as well as fish eggs, crustaceans, floating carrion, and some discards from fishing boats.

Incredibly, adults with chicks to feed take foraging trips that last up to 17 days and travel 1,600 miles away from their nest during this time. The trip must be completed before the chicks die. These are incredible numbers, often confirmed by satellite tracking transmitters on the birds.

No one pretends to know their methods of navigation while making these long flights at sea. Some sightings have been reported where this big bird ranged up to 1,700 miles on a fishing trip to feed young ones. They land and ride the waves sometimes; at other times it rides just above the waves that makes his speed greater than the water wave by using wave gradients. He seems to sail along at hundreds or thousands of miles with hardly a wing flap. Some say he even sleeps while he sails along. By this dynamic soaring distances, they expend about the same energy as they do when resting, judging from their heart rate.

Many sailors consider the albatross as bringers of bad luck. They are considered good luck if they are not harmed, but harming them brings bad luck. They can therefore alter the outcomes of the games of chance. They are to be respected and allowed to stand aloof.

The albatross uses its unique characteristics to fly much faster than the ocean waves propelling him. This allows them to use the ground effect in flight where the slopes of water waves allow the bird to extract energy from the wave slopes.

This regime is by far the most sophisticated method of distance flight. It is the wave-slope flying as practiced by albatrosses. This allows the bird that has formed its preferred configuration, particularly of the wing chords, to lock in place a stiff membrane across his wings. He can then sense wave motion of the water and propel himself with the slope of the water wave and its ground effect up to several hundred feet altitude. He can then thrust forward by the gradient of the water wave, even flying directly into the wave slope. It is said that these birds can sleep on the water or in flight. Measurements indicate they can fly vast distances, thousands of miles, while expending only the energy used with the bird at rest. The membrane locks the wings in the most efficient regime of flight with no energy wasted by constantly reshaping the wings. Wave-slope flying propels the bird at speeds much greater than the water wave speed.

Vultures are also big birds that play a prominent role in African folklore. Their ability to show up whenever there is a carcass leads many to believe they dream the location of food or use some kind of mental telepathy to pass this information between birds. It seems that only supernatural communications accounts for this. These sightings have often led to superstitions and other tales ranging from good luck to death. Voodoo is cited as the host of many of these beliefs for areas of Africa and the Caribbean Islands. It is easy to assign supernatural powers to big birds. It is easy to fantasize magical attributes such as magic and magic carpets.

Albatross birds occur in great abundance on both Wake and Midway Islands. The bird's bill is composed of several horny plates, and along the sides are two "tubes", or long nostrils. These tubes allow the albatrosses to measure the exact airspeed in flight; these nostrils are analogous to the pitot tubes in modern aircraft. The albatross needs accurate airspeed measurement in order to perform dynamic soaring.

Albatrosses have a need to excrete the salts they ingest in drinking sea water and eating marine invertebrates. This amounts to a salt gland. Scientists know in general terms that it removes salt by secreting a saline solution that drips out of their nose. They extract fresh water by this method from salty seawater. I wander why technologists can't use the same method to filter salt water on an industrial level. If sufficiently efficient, this would answer a fundamental requirement of life where man's great hope has always been to extract fresh water from seawater.

Albatross birds are aided in soaring by a shoulder-lock, a sheet of tendon that locks the wing when fully extended, allowing the wing to be kept outstretched without any muscle energy expenditure, a morphological adaptation they share with few other birds.

Taking off is one of the main times albatrosses use flapping wings to fly, and is the most energy-demanding part of a journey. The only effort expended is in the turns at the top and bottom of every loop. This maneuver allows the bird to cover about 623 miles a day without flapping its wings. Slope soaring uses the rising air on the windward side of large ocean surface waves. Albatrosses have high glide ratios, around 23-to-1. Thus, for every foot they drop, they can travel forward 23 feet.

Albatrosses range over huge areas of ocean and regularly circle the globe.

They combine these soaring techniques with the use of predictable weather systems; albatrosses in the Southern Hemisphere flying north from their colonies will take a clockwise route, and those flying south will fly counterclockwise. Albatrosses are so well adapted to this lifestyle that their heart rates while flying are close to their heart rate when resting. This efficiency is such that the most energetically demanding aspect of a foraging trip is not the distance covered, but the landings, takeoffs and hunting they undertake having found a food source. When taking off, albatrosses need to take a run-up to allow enough air to move under the wings to provide lift.

This efficient long-distance travelling underlies the albatross's success as a long-distance forager, covering great distances and expending little energy looking for patchily distributed food sources. Their adaptation to gliding flight makes them dependent on wind and waves. However, their long wings are ill-suited to powered flight and most of these species lack the muscles and energy to undertake sustained flapping flight. Albatrosses in calm seas are forced to rest on the ocean's surface until the wind picks up again.

Alternatively, the North Pacific Albatross can use flap-gliding, where the bird progresses by bursts of flapping followed by gliding, a regime favored by pelicans.

They can live to 60 years and beyond; they mate for life and some do not find another if their partner dies. In 2005, an albatross was tracked through 13,670 miles around the world in the Southern Hemisphere in 46 days. Some albatross species can spend up to five years at sea. By repeatedly using these flight regimes, the birds can travel thousands of miles without flapping their wings. This allows the Wandering Albatross to achieve the necessary power of 81 watts or one-tenth horse-power for flight at 43 mph. That much power is required for its 19-pound body.

Dynamic soaring involves the birds gaining height by angling their wings while flying into the wind. They can then turn and swoop along for up to 62 feet at speeds of up to 67 miles per hour.

Students of the albatross's flight understood early on that the bottom-most layer of wind blowing above any surface, including that of water, will incur friction and thus slow down. This layer itself then becomes an obstacle that slows the layer just above it. This result is a 120 to 240 foot high region known as a 'boundary layer' through which the wind speed increases smoothly the higher you go in the field. Dynamic soaring maneuvers extract energy from that field, enabling the albatross to fly in any direction, even against the wind, with hardly any effort.

The Wake Island rail is classified as extinct. Its inability to fly and the island's geographic isolation, combined with the bird's inquisitiveness and lack of fear of humans, made it an easy victim of over-hunting. It is now known that the extinction event occurred specifically between 1942 and 1945. This was as a direct result of the presence of thousands of starving Japanese troops stranded on the island, combined with the inevitable habitat destruction resulting from military alterations of the environment and extensive aerial bombardment during World War II.

CHAPTER 21

GRAND SOVIET EXPERIMENT

It is difficult to view the grand sweep of history without conceding the dual metaphors of life for a person's biological and behavioral evolution.

One is the biological Wheel of Life, as observed in Oslo's Frogg Park, for his procreation and for the cycle of birth, youth, maturity, and death. The other is the Behavioral Drive of Life toward curiosity, exploration, and migration.

Some say the Soviet state was history's grand social experiment. It was implemented in 1917 by Lenin and his Bolsheviks in a coup d'état against the short-lived Kerensky Republic, and carried to its logical conclusion by Stalin during his reign and later leaders. This was after Lenin's death in 1924 and until Stalin's own death in 1953. The Soviets continued their rapacious policies until their demise in 1991. Lenin or his policies had hundreds of thousands of Russians murdered. Some say millions. Stalin or his policies killed over ten million more, as is well known. Stalin and Hitler had initiated World War II by partitioning Europe by the secret protocols of the Molotov-Ribbentrop Pact that only became known long after the war. Hitler later attacked the Soviet Union, as pre-shadowed in his book, *Mein Kampf*, to gain 'lebensraum'. The war cost the lives of perhaps 40 million people, 20 million of them Russian. Stalin gobbled up most of Europe and major parts of the world, at first because of the war and later because of his rapacious state policies and the voracious Soviet appetite.

In the end, the Soviets lasted 75 years. It was a grand social experiment enveloping all of society for all that time. The Soviets were responsible for the deaths of about 60 million people during their tenure. Further, it was a failed economic experiment.

CHAPTER 22

COLD WAR ONSET

In 1948, the Americans formulated the Cold War or formally stated a policy of "*Containment*" to curtail the voracious appetite of the Soviet Empire. Later, President Reagan called it the Evil Empire. These *rapacity versus containment* policies, defined the Cold War or super-power conflict for the next 43 years.

America's containment policy put major strains on the Soviet system, as did other external factors late in its life. The Soviet Union collapsed from the wars and stresses of containment and from its economic and political failures. In the end, as was demonstrated in Moscow's stores, it could not provide bread for its people.

The Soviets allowed some tourists into parts of Russia in 1989. I took a tour then. The tour bus entered from Poland in the east, through Minsk, Moscow and St. Petersburg. I saw the long lines at the grocery stores in Moscow, even though there was little to be had in them. A Soviet citizen often stood for hours for a single item. Finally, entry to the stores was blocked while a single item such as bread was sold at a door or window; cabbages were sold at another window with a different line to be endured.

The gross domestic product, or GDP, comparison between U.S. and Russia was very different. In 1998, the U.S. per capita GDP was reported for 1998 by *The CIA Fact Book* as $21,000 while that of the Soviets was $9,186 as reported by the Soviets and repeated by the fact book. I saw no evidence in Russia to support this.

My estimate of the Soviet GDP, based observation, was $1,150. I made this observation by assessing the life of a few individuals, and then extrapolated this into the whole total population to determine the national GDP. This was a clumsy method that violated all rules of statistics but it had to yield better results than those being passed out as government data, by both The Soviets and by Washington. *The Guinness Book of Answers* estimated $950. When the Soviets fell in 1991, the economic statistics in produce, electrical output, oil and coal and others projected the same rosy outlook as before the fall. The Soviet bureaucrats could look out their windows and see the collapse of the Soviet Union. Yet, they continued their rosy statistical economic reports long after the fall. Even in the face of unquestionable facts, one must remember this: Communists lie. And in many cases, Americans repeat the lie

That often seems a characteristic of liberal organizations. They promise fantastic results and then lie when they underperform.

What is this? Charlie thought to himself. *The power is off most of the time. The people cannot stand in line long enough to get sufficient food. When the pumps don't work for lack of power, the water system gets interrupted. This place is collapsing.*

A metaphorical thread in this story is the threat to sedentary people across Russia from pastoral barbarians or nomads, who kick up dust clouds on the steppes beyond the horizon. Were these minor dust devils, or did they portend the coming of the barbarian horsemen to rape, pillage, and lay asunder? This fear lasted for millennia. However, in about 1700, gunpowder and guns found their way into the hands of the settled people, and thus the barbarians were stopped. In metaphorical symbolism, after WWII, Stalin, acting the barbarian, closed his borders and used this fear to bluff and have his way. Often, it was not a bluff! In response, the Americans looked into the metaphorical dust clouds. They flew Low-Flyer and High-Flyer aircraft and spacecraft around, into, and over the steppes, with electronic eyes and ears and exotic sensors. These electronic intelligence wars stopped Stalin's neo-barbarians.

Finally, Soviet aggression prompted a response.

This response became the Cold War. It developed slowly at first. There was no rallying cry or outburst. However, Churchill noted in 1946 that an Iron Curtain had come down around the Soviets and their acquisitions. The Berlin Airlift sent shivers as country after country fell to them. Even before Korea in 1950, it was clear that the various actions taken by America and the West amounted to a containment policy.

This policy had several important aspects. The most obvious was the military response, as demonstrated in the Berlin Airlift in Germany, in continued involvement in the Chinese Civil War, in Greece and Turkey and a hundred other places. The military response required holding a large military organization, keeping it deployed and ready to fight at a large number of strategic places around the world, designing and building weapons to keep up with the escalating requirements, and continually finding, developing and deploying ever newer and more effective weapon systems.

Another was the diplomatic aspect in which NATO, SEATO, and other organizations, pacts, and treaties were formed. This strengthened the governmental cooperation between countries and increased the general resolve to resist the Communists even while ever-larger popular votes in France, Italy, and most Western countries were installing substantial Communist components. A heavy economic component included Greek, Turkish and Iranian assistance under the Marshall Plan, to name a few.

All of these required information about the Soviets, their capacity, and their intentions. Thus, the U.S. placed a premium on intelligence, invested vast sums in the military and civilian intelligence arms of the U.S. government, and invested and encouraged the investment similarly by their allies. Intelligence and electronic wars would be known euphemistically as Technical Intelligence or Intel Wars.

The Containment policy, in truth, gave a singular name to the dedication of the U.S. and the West in checking the spread of the Soviet Empire and diminishing it where feasible.

The word *containment* described the environmental conditions seen by the West. This environment required a number of policies and actions, but they were not obvious in the term. The West was under a severe handicap since it never invented active words or expressions to define their position.

Soviets shouted with clinched fists, "*Workers of the world, unite! Throw off your chains!*" These active verbs are a clear call to action. Man responds to active verbs, just as most men respond to martial music and drumbeats. It is embedded in a man's genes somehow. However "Containment" and "Cold War," what kind of call to action is that? No music plays and there are no drumbeats. The genes remain dormant. "*Kill the Huns!*" Now those are words to live by! "*Liberty, Equality, Fraternity!*" These drove the French radicals mad, although the active verbs, "*Give me*," were only implied.

In 1948, The Soviets closed the roads and railroads into Berlin to starve the people out, and thereby the Allies. Britain, France and the U.S. flew thousands of planes in with sufficient material to keep the city alive. There was food, coal, everything. They flew into Templehof Airport in the middle of Berlin. It was a constant stream of airplanes.

The whole operation lasted from May 1948 to May 1949, when Stalin, for whatever reason, stopped the blockade. The West celebrated saving Berlin. However, who knew the Kremlin's purposes and who knew if those had been accomplished, which would have meant the Kremlin had won. Some said the Berlin blockade was to prevent the West from coming to the aid of the Chinese Nationalists as the Communists won their civil war and Chiang was driven to Taiwan in 1949, but who knew? In the distant future, Berlin was to stay free and China was to remain Communist, but who knew what was cause and effect and who knew intentions? Victory was hard to assess.

That was really a scary time. People did not think Stalin had the bomb, but no one was sure with the Rosenbergs executed as Russian spies and all that. There was also the greatest fear that Russia had these enormous numbers of Army divisions to roll across Europe. Russia denied they were weak, but it was said later that over 20 million Russians died in the war. They were in no condition to roll across Europe, but who knew it? It was another Stalin bluff. He pulled it off until 1949 when he exploded his first A-bomb, and then the Soviets got the H-bomb four years later. He did not have to bluff again until he died in 1953.

Meanwhile, Stalin owned the Soviet Union; he was a God-figure beyond any Czar. He was the Godhead without spirituality and his subjects were mere chattel, of no account. Stalin had killed all his opposition long ago, had stilled all the dissent in the 1930s. Untold rivers of blood and armies of corpses filled the woods around Moscow, even before the war. The corpses included all his fellow revolutionaries, and his peers who might think of competing or not blindly following, and all their families. They included all those who could give evidence for the defense of his real or imagined enemies, or for his friends or peers. Included were all the young who might someday question him as a God-figure, or any history that led to his exalted position. He sent millions to death as he enforced mass collectivization. His Soviets confiscated the peasants' food and left them to die in the Russian winters. Many Russians considered WWII when it came, a blessing. However, the Germans spilled Russian blood even faster than Stalin did. Soon, the various ethnic groups, the Ukrainians, and the Russians themselves realized this invasion was nothing short of Apocalyptic. They steeled themselves to a long and bloody war against a German foe that was causing a land of far more bloodletting and savagery than they had known, even under Stalin. This Apocalypse cost the Russians 20 million dead in five years, an incredible number.

"And why did the Americans ally themselves with Stalin?" It was often asked. Stalin and Hitler started the war. This was only one week after his non-aggression Molotov-Ribbentrop Pact with Hitler and its secret protocol. Hitler then attacked Poland on September 1, 1939. Stalin and Hitler, under the secret protocol, agreed to dismember Poland and to divide it and Eastern Europe between themselves. Hitler attacked first, but Stalin attacked after a couple of weeks and annexed two-thirds of Poland as his part of the deal. England declared war on Germany. She later allied herself with Stalin in an astonishing turnabout.

It was two devils loosing the Horsemen of the Apocalypse, and the British chose one. In the next two or three years, the German devil gobbled up all of Europe. However, the Russian devil in the next five years gobbled up half the world!

Yes. And this devil isn't through yet. This was thought through the 1950s and 1960s.

The West had reason to fear after the war. They also soon realized they had been premature in their rush to demilitarize. The world is a terribly dangerous place. People were not naïve enough to believe after WWII, as they did after WWI, that the war was fought to end wars. However, after the nuclear explosions in Japan and with the later advent of ballistic missile carriers, it was thought that major wars were too dangerous to fight. The nuclear umbrella was encompassing, it was thought. By this, many of the horrors of the past could be avoided, but wars proliferated underneath the nuclear umbrella, and government-caused murder increased explosively. They soon relearned that just as police must be vigilant and fight an unending crime spree where they often die heroically, so the military must be vigilant and fight with unending violence and die heroically. This violence is usually caused by state against state, but is more often caused by governments against their own people. This is especially true of totalitarians. Since WWII, hundreds of millions of people have died violent deaths at the hands of government. Political scientists often call this "democide."

> Leon Trotsky once said, "*You may not be interested in war, but war is interested in you.*"

Spying is as old as man. In history, Moses sent spies under the leadership of Caleb unto the land of Canaan to evaluate the land and its people. They came unto Hebron, now celebrated by Muslims and others for the cave of Abraham. They returned with huge grape clusters on poles between them and later reported, "The land flowith with milk and honey," and the Israelis plotted to take it.

On returning, they reported that, "The Lord hath delivered unto Israel's hands all the lands." This was because the inhabitants seemed weak. Joshua then "fit the battle of Jericho" with priests and ram's horns. One can walk on those disinterred walls today that are 20 feet thick and question the siege with ram's horns. Nevertheless, the spies were reported to be reliable and accurate. Jackson was mindful of this and other biblical stories. His knowledge was based on 'Sunday School Classes' that he attended while a young man or in high school. He had the ability to recite an applicable story and often did so. His associates or friends responded by rolling their eyes. Not everyone appreciated the references he threw into everyday conversation.

Such human intelligence has been practiced throughout history. History is generally segregated into periods of war. This gives the impression that state killings are defined by warfare, but this hardly reaches toward the enormous numbers of state killings, or those of genocide, imposed starvation, and general policies imposed where premature death is inevitable. This certainly occurred when millions were banished to Siberia or were placed in concentration camps with little food or sanitation. Prof. R.J. Rummel estimates the number of military and civilian deaths in wars since WWII. His estimates are widely quoted but there are no generally accepted numbers.

Rummel estimates those directly killed because of wars in the world from 1945-2000 are about 77 million souls or about 1.4 million per year. This excludes about 20 million estimated deaths in WWI and 55 million in WWII, where all these numbers are greatly dependent on definitions. He estimates that government murder, or deaths caused by famine and war against its own people, to be about 262 million for the twentieth century or 2.6 million per year. His estimates include 38 million dead during the Chinese civil war (the warlord period) and another 38 million dead during the Chinese Communist government-caused famine of 1958-1962. This was Mao's "Great Leap Forward" after the civil war. The Civil War was fought from 1945 until 1949 at which time Chiang Kai-shek fled with his army to Taiwan. The Soviets supported Mao's army during this time. President Nixon and Henry Kissenger negotiated with Mao that made them powerful architects of today's world.

The West likes to think of themselves as sparing women and children from the ugliness of death during wars while the enemy does the opposite. Yet, think of WWII where the U.S. and Britain imposed a policy of "carpet-bombing" for three years or so. This policy bombed women and children day and night, every day, and there was no attempt to limit it to military targets. The killing of innocent women and children was the object of the policy, although the policy was always stated in nicer terms. Britain's "Bomber Harris" and America's General Curtis LeMay leveled most of the important cities of Europe and much of the countryside. War is a nasty business. However, state murder is far worse.

Rummel also finds that between 1945 and 2000, 205 wars occurred between non-democracies, 116 between non-democracies and democracies and zero wars between democracies. Democracies appear to reason together and avoid major strife; yet totalitarians still claim to be democracies. It is a veil that must be pushed aside. He finds the greatest number of post-WWII deaths were caused by Communist regimes; about 87%. He concludes that totalitarian regimes are the least constrained by their citizens, and are the most prone to murder. Democracies are most constrained, and are therefore the least likely to murder its own or other citizens. The power in democracies is most diffuse, depending on constitutions, citizens with voices and votes, and term limits.

Yardley's book, *Secrets of the Black Chamber* popularized interceptions and code breaking around the world. It not only told what the U.S. had done during the conference, but also described in detail how codes were broken. It explained the mathematical and statistical underpinnings of codes and how to use them. The book sold very well in Japan, with even more copies than were sold in the U.S., and caused further infuriation in the Japanese government. Even so, he was invited to Japan to train their code breakers and was paid handsomely for this. Some in the U.S. called this treason but the law never interceded.

With this background, it is incredible that the Japanese would lose the Battle of Midway in 1942, which was the turning point of WWII. It depended almost totally on the U.S. deciphering the Japanese naval code. Even with the Yardley background, the Japanese did not believe their codes could be broken.

Yardley not only broke the codes, but also put code breaking on a statistical and mathematical footing that paved the way for its future, and its critical contribution to the development of digital computers. He is considered now to be an erratic father of cryptography. The Enigma code, the Purple code, and other codes that were broken with these techniques later, gave the

U.S. and the Allies in WWII a very distinct advantage over both Germany and Japan, and certainly changed the nature of the war and, some say, the eventual outcome.

We profit from cipher technology every time we use a cell phone, shop on the internet, or use an ATM. Hedy Lamarr, the movie star, claimed to be the inventor of spread spectrum using similar techniques on torpedoes and she certainly holds an early patent on the technique.

I was ruminating about people in general.

One thing I have learned. People are generally not interested in history. If one wants to capture a small niche in history, he is barking up the wrong tree. If I ask someone at less than 60 years old about the event, they often respond that they have never heard of it. "I was not even born," they respond.

I was born after the Civil War but I know a lot about it. These people seem immune from history, from what life is all about and how they got here. The Old Testament of the bible responds to these hard questions although it is difficult to see the connections. One finds a hardness there, harsh judgments by a God that sometimes demands the sacrifice of one's own child. The Old Testament dates far back in history, so it is more primitive and far more demanding. The New Testament advocates love as the best answer for these questions. Throughout, we find the poetic centrality of these two paths: the Old Testament responding to draconian demands or the New Testament advocating love. Europeans seem to know much more of history than Americans. I'm sure that is a reflection of interest rather than intelligence.

Charlotte and the Lees didn't pay much attention to religion. It was barely a part of their lives.

On the other hand, Bianca Bravo found it to be a necessity in her life. She was a Catholic. Being of Italian heritage and an Argentine family, it was almost inevitable that she would be a Catholic. Further, she was a practicing Catholic. One could rely on her going to mass regularly. When someone made a disparaging remark, she would be silent as if she had not heard it but she stored them up. This was certainly not unusual in a South American country.

CHAPTER 23

BERLIN AIRLIFT

After WWII, the relationship between the U.S. and the Soviets was strained, particularly since the Soviets rolled across Eastern Europe during the war and continued to occupy the captured land afterwards. Winston Churchill condemned the Soviet Union policies and declared in a 5 March 1946 speech, "From Stettin in the Baltic to Trieste in the Adriatic," he declared, "an iron curtain has descended across the continent."

His speech is considered the opening volley of the Cold War. This was expanded in a *Foreign Affairs* article in July 1947 by George Kennan of the State Department.

The Soviets implemented a Berlin blockade 24 June 1948 until 12 May 1949.

Berlin was in the center of four occupied regions and was about 100 miles from the nearest 'open' border. The Soviets closed railroads, roads and canals. Only air routes were open but their low cargo-hauling capacity was considered greatly inadequate to supply a city of 2.5 million Berliners.

Even so, the Allies determined to bypass the blockade by airlift. This was to be a daunting task. The only aircraft the Americans had available in quantity were Douglas C-47 Skytrains, which would only haul 3.5 tons each compared to the C-54 at 10 tons each.

Berlin was surrounded by the Russian East Germany and was divided into four sectors including the American, British, French and Soviet. The prime American airport was Tempelhof, a very congested field in the center of Berlin. The field was surrounded by multi-story apartment buildings. To land, one must descend between two buildings or drop propitiously between them. It had been agreed before the blockade that there would be three 20-mile wide air corridors providing access to the city. These providentially provided the air routes to enter and exit Berlin and the Soviets honored the previous decision to maintain these. These channelized air routes accounted for the success of the airlift.

In early 1948, the United States and Allies secretly began to plan the creation of a new German state made up of the Western Allies occupation zones. In March, when the Soviets discovered these designs, they withdrew from the Allied Control Council, which had met regularly since the end of the war in order to coordinate occupation policy between zones. In June, without informing the Soviets, the West introduced the new Deutschmark. The purpose of the currency reform was to wrest economic control of the city from the Soviets, enable the introduction of Marshall Plan aid, and curb the city's black market, which was rampant. Soviet authorities responded with similar moves in their zone. Besides that, the Soviets blocked all major road, rail, and canal links to West Berlin, thus starving it of electricity as well as a steady supply of essential food and coal.

The drawdown in U.S. and British combat forces at the end of WWII, left the Red Army around Berlin dwarfing the Western Allied military presence. This restricted the options left to America. The only connections to Berlin left to the Western Allies were three air corridors from West Germany into Berlin.

On June 26, the first C-47s landed at Tempelhof Airfield, foreshadowing the great operation that was to come.

It was determined that in total supplies, 3,475 tons would be needed daily to keep more than two million Berliners alive.

Initially, General Clay who was in charge, determined that, with the limited number of airplanes available to him, he could haul about 300 tons of supplies a day, while the British effort was estimated to be capable of 750 tons a day. This left a 2,425-ton deficit daily. Since this kind of tonnage could not be achieved using C-47's, Gen. Clay and General LeMay made requests for more C-54's, since they could carry over three times more cargo than C-47's. On June 27, an additional 52 Skymasters were ordered to Berlin.

President Harry Truman decided that we would stay in Berlin. Military action with its risk of a hot war, and especially a nuclear war, was just too great for any other military action.

By July 1, C-54's were slowly taking over airlift flights, and they were operating 24 hours a day. Rhein-Main Air Base in Frankfort was made an exclusive C-54 base, and Wiesbaden was a mix of C-54's and C-47's. To accommodate these two different aircraft, General Smith established a block system, giving the bigger, faster C-54's priority. The size of Templehof was about 840 acres with 2 runways; one was 6870 feet and the other slightly shorter. This is similar to central park in Manhattan with 900 acres and with dimensions of 2.5 by 0.5 miles. Most modern airfields today have runways of 10 to 15 thousand feet long, twice as long as Templehof.

A string of C-54 aircraft rotated in and out of Templehof. Coal was the primary load. It kept Germans warm but its primary use was keeping the German industrial wheels rolling. The pilots were allocated 30 minutes on the ground. The aircraft crews were ordered to remain in their planes during unloading to avoid loitering delays. This string ran 24 hours a day. When there was a mechanical problem, that plane was dropped out of the string and the continuity of the loop was maintained.

During the Berlin airlift, an Allied supply plane took off or landed in West Berlin every 30 seconds. The planes made nearly 300,000 flights in all.

The airlift was supposed to be a short-term measure, but it settled in for the long haul as the Soviets refused to lift the blockade. For more than a year, hundreds of American, British and French cargo planes ferried provisions from Western Europe to the Tempelhof in the American sector and lesser airfields. At the beginning of the operation, the planes delivered about 5,000 tons of supplies to West Berlin every day; by the end, those loads had increased to about 8,000 tons of supplies per day with over 100 aircraft. The Allies carried about 2.3 million tons of cargo in all over the course of the airlift.

Life in West Berlin during the blockade was not easy. Fuel and electricity were rationed. Still, most West Berliners supported the airlift.

It is cold in Berlin, it was said, but colder in Siberia.

Charlie to Berlin

It should have been a bolt out of the blue when I received orders to report to Dover Air Force Base in Delaware, but it was not. This was a waypoint that sent me directly to Berlin. The struggles by the Truman administration had been documented well in the news media so I expected it to be coming.

I had been serving in an intelligence slot in the pentagon after WWII. However, the U.S. was desperately short of both cargo planes and crews. Orders went out from the pentagon to move to Germany as many C-47s and C-54s as could be found and their crews. I was a pilot so I fell into the category desperately needed. I was swept away to Dover Air Force Base and then to Wiesbaden, Germany. I became one of the hundreds of pilots and crew flying C-54s in the airlift. To indicate the seriousness to the Soviets, B-29 bombers were flown to Britain as a threat.

There was a scramble to get me to Dover from Washington where I was stationed. To Charlotte, this was just one more unforeseen order that moved me around. At least, in this case, she could follow what was happening since the newspapers tracked every angle of the airlift. It was bedlam getting my things packed and preparing my travel plans. Charlotte was not her usual self. She cried and mumbled how she hated the military. This was confusing and out of character. I was placed in a crew as a copilot on a C-54, mostly hauling coal.

The operation was somewhat chaotic when I first flew into Templehof. There were far fewer aircraft than needed and the same applied to the crews. General LeMay and the top brass worked on the problem long into the night. Finally, orders were given that moved mostly C-54 aircraft to the airlift. The crews were lackadaisical, sauntering to snack bars and returning to their aircraft late. As a new regime of operations, crews were ordered to stay aboard their aircraft while they unloaded. All aircraft had to fly instrument flight rules all the time. Special stacking arrangements were imposed whereby laggards had to drop out, return to base, and try it another day. German army mechanics and off-loaders were used, Often they volunteered to keep the planes flying. The average time for offloading was about 30 seconds.

I had seen some of the worst of the Germans but now a different light illuminated them. The Germans came to look on the airlifters as friends and both were heroes, intent on defeating the Russians and saving themselves.

Even a chocolate army was enlisted for kids. Someone tied the four corners of a handkerchief to hang below as a makeshift parachute. The kids loved it and met around Templehof to cheer the planes on and grab the chocolate.

By the spring it was clear that the Soviet blockade of West Berlin had failed. On May 12, 1949, the Soviets lifted the blockade and reopened the roads, canals and railway routes into the western half of the city. The West had won a critical victory.

I then returned to Weisbaden. It had been a wonderful excursion but the drudgery of the Pentagon beckoned and I could not escape it.

CHAPTER 24

NUCLEAR WEAPONS TRIAD

After 1946, the military formed a nuclear "triad." The Air Force sponsored the Strategic Air Command as a deterrent that no aggressor could ignore. This triad consisted of B-52 manned bombers, Minutemen ground-launched ICBM's and the Navy's submarine-launched SLBMs. All these carriers were to deliver nuclear weapons. These would characterize the nuclear triad for years to come. By the late 1960's, the number reached hundreds of bombers, 1000 ground-launched Minutemen missiles and 656 submarine-launched Polaris/Trident SLBMs.

SAC also controlled all strategic intelligence or reconnaissance aircraft. The world filled with nuclear weapons. Launchers were not useful if they could not be targeted for lack of intelligence. Again, one needs to continually assess capabilities and intentions.

All USAF aerial refueling aircraft for the bombers were under the control of SAC. Air refueling gave the bomber leg of the triad the ability to fly for days and for very long distances.

All strategic airborne command post aircraft were also under the control of SAC. This gave command and control to the triad even after a hypothesized nuclear strike.

The Navy and its 16-24 missiles on each submarine was a separate command.

Each missile or bomber in the triad carrier could deliver multiple independent reentry vehicles, MIRV, or multiple warheads where each was independently targetable.

The triad was America's response for decades.

SAC bombers by the late '60s were on a 10-minute alert. To achieve this, a dozen aircraft were in the air at all times. These circled on a route that often lasted for days and required multiple refueling by airborne tankers. Each aircraft had waypoints that were on the edge of Russia.

The Navy could launch all their missiles within minutes. Their maintenance transportation requirements were satisfied inherently by the submarine on-board capability or their return to a home port. Two crews deployed sequentially with each submarine where a deployment for each crew lasted one month.

SAC and the Navy both reported to the president.

Then, the Soviets got ahead of themselves. They shot down a Navy Privateer aircraft in 1950.

Many said this was intentional. Some said it was an unintentional shootdown. In every respect, the plane was lost with all members of the crew. One could only conclude that the entire crew was dead. None were ever found. The Cold War took on a renewed seriousness.

Nuclear Accidents

A friend and I were sitting in the Officer's Club one day and the subject of nuclear accidents came up. This was a subject that did not often come up in the conventional forces and even less often with the nuclear forces. I was despondent and missing the companionship of Charlotte. My sun tended to rise and fall with her but the military shifted everyone regularly.

I held that the consequence of accidents with conventional weapons become pitifully small compared to any that occur with nuclear bombs. Unfortunately, there is sufficient evidence of such episodes to have grave concern about the future. The information is weak since the first reaction to a nuclear accident is to cover it up with military secrecy.

When one thinks about vulnerabilities to attack, one usually thinks of the targets. Where are sites that are likely targets for nuclear weapon attacks? The target will be Washington, D.C. or some similar place with concentrated buildings, command and control facilities or other high value targets. One may say, "I live in Virginia farmland where there are no obvious targets so I am safe." Many believe that is wrong. Nuclear explosions, when they occur, will be from our own unintended explosions, and those explosions or launches will be by our making a foolish mistake of some kind and our safe-arm mechanisms will be inadequate in preventing the Armageddon.

The problem is when the enemy is us. At the end of the cold war, we reportedly had over 40,000 nuclear weapons. Those with the Air Force ranged as high as tens of megatons each. This explosive number is relative to the amount of TNT yielding the same explosive power. Aircraft bombs or warheads seem to be about one megaton each. A small mistake may cause inestimable damage. We have safe-arm devices attached to the bombs to prevent accidental explosions. Mind you, an initiator charger of conventional explosives is necessary to set off a nuclear bomb. This initiator may be 7,000 pounds or more of conventional explosives. We have accidentally dropped several bombs like this where the initiator or starter exploded but the warhead did not. The relative difference is 1,000 kilotons versus about 3.8 tons. Nuclear warheads are either of the gun, or canon, type used on Hiroshima or the lens, implosion, type used on Nagasaki. The gun type is simpler but lower yielding. The above ratio is for the improved Fat Man bomb as was dropped accidentally near Goldsboro, N.C. The Hiroshima A-bomb canon was 15 Ktons while the Nagasaki lens bomb was 21 Ktons. Today's Hydrogen warheads are pedestrian at typically 1 megaton.

We all know of the enormous effort made in the design of the Atomic (fission) and Hydrogen (fusion) bombs, the number of people working on it and the Nobel prize winners dedicated to making this a reality. The goal is to provide the enormous energy and destructive power. The safe-arm mechanism is implemented to explode when intended and to prevent the bombs from exploding or releasing their energy if not intended. We are confident that the bombs will explode as intended as has been demonstrated in tests and by the Hiroshima and Nagasaki experiences.

Thus, a high probability of success for explosions of enormous power is expected of the bombs and we can surely tolerate a reasonably small drop in probability of detonation by using several bombs. One could argue that a safe-arm mechanism is to prevent an unintended explosion or provide an infinitesimally small probability of an unintended explosion, as a necessity to save mankind. Surely, the safe-arm mechanism deserves a herculean effort, at least to be treated with the same herculean effort as the initial design of the bomb. We cannot depend on a few primitive preventive mechanisms. The bomb may be acceptable with only a few percent probability of exploding. Yet, the safe-arm should have the reciprocal of one in billions likelihood of performing as intended after an accident. For this, we also include the system of human beings and mechanisms that address maintenance, shipping, natural phenomena, unknown and unauthorized shipments to surprising addresses, floods, earthquakes, and the list continues forever. If the bomb weighs ten thousand pounds, surely it is reasonable that the safe-arm devices also weigh some large percentage of this, say 10 percentage of that much as an upper limit. We are not advocating large safe-arm devices, only far more effective ones.

We haul nuclear weapons all over the U.S. or the world by planes, submarines, by ship, rail and truck and by all forms of transportation. We have far too many bomb accidents that prove the danger of our present practices based on old data and a single mishap of September 2007. The best information that is public indicates about 1.3 serious mistakes per year in the 1960s. That is the number of such mistakes from nuclear bomb releases based on data for 1957 to 1968. The most common error was caused by the aircraft transporting the bombs crashing or jettisoning before the crash. They often jettison or crash over rivers, fields and oceans.

The nuclear bombs contain the nuclear material and mechanisms and require considerable high explosive material that is necessary as an initiator of the nuclear event. These initiator conventional explosives are quite dangerous in themselves and often explode on ground impact, doing considerable physical damage and spreading radiation in a confined area. It implies the safe-arm of the nuclear device is working since it survives impact and perhaps hundreds of feet interment on land. They survive raging fires and serious contortions, as they are part of the aircraft break-up while twisting or bending violently. We have been lucky with our safe-arm mechanisms, but nuclear luck is no more dependable than the probabilities of Las Vegas games.

The two hydrogen bombs dropped near Goldsboro in 1961 have never been fully recovered. One correctly opened a drag parachute and did not penetrate too far. The other one did not open the chute and buried itself in the mud of N.C. The nuclear components are buried 180 feet below ground. The water table in the marsh is almost at ground level and the Air Force and its contractors could never pump water out of the hole fast enough to reach it. Many of these or their nuclear parts are laying dormant 30 or 40 years later. The enemy might not be over there. He might be right here. This enemy is far more tangible. He operates amidst the transportation networks we implement and he pushes the probabilities of a serious accident ever upward. This enemy has the potential of destroying civilization. And this enemy works every day in pursuing accidental detonation. This is a new enemy, the likes of which we have never faced before. The data here suggests we are doing phenomenally well but it is woefully short of being adequate. This is a real enemy.

"For instance, the following story was seen in CNN news reporting of 12 June 2014. It is reporting an event in Goldsboro 24 January 1961. This was old news by this time; nevertheless, it was news.

"The event of two nuclear bombs dropped near Goldsboro, North Carolina occurred 24 January 1961. Very little information was released by the military at the time." Nevertheless, there is now considerable information about the Goldsboro incidents. Reports were made by *CNN News* and Freedom of Information (FOI) releases that show the 1961 reports are still valid.

The nuclear accident of January 24, 1961 was a B-52 crash near Goldsboro. The plane was from the Seymour Johnson Air Force Base in Goldsboro, a SAC field at the time. There was physical destruction by a nuclear bomb and loss of nuclear materials. A USAF B-52 bomber caught fire and exploded in midair due to a major leak in a wing fuel cell 12 miles north of Seymour-Johnson Air Force Base after airborne refueling. Five crewmen parachuted to safety, but three died—two in the aircraft and one on landing. The incident released the bomber's two Mark 39 hydrogen bombs. The safe-arm device on one of the bombs activated, causing it to carry out many of the steps needed to arm itself. The drag parachute on the other bomb allowed the bomb to hit the ground with little damage. The second bomb plunged into a muddy field at around 700 mph and disintegrated. Parts were discovered about 20 feet down and much of the bomb recovered, including the tritium bottle and the plutonium. However, excavation was abandoned due to uncontrollable ground water flooding. Most of the thermonuclear stage, containing uranium, was left embedded in the earth. It is estimated to lie around 180 feet below ground. The Air Force reportedly purchased the land and fenced it off to prevent its disturbance, and it is tested regularly for contamination, although none has so far been found. Some contest the actions in the last sentence, so it is not confirmed.

This was astonishingly close to a disaster that could have been worse than the devastation wrought in Hiroshima and Nagasaki. This could have befallen the United States that night. But it didn't, thanks to a series of fortunate missteps caused by the mechanical contortions of the arming circuits.

The Guardian reported that they found many of the details of that accidental drop through a FOI document they received from the military 20 September 2013 after being requested. The B-52 carrying the bombs dropped them in an accidental release following the aircraft disintegration. No nuclear explosion occurred but it was indicated that the safe-arm device was defeated by wires being stripped as the plane broke up.

The Stockholm Institute, in its *Brush with Catastrophe?* has called the Goldsboro incident "perhaps the single most important example in the published literature of an accident which nearly resulted in a catastrophe."

This claim appears to be founded on yet another hair-raising claim in the 1961 Lapp book. Lapp wrote in *Kill and Overkill* that each device involved in the Goldsboro incident was equipped with "six interlocking safety mechanisms, all of which had to be triggered in sequence to explode the bomb." Lapp said that "five of the six interlocks had been set off by the fall..." and thus, "only a single switch prevented the bomb from detonating and spreading fire and destruction over a wide area."

The exits from the bomb bays by the bombs were chaotic and destroyed most of the arming wires and that defeated their purpose. This was reported as preventing a nuclear detonation.

Several bomb accidents were reported in the 60's but none after 22 May 1968. That is what makes the 2013 Guardian Freedom of Information so important.

There was a classified report that two nuclear bombs nearly detonated in North Carolina on that earlier date. The Goldsboro accident was one of 32 pre-1980 accidents reported by the military involving nuclear bombs. Incidences continued to be related where nuclear accidents took us to the brink. It seems the Goldsboro event is a baseline for such accidents.

Both Goldsboro bombs were far more powerful than the bombs dropped on Japan. The Hiroshima Little Boy Uranium gun bomb was 15-Ktons of TNT while the Nagasaki Fat Man lens Plutonium implosion bomb was 21-Ktons. Both were extremely large and heavy. The Goldsboro bombs were each 3,800-Kton Mk39s. They actually dropped near Faro and Pikeville, a few miles north of Goldsboro and 40 miles or so east of Raleigh. Both were Hydrogen bombs.

A document was uncovered by Eric Schlosser as part of his research into his book on the nuclear arms race, *Command and Control.* Using Freedom of Information data, he discovered that at least 700 "significant" accidents and incidents involving 1,250 nuclear weapons were recorded between 1950 and 1968 alone.

According to the Schlosser report, two bombs, 3.8-Mtons each, fell in Goldsboro in 1961.

The first bomb deployed with its parachute as expected. The conventional initiator explosive was 7,600 pounds or 3.8 tons. It did not detonate.

The second bomb with the unopened parachute, landed in a free fall. The impact of the crash put it in the 'armed' setting. Fortunately—once again—it only damaged another part of the bomb needed to initiate an explosion. Three of eight crew members survived the aircraft crash.

While it's unclear how frequently these types of accidents have occurred, the Defense Department has disclosed 32 serious bomb accidents involving nuclear weapons between 1950 and 1980.

There are at least 21 declassified accounts between 1950 and 1968 of aircraft-related incidents in which nuclear weapons were lost, accidentally dropped, jettisoned for safety reasons or on board planes that crashed. The accidents occurred in various U.S. states, Greenland, Spain, Morocco, England, over the Pacific and Atlantic oceans and the Mediterranean Sea. Another five accidents occurred when planes were taxiing or parked.

Two months after the close call in Goldsboro, another B-52 was flying in the western United States when the cabin depressurized and the crew ejected, leaving the pilot to steer the bomber away from populated areas, according to a DOD document. The plane crashed in Yuba City, California, but safety devices prevented the two onboard nuclear weapons from detonating.

We cannot tolerate even a very small percentage of that rate. Safe-arm mechanisms may be almost perfect but the men handling the actual bombs are far less than perfect. They are humans that do human things. In that, we are far less than perfect. A look at the failure rate of the overall system shows we are prone to mistakes and they happen often.

The Goldsboro event appears the most ominous. Like many of the missile silos in the western U.S., the surrounding area was assumed to be the only area vulnerable to direct shock. The opinion of that has changed. Some thought they were living in a backwoods area of a backwoods state. Nothing could be further from the truth. Goldsboro seems to be the accident danger capital of the nation when considering the transport and training with nuclear bombs.

Of course, that may be a skewed view of the world since little data has been given the public since 1968. Not too much was shared even then. We now get a smattering from FOI coercion.

Nuclear Transport

It appears most events are from transporting weapons back and forth. Although conventional initiator explosives suitable for setting off the nuclear device may explode, in these events no known nuclear explosions have occurred.

Most bomber crews including this author have experienced thousands of hours of flight. Much of the training used bombs where the explosives were replaced by concrete or inert material. This is a realistic preparation for war and it does not require an actual nuclear war to prove that we can safe-arm a device and prove it without blowing up the entire world."

The Air Force set up the Strategic Air Command, or SAC, soon after WWII. During the 1950s and 1960s, SAC kept at least 12 strategic bombers in the air for 24 hours a day or at all times. Each bomber carried either two or four thermonuclear bombs (H-bombs), approximately a megaton each. This is compared to about 15-kTons for the Hiroshima bomb. This guaranteed our nuclear retaliation certainty as part of the Cold War.

Each bomber spent about 24 hours a day in the air and was refueled on average of twice a day. They flew orbits that traversed the Atlantic to the south and to the north and overflew Thule, Greenland twice a day. They also had an orbit that circled over Greenland continuously. Part of each orbit was close to the Soviet Union so we advertised our intentions well. Needless to say, this put an enormous strain on the aircraft, their maintenance and the crew. One could expect such a tasking to cause serious maintenance problems and errors. This requirement was christened as 'Chrome Dome' and it lasted until 1968 at which time the nuclear weapons were removed from all the aircraft under pressure from our allies, the international community and the Soviets.

Mars Bluff Warning Light

In the Mars Bluff event near Florence, S.C., the flight had barely begun when a small, red warning light came on in the cockpit. It indicated that the bomb wasn't properly secured in the bay. A crew member later said that the copilot thought the red warning light was a 'glitch'. He hit the light with the butt of his service revolver, and the light went off momentarily. When the red light returned, he figured something was wrong.

The copilot went back to the bomb bay and discovered that the egg-shaped bomb wasn't locked into place. He pushed a button he thought would engage the bomb lock. The man hit the wrong button. The bay doors opened, and the nuclear package fell to Earth.

The bomb was a 26-kiloton Mark 6, a more modern version of the Fat Man dropped on Nagasaki. It mistakenly fell out of a B-47 jet, dropping 15,000 feet. The plutonium core didn't explode, but the 6,000 pounds of initiator explosives detonated.

That, in itself, prompts us to use extremely reliable safe-arm techniques for the starter as well as the nuclear detonator. That explosion puts the nuclear material at risk; at least a risk greatly higher than it was without the accident. Many of these have been reported after the bomb fell off airplanes, the planes broke up in the air, they crashed sometimes with parachutes, and sometimes with none. There is solid evidence that the initiator is vulnerable to these accidents even if they can be tolerated.

Darned! We have nuclear bombs dropped, mishandled, being part of aircraft breakups, crashes, fires, explosions of the starter with tons of TNT and lost. This is not to mention the nuclear tripod described later as being transported from North Dakota to Louisiana while later being left unguarded on an airfield. But the reporter and retired general think that is not a danger.

"This is serious business, but it was not dangerous business," said the general.

I think I am dreaming. There has been no accidental nuclear explosion but we can only tolerate zero such events. That seems to have been forgotten.

One can risk a miniscule probability that a launched device may not detonate, when we have thousands of them. Yet, to risk even an infinitesimal probability that one might accidentally detonate a nuclear bomb cannot be tolerated. The determination of the actual size of 'infinitesimal' is not to be left in the hands of a few aviators, nor should it be in the hands of thoughtless generals. These have proven time and again that they are accident-prone and our safe-arm strategies are woefully inadequate.

What in the world are we thinking to risk it all when not necessary? One should stop the sequence of accidents now before we extinguish the planet. This is not a cry for passivism. It is a cry for rational thought and life.

Now, this was a fine how-do-you-do, I thought. *I'm a pilot of a transport aircraft and I have to contend with hauling nuclear bombs around. The bomb factory is turning them out as fast as they can and I have to haul them wherever the waybill says. The more we build, the more we fly them to be deployed, to be modified, to be repaired, to be refurbished and to be mishandled.*

Recent Cruise Missile Incident

Another incident is presented to indicate how close we are to Armageddon and how little we appreciate a doomsday happening.

On September 2007 a CNN headline and article appeared as follows:

> **Six Nuclear Warheads on Cruise Missiles Were Mistakenly Carried on a Flight From North Dakota to Louisiana Last Week**
>
> The plane took the cruise missiles with 6 live nuclear warheads (3 on each tripod) from Minot Air Force Base in North Dakota to Barksdale Air Force Base in Louisiana for decommissioning the Air Force said. The warheads were to be removed at Minot where dummy warheads were to replace them before they were attached to the B-52 bomber. The flight crew was unaware that the plane was carrying nuclear weapons, the officials said,
>
> "This is a major gaffe, and it's going to cause some heads to roll down the line," said Don Shepperd, a retired Air Force major general and military analyst for CNN. The mistake was discovered after the plane's flight to Louisiana, 36 hours later. Therefore, the aircraft and nuclear weapons were left unguarded on a ramp for most of this time.

> Once the mistake was discovered, the Air Force immediately began an inventory of all of its nuclear weapons, a military official said.
>
> Major Gen. Douglas Raaberg, director of Air and Space Operations at the Air Combat Command in Langley, Virginia, has been ordered to investigate how the nuclear-tipped missiles were flown across the country without anyone knowing, officials said.
>
> A military official told CNN there was no nuclear risk to public safety because the weapons were not armed. Officials believe that if the plane had crashed or the missiles somehow had fallen off the wings, the warheads would have remained inert and there would have been no nuclear detonation, though conventional explosive material in the warhead could have detonated.
>
> The retired Air Force and CNN consultant, Major General Shepperd, said the United States had agreed in a Cold War-era treaty not to fly nuclear weapons. "It appears that what happened was this treaty agreement was violated," he said.
>
> If we did agree by treaty, then how do we transport the thousands of warheads in our inventory? Are trains or trucks safer than airplanes, one wonders.
>
> Military officials also say the missiles could not have been launched because of multiple security procedures required to be enacted before any launch would have been authorized. Shepperd agreed with military officials that the situation could not have caused a nuclear detonation. But he added, "Any time you have nuclear material on board, if the airplane crashes, nuclear material can be spread in the immediate area of the crash, so you get radioactivity in the immediate area. This is serious business, but it was not dangerous business," Shepperd said.

This event prompts multiple reactions on different levels. This apparently became news in 2007. It appears the Air Force did not volunteer the information. One suspects an enterprising reporter heard about it and rooted out the story. We know about the nuclear accidents through 1968 but how many could there have been in the intervening years?

There is also this business that there can be many detonations over the years of the conventional initiator needed as a starter to set off the nuclear explosion but no nuclear explosion occurred. The cruise missile carried 3 tons of conventional starter initiator for a 26-Kton nuclear bomb.

One nuclear bomb will probably change our form of government. It certainly did in Japan. It will change our social structure. God only knows what else will be changed but it will be beyond our imagination.

When it comes to the nuclear bomb issue, let's consider the problems caused by a large number of bombs. One must consider the maintenance problem. One cannot produce a large number of bombs, put them into storage and leave them. After all, plutonium is one of the most corrosive materials known to man.

The bombs must be maintained. Like any product, they degrade. They become less reliable. They must be monitored. Mechanisms must be monitored in storage. They must be brought up to certain specifications. When this cannot be done in the field, they must be shipped to a maintenance depot. Many cannot be fixed at the depot and must be shipped to the manufacturer. Even with 1000 bombs, they must be deployed or transported to their initial deployment sites. Think of the transportation problem with 1000 units being shipped to numerous installation sites around the world. Maintenance requirements then cause multiple movements around the world. There are movements to the maintenance depot, not to mention those to the manufacturer. How often must these movements occur? These are not static devices that do not degrade. These are made of fissionable material with specified half-lives. Radiation is continuous. The transportation problem must be addressed. Do we haul them to the various bases on military aircraft where we are aware of the dangers in military flight? Do we haul them on railroads that meander through towns across the nation with the dangers known there? Do we haul them with trucks? Again, these must pass over questionable infrastructure roads and bridges through the towns and cities of America?

The same questions must be asked with overseas deployments. Do we fly them, or ship them?

Even with a small number of bombs, the interconnecting transportation paths are phenomenally large. They grow exponentially with the number of bombs.

There is no doubt that humans on these paths make mistakes. It stands to reason. We know it from the experiences with the bombs. We look to the safe-arm mechanisms to save us, to disable the explosive accident. We do not know the effectiveness of these devices but we do know they are critical. They were effective in our many nuclear accidents but barely. These save us from the Armageddon.

The story here centers on America and her bombs. This ignores the compounded likelihood of accidental explosions when numerous countries have operational nuclear bombs and delivery systems to use them. The system of each country is different, there are procedures and protocols but they are different with each country. There is no doubt that these various systems make us all vulnerable to a multitude of accidents. That must be taken into account. If we are comfortable with our situation, we must assume a deficiency in our expository abilities.

As said, the number of errors in the nuclear bomb field overwhelm any others in different fields. Admirals and generals have especially heavy responsibilities.

From what we do know, the nuclear regime is rife with daffy episodes. There is no room for daffiness in the nuclear arena. This must be stopped.

There was a time when people thought there was a defense against nuclear weapons. In the 1950's and 1960's we tested these weapons and flung radioactive materials into the atmosphere with abandon. We advised little children to get under their desks in school and avoid standing in front of glass windows.

"Those days appear to be gone," I say. "You know, many foreigners did not feel the same way about things. They hardly knew of nuclear radiation and things like that. They just went on with their daily life and ignored those military things. Everything changed if they came to America.

"Columbia University marched to a different drummer, it was said. It was difficult to be on that campus in Manhattan and not feel the winds of the times wafting through. Suddenly, we were all thrown into the seriousness of the war. That was followed by black headlines in the newspapers that the Americans had invented and used an Atomic Bomb. All our worlds had changed overnight. Mankind was thrown into a dangerous maelstrom and we were all a part of it.

"Throughout the time of the Cold War, things appeared to change. Now, nuclear weapons were for someone else to think about, not us. We have the knowledge that things are deadly serious but we kind of ignore it. No one knows what to do other than continue our lives as if we are in control and we can shut out things that are unpleasant. So we do that.

"We know that the bombs carry more and more power, reaching many megatons TNT equivalence. We know many nations now have nuclear weapons. Yet, what can we do? We ignore these facts and hope someone else is worrying about those things. Life goes on."

We were not concerned about weighty issues like this. Most of our conversation was not about these things but about girl-things, as Charlotte would say. We discussed boys, their families to be, clothes, shopping, and social affairs. My wife, Charlotte, affirms this. Girls tend to talk about girl things. Men talk about golf or football.

My sidekick was George Grayburn, and he had dated Bianca several times during the war. Afterwards, they got married and also had two children. They bought a house near Larchmont in Westchester County. Although George was almost always gone, Bianca made the most of her life. She also had the advantages of New York enjoyed by Charlotte. Bianca and Charlotte continued their close relationship for many decades.

Bianca was more stable than Charlotte. Charlotte had a wild side but Bianca never showed these characteristics. She lived a nice, even life. She visited her aunt, Maria Rossi, often as well as Charlotte's family.

Life with the bombs continued.

CHAPTER 25

RUSSIANS SHOOT DOWN PRIVATEER; NAVY PLANE OVER BALTIC

In April 1950, the Russians shot down a Navy PB4Y2 Privateer aircraft. It was based in Port Lyautey, Morocco. It was flying over the Baltic when the Russians shot it down. The Russians said it was an intelligence plane. There was a big conflict. Finnish fishermen said they sighted the plane in the water but no crew was found. There was a lot of speculation that the Russians had captured them. That question was to haunt the Americans to the Soviet's final days. Many were to think they were still prisoners of the Russians; that they were still somewhere in the Siberian Gulag Archipelago.

This is often cited as the onset of the Cold War. In the twelve-year period that followed, numerous U.S. planes, mainly reconnaissance aircraft, were destroyed in one-sided fights with Russians.

Even in 1992, 42 years later, Boris Yeltsin was to tell the Americans that some of their aircraft crewmembers were still in Russian prisons. Some suggested that the crew of the Privateer was that referred to. Several news organizations told this story and it was to be retold on national television. Unfortunately, neither crewmembers nor data were ever found.

Jackson and his squadron of Privateers were in Washington at the time. They quickly received orders for his squadron to relocate to Port Lyautey. They would replace that downed aircraft. These were to patrol around the

Soviet Union with all their guns loaded. They had six dual turrets or a total of 12 machine guns on each airplane.

Traditional operatives or spies continued to provide what was known as Human Intelligence. However, the world increasingly turned to electronics to provide the necessary information. America not only watched the dust clouds, but also investigated them, probed them, evaluated the capabilities of those on the steppes, and tried to analyze their intentions. The world was far too vulnerable and the Soviets were far too dangerous to leave them unobserved beyond horizons or borders. It was Stalin's will to close his domain tight with an iron curtain; it was America's resolve to look through that curtain for all the years of the Cold War. Aircraft sensors were the primary source of information during the entire Cold War.

The Americans declared their intelligence aircraft were outside the international borders. The Russians always said they were inside the borders and shot them down. The border historically was three nautical miles, later twelve miles and sometime others defined by treaty. Free passage is guaranteed outside these limits, but who was to enforce it.

The Russians kept shooting down American planes around her borders. America said they were in international waters off Russia. They were on legal flights and behaving legally under international law. The Russians shot them down anyway. The Russians did not announce it. America also seldom announced it. It was a silent shooting war, and America and its airplane crews always lost. The Russians pitted their fighters against America's reconnaissance planes, and the crews silently paid the price.

As many as 30-50 American planes were reported to have been shot down with impunity by the Soviet's by the time of the Soviet fall. They were not discriminate. Usually, they shot down military planes, but sometimes, they shot down fully loaded passenger planes on international commercial flights.

America's allies also flew such flights into the Asian mainland. Chiang's Nationalist Chinese retired to Taiwan in 1949, but they operated intelligence and other flights of their own against the Chinese Communists through much of the Cold war. This was part of their ongoing struggle for their homeland, still part of the Chinese Civil War. They, too, were shot down and their crewmembers killed. The electronic wars had to go on.

One supposes every air force in the world flew similar missions, even if they were very benign forms of the flights. However, one supposes their penetrations of international borders were probably very, very restricted.

Technical Intelligence In, Around and Over

The Low-Flyers continued to poke around the edge of the Communist world, or Iron Curtain as Churchill called it. They usually flew twelve miles or more offshore in international waters where it was legal, sometimes at high altitude, or at times they dropped to low altitudes. Their main purpose was to take continuous photographs with telephoto lenses and to capture electronic signals with electronic intelligence systems.

In the mid-1950s, the High-Flyers changed that paradigm. The edge-flyers left too much to the imagination; the world had become too dangerous for that. Missilery made it imperative that the interior be known. The High-Flyer traversed the Soviet Union from border to border while taking photographs on film with spectacular clarity and fidelity and while recording electronic intelligence all the while across the entire short-range microwave frequency spectrum. It would fly so high that no existing weapon could reach it and knock it down. The project was a spectacular success. The High-Flyer aircraft would continue its usefulness even well into the next century, more than forty years later!

Naturally, both Jackson and I had great interest in this new plane. I was especially inquisitive about this new technology and sought out any information he could find. However, the information was very closely held and he could not pierce the security blanket thrown over the project. It was one of the blackest programs.

CHAPTER 26

SOVIET RAPACITY

The Soviet Union did well in the acquisition of real estate during and following WWII. Even before the war was well underway, the Soviets took parts of Finland, eastern Poland, all of Estonia, Latvia, and Lithuania. At the end of the war, the Soviets extended their boundary deep into eastern Hungary and Rumania. Then they installed puppet Russian Communist governments in Poland, East Germany, Czechoslovakia, Hungary, Rumania and Bulgaria. They also installed or approved a Communist government in Yugoslavia but Tito proved to be a renegade and political heretic. The Soviets continued a love-hate relationship with him for 40 years but could not reduce him to puppetry. Afterwards, Albania became a rabid Communist state, completing the European satellites. The war saw Soviet Communists installed in North Korea and Outer Mongolia. All of these countries had local communist governments that were totally servile to the Soviet Union."

The Chinese civil war continued, and the Communists were assisted by the Soviets from 1946 until 1949, at which time Chiang was driven to Taiwan and a Communist government was installed in China. North Vietnam had fallen under the control of the local Communists who were waging a protracted civil war with the south."

With the massive Soviet acquisition of empire, the U.S. became alarmed. At that time, the U.S. produced fully one-half the industrial output of the entire world. It was the only nation with the ultimately powerful A-bomb. It was virtually unscathed by the devastation of WWII."

Yet Stalin believed that a state of continued belligerence had to be maintained with the West, or else the Americans would endanger his Soviet state. He made the ultimate bluff to shield his Sovietizing Eastern Europe and elsewhere. The Soviets encouraged the myth that they had hundreds of tanks in mechanized divisions behind their borders, ready to fall down on free Europe at a moment's notice. He purposely threw up these dust clouds over the horizon; he knew their effect in the marrow of our Western bones. The Soviets gave the impression that Soviet losses had been light during the war. There was an implication that Communist sympathizers, spies, and brilliant Western scientists had delivered bomb technology to them and their detonation of a test bomb was imminent. They indicated they could squeeze the Americans in a hundred places and bleed the West if it were not ready for war.

The bluff worked. Europe was in no mood for bloodletting; they were also in no position to defend against massive tank armies out of the east. With the Rosenberg executions and evidence in America of massive security leaks and a torrent of bomb secrets flowing into the Soviet Union, who knew what they knew? With fully one-third the French and Italian voters opting for Communist governments, the West looked vulnerable indeed. The Berlin Airlift crisis demonstrated Stalin was right and the West was vulnerable if it was not ready to fight — and it was not ready to fight.

The Soviets kept holding out the specter of thousands of tanks spilling through the Fulda Gap toward Frankfort-a-Main, Germany. NATO and the West bought into the bluff as often as not and this threat was used for seven decades.

"That's right," I said. I was talking to several casual friends I had made in the Air Force Officer's Club. "The Soviets thought they won the war and they did it with tanks. Their tank battles in the Ukraine convinced them and the Allies. The Russians only had to raise the specter of all those tanks sweeping across Russia and Germany and it seemed real to both sides.

"The same thing could be said about the missile gap," I said to my friends. "The Allies raised the specter of Russian missiles filling the skies on the way to the West. It seemed real. For generations, it seemed that the Russians had huge numbers of missiles and ICBM's while the West squandered its opportunity with pitifully small numbers. This missile gap was endorsed by the American president, the State Department, the Defense Department and others that should have known better. It was mostly a hoax. This did not mean, however, that the U.S. was not vulnerable. Nuclear annihilation is not a matter of numbers. When hit by a few Hydrogen bombs, the rest hardly matters. These have changed the world."

I was not a pacifist, far from it. But nuclear realities weighed heavily on me. I had witnessed the horrors of WWII and the Korean War. My thinking was profoundly changed by these wars. The holocaust ovens in East Germany and Poland particularly affected me. These terminated six million Jews and about that many non-Jews. Humans clearly have the will for extinction and nuclear technology suggests they have the means.

The specter of thousands of Russian tanks was all a monumental Stalin bluff. The Russian losses in the war were not light; she lost more than 20 million dead; her population was decimated. There were no hundreds or thousands of mechanized divisions; the Soviets had to bow to the manpower and economic realities, and deal with the demands of their devastated industry and housing; 25 percent of their population was homeless at the end of the war. Although the Soviets built city after city with 20 story apartment buildings across the whole skyline, the buildings were inferior and needed brick catchers at ground level to protect passers-by. Even so, the tiny apartments were vastly over-crowded. Stalin did not have a bomb, although the Soviets would astonish the world by detonating an A-bomb in the fall of 1949 and an H-bomb in 1953. Even so, it would take some time before a militarily significant number could be operational and a delivery system perfected. Thus, Stalin imposed his massive bluff and the world operated from 1945 until his death with military reality as he had willed it, as he would have it be. He manipulated his Potemkin Army, created his images of tanks and armies and nuclear rockets, and the world shared his images; the world saw them too, just as he pictured them with real three-dimension solidity. To them all, in the new world of unthinkable horrors, Stalin's images became the reality.

The American response was timid, but in the end it prevailed. In 1947, the Marshall Plan was instituted to infuse massive financial aid to the Western economies. Greece was being buffeted by internal Communist insurrection and Turkey was being subjected to massive Soviet pressures for territorial concessions; so the Truman Doctrine provided financial and military assistance to both.

In March 1946, Churchill had made his famous Iron Curtain speech in which he likened the Sovietization of Europe to an Iron Curtain. This view was severely criticized by liberals, for it was calling for the West to acknowledge the confrontational stand of the Soviets instead of the cooperative stand they had all wished for during the war.

Churchill's speech was followed in February 1948 by a famous article by George Kennan in the magazine, *Foreign Affairs*, defining a U.S. policy of patient, determined, and vigilant containment of the Soviet expansive drive, until the Soviet power structure became permanently altered. That containment became the essence of American policy toward the Soviets for the next half century.

A test of the policy came head-on within the year. The Soviets blocked all road and railway access to Berlin in May 1948. Some say Stalin wanted to force the West to recognize his European acquisitions and the borders the Soviet Union had imposed on Poland and the East Germany occupied zone while others said it was to prevent the formation of a West German government then being sponsored by the Western allies, Britain, France, and the US. Berlin was a political island, surrounded by the Soviet-held East German zone. The West avoided direct confrontation that would have resulted by attempting a military relief column or forceful removal of the blockade. It responded with a massive airlift. It brought in all the food, coal, and other critical resources needed to sustain Berlin life. The Soviets did not foresee this response. It indicates a surprising resolve and exceptional reaction capability by the West. The Soviets lifted the blockade in May 1949. The West then completed the formation of the Federal Republic of Germany while the Soviets responded by implementing a puppet Communist regime called the German Democratic Republic.

"Come on now!" I waved my hands into the air and spoke to no one in particular. Like Jackson, I often argued about many views of history. Naturally, our views did not coincide. I was trying to answer George's charge about oracles. I said, "All we oracles and gurus are ancient. How do you think we get so wise? When Dorothy opened the drape and discovered that the Wizard of Oz was really old Frank Morgan, didn't he have white hair and wasn't he ancient? He wasn't even a real wizard. He had no magic. He did it all by trickery, by pulleys and levers and belts; he was only an engineer, an inventor. What a letdown. Oracle or fakir, we all have to appear ancient. So I do it by fakery!"

"On this point they did agree. Engineering made the world go round and it just looked like magic."

At the end of the war, the Soviets controlled Korea north of the 38th parallel. They sponsored a Communist government that prompted the U.S. to respond with an independent government in the south. Stalin then tried repeatedly to participate in the occupation of Japan, his old Far Eastern enemy. He had declared war on Japan in the last few days of the war. However, the Americans rebuffed his participation in the ensuing occupation.

Frustrated and wanting a bigger role in Asia, he either ordered or encouraged North Korea to invade and absorb South Korea. The North attacked on June 25, 1950. The Americans and the United Nations came to the fighting assistance of South Korea. They were first beaten back to a toehold around Pusan on the South coast. Then, the Americans launched a counter-offensive with massive forces and drove the North back to the Yalu on the Manchurian border. The Chinese then came into the fray with massive infantry forces. The war ended in a stalemate on the 38th parallel in 1953, where it stands to this day.

The Korean War saw 2.5 million Chinese troops enter Korea and at least 400,000 casualties although some say they were as high as one million. Chou En-lai often confided that Stalin had outwitted China. Only Stalin's death made the armistice possible in 1953. Still, Stalin's Killing Machine ground on with Chinese, Korean, Americans, and Turks providing the grist.

Stalin had remained true to himself in the Sovietization of East Europe. When the Communist governments were installed, some degree of autonomy was hoped for. This hope did not last long. Tito of Yugoslavia hastened the demise of even a small degree of autonomy. He had the good fortune of a buffer from the Soviets with a limited common border so by guile, good fortune, and political maneuvering he managed a degree of independence and defiance until his death. Stalin reacted to this by tightening the Soviet grip in the other Satellite countries. He orchestrated, primarily in 1950, or had orchestrated, massive public purges of "Titoists" throughout Eastern Europe. Stalin put thousands of the leaders in the docks. They attributed these to the prompting of Tito, the CIA, other intelligence agencies, or international Zionism. The climax was usually execution. Stalin thereby exported his purges and show trials of the thirties.

Meanwhile, Beria remained head of his secret police and the state security apparatus. He masterminded the purges on Stalin's behalf, and bestrode Europe like a Goliath. Europe was awash in state killings, kidnappings, murders, "suicides," spies, and counterspies.

Stalin became more and more erratic. He denounced Molotov, the foreign minister, as a British spy and sent his wife to a labor camp. Stalin denounced Voroshilov as a British spy. Mikoyan was branded as a Turkish spy.

Stalin Dies

But then, on March 5, 1953, Joseph Vissarionovich Stalin died, at the age of 74. The Killing Machine ground to a halt. Neither the Apocalypse, the final Day of Judgment, nor the Kingdom of God appeared. Stalin was not God, but a mortal. He was merely struck down by mortal death. His evil dictatorship remained.

Lenin had created this sadistic, maniacal Killing Machine. He had created the omnipotent party; he had placed Stalin in supreme power as Secretary of the Party; he had created the ubiquitous secret police, the state security apparatus. It was all pre-ordained by Lenin's coup d'etat with Bolshevik terrorists.

I continued talking with George Grayburn in our long-running conversation about Russia and German.

"This indicates the ideological underpinnings of Stalin's regime and how it rebuffed the theoretical writings of Trotsky. After Stalin assumed power, the fight between him and his main opponent, Leon Trotsky, became ever more vitriolic. Stalin later exiled Trotsky.

"Trotsky's assassination was not just a malicious afterthought or loose end on the part of Stalin. It was the culmination of a systematic and bloody terror directed against a whole generation of Bolshevik leaders, and against the young revolutionaries of a second generation prepared to defend the ideas of Marxism against the bureaucratic, repressive regime developing under Stalin.

"Trotsky favored an idea of permanent revolution as opposed to Stalin's bureaucracy notion of building socialism in one country."

"Why, if Trotsky was one of the foremost leaders of the Bolshevik party and the head of the Red Army, did he allow Stalin to concentrate power in his hands? Why did Trotsky not take power himself? Stalin had the power so why did he not have Trotsky killed early in the revolution?

No, no. Their difference was a fundamental struggle about the nature of the revolution and the revolutionaries. Both had some sort of ideology that strongly influenced them. Trotsky was essentially the ideological theorist of the Party, who wrote and published innumerable tracts. Stalin had different views that were much more pragmatic, even if they were the practical ideology of dictatorship.

"Clearly, from a Marxist standpoint, it is superficial to think of the conflict which developed after 1923 as a personal struggle between rival leaders. Stalin and Trotsky, in their different ways, personified conflicting social and political forces, Trotsky in a conscious way, Stalin less consciously. Trotsky opposed Stalin with theoretical and political means; Stalin fought Trotsky and his supporters with state-sponsored terror. 'Stalin conducts a struggle on a totally different plane' Trotsky once wrote. 'He seeks to strike not at the ideas of the opponent, but at his skull.'

"Lenin appeared to be a duality in his personality and leadership. On the one hand, he was a dictator employing all the devices of state terror to win his way regardless of the consequences. On the other, he was an intellectual who could state his methods in theoretical and intellectual terms. He was dictatorial within Russia. However, his founding of the Comintern and preaching to other countries was very attractive to them and made his movement respectable on the surface.

"With Lenin's health failing, he accommodated his bloody side by supporting Stalin as leader of the Party and thereby the apparent successor. Stalin was the ultimate expression in the dictatorial side of the Bolsheviks, unbridled in his use of terror when operating the apparatus of the state. He expressed his contempt for theory and the intellectualism of foreigners,

"Trotsky had long appealed to Lenin's intellectual side. He was the effective theoretician of the party, having written continuously during his long exiles with Lenin and other party leaders. He put a relatively benign face on the party with foreigners. He gave a pseudo-intellectualism to Communism, and made it appear respectable, more or less. The party and Trotsky put a lot of effort in wooing foreign intellectuals to their cause. They especially pursued foreign politicians, artists, academics, scientists, filmmakers and news organizations.

"Stalin's theory of bureaucracy manifested itself eventually as a *privalegencia* in which the party, Stalin, decided and implemented, with exile, mass murder, and all the fruits of his will. Stores for the *privilegencia* were cornucopias while those for others were barren, primitive, and lacking.

"Paradoxically, Trotsky, artists and intellectuals, all helped propagate the myth of Communist intellectualism and respectability and hid the ultimate obscenities committed in its name. This made them co-conspirators with Stalin, the opposite of their intentions. One must be careful when '*fellow traveling*.' Many devils lurk along the way."

There was a lot of political talk and even demonstrations on the Columbia campus. Bianca and Charlotte saw each other every day. They often discussed these rallies but never participated in them. Both had their special terms. Bianca was an Argentine that had to watch her political activities where there was someone always watching. Charlotte's father was the ambassador to Argentina so she had a social position to watch as well as being vulnerable to political activity.

Nakita Khrushchev as Leader

After Stalin's death, there was a grab for power. Beria and Malenkov arranged the Leningrad Purge to eliminate the Leningrad leaders from contending for power, the evidence shows. Beria then made a play for power by declaring the Jewish doctor's plot had been a hoax arranged by one of his assistants under Stalin's direction.

Before Beria could consolidate his position, Krushchev got the support of the military, including Marshals Zhukov and Koniev. They arrested Beria in his offices in the main secret police building on Dzerzhinsky Square near the Kremlin in Moscow. Beria was summarily tried and executed. Several of his aides were arrested and shot on the spot. Nikita Khrushchev's Soviet dictatorship was assured. The Soviet state remained true to itself while the world intellectualized on the mysteries and mysticisms of Communism.

In February 1956, Khrushchev decided to dissociate the party from Stalin. "This would give the illusion of normalcy and stability and reform. He thus made his secret speech to the 20th Party Congress revealing many of the 'excesses' of Stalin. This was a sensation. It undermined not only the Soviet government but also those of the satellites that were still ruled in a Stalinesque fashion.

Khrushchev quickly realized his reforms were undermining the dictatorial basis for the whole Soviet regime. He was neither an educated nor a sophisticated man, but he understood power and how to manipulate it. He let the reforms slip by and kept the tyrannical Soviet power in place.

Keeping the dictatorial and communistic regime in place was the goal of the leaders from Lenin to the installation of Gorbachev. Gorbachev miss-read the whole thing and attempted to reform the party and government. In this, he was a dolt and almost single-handedly brought down the Soviet system. For this, he is held as a hero in the West. Nevertheless, few Soviets or ex-Soviets see it that way.

Polish factory workers rioted in June 1956 for 'bread and freedom,' causing more than 50 deaths. In a confrontation with Khrushchev, a degree of independence was granted which proved to be a harbinger for the future.

The Poles were to be the central figures in pulling down the Soviet temple.

1956 was a watershed year for military action at the grass roots level. The Russians invaded Hungary while Britain and Israel invaded the Sinai with thousands of tanks and they threatened Cairo.

In October, the Hungarians rioted in sympathy with the Poles. Both the Hungarian secret police and Soviet Troops fired on them. Rioting spread throughout the country. After extensive political and military maneuvering, the full might of the Soviet Army swept into Hungary on November 4 and crushed all resistance within a few days. Over 3,000 people were killed, 15,000 imprisoned, and over 200,000 fled the country before order was established.

In the midst of this, in October 1956, Israeli, British, and French troops attacked Egypt over differences on the Suez Canal. Khrushchev threatened to intervene with nuclear weapons and rockets if they did not withdraw. The U.S. also demanded a withdrawal, which was quickly affected. The U.S. refused any aid to Hungary during its trials. America's message during all of this was mixed and unclear.

By this time, Jackson was working in a California defense company. He and his friends at work had intense interest in the Hungarian debacle and in the Suez escapade. This made wonderful lunchtime conversation since the news rolled on like a military movie.

On August 23, 1958, the Chinese began the bombardment of Quemoy and Matsu Islands, Chinese Nationalist Islands in the mouth of Chinese mainland Amoy harbor. This was followed with numerous dogfights between the Nationalists and Communists with jet fighters along the Taiwan Strait in which the Communists suffered heavy losses using Russian-made aircraft. It is thought that the Chinese were testing both Russian and American resolve.

In the end, America stood up with considerable resolve after lifting huge numbers of American troops onto Taiwan and placing the American Navy along the Taiwan Straits in the way of the Communists. Then America indicated a willingness to go to war if the Chinese insisted. The incident was allowed to recede, but the Chinese Communists had been humiliated.

Jackson was in Taiwan during this time and witnessed many of the events directly.

He was seriously involved with the technical intelligence gathered in Taiwan. The airborne equipment that he was responsible for needed attention now and then. For this, he had to be aboard the aircraft and have access to the antennas and systems in the aircraft.

Jackson had access to the over-flight aircraft. He sometime served as a temporary crew member. This was in recognition of his status as a contractor that was needed to maintain the special equipment. Some of his flights were just off the mainland along the Taiwan Strait. He flew these trips to align and work on his equipment. The aircraft would fly hundreds of miles down the Straits, then retrace its steps. Sometimes these were flight tests of the aircraft and stood off a safe distance from shore. At other times, a mission was assigned to an aircraft that then flew just outside international waters, along the edge of China.

These were avionics experiments with ultimate realism. In this, he could manipulate antennas, trouble-shoot equipment, optimize their configurations and quickly determine results. He was thrilled with being able to control the experiments so closely. He always had a series of experiments he wanted to run to prove this or that hypothesis.

As to the danger of these flights, they were down the coast at 12 miles or so offshore in international waters. There was freedom of the seas in these waters in that the law supported free passage. Unfortunately, the Chinese Communists saw things differently and tended to support their own laws. One never knew when they would send fighter jets down the Strait to punish the flyers. By this time, both the Communists and Nationalists operated jet aircraft. It was not difficult to predict whether these or WWII reconnaissance aircraft would prevail in any conflict. In other words, there was always an element of risk in these Strait flights.

This did not deter Jackson.

Far more risk was to occur on over-flights into the mainland. Jackson wanted to go on an over-flight. He did go on at least one. He could then manipulate antennas, optimize their configurations and quickly determine results. He was thrilled with being able to control his system so closely. Except, in this case, real missions were performed. The Communist government was sure to contest these flights with machine guns, canon and rockets. These were usually performed at night with darkened aircraft.

It was known that part of Chiang's army diverted to the Burma jungles in the 1949 Civil War. These units maintained contact and structure with the Taiwan headquarters so it was not difficult to accept that there was transport across Asia to fulfill this role. These were kept separate from the intelligence flights.

The world then knew or should have known that flights of various kinds were taking place across Asia to support these vast distances.

Jackson was sometimes aboard the aircraft while it was flying down the Taiwan Strait just off the international border of China. These were low-level flights so there was only a limited risk in doing this it was thought.

Jackson knew that the more accurately frequencies were known, the narrower channel bandwidths had to be for monitoring. He therefore made measurements on these Strait flights. This allowed very narrow channels and this increased the distances that could be achieved. Further, antenna adjustments were very sensitive. He made several flights like this and was able to gather a striking amount of low altitude technical intelligence. His reach extended deep into China, even if the flights were at a low level.

Alex also had equipment on these aircraft. He did not participate in penetration flights. He and Jackson continually discussed improvements and experiments that were often incorporated into their equipment.

I was very proud of the flights I made. I assumed my participation was important and I made a clear contribution to the Cold War.

At about this time, in 1960, Khrushchev's forces shot down the unarmed U-2 High-Flyer reconnaissance aircraft near Sverdlovsk with a missile, deep within the Soviet Union. Soon thereafter, they shot down an unarmed RB-47 in the Arctic Ocean. Both of these occurred in the last days of the Eisenhower presidency and both were reported in the world press.

The Soviets had treated Mao as a client or junior partner. They had given him equipment, international political support, and both military and technical assistance. China said nice things about the Soviets and vice versa. Yet, there were fundamental differences that eventually caused a schism. In 1960, the Chinese resented the historical Russian encroachment on their borders and still do to this day. They had more people than any other nation, and they would not see themselves forever as a junior partner. They felt they fought Russia's war in Korea. There was also reason for them to resent the lack of Soviet support in the Taiwan crisis. This was to be compounded later, in 1965, by the Soviet support for Vietnam, which they felt was in their sphere. There was also the American and South Vietnam war on their border, which was to threaten again U.S. retaliation against China, not the Soviets, as in the Korean War.

In any event, the issues came to a head in 1960 with overt verbal attacks by the Chinese on Khrushchev and Soviet policies. An article, *Long Live Leninism*, appeared in the Chinese organ, Red Flag. It was attributed to Mao. It stated the Communists should not launch nuclear war; but if the West did so, he proclaimed, "On the debris of a dead imperialism, the victorious people would create very swiftly a civilization thousands of times higher than the capitalists, and a truly beautiful system for themselves."

This and similar nonsense formed the central verbal issue between China and the Soviets, a proxy for the hostility between the two regimes. As the controversy escalated, in 1960 the Soviets abruptly withdrew all 1,390 technical experts assisting China on 247 projects, often sabotaging them or taking the blueprints with them. China was undergoing a crippling famine at the time where millions were said to be starving. This public schism and the future hostility portended between the two Communist super-powers was the most important occurrence of the many dramas of 1960.

John Kennedy was inaugurated in January 1961. In April, he backed the invasion of Castro's Cuba by Cuban refugees. This was a disaster for the U.S., in that the U.S. Navy delivered the invasion forces, but Kennedy ordered its withdrawal when the forces ashore met stiff military resistance and were in desperate trouble. Most soon perished. This debacle became known as the Bay of Pigs invasion. A summit was held in June 1961, where Khrushchev sized up Kennedy as a lightweight, a playboy, and presented him with demands to withdraw from Berlin.

Kennedy supported the East Germans in constructing the Berlin wall to staunch the flow of skilled workers and professionals from East to West Germany. It was started in August 1961. The Soviets then resumed atmospheric bomb tests, escalated their rivalry with China, and multiplied their adventures in the Third World. This led to the Cuban Missile Crisis in October 1962, with the placement of Soviet missiles in Cuba and the U.S. Naval blockade of Soviet ships; both countries threatened nuclear retaliation. Armageddon was avoided when Khrushchev backing down and was publicly humiliated. He was ousted in 1964 and replaced by Leonid Breshnev.

The Vietnam War was sharply escalated when President Johnson committed to the defense of South Vietnam in the spring of 1965. This was America's second full-scale war with a Soviet proxy in a single generation. It was to last for eight years — arguably the longest war in American history — and have a profound effect on America and its people.

"Breshnev died in 1982, and was replaced by Y. V. Andropov, to be followed by K. V. Chernenko in 1984. Gorbychev was installed in 1985, where he served until 1991 and the overthrow of the Soviet Union by Boris Yeltsin.

CHAPTER 27

SOVIET RAPACITY IN CHINA

The Soviets declared war on Japan on August 8, 1945 just five days prior to the end of WWII, on August 14, 1945, after massive military preparations along the Manchurian border. They attacked across the whole border, quickly overwhelmed the Japanese and occupied the area. The Soviet attack and the handover of Manchuria to the Communists were decided at Yalta early in 1945, to the chagrin of the Nationalists. The Soviets handed over to the Communists most of Manchuria, the arms of the eight hundred thousand Japanese military force, and huge hidden arms caches. In 1946, The KMT and Chinese Communist Party, CCP, armies began widespread war on each other across China. Most called this the Chinese Civil War.

For this, Soviet Russia appeared to totally commit to the Chinese Communists. On the other hand, America's support for Chiang, even during WWII, was in fits and starts, first under Ambassador Patrick J. Hurley and then under Gen. George C. Marshall as Roosevelt's Secretary of State and Special Envoy. In a standard U.S. diplomatic ploy, the Americans pressured Chiang and Mao to accept a cease-fire while negotiating, and then to accept a coalition government with each sharing power. Several times, both agreed to an American-imposed cease-fire while negotiations took place. Assumedly, the U.S. acted in good faith, but we have seen how Stalin and the Communists implemented this concept across Eastern Europe. There should have never been a doubt that coalition meant a totalitarian government reporting to Stalin in Moscow. The CCP accepted the cease-fire and coalition government proposed for negotiations, then worked to undermine it and to seek advantage on the battlefield. Afterward, when the situation was advantageous to them, they ignored the cease-fire, attacked, and continued the war. Then, under prodding by the U.S., the process was repeated.

Although the West often refers to Chiang as a dictator, this cannot be sustained by logic. Chiang was deeply involved in uniting his country according to the democratic principles of Sun Yat-Sen from his earliest history until his death. Chiang was on the right side of history. The Communists perverted his position. Nixon and Kissinger apparently bought into this perversion and abandoned Chiang in 1972. Many say that America can be an untrustworthy ally, based on her experiences in China.

Many of his decisions and policies did stem from a strong mentality, but he was always restrained by the multi-faceted KMT political party. However, he never veered from his belief and conviction in the three principles championed by Sun Yat-Sen for the KMT. These were the three stages of the revolution, namely, 1) military unification, 2) political tutelage, and 3) constitutional democracy. He judged that by 1940 most of the revolution had passed from the first stage into one of political tutelage. The KMT implemented some teaching teams to train the populace in the fundamentals of democracy. One can argue against this, but after the exile to Taiwan in 1949 with two million of Chiang followers, the KMT evolved into a multi-party democratic government, as advertised.

Chiang's son, Chiang Ching-kuo, became the president of Taiwan in 1980 and initiated reforms. One of these was to convert from a single party system to a multiparty system by election. These were adopted by Chiang's successors through 2000 and beyond. Many consider Taiwan and its 25 million people as the first democratically ruled nation in Asia.

What happened at the end of the Civil War? There was a paroxysm of killings. When this peasant mass and army entered a city or village, they killed officials, police, teachers, doctors, professionals, peasants and village elders. There were mass killings like this across the whole country.

It's estimated that 2.4 million people were killed in the Chinese Revolution. According to some, the Civil War in 1928-1937 saw 2 million dead. The Civil War from 1946 to 1949 caused 1.2 million deaths. These seem awfully low estimates from what is known."

But this was just to inaugurate the Communist system. What happened under their rule?

Well, Mao's "Great Leap Forward" from 1958 to 1961 sent the non-peasant class into the fields and rice paddies. In addition, every group had a backyard forge to melt down pots and pans to jump to Mao's industrial nation. This nonsense caused famine and hunger, where it is reported about 38 million died.

To punctuate this, Mao's "Cultural Revolution" from 1966 to 1969 overturned all civil code and social rationality. Mao's Chinese turned class against class and generation against generation. This holocaust killed about 11 million more Chinese.

PART 3

CHAPTER 28

INTEL WARS: LOW-FLYERS, HIGH-FLYERS AND SPACE-FLYERS

The High-Flyer had been the blackest of the black.

It was America's most famous intelligence craft. I remembered those sleek, glider-like jet airplanes, those High-Flyers. When they began their run down the runway, they were ungainly with their little outrigger wheels and long, drooping wings. Then, those wheels dropped off, and the long, long wings with the skids on the end lost their ungainly droop and lifted up; now they reached gracefully upwards. The silvery bird was now long and willowy with great, outstretched wings. It was beautiful. The nose and cockpit stretched out, out beyond the wing roots in a long thrust forward. The only contact to the ground now was two inline wheels, just below the belly. Then it lifted off. It never did fly. It slowly rotated until the nose pointed straight up and it just zoomed and zoomed and disappeared straight up. Almost immediately, the sound was gone. The only evidence that it had existed were two or three attendants standing on the end of the runway, and a pick-up truck retrieving the little outrigger wheel struts. God, what a plane!

It continued its climb until it was over 70,000 feet in the air. It flew across continents at over 500 miles per hour. All the while, it listened and looked and determined if the closed, secret society was an immediate threat to her neighbors, to the world. It was too high to be shot down, too high to violate the sovereignty of its day. It was a wild thing that could not be reached. The Soviets were having their way everywhere, but with this, they could not have their way. They could not rape Europe by surprise, or the world, and they could not slaughter their own people and ravage their countryside without it being known. It put a light on the dark recesses of the Soviet soul. Best of all, the Soviets had no way of stopping this wonderful machine that heard and saw. It was the eyes and ears of America's defense.

Without this machine and without the electronics listening posts all across Eurasia, a vulnerable world could stand at the ramparts, but could not see beyond the horizon. That would have remained true even as armies of the Soviet Huns kicked up the dust to strike terror in the West's sedentary hearts.

The Soviets were furious. They were furious on two counts.

One, they could watch the High-Flyers go over on radar but they couldn't do anything about it. Their fighters would rise up to meet the High Flyers. They would climb up, up towards it. Then their controls would get mushy as they reached their upper altitude limit. They would hang there on their engine, mushing along. Then they would fall away as the wings and engine had to acknowledge aerodynamic reality. The High-Flyer would watch these abortive attackers over and over as it continued its steady cruise high above as if nothing was happening below it. Just a few dogs now and then chasing hubcaps, and the Soviets stewed and stewed, but they could only chase the hubcaps.

Two, the Soviets could not tell anyone about it, or their subjugated satellite states would recognize this impotence. Who knew how they would take it? Therefore, the Soviets fumed. Every once in a while, a short statement by a Soviet revealed this fuming, but you had to know how to read the enigma. Otherwise, it sounded like another Russian inanity. It was an ultimate inside joke to those in the know. It was the blackest of the black state secrets to them and to us.

Even Khrushchev, after the famous 1959 kitchen debate in Moscow with Nixon, made a remark that was obviously inane, something about those damn Americans with their special aircraft provocations. He swore they would get theirs as he clinched his fists, gritted his teeth and turned red. Khrushchev said this to reporters after the debate, but they did not make any sense of it. One reported it in an American paper, the Los Angeles Times, as another bit of Khrushchev nonsense. Jackson saw the short clip in the paper, and he knew. Khrushchev knew! Nixon, although the remark was not made to him, knew! However, there was no acknowledgment and no flicker of recognition by anyone. Eisenhower knew! In the important world capitals, they knew!

These kinds of remarks were made by the Soviets several times and reported, but at no time was there the least indication that anyone recognized the significance of the inane remarks.

Thus, at least a tiny few could sleep soundly because they could examine the Huns' dust. They could evaluate the threat. Thereby, they could repel it. Meanwhile the Huns writhed in their indignation and impotence. Their armies could not arrive from over the horizon to ravage an unsuspecting sedentary land without warning.

Then one day in 1960, Khrushchev succeeded. He knocked one of the High-Flyers down with a new missile. Khrushchev got the pilot alive, the talking truth. The world writhed in the uncovered reality that had required such elaborate guises. Khrushchev gloated. The Soviets could now hide behind their cloaks and the world had no recourse.

Wait! The world of 1960 had changed from the earlier world. It was a new age. The age of space had dawned. The new truly High-Flyers were now Earth Satellites beyond the 14 miles altitude and 500 mph of the High-Flyer; they were now at a little over 100 miles altitude and 18,000 mph velocity of earth satellites. What was a sovereignty question at 14 miles was not a sovereignty question at all at 100 miles height. The world recognized that satellites were legal eyes and ears. We could now legally see and hear the Huns. For all future time, we would see through the dust clouds over the horizon and follow the moves of the Huns.

And just as gunpowder and the gun had ended the tyranny of the horseman of the steppes for sedentary people, High-Flyer aircraft and satellites had ended the military allegory of the steppe in that all the earth is now watched from above, and the meaning of military surprise by modern Huns is redefined forever. The tyranny of the steppe is gone, for both the ancient and the modern Huns of the world.

There is no doubt now that there is an international right to fly satellites at 100 miles height or greater over any nation. We do it. The Soviets do it. England, France, China, Japan, and on and on, do it. We all do it. It's now an international right, as there are international rights of navigation on the high seas, challenged only by pirates and criminal nations. The Soviets fell into that latter category, internationally as well as domestically, as it knocked down one after another American reconnaissance planes, and an occasional passenger plane.

The High-Flyer had served its purpose. For five years, five critical, watershed years, it provided a transition through the introduction of intercontinental ballistic missiles (ICBMs) to reconnaissance and spy satellites. The satellites and missiles are now ineluctably connected for offense and defense. It is the Yin and the Yang. However, the transition for the defense before that time was the High-Flyer. Khrushchev had succeeded, but his victory was hollow, his quarry had transitioned into a new era, and was now the spent casing of the projectile. The Huns were pushed further into the hinterlands, but just as with his puzzling remarks, only a few were equipped to know.

Even so, the High-Flyers had special capabilities that would continue to make them indispensable in every crisis for decades to come, even well beyond the turn of the 20th century.

Stalin's reign was one man's will to re-impose the nomadic-sedentary culture of the steppe whereby his Russians would secrete themselves beyond the self-imposed horizon. Then, they had the option of falling on an unsuspecting and unprepared Europe and Asia with scores of mechanized cavalry divisions, or throwing themselves at the Americans, or at anyone in the world with submarines, ships, aircraft, and missiles. Men with gunpowder stopped the nomads of the steppe in the years around 1700. This demonstrated that the only course for rational men was to use technology to rid themselves of this Soviet scourge. This denied Stalin's re-imposition of the steppe anachronism, of the dust-devil metaphor, after about 1965. The High-Flyers were a major response of rational men.

This was the ultimate inside joke. Like all really good inside jokes, it is compartmentalized and clique-oriented, and can never be fully known or appreciated. It is too convoluted and filled with irony.

Low Flyers In and Around

Jackson then went to Taiwan and spent the next several years there with Chiang's Air Force.

When Chiang Kai-shek had to abandon the mainland in 1949, the Communists had finally won the Chinese Mainland. There were attempts by the Communists to follow Chiang to Taiwan and defeat him, but they couldn't pull it off.

Afterwards, the Kuomintang (KMT) Government, under Chiang, had to fly into the mainland to assess the developments and particularly look for military concentrations and movements that looked preparatory for an invasion of Taiwan. They had to assess what kinds of weapons the Chinese Communists were building or getting from the Russians. At that time, there was a honeymoon between the U.S. and Taiwan, and those same questions were of paramount concern to us Americans.

The importance of this had been made clear in the Korean War when we fought a war with the Chinese Communists, and later in Vietnam, where we fought another proxy war with them and the Russians. In 1958, there was a major skirmish between Taiwan and the mainland, and there could have been an invasion of Taiwan.

This was the Taiwan Quemoy-Matsu crisis?

Those are two islands off Fukien Province across the strait from Taiwan. The Nationalist Government on Taiwan controls them; they're essentially in the Amoy harbor mouth, only a couple of miles from the mainland. The Chinese Communists started an intense shelling of the islands and made a major buildup of army troops next to them. The Nationalists poured troops and supplies onto the Islands. The Communist Air Force came zooming into the Straits and South China Sea, challenging and shooting down Nationalist aircraft. They had Russian MIG-15s and the Nationalists had American F-86s. A major air battle then was joined which lasted a month or so. It looked like the invasion was on.

Then the American military responded. American cargo planes started arriving in large numbers. The American planes would taxi up and hundreds of troops would pile out fully armed and in full battle gear, in jungle greens. They pitched tents on the grass right on the field; soon there were thousands of them in a major battle bivouac. This happened all over the island.

As it turned out, Quemoy and Matsu withstood the shelling, the Nationalist navy continued to operate, and the navy and air force continued to resupply them. The Nationalist air force overwhelmingly defeated their challengers in dogfights. One forgets actual numbers, but about 50 or so Communist aircraft were shot down to only a handful of Nationalist aircraft.

"Charlie, you should have been there. Jackson told this story to me the next time I saw him in Larchmont. The whole island went on a war footing while Jackson and his friends had a front row seat. We all sat on the midfield grass and watched it all unfold.

But, most important of all, Eisenhower had demonstrated America's resolve in containing the Communists once again. Our Navy and Air Force and Army and Marines had interposed themselves between the two Chinas. That was required under the terms of our treaties, and made clear we were going to live up to that commitment even if it meant war. The Communists backed down. That was the most significant threat we've had over Taiwan.

It was funny how things happened. In many respects it was business as usual on Taiwan during this time, although thousands of troops came pouring onto the Island. At the officers club, the newcomers were turned away from the Saturday night dance. "Only dress uniforms," the doorman said.

The newcomers were, naturally, in jungle green battle dress. They argued long, hotly, and with logic. "Only dress uniforms," the doorman said. Military police were on hand to enforce the rules. Therefore, they didn't get in.

After a month or so, things returned to normal. The troops left. The American fighter planes and transports disappeared and everything went back to the way it was before. The Chinese Communists haven't made a frontal attack on Taiwan since then.

Did your Chinese Air Force planes go into the mainland?

Of course. The Nationalists maintain they are the legitimate Government of China, and it is their country. Why shouldn't they go in?

Everything was kind of goofy. The Communist air defenses would monitor the entry, and they'd try to shoot the plane down all across China. They shot missiles from aircraft, from the ground, from guns; you name it. Naturally, the planes were painted solid black, and they flew at night. There were no lights. They always had to fly low, often in the trees, or that is how it seemed. It sounds like a fairy tale to me.

Everything was a fairy tale in China. Things have changed now. However, others and I were in on this joke, although we could not tell one another how funny and ironic things really were. Nixon and Khrushchev were also both in on this joke!

I said, "I usually stayed in Tokyo when going to Japan, but I also spent a lot of time at airbases,"

"Doing what?" he was asked.

"He didn't say," he laughed and giggled since he was in on the joke.

It's like that Spike Jones song, *Cloe*, in the movies where the band yells, "Cloe, where are you, you old bat?"

The phone rings and Spike's man answers it. "You don't say," he says.

"You don't say. You don't say," he says.

"Who was that?" the band asks.

"He didn't say," his man answered.

"And so it was. He didn't say."

Jackson laughed. Those in on the joke always laughed, but each had to make up his own punch line. It was the rule of the game. It was part of the joke!

Space-Flyers

Everything is different now, Jackson thought. With a plane, one makes a pass only occasionally. Then, the results may have been just a fluke, nothing was happening. It's a bigger, riskier operation, but you can use a decoy to flush them out, run it in to shake them up and get them to respond; then you follow this up with the real thing, the intelligence collection aircraft, while you collect the data on their response.

When a really big thing occurs and you need continuous information, you can fly continuously but it's enormously expensive and risky, like the Cuban missile crisis. We ran plane after plane, kept them flying, and some were shot down. For every plane you've got in the air, you need two or three more in the repair and preparation cycle. That gets expensive and requires a lot of support and people. Again, you pass over and then you're gone. They are free to fiddle until the next one comes over and that has to be for a very short time and is infrequent.

Therefore, airplanes are miraculous, but there's a limit in what they can do. Besides, there are very severe political consequences of aircraft over-flights. There's still not a clear definition of what altitude a nation's sovereignty ends, but it's pretty clear that sovereignty doesn't reach up to orbital altitude, which is a hundred miles or so; but countries still insist it does reach aircraft altitude which is up to 20 miles or more.

With satellites we don't have the over-flight sovereignty problem. There are basically two kinds of satellites, the orbiting and the synchronous. The orbiting satellite allows you to get down as low as a hundred miles or so, but it decays from there in a few days, so you usually get up to a hundred and twenty miles or higher. A circular orbit is reached with about 18,000 miles per hour and takes a little over an hour to complete. If the spacecraft goes faster, it moves out or starts an elliptical orbit which moves it to the far away apogee for part of the cycle and then to the perigee or to a low altitude for the opposite part of the cycle.

The other type is the synchronous satellite. If you put it at about 25,000 miles up at the equator at the right speed that is about 23,000 miles per hour, then it will circle the earth once as the earth rotates once, or it stays exactly overhead. Putting this into position is a lot trickier and takes more energy, fuel, or velocity than the orbiter. The communications problem is worse, since it is further away, 25,000 miles versus 120 miles, say.

The orbiter is great, since it is close, but it only comes around every hour or so and is in sight slightly over ten minutes. It precesses, so it's just seldom over where you want it to be and when you want it to be there. You can put up more and more of them to give you a better chance.

The synchronous satellite is really fantastic, since it always looks at its fixed area. You can move it around the equator to look at a particular hot spot. There's an exception. Your antennas have to be much bigger now, to make up for the huge distances.

In all reality, the moon should be studded with hundreds of optical and radio telescopes and radars looking down at the earth to prevent military surprises. What the world needs to do is shine these bright lights into every corner. Deny the dictatorships and tyrannies the cloak of secrecy. That will happen sooner or later. It will not stop tyranny, but it will make it more difficult.

But, thank God for the Space-Flyers and those who run them! I was serious about this.

Chiang's Air Force; In and Over

China under Chiang Kai-shek had a history of using foreign air forces to support weaknesses in the Chinese Air Force. He sought help from both the Soviets and Americans when his Japanese war began in 1937. Only the Russians responded with their Russian Volunteer Group (RVG), analogous to the American Flying Tigers. They provided 700 planes and 2,000 pilots in 1938-1940, many fresh from the Spanish Civil War. They were credited with downing 425 Japanese aircraft. This effort was discontinued when the Germans attacked Russia and all were recalled.

China then asked the U.S. to provide similar support. The response was the American Volunteer Group, or AVG, better known as the Flying Tigers. They arrived in China in 1941. They were credited with 229 downed Japanese aircraft. They were converted to regular U.S. Army Air Corps units in 1942, after America entered the war.

Taiwan has recently acknowledged some of their roles in operating intelligence aircraft. The acknowledgements were by both high government officials and by newspapers in Taiwan. Even the Associated Press was involved with these releases. These were made to coincide with the opening of a museum honoring the heroes that participated in the program.

Chiang's Chinese government in Taiwan is said in recent web pages to have operated one Low-Flyer and one High-Flyer squadron, known as Black Bats and Black Cats, with support by the Americans. Black bats sweep back and forth near the bushes and trees at night while black cats sit arrogantly and stoically like Cheshires above it all. Both accomplish their missions. Thus, the Nationalist Chinese continued their admiration and adoration of American flyers and aircraft for a long time.

The recent web pages indicate Black Bats flew missions over Mainland China, dropped agents and gathered military signal and photographic intelligence around military sites. The squadron was formed in 1953 and the last operational mission was flown in 1967. The internet pages indicate they flew several types of aircraft, such as the B-17, B-26, P-2V, P-3 and transports, it is said. The squadron specialized in very low-level airspace penetration, usually at 300-600 feet altitude. They hugged the ground in order to evade radars, fighter interceptions and ground-launched missiles.

According to Annie Huang of the Associated Press, as paraphrased in the following paragraphs, the Black Bats' story emerged in Taiwan in 1992. This occurred when China repatriated the remains of 14 crewmembers that died when their plane was shot down over the mainland in 1959. A few books on their exploits were published in subsequent years, including one by the Taiwanese Defense Ministry detailing their clandestine China over-flights. However, the Bats had remained largely anonymous until the gathering early in June at Hsinchu's National Tsing Hua University, where hundreds of Taiwanese observed a minute of silence for the 148 Black Bats who did not return from their missions and paid an emotional tribute to the few surviving members of the group.

Seventy-seven-year-old Chu Chen was one of about 10 surviving Black Bats pilots. Like others in the group, he kept his exploits secret until recently — even from members of his own family. "If we had disclosed anything, we could have been shot as intelligence agents leaking secrets," he said. It may have been so. One can never be too sure about these things.

The Black Bats' major function, it was reported, was to drop Taiwanese spies to incite mainlanders to rise up against communist rule. A former navigator recalled numerous parachute infiltration missions and extolled the bravery of the agents. "They tossed their weapons out first and then they jumped," he said.

A pilot said, "Unarmed, we broke through the Iron Curtain in the darkness of the night. Each time, we were confident that we could get the mission accomplished."

It was said that besides inserting agents, Black Bat aircraft also flew near Chinese radar installations to obtain their electronic signatures in preparation for possible conflict with the Communists. They gathered electronic intelligence on radars, missiles, and weapons in general, and especially on Communist air defense systems. Crews also helped the U.S. monitor Chinese nuclear weapons programs in the early 1960s by collecting air samples from suspected Chinese test sites.

A Taiwanese defense expert, Andrew Yang of Taipei's Council of Advanced Political Studies, said programs like the Black Bats provided Washington with valuable intelligence about China's secretive nuclear weapons program when the mainland was largely isolated from the rest of the world. "Taiwan was an important source of information for the U.S., enabling it to avoid taking actions arising from misjudging the situation," he said.

Taiwan's Defense Ministry said that both the Bats and the Cats made "important contributions."

"They ... provided crucial strategic and military intelligence that helped stabilize the Taiwan Straits situation," the ministry said in a statement. "We will never forget this chapter of our history."

From 1953 to 1967, the squadron flew 838 missions and 148 crewmembers went down with their planes. A few were captured after being shot down.

The web pages indicate that the Black Cats flew 102 High-Flyer surveillance flights over Mainland China between 1962 and 1974. These squadrons gathered significant intelligence during the Cold War that was shared with the U.S. The intelligence gathered included evidence of a military build-up on the Sino-Soviet border in western China in the late 60s.

When President Nixon visited China in 1972, he and Secretary of State Kissinger made briefings to the Chinese in Beijing on the Soviet's deployment. This was to convince the Chinese leadership of American sincerity and that the U.S. wished them as allies as opposed to the Soviets. The briefings exposed the extent of U.S. intelligence gathering. They were made without the knowledge or approval of any U.S. or Chinese intelligence organization, apparently. In a web page transcription of the meeting recently released, Nixon said that no one knew of the briefings except the persons in the room. This is said to have startled the top Chinese military brass who were invited on Nixon's request.

This was another giant step in the abandonment of our WWII allies to the advantage of the Communist Chinese. Nixon's dealings were with Mao's government whose policies from 1949 had resulted in 40–60 million deaths. These occurred during the Great Leap Forward (1958–1963) with an estimated death toll of around 45 million from starvation and the Great Cultural Revolution (1966–1976) with an estimated death toll of 3-20 million. Even so, the American officials supported China joining the United Nations and taking a seat on the Security Council. Taiwan was ejected from the U.N. and has little official representation in international bodies. It has no vote.

Apparently, Nixon also agreed to have both the Low-Flyer and High-Flyer missions discontinued. In 1974, these squadrons were said to be dissolved or had discontinued their operations. A museum is said to be operating in Taiwan now celebrating the achievements of the squadrons. The museum credits the intelligence as having been necessary for the détente, since it could not have been achieved without U.S. knowledge of the strength and disposition of Soviet military forces and the capabilities of their weaponry. "These were all pieces of the electronic intelligence game. Put eyes and ears in space over them, in aircraft around them. Put them in the water about them, and put them wherever they might go. The only way to handle the vermin is to put a bright light so they can't hide in the dark. Expose them and let the world see them.

By this time, Charlotte and I were married and had two children. We lived in Westchester County of New York. She had finished Columbia with Bianca Bruno. Charlotte was married to me shortly after WWII. She was an aggressive girl and knew what she wanted. Her mother and father, the previous Ambassador to Argentina, lived in their old house in Larchmont. Charlotte visited them often. Even so, Charlotte went her own way and was not deterred by her family although the Ambassador was a strong character in his own right. She made the most of her situation. I traveled all the time with the military. Even after I retired from the military, I stayed on the road more than ever. My business was airplanes. I had the experience of the military as a pilot and a degree in Aeronautical Engineering that placed me in constant demand by aircraft and avionics companies. She had to make a life of her own. Since Larchmont is on the New Haven railroad line with its own station and parking, it was extremely convenient to hop on a train at Larchmont and be delivered directly to Grand Central Station in the heart of Manhattan. From there, she could see shows, go to clubs, attend conferences, go to trade shows or do a million other things. She worked for two-or-three companies but that was on her terms. It always kept her occupied.

Bianca was also an accomplished girl. She also had two children. She had remained in the U.S. after finishing her degree at Columbia. This occurred several years after WWII. She also became a naturalized citizen.

CHAPTER 29

TAIWAN; VIGNETTES

This story has now come full circle. The last chapters here are really about Jackson leaving Taiwan and returning to Los Angeles. The final several chapters are about Jackson Lee living in Taiwan and his making an over-flight Into China.. My story was intertwined with Jackson's. In many respects, My life was what Jackson wanted his to be. I was an unsuspecting mentor.

Jackson arrived in Taiwan in the mid 1950s. He thereby inherited a fluid historical milieu. To put one in the picture somewhat, one must address a little of the history here and the physical environment into which Jackson walked. This is sometimes described as a milieu of facts, efforts and images that weave a multi-dimensional tapestry. This tableau describes or defines a locality or circumstance.

Jackson's tour in Taiwan was in the mid-1950s. Chiang Kai-shek had escaped China in 1949, ending the second Chinese Civil War. The troubles on the island were ending by this time and things were reasonably stable if one discounted China's belligerency. One also made continuous threats and attacks on Chiang's Air Force in the Taiwan Strait. There was off and on artillery shelling of Quemoy and Matsu and other islands by the Chinese Communists. China continued to threaten Taiwan with military action to pull her back into China's fold. This continued for at least six decades.

When Chiang's Nationalists fled the mainland in 1949, there were about two million of them. This is compared to about eight million Han Chinese that were then living on Taiwan and were the population that had been there for over three centuries. These had escaped a previous civil war ending in 1620. This also included a handful of aboriginal Taiwanese that were distinct from the Han Chinese. Further, the aborigines had little say politically compared to the Han population. The Taiwanese were not thrilled with the Han Chinese Nationalists that fled China. This looked to them like an invasion of Taiwan by an occupying army, which it was. This caused insurrections on the island and many troubles with bloodshed.

Taiwan had been ceded to Japan by China in 1895 as a concession after losing the Sino-Japanese war. The Taiwanese were modern Chinese. They had prospered under the Japanese. The Japanese had become very popular in Taiwan as it now became a province under Japan. The Taiwanese liked the language, schools, and general culture that became very popular in Taiwan. Naturally, the popularity of the Japanese on the Island was one of many barbs to be endured by Chiang's Chinese.

The Chinese announced the new government of Taiwan was actually a government to cover the entire Chinese mainland or a continuation of the civil war. This assumed the previous Taiwanese status was as a prefecture that had simply been transferred to the Nationalists. This caused troubles with both the Taiwanese and the aboriginals, but these were soon slapped down. Taiwan had been a prefecture before it was occupied but it now had bold ambitions.

A New Adventure

When Jackson arrived just over half a decade later, after the 1949 Civil War ended, this was a backwater, a little province that was quite poor. The housing was substandard and crowded. The farm population seemed to be the majority by a large amount. A large segment of the people consisted of bureaucrats and civil servants from the mainland. As was said, the island was administered as if the government covered the whole of China. This caused a lopsided political representation that satisfied no one.

Jackson was naturally anxious to see the island the best he could so he began an exploration from north to south. He began the exploration a little at a time. After all, one cannot take in the ten million people population as if they were simple *Lego* pieces.

This produced vignettes or small stories or anecdotes. This was his way of drawing conclusions about a place and the vignettes themselves suggested snapshots that revealed its true nature.

The history of Taiwan dates back thousands of years. The appearance of an agrarian culture around 3000 BC is believed to reflect the arrival of the ancestors of today's Taiwanese aborigines. The Dutch colonized the island in the 17th century, followed by an influx of Han Chinese. The Chinese name of the island derives from an aboriginal term; in the past (from the 16th century), the island has been called "Formosa" from Portuguese. It was known as *Ilha Formosa*, "Beautiful Island" by the west. In 1662, Koxinga, a loyalist of the Ming dynasty, defeated the Dutch and established a base on the island. Zheng's forces were later defeated by the Qing dynasty in 1683. From then, parts of Taiwan became increasingly integrated into the Qing dynasty before it ceded the island, to the Empire of Japan in 1895, following the First Sino-Japanese War. The modern Chinese used the term "Taiwan" while many still used the term Formosa.

The island produced rice and sugar to be exported to the Empire of Japan, and also served as a base for the Japanese colonial expansion into Southeast Asia and the Pacific during World War II. Japanese imperial education was implemented in Taiwan and many Taiwanese also fought for Japan during the war.

In 1945, following the end of WWII, the Republic of China (ROC), led by the Kuomintang (KMT), became the governing polity on Taiwan. In 1949, after losing control of Mainland China following the Chinese Civil

War, the ROC government under the KMT withdrew to Taiwan and Chiang Kai-shek declared martial law. Japan formally renounced all territorial rights to Taiwan in 1952 in the San Francisco Peace Treaty. The KMT ruled Taiwan, along with Kinmen and the Matsu Islands in the mouth of Amoy harbor on the opposite side of the Taiwan Strait.

It was ruled as a single-party state for forty years, until democratic reforms were promulgated by Chiang Ching-kuo, the son of the Generalissimo, in the 1980s. The reforms were continued by Chiang's successor, which culminated in the first-ever direct presidential election in 1996. In 2000, Chen Shui-bian was elected president, becoming the first non-KMT president on Taiwan. Most consider these developments a shift to a multiparty system of rule or the first democratically ruled nation in Asia.

The history of Taiwan is divided into three tiers of the social order. The first tier is composed of the native people to the island, the aborigines. They are distinctly different from the other two tiers in that their physical makeup and appearances are different from the later Chinese that immigrated to the island. These are darker in complexion with bone structures suggesting an earlier period. They have their own language that sounds more guttural than the sing-song speech of the Han Chinese.

Their body structure seemed larger and different from the Han Chinese. They did not seem to have the agility required for modern competition. Therefore, the athletic prowess of the aboriginals was questioned. Then, one of them qualified as an Olympics runner. This was C.K. Yang, better known as the "Iron Man of Asia." Yang attended UCLA. He won the gold medal in the decathlon at the 1954 Asian Games and he again won the gold medal in the decathlon in the 1958 Asian Games. In addition, he won the silver medals in both the 110 meters hurdles and the long jump, and the bronze medal in the 400-meter hurdles. He excelled athletically. One afterwards never heard the athletic ability of the aboriginals questioned.

The second tier is composed of the Taiwanese. This was a Han Chinese group from the Qing Dynasty that in 1620 replaced the Ming Dynasty. This resulted from a civil war in China that placed a new government in power. Many of the old regime immigrated or escaped to Taiwan. Those of this second tier were known as the Taiwanese.

A third tier was composed of modern Han Chinese that escaped from China to Taiwan as a result of the Civil War of 1949. This placed the Nationalist government of Chiang Kai-shek in power in Taiwan following their escape. These were government functionaries and many of the elites in present-day China. They brought treasure, priceless art works, a government and social order along with them. This third tier is known as the Han Chinese on Taiwan.

Taiwan was a one-party rule (Chiang Kai-shek's Nationalist Kuomintang party). Taiwan under Chiang was an autocratic government with effectively a one-party rule until the 1980s. Then, Chiang Ching-kuo, Chang Kai-shek's eldest son, orchestrated a change to a multiparty system that allowed Taiwanese rule through the ballot. Thus, the son is recognized as implementing the first democracy in Asia.

Taiwan Description

One can attempt a Taiwan description by beginning with Taipei's real estate or the city skyline.

In the early times or that of WWII, most of the people of Taiwan were farmers or fishermen. Thus, the population was thinly spread across the whole inhabited countryside. This was not so easy in Taiwan since the island has high mountains along the entire east coast. These were over 19,000 feet high which is a very respectable mountain range. The west side faced the Chinese mainland that was about 100 miles away. The island sloped down to the Taiwan Straits or East China Sea and this area was amenable to farming. The mountainous region constituted about two-thirds of the island area, leaving about one-third that was habitable for the population of 10 million people in 1960. It is said to have about 25 million residents in 2014.

The Taiwan map is leaf-shaped. It is about 100 miles from the China mainland, about 80 miles from the Japanese Ryukyus or Okinawa Islands in the north and 230 miles from Luzon, Philippines in the south. As nature would have it, there are numerous small islands strewn in this area. Oil is promised on the seabed around the islands so there is continual military aggression to claim the islands by half a dozen or more nations in the area.

The Island itself is about 240 miles long in the north-south direction and 90 miles wide.

Taiwan had the tallest building in the world in 2014 but within a year, that building became second after one in Dubai. The skyline is very distinctive in that there is a huge section of buildings of about 10–20 stories or 100–200 feet high. Then, a huge geographical anomaly occurs in the skyline since the tallest building is in the center of the section and goes straight up to a height of 1329 feet, not counting non-architectural radio antennas, flagpoles, etc. The anomaly when comparing New York is that Manhattan rises somewhat as a bell curve where buildings are tall but they are most all in the vicinity of other buildings of similar height. The tallest building in Taipei rises almost vertically as a lone building.

The farm families and even urban dwellers in Chinese culture allowed the eldest lady or grandmother to rule the roost. They thought the men were carousers that spent their time in games, cards and worse. The women therefore more or less took over the finances and thereby ruled the family. When sons married, the grandmother had to acquiesce. She and the family then moved the son and his bride into the communal house. This usually required building an attached room or living quarters for them expressly. As he had children, further quarters were built as house attachments for the newlyweds. After a while, the house became a large structure and the longer the family stayed together, the larger the homestead became.

The Chinese provided Jackson with housing, servants, transportation with drivers and general travel arrangements.

He shipped a little sports car to Taiwan and used that often. This occurred generally when he was in Taipei. This usually was during weekends. This was a British car, an MG-TF. This is quite rakish and provided many hours of pleasure. Jackson loved that little car.

One can see the opportunities for dream versions of reality when viewing the car.

The population of Taiwan since WWII has been dominated by urban areas. The major city was the Capitol, Taipei. Keelung was also a major urban area. It was a seaport, on the north point of the island. Other cities consisted of Hsinchu, about 50 miles south of Taipei, Taichung, near the center of the island and Kaohsiung, nearly the south end of the island. These are all on the west coast, shunning the massive mountains to the east of the island and running from one end of the island to the other. All but Hsinchu have populations of about 2.7 million in 2015 for a total population of about 25 million. The population of the island was about 10 million in 1960.

Many people remember the old China that fertilized their fields with human dung. Dung buckets were provided throughout to collect the fertilizer before spreading it across their fields. The hot summers in China exuded an odor that was barely tolerable.

Taiwan, being part of the Chinese milieu, used the same bucket practices. The north end of the island was bearable during the hot summers but the south end of the island, being in the tropics, was beyond bearable. Kaohsiung was a large urban area. Ironically, the beautifully named *Love River*, spread gasses in all directions that often left one retching, a victim of this most unhealthy practice.

Jackson and his friends sometime hunted for boar and doves in the Kaohsiung area. Although it was in autumn, the gasses lingered on. It was enough to bring a good man to his knees. We hoped our food did not come from there although one was sure part of it did.

The typical way of building a town was to construct reed fences around one's entire property. These were about 7 feet high. Thus, when you looked down a street, all you saw was this sequence of fences stretching out. To visit someone, you rang the doorbell while standing in the street. This was usually answered by a houseboy (a male servant). One also usually had an Amah, a female servant. China often favored calling them both servant-friends but they still were looked on as house servants. Both often stayed as a part of the house even when the property was rented or resold. There is usually a small apartment behind the house that houses two or three servants and provides them cooking arrangements, bathrooms and sleeping quarters.

When the massive migration occurred in 1949, many professionals, educated civil servants and other elite civilians, found it difficult to get a job in Taiwan. This prompted many professionals to take jobs as house servants for which they were greatly over-educated and it was clearly beneath their earlier station in life.

Jacksons houseboy was like that. Everyone said he was a doctor and professor at a prestigious university in Beijing. He did not know if that was true. He certainly did not ask him directly nor have a conversation about it since it was thought it would be too embarrassing to him. Yet, there was no reason to doubt that it was true. He was an elegant, lithe character who never gave a cause for complaint.

The Amah was clearly a little country girl. She was Taiwanese having been born on the island. Her family still lived near Taipei on the seashore. She was uneducated but competent in her duties. Jackson had no reason to complain about either. In fact, there was not a serious issue with either one.

He shared the house with another American. They got along together with no issues. They usually only saw the other one on weekends. Even then, Jackson was often down-island on many weekends so they were seldom falling on each other or one getting in the other's way.

English Lessons

It was desirable that the Chinese fliers speak English as well as possible. Many of the officers spoke passable English but that was not good enough. They were stationed in the East China Sea and the South China Sea effectively, so they came in contact with other Chinese fliers in that neighborhood. This included the Philippines, Japan, Korea, Russia and other areas. Although English was the official aviation language, one worried if their language was sufficient to be clear on the communications loops. When Koreans spoke English to the Japanese, for instance, there was always room for ambiguities, mistakes and misunderstandings.

The Chinese Squadron Commander worried about this and decided to do something to improve his pilots' English. He believed that better English would ameliorate this problem and he thought he had a solution.

He would pick an American from our group and assign him to teach English. This was to be one hour every day with the American instructor and some of the students were coaxed outside our formal classroom when their English needed tutoring to bring them up to standards.

It came as a complete surprise to Jackson that he was being considered for the teaching job as were the rest of the Americans. By the time Jackson was notified that they were considering him as the instructor, it was too late to decline. Jackson was chosen and that was it. It would be more correct to say he was appointed.

From then on, the Chinese called Jackson The Professor.

Jackson had traveled a lot and this affected his speech. He never did sound like a Southerner with long, drawn out, almost syrupy speech. He had traveled the world so he thought most of his colloquialisms and regional language was gone. In other words he was free of those expressions and words that identified the origin of the speaker. Years later, he took a plane from Raleigh. He made some remark to his seatmate during takeoff that implied he was from the north. Clearly, his seatmate was from Long Island or thereabouts. The seatmate asked without further prompting what area of North Carolina did Jackson grow up in. Damn! There went his unintentional language disguise. Clearly, he was not as sophisticated as he imagined. Maybe he was a provincial after all.

At any rate, from his college days, he knew that his English needed some polishing. He was good with words, with sentences and with coherent stories. However, his grammar left a lot to be desired. The students used English textbooks that were part of their tool kits, part of their ongoing responsibility. This encouraged them to think that English consisted of the mechanics of the language, the rules and the grammar requirements. The students found it easy to back him into a corner based on the grammar tools. It was not easy to free himself. In the early stages, several students did this. They proved that the sentence required a certain structure.

It finally went too far for the Squadron Commander. This man spoke English better than most but he still needed work.

He jumped up and said something like the following:

"Look. The Professor is here not for his grammar but for his ability to speak English. We all need our speaking ability improved so we can be understood better, particularly with radio communications in English, and others can understand us. Forget the grammar. You can study that later on by yourself. He is here to speak conversational English with us. If he improves us just a bit, we will be thankful. Is that understood?"

The classes went on and their English did improve. Our grammar analysis did not seem so important after the Commander had spoken. For that, Jackson was very grateful.

Army on Maneuvers

As discussed earlier, Alex and Jackson often took rides around the island in the MG-TF. They became familiar with much of the island. Mostly, these were drives onto the mountain edges on the north end of the island, toward the center. These extended sometime to the southern end of the island, particular if they were out hunting. There was no particular route or reason for drives they took; it just appeared that some general direction looked interesting. So, once they found an interesting direction, they drove along mapped roads to see what it was like and what was there. Sometimes they got more than they bargained for. Once they flushed out a whole army battle group that was dug in and camouflaged.

If they took a north-south road, they could depend on it going for some distance. If they chose an easterly direction, they knew it would last for a relatively short distance as the road played out to rising mountains. The paved roads then became dirt roads, then wheel-rucks and finally water buffalo tracks. These often became footpaths across rice paddies.

One evening after work south of Taipei, Alex and Jackson decided to take a ride or explore the area in the MG-TF. There was plenty of light but the sunlight was fading. They just picked a road at random that ran to the east. True to form, the road ran up an incline on the side of the mountain. There was deep foliage, especially as the incline became sharper. They followed the road and then the dirt track that was rounding a sharp hill. It was a remote area and they had no reason to suspect anything out of the ordinary. They proceeded slowly and quietly. There was not a sound anywhere.

The car had a manual shift so it also was running very quietly.

All of a sudden, three soldiers in full battle fatigues stood up in front of the two Americans and pointed their rifles or machine guns directly at them. We were so astounded that they could not describe what they saw to this day.

Jackson stopped the car that was barely moving anyhow and they both were otherwise frozen.

Then, an astonishing thing happened. The whole mountainside of soldiers in camouflage stood up with their weapons. There were hundreds of them or maybe thousands. The uniforms were in jungle green. They had branches and tree limbs attached to themselves and to their helmets. Even after they rose up, they still blended into the woods or semi-jungle in the failing light.

Jackson looked around, and to his amazement there were dozens of tanks that were dug in on the mountainside. Apparently, the soldiers had dug earthen-works. Then the tanks were backed into the earthen-works and recessed so that they did not stand above the general hill. All wore green camouflage. This was a combination of paint and foliage. Tree limbs and vine runners had been cut and laid over the tanks. The tanks and soldiers surrounded us. The only thing that was seen was the barrels of the tank cannons. These were mounted on the tank turrets. The barrels rose to the sky as the tanks and drivers made themselves known by commanding the cannons to rise upward.

The soldiers were far more ominous appearing than the cannons somehow. They also had tree and vine foliage on their jungle uniforms and helmets. Clearly, we were in the wrong place and wanted to get out of there.

While not a whisper could be heard, Jackson slowly backed the little MG in reverse as the original three soldiers followed him by his front bumper. After raising their cannons, the whole army was motionless. They just stood up in what appeared as green jungle camouflage. This army seemed ready to fight.

Slowly, slowly He backed up. He never spoke to Alex nor looked at him. He just backed up without turning his head this way or that.

Finally, he backed up to a sizable flat spot to turn around. He changed gears trying to be totally silent. There was no fumbling or fiddling around. He wanted to get out of there with dispatch.

Apparently, it was an army on maneuvers. It was a place for brave men ready to fight. It was not a place for us to be.

CHAPTER 30

PAPPY BOYINGTON'S FLYING TIGERS

It is said that the Civil War from 1945–1949 killed 1.2 million people, Mao's *Great Leap Forward* killed about 38 million people from 1958 to 1961and his Cultural Revolution from 1966 to 1969 killed another 11 million people. President Nixon and his Secretary of State, Kissenger, saw the light. In 1972, they visited China and initiated the détente. Subsequently, the Americans effectively dumped the Nationalists on Taiwan. In 1979, America formally recognized China. The Central Nation was back in business!

During WWII as a boy, Jackson read a book on the Flying Tigers in China. One of the things that stuck with him was a vignette of an argument between the support people over whether water buffalos were dangerous to Americans. The author, a Flying Tiger himself, declared that the whole question was nonsense since there was no difference to the buffalo between Americans and Chinese. However, a multitude of Chinese people walked along the highways with numerous buffalos passively included in the crowds. There was no reaction by the buffalos.

Jackson lived in Taiwan several years starting about a decade after WWII. That was then a rural country with almost no tractors and those that did exist were little hand-held things. There was on main highway running north/south down the island. There were essentially no cars. The farmers walked several abreast down the highway and near a city they would about half the highway. There were numerous farmers and a number of buffalos walking bunched together. The animals were clearly tamed, placid and part of the crowd. Almost every farmer had a buffalo so there were many. Of course, Americans had cars so there were none plodding along with the farmers.

The two of them with Robert, an Old China hand that they knew and worked with, went hunting on the south end of the island. While walking along a narrow path in a flooded rice paddy we saw two farmers with a buffalo coming toward them. The Old China Hand got off the path and went 20-30 steps into the paddy. We followed. "Why did you do that?" Jackson asked.

"Wait and you'll see," Robert said. When the buffalo got downwind from them, it sniffed, threw it's head into the air, snorted and kicked a couple of times. It clearly did not like the smell.

Jackson later related the story to a Chinese friend he worked with. "That's not true," he said. Jackson then told him to slap a buffalo grazing nearby and see the reaction. Meanwhile, Jackson stood downwind from the animal so the wind was blowing away from the buffalo. He walked over, slapped the buffalo on the rump and shouted at the same time. The animal looked slowly around, then continued to graze.

"See," my friend said.

Jackson asked him to do that again. Then he walked upwind from the animal and reached there about the time my friend slapped him. The animal snorted, threw his head into the air and with his horns lowered chased my friend into a nearby building.

"Gee," the friend said. "I've never seen that before. I don't know what got into him." Jackson never told him that he had prompted it by using the wind to impart his smell. The WWII book and its author were wrong.

Everything changes, of course. The last time Jackson was in Taiwan, only a few years ago, he saw few farms and only a couple of buffalos from his railway window. He suspected each of those was kept by some sentimental farmer as a pet. But, in those days, our soap or something gave us away as Americans, at least Europeans. Buffalo's smelled us, at least, back then.

CHAPTER 31

CHIANG KAI-SHEK'S CONVOY

Jackson had never met Chiang Kai-shek but he almost did in 1958. Jackson was living in Taipei at the time and had an MG-TF sports car. He was driving in early evening down the main street of Taipei, he thinks it was spelled like Chung Ching Bai Lu. This was a 4-lane thoroughfare. It also had traffic circles spaced about one mile apart. He had Chen Bai, his good girl friend, in the car. They had been to the Officer's Club.

He approached a 3-limo convoy proceeding in the right lane. The limos were from the 1930s. They were long, black touring cars of the kind used by Chicago mobsters. He had seen the same kind of cars in Japan used by Japanese mobsters known there as the *Yakuza*. He could only guess that many in China and Japan saw American movies and assumed American mobsters still lived as they did in New York, Chicago and particularly, in Joliot, Illinois. It did not mean that the Chinese touring cars were only used when owned by mobsters, just that Asians were clearly very impressed by American movies and imitated them wherever possible.

Anyway, as Jackson pulled into the left lane, the convoy swerved into that lane ahead of him. Well, he moved back into the right lane, into the convoy. The limos jumped back into the right lane cutting him off. He in his sports car mentality could not take this so he jumped into the left lane again. This time, the convoy jumped into the left lane and much to his surprise, about six Chinese dressed in black stuck their bodies from the waist up out their windows and raised submachine guns into the air. Naturally, Jackson slowed down and dropped back. There was more to this than met the eye. They then sped away with great concern. He was no fool. He got the point. My friend kept saying, "No, no. That's the G-Mo." This was a shortening of the title of Generalissimo applied to Chiang Kai-shek.

Jackson drove slowly and sheepishly behind them as his friend and he were frozen in anxiety. When they got to the next traffic circle, police officers came running from every direction. They stopped all traffic in the circle and descended on my car. Jackson did not speak enough Chinese to understand them nor to get him out of the mess and perhaps there was some foul language and some cursing used by them. His friend talked a mile a minute to get them out of the mess and convince them they were not terrorists. All traffic was held in the circle for the next half hour. Finally, they were told to get out of there and not to irritate black limos again.

The following is stretching the truth a little but not much. Jackson was in Tokyo once when there was a typhoon. He and a girlfriend were in an expensive after-hours club. Mitzi Gaynor and her entourage came into the bar and wanted a seat in the audience. The manager told her there were no more seats. They asked the conventional question, "Do you know who this is," the entourage asked? Well, yes, they did. But there are no more seats the manager said and left them to sit at the bar or stand by the rails to see the show.

At any rate, it was early morning and the lights went out. Actually, they went out all over this section of Tokyo. Jackson's girlfriend and he decided to walk and perhaps a taxi would come along. This was doubtful since there was no traffic. Anyway, they left the club and took their chances.

Finally, a long, black limo that looked just like the G-Mo's pulled up beside us. "Can we give you a ride," they asked. We looked at the characters inside and they looked just like the hoodlums they probably were. We thought about it but finally declined. We did it nicely since we didn't want to irritate. Jackson thought he had seen them at a table in the club. They usually were theatrical when they entered or left. There was little doubt they were just hoodlums playing the roles of mobsters, but one could be wrong. The Japanese have a name for these organized hoodlums. It is *yakuza*. These are socially somewhere between union members and out-and-out mobsters.

They dress to fit the image by wearing dark suits, black shirts, flowery ties and hats with silk corsages and boutonnieres. These are wonderful period pieces. However, one did not want to get on their wrong side. Some Asians play the role even beyond the Japanese.

Finally, the lights came back on and traffic began to rumble past them. They soon caught a taxi and that was the end of the adventure.

It was confirmed later and the best we could that the convoy in Taiwan was Chiang's convoy.

Jackson had heard about a similar incident that occurred previously with an American. The G-Mo lived in a compound high on Green Mountain. He periodically rode with his convoy down to various meetings and social events in Taipei. At least, that is what they said.

In that incident, the convoy was proceeding up Green Mountain. One assumes he was returning to his complex. The American tried to pass the convoy so the convoy ran him into a ditch. After several days, the Chinese paid for the minor damage to his car and that was the end of it.

CHAPTER 32

SOVIET AIR IN CHINA

Russia and Japan collided in Korea and Manchuria. Their conflicting ambitions sparked the Russo-Japanese War of 1904, which ended in a stunning victory for Japan in 1905. In 1918, following the disintegration of the Soviet Army the Czarist empire and the Russian Revolution, the Japanese army occupied Russia's far eastern provinces and parts of Siberia. The consolidation of the Communist regime, however, compelled a reluctant Japan to withdraw from those territories in 1922. Japan resumed its westward march in 1931 with the occupation of Manchuria and the establishment of the puppet state of Manchukuo. In 1937, the Japanese invaded China, seizing Shanghai and Nanking.

Incidents along the 3,000 miles of the ill-defined border between Manchukuo and the Soviet Union numbered in the hundreds from 1932 on. In the summer of 1938, a major clash erupted at Lake Khasan, 70 miles southwest of Vladivostok at the intersection of the Manchukuo, Korean and Soviet borders, leaving the Soviets in possession of the ground. The lifeline of the Soviet position in the Far East and Siberia was the Trans-Siberian Railroad, which was the only link between those regions and European Russia. Outer Mongolia was the key to strategic control of the Trans-Siberian Railroad. To ensure the protection of that vital artery, the Soviets had established their puppet Mongolian People's Republic (MPR) in Outer Mongolia. A treaty of mutual assistance between the Soviet Union and the Mongolian Peoples Republic had been signed in 1936.

The Kwantung Army's staff was convinced that they enjoyed a decisive logistical advantage in that remote area. Japanese railheads were located 100 miles east of Nomonhan. In sharp contrast, the nearest Russian railhead was 434 miles away. The Japanese were sure that the Russians would not commit more than two infantry divisions to operations in that area. The Japanese were also convinced that Stalin's Great Purge of 1935 to 1937 had effectively crippled the Soviet officer corps.

On June 2, General Georgi Zhukov, one of the few general officers to survive Stalin's purges, was entrusted with the command of Soviet and Mongolian troops at Khalkhin Gol. Reflecting the conflict's importance to the Soviet premier, Zhukov was instructed to report directly to Stalin. Upon his arrival, Zhukov thoroughly organized his command facilities and communications networks. Another hallmark of his leadership, discipline, was ruthlessly enforced among the men of his remote army.

As befitted a battlefield with little or no ground cover, much of the early fighting between Zhukov and Japanese forces were focused on securing the air. Initially, the Japanese enjoyed an advantage in these encounters. Japanese pilots were experienced veterans of the air war over China.

Among the Soviet fliers dispatched to Mongolia were veterans of the Spanish Civil War. With experienced leadership and new fighters, the Russians turned the air war to their advantage as the summer wore on. Japanese aces rang up fantastic scores during that period — including 58 kills by one ace, a Japanese army record.

Without prior knowledge or approval of the high command in Tokyo, the Kwantung Army unleashed major bombing raids on June 27 against Soviet air bases, deep in the Soviet rear. Infuriated by such rank insubordination, the officers in Tokyo delivered a blistering rebuke. Orders were issued forbidding attacks upon airfields in Soviet rear areas. The incident illuminated the deep division within Japanese army leadership at the highest levels. Deeply concerned about commitment of Japanese forces in China, the army general staff in Tokyo was beginning to view the escalating conflict in Mongolia with growing alarm.

Chinese Civil War

The Chinese Civil War was fought between forces loyal to Chiang's Kuomintang (KMT) Republic of China (ROC), and forces loyal to the People's Republic of China (PRC) The war began arguably in August 1927, with Chiang Kai-Shek's Northern Expedition. Many argue that the war was defined from 1945-1949. The conflict eventually resulted in two de facto states, the ROC in Taiwan and the PRC in mainland China, both officially claiming to be the legitimate government of China.

The war represented an ideological split between the CPC and the KMT with its own brand of Nationalism. Chiang's forces were weakened in his fight against Japan. Meanwhile, the Communists conserved their forces wherever possible. They also targeted different groups, such as peasants, and brought them to its corner. Strong initial support from the U.S. diminished with the failure of the Marshall Mission, and then stopped. Communist land reform policy, which promised poor peasants farmland from their landlords, ensured popular support.

Stalin had joined the Brits and the U.S. but he refused entry into the war against Japan. He only declared war there four days before the surrender of Japan. Their strategy was to accept the surrendered weapons, which were sufficient to equip about 750,000 Japanese. Naturally, one can assume these fell into the hands of the Chinese Communist Party, a major equipment reinforcement. This allowed it to take control of territory in Manchuria. Hyperinflation and continued land redistribution resulted in the ROC losing the war. The interference, irregular and biased support of the Americans did their fair part of in losing China.

To this day no armistice or peace treaty has ever been signed. Both governments officially adhere to a "One-China" policy. The PRC still actively claims Taiwan as part of its territory and continues to threaten the ROC with a military invasion if the ROC officially declares independence by changing its name to the ROC. They both continue the fight over diplomatic recognition. Today the war as such occurs on the political and economic fronts in the form of cross-Strait relations; however, the two separate de facto states have close economic ties.

In 1923 Sun Yat-sen sent Chiang Kai-shek, one of his lieutenants, for several months of military and political study in Moscow. By 1924 Chiang became the head of the Whampoa Military Academy, and rose to prominence as Sun's successor as head of the KMT.

The Soviets provided much studying material, organization and equipment, including munitions, for the academy. They also provided education in many of the techniques for mass mobilization. With this aid Sun Yat-sen was able to raise a dedicated "army of the party," with which he hoped to defeat the warlords militarily. CPC members were also present in the academy, and many of them became instructors, including Zhou Enlai, who was made a political instructor.

After much bickering and fighting, the Communist army began its long march toward the north-west of China. The massive military retreat of Communist forces lasted a year and covered what Mao estimated as 78 hundred miles. It became known as the Long March. Along the way, they confiscated property and weapons from local warlords and landlords, while recruiting peasants and the poor, solidifying its appeal to the masses. Of the 90,000-100,000 people who began the Long March from the Soviet Chinese Republic, only around 7,000-8,000 made it to Shaanxi. The remnants of Zhang's forces eventually joined Mao in Shaanxi, but with his army destroyed, Zhang, even as a founding member of the CPC, was never able to challenge Mao's authority. Essentially, the great retreat made Mao the undisputed leader of the Communist Party of China.

During Japan's invasion and occupation of Manchuria, Chiang Kai-shek, who saw the CPC as a greater threat, refused to ally with them to fight against the Imperial Japanese Army. Chiang preferred to unite China by eliminating the warlords and CPC forces first. He believed that he was still too weak to launch an offensive to chase out Japan and that China needed time for a military build-up. Only after unification would it be possible for the KMT to mobilize a war against Japan. So he would rather ignore the discontent and anger among Chinese people at his policy of compromise with the Japanese, and ordered KMT general Zhang Xueliang to carry out suppression of the CPC; however, their provincial forces suffered significant casualties in battles with the Red Army.

On December 12, 1936, the disgruntled Zhang Xueliang and Yang Hucheng conspired to kidnap Chiang and force him into a truce with the CPC. The incident became known as the Xi'an Incident. Both parties suspended fighting to form a Second United Front to focus their energies and fighting against the Japanese. In 1937 Japan launched its full-scale invasion of China and its well-equipped troops overran KMT defenders in northern and coastal China.

The alliance of CPC and KMT was in name only. Unlike the KMT troops, CPC shunned conventional warfare and instead engaged in guerrilla warfare against the Japanese. The level of actual cooperation and coordination between the CPC and KMT during World War II was at best minimal.

Despite the intensified clashes between the CPC and KMT, countries such as the U.S. and the Soviet Union attempted to prevent a disastrous civil war. U.S. President Franklin D. Roosevelt sent special envoy Lauchlin Currie to talk with Chiang Kai-shek and KMT party leaders to express their concern regarding the hostility between the two parties, with Currie stating that the only ones to benefit from a civil war would be the Japanese. In 1941 the Soviet Union, with its closer alliance to the CPC, also sent an imperative telegram to Mao warning that the civil war would also make the situation easier for the Japanese military. Due to the international community's efforts, there was a temporary and superficial peace. In 1943 Chiang attacked the CPC with the propaganda piece, *China's Destiny*, which questioned the CPC's power after the war, while the CPC strongly opposed Chiang's leadership and referred to his regime as fascist in an attempt to generate a negative public image. Both leaders knew that a deadly battle had begun between themselves.

In general, developments in the Second Sino-Japanese War were to the advantage of the CPC, as its guerilla war tactics had won them popular support within the Japanese-occupied areas, while the KMT's had to defend the country against the main Japanese campaigns to take over the country, since it was the legal Chinese government, and this proved costly to Chiang Kai-shek and his troops. In 1944, Japan launched its last major offensive, Operation Ichi-Go, against the KMT that resulted in the severe weakening of Chiang's forces.

Under the terms of the Japanese 'unconditional surrender' dictated by the United States, Japanese troops were ordered to surrender to KMT troops and not to the CPC, which was present in some of the occupied areas. In Manchuria, however, where the KMT had no forces, the Japanese surrendered with their Japanese weapons to the Soviet Union. Chiang Kai-shek ordered the Japanese troops to remain at their post to receive the Kuomintang and not surrender their arms to the Communists.

In the last month of WWII in East Asia, Soviet forces launched the mammoth Manchurian Strategic Offensive Operation to attack the Japanese in Manchuria and along the Chinese-Mongolian border. This operation destroyed the fighting capability of Japan's Kwantung Army and left the USSR occupying all of Manchuria by the end of the war. Consequently, the 750,000 Japanese troops stationed in the region surrendered. Later in the year Chiang Kai-shek realized that he lacked the resources to prevent a CPC takeover of Manchuria following the scheduled Soviet departure. He therefore made a deal with the Russians to delay their withdrawal until he had moved enough of his best-trained men and modern material into the region; however, the Russians refused permission for the Nationalist troops to traverse its territory. KMT troops were then airlifted by the U.S. to occupy key cities in North China, while the countryside was already dominated by the CPC. On November 15, 1945, an offensive began with the intent of preventing the CPC from strengthening its already strong base. The Soviets spent the extra time systematically dismantling the extensive Manchurian industrial base (worth up to $2 billion) and shipping it back to their war-ravaged country.

By the end of the Second Sino-Japanese War, the balance of power in China's civil war had shifted in favor of the Communists. Their main force grew to 1.2 million troops, with a militia of 2 million. Their "Liberated Zone" contained 19 base areas, including one-quarter of the country's territory and one-third of its population; this included many important towns and cities.

Moreover, the Soviet Union turned over all of its captured Japanese weapons and a substantial amount of their own supplies to the Communists, who received Northeastern China from the Soviets as well.

Xi'an and the 50-Year House Arrest

The warlord period in China produced some really extraordinary situations. One of these is related here that gives some sense of how things were in the 1915–1945 period.

Jackson was in Taiwan concurrent with the mid-phase of the Xi'an incident. Jackson heard of the prisoner that was under house arrest since 1937 and his transfer to Taiwan at the end of the Civil War. A friend of Jackson had some influence in the KMT government. This led Jackson to presume he may be able to arrange a meeting with the warlord and hear more of the story. After all, many outlandish things happened in China so Jackson would take a chance. This was squelched in short order. There would be no such meeting.

Jackson was introduced to a man who was a puzzle. It was said that in the Chinese government before the warlord period reaching into the early 20th century, had an emperor and underneath that layer of authority were several 'Kings'. A meeting was arranged between Jackson and one of those Kings in Taiwan. This was under the auspices of a professor in the University of Maryland that taught college courses in arrangement with the American military. This King was a phenomenon in dress and appearance.

This Chinese man was very effeminate. He wore a colorful silk gown that reached from head to toe. It was obviously very expensive. His fingernails were long and painted. His facial features were crystalline. His skin was also of this crystalline quality. He appeared very fragile, as if he was about to break. He had rouge on his face. One would not choose him to drink beers with. However, he was interesting.

The Xi'an incident that transpired here was one of the most bizarre events in history. As things played out, General Zhang Xueliang, a warlord in the northwest of China, was arrested by Chiang Kai-shek. The repercussions for Zhang lasted for more than 50 years, from 1936–1993. He afterwards exiled himself to Hawaii until his death after another seven years.

Zhang Xueliang was a powerful War Lord who ruled Manchuria and the northwest area of China. He decided that he would be a peacemaker between Chiang, who was known as the Generalissimo, and the Communists. His intent was to form a United Front between the two governments that would concentrate on fighting together against Japan, the invader, and not each other.

A meeting was set up between Zhang and the Generalissimo to present Zhang's case. The meeting degenerated into gunplay and Chiang escaped barefooted through a window in the cold. Zhang and his fellow generals took Chiang or effectively kidnapped him. Chiang, under prodding by Zhang, reluctantly agreed to the terms whereby Chiang would be released if he promised to concentrate on the Japanese invaders in concert with the Communist government. Zhang soon felt remorse for his role in this since it was treason. He volunteered to go to Chiang's capitol, Nanjing, with Chiang to explain himself. When they were away from Zhang's loyal generals on their airplane, Chiang placed Zhang under arrest. Jackson Lee heard that General Zhang was under house arrest in the late 1950s and he was in Taiwan. Being a student of history, Jackson could not forego the possibility of meeting the warlord and interviewing him. Actually, there were reasons that this may be pulled off because of mutual friends in unusual places. Jackson worked on this and for a time or two it looked like he may be able to pull this off as a coup. By this time Zhang had only been a prisoner for a couple of decades. How long could it go on?

Finally, the definitive word came down. There was to be no meeting between Zhang and Jackson nor his friends. In this murky world at high places, there was a limit on what could be done. Jackson had to reconcile himself that the possibilities had been shut off. There was to be no such introduction. Jackson was very sad about this but it was a very long shot in the first place.

General Zhang's father was Zhang Zuolin, a major War Lord in Xi'an and Northwest China. He was assassinated by the Japanese, who dropped a bomb from a railroad overpass onto his train as it swept past the bridge in 1928. He was known as the 'Old Marshall' while the son was known as the 'Young Marshal'. Zhang replaced his father that year.

Zhang Xueliang was not a promising commander. He was a womanizer and a dope addict, being hooked on Opium. Sometimes before 1933, he became more stable and overcame the heroin addiction. His character became stronger than anyone had expected. The number of troops under his command reached about 400,000. In December of 1930, Chiang sent his troops to capture Zhang but this was not accomplished. Zhang then arranged a meeting with Chiang in Xi'an, Zhang's capitol. His intent was to force Chiang to accept a promise of a coalition government that would jointly fight the Japanese instead of each other. In April 1936, Zhang Xueliang had met with Zhou Enlai, an accomplished minister for the Communists, to arrange a joint effort against the Japanese, thus putting the Civil War on hold. This did not occur.

Chiang thought the Communists posed a greater danger to his government than the Japanese. He considered the Communists a cancer while the Japanese were a superficial wound. His strategy was to fend off the Japanese the best he could without committing to major battles while he used his power for the fight against the Communists.

Zhang lived in these circumstances until Chiang lost the Civil War in 1949. He was then taken by Chiang to Taiwan, where he continued under house arrest until Chiang's death in 1975. He was allowed to migrate to Hawaii in 1993 to spend the rest of his life with his descendants.

His house arrests in both China and Taiwan were very benign. In Taiwan, he lived in a rich compound of three houses where he had servants, valuable artworks and all the accouterments of a rich lifestyle.

He became a national hero due to his unselfish attempt to resolve the differences between the Nationalists and Communists and wanted to implement a United Front or coalition government in fighting the Japanese.

Zhang disappeared from public view and remained so for over 40 years. He whiled away his time reading the bible and studying history.

In 1949, Zhang was transferred to Taiwan where he remained under a loose house arrest for the next 40 years. During this time he was answering to Chiang Kai-shek. Chiang's son was Chiang Ching-kuo. He was a powerful politician and generally took care of day-to-day business for his father in the Taiwan years. The Chiang family was close to Zhang. The son actually chose the compound in Taiwan for Zhang's house arrest there. Chiang Ching-kuo became the leader of Taiwan after his father's death in April, 1975. He is credited with installing a democratic form of government after his benign dictatorship for a decade or so.

Zhang's status was murky during part of this time. He continued to live a life of luxury but also seemed to enjoy increasing freedom during Chiang Ching-kuo's rule. By 1993, he was released and relocated to Hawaii where he lived with his descendants until his death in 2000. He and his wife became devout Baptists while living in Shilin (Green Mountain) a Taipei suburb that also housed Chiang Kai-shek's family.

For most of his confined life, he studied Ming dynasty literature, Manchu language, and the Bible. He collected Chinese fan paintings, calligraphy and other works of art by illustrious artists. His collection consisted of more than 200 works.

He died of pneumonia at the age of 100 and was buried in Hawaii. His papers included an extensive oral history and paintings by his friends. These included art works by both Chiang Ching-kuo and Mme. Chiang Kai-shek, testimonials to their friendship and loyalty.

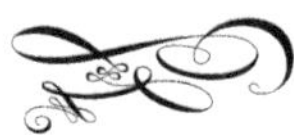

What are these dates? What does it mean to elaborate about 1927, 1934, 1941 and similar dates? That represents a generation that held power then. They were sweeping out their role in history. Yet, we must keep it all in context. I am the main player in this narration but I am only 17 years old at the Pearl Harbor debacle. In fact, it makes more sense to relate the activity as generational. Wars are fought by youngsters, by teenagers. Sure, there are the oldsters that leak through the process and join a fighting group but that is exceptional. The fighters are boys, really. It is amazing how they can suddenly lose their youth and become highly responsible for their role. Many men, perhaps thousands, accept them as the mature adults that make the organization work.

Charlotte and Bianca always remember that and appealed to the men as If they are wizened adults. But, they were only boys, they would say. On the rare occasions that they could get together, their men wanted to act with restraint as adults while the girls wanted to treat them with motherly care. It was difficult for all of them to accept that their generations had split.

CHAPTER 33

HAN CHINESE AND TERRA COTTA ARMY IN XI'AN

Many Chinese scholars believe that the concept of a Han ethnicity is an ancient one, dating from the Han dynasty itself. The Warring States period came to an end with the unification of China by the Qin dynasty after it conquered all other rival states. The King of Qin declared himself the first emperor, using a newly created title "First Emperor of Qin", thus setting the precedent for the next two millennia. He established a new centralized and bureaucratic state to replace the old feudal system, creating many of the institutions of imperial China, and unified the country economically and culturally by decreeing a unified standard of weights, measures, currency, and writing.

However, the reign of the first imperial dynasty was to be short-lived. Due to Qin Shi Huang's autocratic rule and his massive construction projects such as the Great Wall. This fomented rebellion among the populace, the Qin dynasty fell soon after his death. The Han dynasty from 206 BCE–220 CE emerged from the succession struggle and succeeded in establishing a much longer lasting dynasty. It continued many of the institutions created by Qin Shi Huang but adopted a more moderate rule. Under the Han dynasty, arts and culture flourished, while the dynasty expanded militarily in all directions. This period is considered one of the greatest periods of the history of China, and the Han Chinese take their name from this dynasty.

The fall of the Han dynasty was followed by an age of fragmentation and several centuries of disunity amid warfare by rival kingdoms. During this time, areas of northern China were overrun by various non-Han nomadic peoples, which came to establish kingdoms of their own, the most successful of which was Northern Wei established by the Xianbei. Starting from this period, the native population of China proper began to be referred to as the "People of Han", to distinguish from the nomads from the steppe. "Han" refers to the old dynasty. Warfare and invasion led to one of the first great migrations in Han population history, as the population fled south to the Yangtze and beyond. At the same time, in the north, most of the nomads in northern China came to be Chinese-like as they ruled over large Chinese populations and adopted elements of Chinese culture and Chinese administration. Of note, the Xianbei rulers of the Northern Wei ordered a policy of systematic Chinese ways, adopting Han surnames, institutions, and culture.

Today, Han Chinese is an ethnic group from China. 90% of the people living in China are Han.

Furthermore, more than 97% of the people in Taiwan after 2010 are Han.

Out of the entire human population in the world, 19% are Han.

The Terra Cotta army has great significance. First, the features and characteristics backward 2500 years are established. Next, it solidifies the claims of that length of time that the Hans are what they say they are. It reinforces the claims that Xi'an has been an important area of China for a long time. It solidifies the claim that the Qin dynasty drove their adversaries to escape to Taiwan, over 400 years before the present time. The 1949 escape at the end of the civil war parallels closely the 17th century escape.

During modern times, or those around WWII, there was the conflict between the Chinese Nationalist Government of Chiang Kai-shek on the one hand and the Communist Government of Mao Tse-tung on the other. Both were fighting against the Japanese, the Communists with little enthusiasm and the Nationalists with great fervor under the circumstances. This difference in military enthusiasm presented a dilemma throughout the period from about 1932 to 1945, the period of the occupation of China by the Japanese or roughly the period of WWII experienced by the Chinese. After WWII, this conflict continued in earnest from 1945 to 1949 as the Chinese Civil War. The Civil War after WWII drove the Nationalists to Taiwan, an island off the Chinese mainland. The Nationalists have remained there to this day

Workers in the city of Xi'an were digging a well outside the city of Xi'an, China in 1974. They struck upon one of the greatest archaeological discoveries in the world: a life-size clay soldier poised for battle.

The diggers notified Chinese authorities, who dispatched government archaeologists to the site.

They found not one, but thousands of clay soldiers, each with unique facial expressions and positioned according to rank. Though largely gray today, patches of paint hint at once-brightly colored clothes. Further excavations have revealed swords, arrow tips, and other weapons, many in pristine condition.

The Terra Cotta figures are life-sized. They vary in height, uniform, and hairstyle in accordance with rank. Originally, the figures were also painted with bright pigments, variously colored pink, red, green, blue, black, brown, white and lilac. The colored lacquer finish and individual facial features would have given the figures a realistic feel, however much of the color coating had flaked off or become greatly faded.

We reach several conclusions from this. The soldiers had taken on Han Chinese looks and characteristics, or facial expressions, long before the soldiers depicted in Xi'an. That is, the people were Han Chinese more than two thousand years ago.

Second, the method of constructing the army was similar to the production line concept that was talked about by Henry Ford and others 2,000 years later. They constructed molds and inter-fitting pieces that accommodated the production line concept making more than 8,000 composite pieces, a significant number that required something approaching a production line. In all, the Terra Cotta Army was a remarkable achievement. Even today, it challenges our abilities.

Soldiers of Fortune

Both Jackson and I were Soldiers of Fortune in a sense. When young or just past their teens, they staked everything on each event, each throw of the dice.

Later, I retired from the military in 1970 and joined a Wall Street firm.

Jackson lasted until the early 1960s. He was always supported by Malinda. They had finally married soon after his return from Taiwan. It was a fitful marriage where one was never sure of his intentions and one could not depend on him. There were instances of anger and rage. He was unpredictable.

When he was in Taiwan before the over-flight, his friends worried about his health and his self-imposed work schedule. They were all afraid he would collapse one day. He was too involved in his projects, in his working through the night and his general commitment. This finally came in 1960 in a penetration flight across north China, Beijing and north.

This proved to be disastrous for Jackson and the rest of the crew. Afterwards, Jackson seemed to be cursed and exhibited symptoms of dementia. This was uncalled for. After all, his losses were only the crew except for Jackson. This could be devastating to some people and not others. Jackson took it especially hard since he was responsible for all their deaths. His moods were fluctuating in that they would come and go. He was sent home to Los Angeles because of this.

For a while, these symptoms could be ignored. They were nowhere near severe. He continued his work in Los Angeles.

That turned out to be an adventure he had not invited nor expected. There was nothing on that trip that suggested how impaired he was. He seemed perfectly normal. That would not last forever.

It soon became clear that Jackson had a mental deficiency. He acted strange and did strange things. He forgot himself, forgot where his car was parked, forgot who he knew. It was clear something had to be done about his long-term upkeep. This started his prolonged battle with the government on his application for disability. This was a mundane necessity of life but one of great importance to Jackson and his managers. He had to have an income. This question dragged on for some time. It was never clear how it was resolved, or if it was. This was not like the French Foreign Legion but it had some of those characteristics.

CHAPTER 34

MOROCCO REMEMBERED: 1950s

Charlie said in a flashback in the late 1940s that he would be back to Africa to see all those villages and architecture. The Maghreb continued its attraction to him, even in this flashback to the 1950s. I, Charlie, was posted in Morocco in 1950 for a few weeks. I always thought of Jackson when I traveled and I realized how important that was to him.

The descriptions of places and people add to historical reality. There is a reality that exists for only a fleeting moment in time. Well, actually that may be a very long moment. Or, it may be a short moment. Even so, one looks at the reality now, the buildings, the farms and they see the city streets, the traffic and people. That appears as a fixed pattern, It seems it will always be so. Yet, there is no reality. We must capture reality the best we can. Hold it, for it will be different before we can capture it. I can freeze the image, Imperfectly, of course. But, I can freeze the image. Now, hold on. Will it be a recognizable Image a few moments from now? Will we be able to replicate our images and environment then? Not really!

We say the Soviet Union fell in 1991. Yet, we struggle to recreate the images of that time. A further example Is today versus 1950 in Morocco. I can recall every detail about that time and about that experience. Says I. I do a search on the internet for that time period and lo, it is all different now. I recall their clothes from my memory, yet the Google search says the clothes were not like I remember. The colors were different. The fabric was different.

The people were different. I can recall data points but the true reality escapes me.

At any rate, I will try to capture moments of 1950 in Morocco.

The time line after the war stretched beyond the Berlin wall that fell in 1990. This was shortly before the fall of the Soviet Empire in 1991.

Well, here it is the 1950's and I have kept my promise sooner than I thought. This I said to no one in particular. Once the Germans left Africa, it became safer to visit various places and even to operate a light plane across North Africa. We were able to do this and found it a godsend for me as I played the part of a tour master.

This was now almost eight years after Rommel's fights in North Africa. Jackson also visited many of the sights across the desert as part of his aircrew duties. He happened to pass Eliot Carson one day as he was preparing to leave the Port Lyautey airbase. Eliot was assigned to a different aircrew.

"Hey, Eliot! What are you doing here and why are you in such a hurry?" Cried Jackson.

"Hey," Eliot replied. "What are you doing here, Fellow?"

After handshakes and profuse greetings, and a number of 'high-fives' Jackson replied. "Do you remember that Privateer recon plane the Soviets shot down last month over the Baltic Sea? "

"Yeah, yeah," Eliot responded.

"Well, we have been ordered to replace it so our squadron is here. We are flying from Port Lyautey. I'm sure you remember Port Lyautey from the war since I remember you were there.

Jackson continued, "We circle the Soviet Union all the time but we usually stay in international waters. They just shoot us down. We will continue to show our flag and let them know they can't just push us around. We will fly with all our guns loaded; hopefully, we can keep our powder dry. Anyway, they want a career intelligence guy so I'm it. I don't mind. In fact, I have to tell them I don't mind, because if you let them know you really want something, they will find lots of ways to deny you. That's the way man works. And this is especially true of the Army."

"I've got it," said Jackson.

They continued talking for a while, then departed with a handshake. They had been the best of buddies for a long time.

Jackson and his crew continued to fly around Russia for several months. Their track was generally to Tunis, Algeria, Libya, Egypt, Greece and Turkey. Many times they would also go to Cypress and Malta where both still belonged to the Brits at that time. There was also Italy, the U.K. and sometime other places.

Finally, our turn ended. They flew all that time with no results. The Russians never challenged us.

Jackson was talking to a pilot in the bar, a Major Rollins of Kentucky. Rollins loved to talk about Kentucky's pretty horses and fast women.

"You know," said Jackson. "People now have a healthy respect for just how dry the Egyptian desert is. One generally thinks that the Sahara runs from Morocco across the top of Africa to Tripoli in West Libya. But it is further than that. In fact it continues right on across Egypt and the Sinai Desert. On the upper Nile, the sand often goes right up to the water on the western bank of the river. The reason for this is that the sand itself is ground granite. It doesn't breathe and store water like other sand. The Nile floods and brings heavy black dirt from Ethiopia and the high desert that keeps the farmland going. I don't know if that is true. He heard this from some of the boys along the Nile that gave one a ride on their Felucca sailboats. Well, when he says they 'gave' me a ride that is overstating it a little.

"But, that's not the point. The pilot was telling us about how dry it was.

We went to an airbase near Tabruk. There had been a lot of fighting by Rommel during the invasion of Egypt and Libya."

There were now lots of planes on this Tabruk-British Airfield that were on their way to the Haj in Saudi Arabia. The British had promised to fly them all to Saudi Arabia for the Haj. Obviously, they were someone of importance to rate this treatment. The pilgrims were there by the thousands where they were to be flown to Mecca. They invariably wore white robes. It was almost like a uniform.

The British rustle up planes and pilots but it is not easy.

The temperature was too much for Jackson. It was in the early summer and the temperature on the base was 120 degrees Fahrenheit. When one breathed, it sucked the air right out of one's mouth and burned when inhaled.

"At any rate, this was eight years after Rommel and his battles in Egypt and Libya but the desert was strewn with the instruments of war. All the equipment lay there in the desert just like it had been when the armies left. Tanks, half-tracks, armored personnel vehicles, packs, clothes. It was just lying there in the sand just like it was yesterday. It was eerie, like a phantom army abandoning the desert from Egypt and Libya. There was no wind to blow away the sand or humidity to cause rust. It was hot to the hand and burned your flesh to the touch. The armies could only fight at night since the armor was too hot during the day. It was just as it had been when it was abandoned eight years earlier. Actually, another artifact of war was abandoned, anti-personnel land mines. The whole desert was full of these. The whole area was marked with strings and little flags indicating that this area was unsafe, mines. There were few areas that did not have these markers.

At night, one could hear infrequent explosions way off in the desert. The local Brit said those were mines being activated by sheep or goats, or they were being set off by the change in temperature or humidity. Jackson said, "You know, I've told that story so many times, I have begun to doubt that it is true myself. Then, about 20 years ago, I read where NASA sent a team of scientists to the desert to determine a ground truth for their instruments as reported in National Geographic. It reported that the scientists were dumbfounded that old newspapers showed no signs of deterioration at all as they reported the news of the Africa Korps and Rommel. The scientists were astonished to find the equipment in pristine condition. Everything seemed perfectly preserved. I guess that is the same theory that holds that the Egyptian Valley of the Kings preserves the mummies for thousands of years. Dry granite is not a good preserver of water.

"This confirmed my experiences," said Jackson. "It confirmed the National Geographic data. And it confirmed our wild claims."

Jackson thought about the girls in Rabat during these times. His impressions came mostly from Casablanca, Rabat and Port Lyautey. As you walked in any of these towns, a large crowd of children would follow and harass for money. They laughed and made a big game of it. You never knew whether they were playing or if it were serious begging. In any event, it was harassing. One never had the impression that the natives, the Moroccans, were friendly. Further, sporadic killings were not unheard of. It always left you with a feeling of danger. You know, something has been on my mind a long time. It concerns the fashion or dress In Morocco.

The young girls almost uniformly had on medium blue Hijahs with veils. At least, Jackson thought that is what they called their covers. These were straight gowns to the ground and longer than the hands to prevent any skin from showing. The material appeared to be wool. There was a hood of the same material covering the head. A veil completed the outfit. The hood covered just the eyebrows, then the veil was across her lower face just below her eyes. The only impression of flesh was around the eyes with the horizontal streak of a real person. As you passed them on the street, especially in Rabat, the capital, they could hardly be seen but their big black eyes often followed you without a turn of the head. Many girls accommodated their modern leanings by wearing stylish and fashionable sunglasses. These were very handsome in an odd sort of way. Now there was absolutely only the vision or image of a woman inside. One would have thought it was a 'paper mache' figure gliding along the road. However, they appeared fashionable and even stylish in this way.

These clothes and this outfit were everywhere in the places Jackson visited. Nonetheless, he investigated the internet later and found absolutely no pictures showing the fashionable blue outfit. What had happened? Had he gone through a wormhole? Everything is now colorful and mostly open with young girls. The modernists are having their way in Morocco. The world is opening. Or, maybe he is simply wrong.

Jackson found the French in France to be much different from the colonials. The cultures in North Africa were such that these colonials were generally richer than the average Frenchman I had encountered in France. They adopted an architectural motif known as French Colonial and these exploited the concepts of the rich and powerful, similar to the American South during slavery. They effectively built a world totally outside conventional Morocco or the other territories. The locals were kept inside their walled villages or cities. This was done commercially and by military force.

Once a demonstration or a riot started, the French backed up several tanks at all the old city gates and lobbed shells into the highly dense homes until the natives recanted. It was very effective. This held the locals in abeyance from 1912 when the French took sovereignty until they departed in 1956, after independence was granted.

The Colonials ruled the outside world, the French Colonial world. Needless to say, the Colonials like others in the empire developed thoughts of their own and they almost always reached for control with conservative attitudes. When France tried to put distance between the Colonials and the French homeland, they were met with civil war. The Colonials of Algeria marched tanks down the Champs-Elysees to confront the government. The wars of liberation after WWII were usually intense and bloody. North Africa was no exception.

The Colonial's attitudes were hard and unforgiving. Jackson was sitting with several others in a typical French sidewalk café once when a kid pushed to sell a shoeshine. The French officer sitting near us with his female companion told him once to get out of there. It was a very authoritative voice but the kid did not respond. The Americans did not quite know what was going on because most of the conversation was in French. Suddenly, the officer jumped up and kicked the kid with a crushing blow in the stomach that knocked the kid into the street as well as all his shoeshine equipment. Naturally, the kid whined and dragged himself away. It was better down the street, he must have thought.

This was a single incident but was revealing. Jackson even had a local Arab come up to him while he stood on the street waiting for a bus. The man was with several friends but he carried a large open knife. He said something belligerent and waved the knife in front of us. His friends grabbed him and pulled him away. They mumbled something about he was drunk and didn't know what he was doing.

"Hey," my friends said. "What did you do to that guy?"

"What did I do?" asked Jackson. "I thought he was after one of you guys." They all laughed but it was hangman's humor.

These instances or those like them were recounted at the base all the time. No one felt safe in Morocco. Helping that along were German Police dogs trained to hate the Arab smell. When they passed walking workers, they had a fit. They growled, barked and slobbered all over themselves to attack the workers. The marine guards held them in check but it seemed they were always about to lose control.

It never was clear who was in control in Morocco at that time. There were the French police, the local police, the French Foreign Legion and the huge black men with swords and sidearms representing the King, one believes. They were as colorful as anything seen in the movies. The King's men were especially recruited for their looks. They were very tall, probably six feet, six inches; they were obviously from black Africa and had the shine of ebony. They wore very colorful uniforms with bright sashes and tunics. Short daggers hung by their side. They also had pistols at their side. The hat was military and very colorful and tall. They had colorful ribbons on their tunics. Their trousers were short and white while they wore full-length stockings.

Then the French Foreign Legion rolled in from the mountains and the Sahara. They were hauled to the cities in army trucks. They looked as belligerent as the dogs. There was never any camaraderie among any of these disparate groups. Some said the Foreign Legion was made up of unemployed Nazis from the German Army. One didn't know but it was better to keep one's distance. They always had a foreign look in their eyes like they were not seeing what was going on.

This unlikely grouping of races, religions, cultures and histories gave an exotic feeling to the whole area. It was with great anticipation every time I caught a train or a public bus there. First of all, there was the totally pervasive odor of the area since they all reeked of French cigarettes. That is to say, only the very cheapest and coarsest tobacco could be found and afforded. There was a great deal of Turkish tobacco mixed in and God only knows what else. The result was a heavy, clinging smell. It is hard to describe the odor since there are so few similar odors. Perhaps one could say that the smell was like newly tanned leather. As known, those smells result from the unique tanning process and a major part of this is uric acid or urine. Camel's urine was thought to be unique and played a major part in the tanning process. The most prevalent product being pushed in the bazaar was ottoman footrests. These were about one foot long cylinders covered with leather. The

American families really liked those and they flocked to the stores to buy them. These smelled to high heaven. There is no doubt that those families really could express their exotic tastes when they introduced these camel-cured ottomans to their friends

The robust smell of tanned leather tends to define the area and our memories of it. The French section of Port Lyautey (later changed to Kenitra) certainly had that quality; but first, let's explain how the French colonials of North Africa lived. The Arabs lived in walled cities that were essentially as they existed centuries ago. There were several gates through the city walls. These led to very narrow, winding alleys that served as streets. These houses were made of a mud or concrete-like composition. They rose generally to about 2-3 stories. The whole family often lived in close quarters here. Horses, camels, goats and all kinds of animals lived somewhere near this area so they mingled as caravans gathered or produce was sold directly off their backs. Everyone seemed to be operating in trade. A stall would be manned by one or two people and would have little boxes of every kind of spice or herb or chickpeas or you name it. There may be 50-100 such choices. Other stalls had something else. There were scores of such stalls. One strolled down the alleys and there was a delight at every turn. Occasionally, a small courtyard appeared and this served as a marketplace. There was no end to the variety one encountered.

Naturally, the heavy tobacco smell permeated the area but now many new odors were added to the 'natural' smells. The areas were often sandy, dusty and dirty. The guttural Arab language was being shouted everywhere. This was a thriving city. This provided all the exotic romance one could expect but seldom found. This was a very exotic place.

Most of the people one encountered were male merchantmen. They wore white robes with an unusual 'pants' that wrapped around them, then was pulled up past the crotch and tied off at the belt-buckle area. This caused a big baggy look at the crotch where the pants fell to the knees. Then the pants were pulled tight around the knee and hips. These were singularly unattractive but they did serve the purpose. They allowed one to get them off as desired and allowed one to escape when necessary.

The downtown area had a French atmosphere. There were large sidewalks with sitting areas under canvas canopies. The traffic was always light. But there was always enough to keep one entertained. The clientele normally consisted of French army officers and their female friends: police officers, the Sultan's guards and bodyguards, Foreign Legion solders and similar assortments.

The lounging in the sidewalk café's was a phenomenon similar to what going to heaven must be like. The weather was balmy; the sun was constant giving a whitewashed appearance to the streets; the drinks were delightful. The perfume from the officer's ladies was unavoidable and consuming.

It was widely believed that the French Foreign Legion was made up of Nazis from the German Army that had been laid off. They were unemployed, one of those in the crowd. Somehow they got a spot in the Legion. They gave a spice to the whole bowl of soup. They patrolled on the edge of the Atlas Mountains or beyond in the Sahara.

One of the things that stands out about the north African desert is the number of flies. They apparently love the desert sands. I noticed this in Morocco. Their presence intensified across North Africa, at Tunis and the ancient city of Carthage representing the Third Punic Wars of Rome and Algiers. They were especially bad at Tripoli. In WWII, there was a huge American air base near the city of Tripoli. Our squadron could not be accommodated so we slept on the desert in tents. These were well prepared in that there were wooden floors and mosquito netting between the lower wall and the ceiling. None-the-less, it was so hot, well over 100°F, that we rolled back the netting to get whatever breeze there was. The tenting only made one hotter. When the sun came up, it was blistering hot and the sun seemed to bore right through one. Each morning, one's face would be a mass of flies. That was really hard to take.

As one moved eastward toward Tabruk and Egypt, the number increased. "Ouch, let me out of here," we cried. But there was no relief. Although I have not witnessed this first hand, I have seen movies of outdoor interviews with the kings of Saudi Arabia and other officials. They were continually swatting flies and trying to protect themselves. If they can't afford to remove the flies; believe me, no one can.

During the Iran-America war in the Persian Gulf, Jackson was once flying as a commercial passenger, from Santa Barbara to Los Angeles. A sergeant was on the plane and had a chest full of campaign ribbons. Jackson started a conversation. The sergeant was just returning from Kuwait he said, so he was expected to confirm the high number of flies in the desert. The soldier looked puzzled when we queried him. "Flies?" he said. "What do you mean?" Perhaps there is a desert area without flies, but I doubt it.

Jackson often tried to confirm facts by questioning people who had been there. This was usually a reliable way to check facts. Either Jackson's theory was wrong or the sergeant was telling fibs.

CHAPTER 35

FLASH-FORWARD, THE WALL 1990

The emigrants from East to West Germany tended to be young and well-educated, leading to the 'brain drain' feared by officials in East Germany. The East Germans wrote an urgent letter on 28 August 1958 about the significant 50% increase in the number of East German intelligentsia among the refugees. Andropov reported that, while the East German leadership stated that they were leaving for economic reasons, testimony from refugees indicated that the reasons were more political than material. Andropov stated, "The flight of the intelligentsia has reached a particularly critical phase."

By 1960, the combination of World War II and the massive emigration westward left East Germany with only 61% of its population of working age, compared to 70.5% before the war. The loss was disproportionately heavy among professionals. The most hurtful professionals were engineers, technicians, physicians, teachers, lawyers and skilled workers. The direct cost of manpower losses to East Germany has been estimated at $7 to $9 billion; with East German party leader Walter Ulbricht later claiming that West Germany owed him $17 billion in compensation, including reparations, as well as manpower losses. In addition, the drain of East Germany's young population potentially cost it over 22.5 billion marks in lost educational investment. The brain drain of professionals had become so damaging to the political credibility and economic viability of East Germany that the re-securing of the German communist frontier was imperative.

On August 13, 1961, the Communist government of East Germany began to build a barbed wire and concrete wall between East and West Berlin. The official purpose of this Berlin Wall was to keep Western 'fascists' from entering East Germany and undermining the socialist state, but it primarily served the objective of stemming mass defections from East to West.

Khrushchev had been emboldened by U.S. President John F. Kennedy's tacit indication that the U.S. would not actively oppose the Soviets building a wall to separate the Soviet sector of Berlin. In August the leaders of the GPU signed the order to close the border and erect a wall.

At midnight, the police and units of the East German army began to close the border and, by Sunday morning the border with West Berlin had been closed. East German troops and workers had begun to tear up streets running alongside the border to make them impassable to most vehicles and to install barbed wire entanglements and fences along the 97 miles around the three western sectors.

Charlie's Tourist trip, West to East Germany (1989)

Several years later, Charlotte and I were on a bus trip across northern Europe and Russia. The Soviets were still in full control. Yet, major cracks in the wall could be seen. We were now agile and mobile but we were both in our early seventies. We would not make such trips for much longer. This trip toured Russia in 1989. The bus went from England to Saint Petersburg. We went first to East Berlin where our hotel was, then to West Berlin and back to East Berlin. The tour bus visited West Berlin. This was through a gate known as Check Point Charlie. You could see through the concrete fence into West Berlin here and there. The West Germans were happy and gay and the city was in full bloom. Once through the Checkpoint, we looked back at the East Berliners. They were deadly serious with no laughing or emotion of any kind. They were mute everywhere he went in East Berlin. You would not like to live in a place like that. He could see West Berlin. The people were happy. They were happily shopping. They were doing what everyone does on a holiday or busy Saturday. The stores and streets were well lighted. The people were brightly dressed.

The people who had arranged the trip told us to avoid making eye contact with the Vopos or East German Police at all times. Further, they said to avoid cameras and taking pictures.

There were several busses in the departure courtyard at Check Point Charlie. The Vopos had machine guns across their chests with their hands on the triggers. The first stepped aboard our bus and glared at us with great hostility. He then chose each person to give a personalized stare. The passengers looked straight ahead without flinching. No cameras were in sight. For all the world, the passengers could have been on their way to Auschwitz or at least to a hanging.

Auschwitz was a gas chamber and crematorium but in May 1942, it also became a slave-labor camp, supplying workers for the nearby chemical and synthetic-rubber works of I.G. Faben. In addition, Auschwitz became the nexus of a complex of 45 smaller sub-camps in the region, most of which housed slave laborers.

After the tour bus passed back across East Germany into Poland, everyone felt like jumping up and cheering. We were free. Even I felt free.

Well, not exactly. Major restrictions on visitors were always present.

Berlin Wall

The Berlin Wall stood until November 9, 1989, when the head of the East German Communist Party announced that citizens of the GDR could cross the border whenever they pleased. That night, ecstatic crowds swarmed the wall. Some crossed freely into West Berlin, while others brought hammers and picks and began to chip away at the wall itself. To this day, the Berlin Wall remains one of the most powerful and pathetic symbols of the Cold War.

Charlie often thought of a flash-forward about the wall when he once visited Berlin. He visited Berlin more than once. He took a trip to Berlin earlier. He said he had always heard of Unter den Linden. It was the continuation of the Charlottesburg Strasse past the Brandenburg Gate and that straddles Unter den Linden. He walked through the world-famous zoo in the center of Berlin, then struck out walking through the Tiergarten in the general direction of the famous street. The walk was long, being a mile or two. He stopped a West Berliner and asked him in halting German how to get to Unter den Lendin. The German looked startled. He finally pointed in a direction but he was reluctant for me to walk there. The same happened with another Berliner. He continued walking. Suddenly, he broke out of the forest to a wide zone with no houses or trees. Just before him was the wall with a guard post about 25 feet high. In it, there were three Vopos holding machine guns and watching Jackson with binoculars while they fingered the triggers.

There were two fences of barbed wire as far as he could see. This formed an open channel of 30 yards or so with the guard post in the center. The dirt and land appeared to have been raked flat. It made a perfect killing field.

"Whoa!!!"

That was scary. Just to the left was the Russian headquarters along with the French, British and American. Entangled barbed wire was everywhere so you could not just walk to where you wanted to go. Charlie assumed the German he had asked directions from knew that. In front of the Russian headquarters, there were two pillars of 150 feet or so. On top of each was a T-64 tank pointing to the horizon across Berlin.

These were massive machines. That must have rankled the Germans to no end.

On 12 June 1987, U.S. President Ronald Reagan spoke to the West Berlin populace in a speech at the Brandenburg Gate. Addressing the General Secretary of the Communist Party of the Soviet Union, Mikhail Gorbachev, Reagan said in his speech, "If you seek peace, if you seek prosperity for the Soviet Union and Eastern Europe, if you seek liberalization: Come here to this gate! Mr. Gorbachev, open this gate! Mr. Gorbachev, tear down this wall!"

On 25 December 1989, less than two months after the Berlin Wall began to come down, the conductor Leonard Bernstein conducted the Berlin Philharmonic in a version of the Ninth Symphony of Beethoven at the then newly opened Brandenburg Gate. The wall had finally come down.

George Grayburn, Bianca, Charlotte, Malinda and I watched these activities on television in Larchmont together with great interest. After all this time, Charlotte and I were still married, and George Grayburn was married to Bianca. We all five watched the television version when Bernstein conducted the Berlin Philharmonic.

Bianca, Charlotte and Malinda cried.

"That was so beautiful," they said.

Bianca agreed. She had long ago applied for U.S. citizenship. It had been granted. It was unusual but all five of them had been in Larchmont at the same time.

It is too bad that Jackson could not be here, they all agreed. The women cried again as they drank champagne toasts to fallen heroes. To them, Jackson had a place in that pantheon.

CHAPTER 36

SOVIET 1991 FALL — THE EXPERIMENT FAILS

Gorbachev brought down the Soviet Union. His dictatorship lasted six years. He was a true believer, but had notions of economics and social reform that set the Union on a fatal path.

Khrushchev had preceded him in reform. He had moved to break with the old ways by denouncing Stalin in 1956, and started various reforms. However, he quickly realized how the Soviet dictatorship and the control of its satellites were being undermined, so he terminated the reforms and imposed the old dictatorial ways, but he did avoid Stalin's worst excesses.

Gorbachev came later. He was a young man with few real accomplishments. He had been a model bureaucrat, had avoided serious mistakes, and in his career trajectory. He was educated, and had none of the baggage of the old-line Communists, none of the blood on their hands. He was a true believer, and acted the innocent about the true nature of the dictatorship, the tyranny. His naiveté brought down the Evil Empire, almost inadvertently and with little fanfare.

There are also heroes of the fall, and they were at work long before Gorbachev arrived on the scene. There were the Americans and their debilitating containment military machine; there was Lech Walesa and the Polish Solidarity trade union movement; there was the Catholic Church led by the

Polish Pope John Paul II; and there was Boris Yeltsin, a maverick Russian politician.

And there were Soviet mistakes; there were economic burdens; there was the debacle of Afghanistan; and there were Gorbachev's glasnost and other naive reforms.

Poland had continued to be problematic after the 1956 riots. Major riots again broke out in 1970. A serious problem for the Soviets had always been their planned economy and the unrealistic pricing system. They set unrealistically low prices on basic consumer items such as food.

The Catholic Church has always had a heavy influence in this predominantly Catholic and very religious country. There had been a consistently abrasive relationship between the Church and the Polish regimes since the Soviets arrived. Several Cardinals and Priests had recurring run-ins with the government, and had to leave the country or take exile in foreign embassies in Warsaw. This made continuous news in Poland and the West, and kept the country in a religious turmoil. Then in 1978, a popular Polish Cardinal was elected Pope in Rome, Pope John Paul II. In 1979, he made a papal visit and traveled across Poland. His popularity, and the popularity of his cause electrified and united the people as no other cause could. This energy could not be contained for long.

The Polish government launched a coup on December 12, 1981, deploying troops and tanks. The Solidarity leaders were arrested and interned."

In April, 1986, the disaster of the Chernobyl nuclear power plant became known as radiation fell on Finland, Sweden, and all over Scandinavia. This was a disaster of the first order. Gorbachev and the Soviets tried to cover it up. They delayed making any kind of admission, but the evidence was hot and in the hands of millions of foreigners; it was in the fields, in the air, in the milk and cows and vegetables. His neighbors were unified; they were horrified and furious. He and his government used the old rhetoric; they dissimulated and obfuscated. Now his own people were becoming horrified at him and his government and previous governments. Tens of thousands knew of the horrors; they had to be moved from the radiation area. He was forced by world opinion and by Russian opinion perhaps for the first time in history, to release information that conformed at least partially to the truth.

As time has gone on, it appears Stalin's drive for nuclear power took a terrible toll on his people. There were few of the safeguards used in the West. Nuclear waste was dumped into rivers that served as city water supplies downriver. As radiation sickness affected thousands downriver, doctors were forbidden to diagnose them or treat them correctly, and they were forbidden to talk. The crime continued.

The world was appalled by the Chernobyl disaster. The Soviets could not deny this. Their disaster raised the fear of the whole world. Gorbachev was on the defensive.

It is said that an authoritarian system is never as weak as when it tries to reform itself. Gorbachev's glasnost, or openness notions, soon began to sound like high state policy. Chernobyl opened the floodgates, and with every new revelation, the gates opened wider. Stalin's excesses and outrages were revealed. More revelations of the Great Terror astonished the world further.

After 1986, the Soviet economy began to unravel in earnest. State planning had always kept food and housing prices artificially low, and this caused disruptions across the whole economy. The agricultural system was breaking down. A closed society can operate this way and tolerate the distortions. However, after WWII and the Sovietization of the satellites, the Soviets looked less and less like a closed economic society. The satellites had trade with Europe and the world; Soviet oil fields and exploration and export pipelines and technology required increasing imports and increasing contacts with the world economies. Its military industrial complex and space program needed computers and chips, high technology materials, and other resources, again from the world economy. The foreign wars drained them; the equipping of foreign armies required large amounts of money, as did the adventures in Afghanistan, Angola, Ethiopia, South Yemen, Vietnam, Cuba, and elsewhere, and the financing of an enormous international spy system. They could not be satisfied with internal promises and debts, and coercions, and extortions, and pillages; only international currency, hard money, would do. The world financial markets force a certain degree of honesty since they do not yield to threats, and coercion, and bloodletting, as Adam Smith foresaw centuries ago. The Soviets were now living in this world market. They were living like drunks on a binge, like there was no tomorrow! The government had been plugging the gap by borrowing from its citizens and exploiting the satellites. It could manipulate the funds to a degree, since the state bank was the only bank, and the Soviets owned the bank. The Soviets didn't own the world banks and there was a limit on how long they could function at a deficit at the sufferance of the world banking system. Soon enough, the disruptions would result in runaway inflation, disruptions, internal disincentives, disillusionment, and an economic breakdown.

The Reagan administration had introduced a massive defense buildup that was responded to by the Soviets. Soon, close to a third of the Soviet product was going into the military buildup.

The Soviets were living far beyond their means. Their expansion into the international market made them vulnerable, and sheer extortion and rapacity would not save them from the brink.

The people professed horror at Stalin's Great Terror revelations, at the Chernobyl horrors, at the way the government had been run. The ruble was collapsing and hard currency was drying up. Their food dropped to a marginal level, especially in the northwest part of the country that housed Moscow.

By then, the state was in total chaos. How did this come about? Glasnost had released a flood of information against the state. The coerced confessions used in the purges were admitted. Stalin's murder of Trotsky in Mexico was admitted. Stalin's murders in the Great Terror were admitted. On and on it went. Of course, none of this was news to thinking Russians. Just as thinking men knew the world was round 2,000 years before Columbus. Thinking Russians knew a great deal of Russian history, certainly the gist of it."

By 1988, it was clear the old history would no longer do. Its departure from the new realities known to the public was too bizarre, even for the Russians. The history books used in their schools had to be revised, but the day-to-day revelations made the revisions too chaotic to follow. Thus, all history and social study classes were canceled for the 1988–1989 school year across the Soviet Union at the high school and university levels, to await new books in 1990!

By this time, even the Russians, the great mass of people, had lost their ability to support the Communists further. It was all too chaotic, too nonsensical, and too bizarre. They were far more interested in how they were going to get a few loaves of bread to eat, coal or oil to put into their stoves, and how to get enough rubles to survive the winter.

The clock was really running out on the Soviets. They began withdrawing from Afghanistan in May 1988. Jonas Kadar was replaced as the head of the Hungarian Communist Party. Once more, Solidarity strikes broke out in Poland, all within the month. This Polish unrest would last through the year.

The Soviets in this climate had no stomach for marching into Poland, so they let the situation take its course. Finally, Solidarity was legalized. In August 1989, Walesa's representative was called on to form a government. There went Poland!

Variants of this drama occurred all across Eastern Europe. In September, Hungary opened its border to Austria, and thousands of East Germans stampeded through it, heading in a roundabout way to West Germany.

After that, the most dramatic of all the dramatic events of the Soviet fall took place. The Berlin Wall came tumbling down! It was breached on 9 November 1989, while 400,000 Soviet troops watched and did nothing.

Only in Rumania was there bloodshed.

Article 72 of the Soviet constitution gave each republic the right to secede, but they all knew the document meant nothing, and was a trap to those citing it. In this chaos, the republics began to use it. Lithuania declared its independence in March 1990. By August of 1991, a full 14 of 15 Soviet Republics had declared their full independence.

Gorbachev was deposed by an unsuccessful, ill-conceived, and ill-prepared coup in August, 1991. He was never to restore his power.

Boris Yeltsin, as the leader of the Russian Republic, became the clear leader of the remaining group by opposing the coup. He led the negotiations for a Confederation of Independent States (CIS) that was declared the successor to the Soviet Union.

As leader of Russia, he commanded the vast majority of the land and population of the defunct Soviet Union.

The ethnics of the Soviet Union were reasserting themselves. Soon, new countries would appear across central Asia, rising from the ashes of the Russian Empire and the defunct Soviet Union. There were names like Kazakhstan, Uzbekistan, Turkmenistan, Kyrgyzstan, and Tajikistan.

The Shadows of History

The reasons for the Soviet fall can be succinctly summarized. There was the debilitating containment military machine of America and her allies. There was the Polish unrest led by Lech Walesa, Solidarity, and the Catholic Church. There were the lack of economic resources to support her empire and international adventures. There was the total bankruptcy of dictatorship and tyranny in this century, regardless of whether they were Communists or whatever other fraudulent shroud hides them. There were the revelations and admissions to the Soviet population and to the international community of the Stalin Killing Machine, blood purges, and outrages of the Soviet regime. There was the revealed incompetence of the Soviets. Last, there was the naiveté of the true believer, Gorbachev.

The Soviet regime didn't fall exactly; it just unraveled. The fabric of the Communist system and the shroud over the hideous crimes came unwoven; each thread lost its relationship to all the others. The structure dissolved, unraveled, or collapsed into a pathetic heap of dust and lint. The mighty Soviet Union and Communist system had become the shadows of history.

They could not know it at this time but it was not too long before the remnants of the Soviet empire could be seen in Murmansk and other naval ports. Rusted hulks of submarines and ships lay in the marshlands, many on their sides. Some still had parts of their nuclear reactors wasting away and scaring all Westerners. The sailors to staff them had been paid off and wandered across Russia looking for work. The army had also pushed out scores of thousands of soldiers who were also looking for work. There were skeletal remains of aircraft and on the airfields after the Soviet pullout from Afghanistan, again putting fliers and those who supported them on the streets.

No less than a tragedy for the military men, the Soviet planned economy and state-sponsored economic theory also found their way to the figurative marshlands. The Soviet experiment for Russia was over. Are you sure that is true, asked Jackson of me.

"Truth is that which I tell you three times," said Alice.

Well, I've told you three times just like Alice asked. First, we've told each other the thousand details of the Soviets and Communism over the years of our lives, and your family's lives, and the long, tortuous details known to history, through books, newspapers, and our own personal experiences. Second, I've told you a long but encapsulated version this morning. Third, I just gave you a concise summary that was clear beyond any misinterpretation.

Anyone can follow such a clear and unmistakable truth.

You should recognize it as the truth; the unadulterated, unmistakable truth!

I sat there in my best oracular pose, looking as best I could like Charlie the Wizard. All oracles and gurus are mystical and impenetrable. Was this analysis just a riddle, or was it an Epiphany, an obscure revelation with a deep philosophical meaning, a solemn portent for the future? Or was it just old Frank Morgan, Hollywood's Wizard of Oz, the architect of the Emerald City and the inventor of magical wonders, hiding behind the Wizard's shroud and manipulating his engineering levers?

Was old Frank Morgan manipulating his engineering levers and just calling it magic?

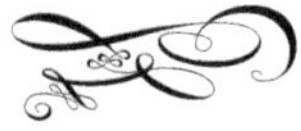

Communism and Philosophy

Early barbarians of the steppe were simple folk. When a leader bound them and the times were right, they came pouring out of the hinterland on flying horseback with their swords held high and their voices raging. They killed, raped, and pillaged in open and frontal assaults.

Modern Huns are more sophisticated. They intellectualize the onslaughts. Hitler quoted Schopenhauer, Nietzsche, and Hegel and evoked the music of Wagner. Hirohito and the militarists brought forth the spirituality of Shintoism. The Bolsheviks quoted Marx. Lenin changed their name and gave it all relevance as Marxist-Leninist Communism. This intellectualized the Armageddon for friend and foe alike, steeling the Huns and confounding their enemies.

Early Communism was hardly more than a shamanist fraud of Lenin; his snake oil for the dispossessed and their champions and radical liberals, while he ravaged Russia and loosed the Comintern discontent and terror on the world. It served as a Utopian mantle for bloody revolutionists and terrorists, a religion for the poor and wretched classes as they and the Bolsheviks savaged and destroyed the existing social fabric. In the West, the resolute were confounded and an intellectual effeteness dissolved resistance.

Bloody Stalin raised Communism to the ultimate colossal fraud. He defied the Apocalypse and pretended to the Czarist Godhead. Bloody Stalin, Omnipotent One of all the Russias, soon reached his goal in an ocean of surviving non-entities. As pretender, he overtly and intentionally took the blood of at least five million Russians and he knowingly and with vengeance imposed policies that took another five million. He went further! He, with the Nazis, co-authored the Russo-German debacle initiating WWII that let the blood of at least 20 million or so Russians.

All the while, Utopians and the merely gullible saw only the mantle, saw Communism as some sort of philosophy and discussed its deep intrinsic meaning. The mantle was to hide the crimes, just as Hitler's ultimate lies teased with and subjugated the truth while his gang stoked the ovens with 12 million humans.

We try to fathom the deep philosophical underpinnings of these colossal frauds!

Our human curse is to intellectualize the Armageddon, the Apocalypse!

It's just another piece of the electronic intelligence game. Put eyes and ears in space over them, in aircraft around them. Put them in the water about them, and put them wherever they might go. The only way to handle the vermin is to put a bright light so they can't hide in the dark. Expose them and let the world see them. Let their acts be seen so clearly that there is no possibility of misinterpretation.

Exposure is the only hope good men have of quelling evil.

CHAPTER 37

FAREWELL CHARACTERS AT EXIT TAIWAN

The plane was cheered, the airfield cleared,
Merrily did we rise
Above the crowds, above the clouds
Above them all, it flies.

Taiwan was, our Cold War location,
Over-flights, our occupation
This tale is told, first chapter first,
A Dada tale, the hero was cursed,

Jackson's departure from Taiwan was both a joyous and a sad affair. After all, he loved the work and the friends that formed a tight cell and he was very sad to see this chapter of his life closing. Alex, a good friend of Jackson, had driven the two of them to the airport. As they arrived, he saw three groups. Two of these were in costume and seemed to represent a slightly earlier time.

"What the heck is this?" Jackson pointedly asked no one in particular but the question seemed appropriate for Alex. The costumed women wore long, brilliant gowns topped off with feathery hats and colorful parasols, many of which were open to block the sun from discoloring their pretty, delicate skin.

They were all there — the girls he knew — including the Dragon Lady and Madam Wu, along with some of his other friends. They were in a festive mood.

Goodbye Taiwan

Long after Jackson came to Taiwan, he got permission to join the crew on an over- flight. He needed to make adjustments to his equipment to make it more effective and this was a unique opportunity. The aircraft was to deploy from South Korea. Unfortunately, a Zombie Lady's curse had followed them. His plane crashed on the flight and he never quite recovered. This aircraft incident was to change all their lives.

After Jackson's stay in Taiwan and his aircraft accident, there were lingering doubts about him that many of his workmates shared. He often displayed odd characteristics and expressions since his return from South Korea. He often laughed when there was no reason for it. He would look to the sky and laugh his heart out.

This was odd.

Further, he often became morose and retreated into a world of his own. He never had these odd characteristics before. It was like a mood change, a personality shift. All were aware of this somehow but no one expressed it. They were feting the old Jackson, the one when he was carefree, young and light hearted.

Sooner or later he had to be sent home. This was clear to his manager in Washington. On this occasion, he had been ordered home. His stay in Taiwan was over as he looked forward to returning to Los Angeles.

Jackson could mostly appreciate the scenes and happenings in theatrical terms. Some call it the Dada movement that received notoriety in the 1920s. Dada was an artistic and literary movement. This movement was put together by several artists of the period including Marcel Duchamp. Even the brother of Isadore Duncan was there. Isadore will always be remembered for her scarf entangling the rear axle of her Bugatti and breaking her neck. Engineers wrapped the axles of later models of the two million dollar sports car but it was too late for the mother of modern dance. Her neck was broken and she died.

Then it came to him. He vaguely remembered describing the Dada movement to a couple of his friends as a "theater of the streets" done in full costume. They must've decided he would enjoy this and somehow arranged this departure show for him. They'd done a great job and Jackson thought this was a perfect sendoff. After all, one could not live in paradise forever.

Taipei Departure

Jackson had a poetic and artistic streak in him. He liked the crazy stunts the artists often pulled and he liked many of the people that floated through the art world. This was mostly from afar, since his contact was only through art museums, books and magazines.

But he was now leaving Taiwan. He had been there several years and it was time for him to go. He said he had better fish to fry back in Los Angeles.

They were all there at the airport. The girls that he knew were there. The Dragon Lady was there. Madam Wu was there. They were in a festive mood and he reveled in this.

Jackson's crowd consisted of three groups of about a half-dozen each. They were dressed to the nines. Not only were they in costume, they each carried a colorful parasol to add color as well as to deflect the sun's rays. Many had beautiful corseted waists with suitable bosoms. They had hats, many with plumed, feathery additions.

Those of each of the three groups coalesced together. The groups mixed in with the numerous travelers of the same flight and their friends and families. Needless to say, Jackson was astonished that his friends were there and especially that they had dressed in costume for the departure. Hollywood could not have done it better. The groups moved around while they waited in the sunshine in the outdoor waiting area. The regular passengers and their friends watched this parade of the ladies with many questions of who they were and what they represented. Nevertheless, these questions were unvoiced as the ladies paraded around in their colorful costumes.

It could not have been orchestrated better. However, it did not just happen without some background. These were indelible trail-markers, leaving traces of Jackson's adventures on Taiwan.

The Girls

Consider the first group. Jackson had become very friendly with the ladies of 'Madam Wu's Bar' while on the island. Madam Wu was the owner and operator of the establishment.

Jackson had a loud and boisterous friend, James, who was an old China hand that liked to sing barrack songs and others reminiscent of Kipling. There were other British and Irish pub songs. He would stand up, wave his beer and burst into song. It was remarkable how he remembered the words but he seemed to know all the verses of those songs and the tunes. Many of these were quite graphic. Yet, many people in the pub joined in and seemed to know most of the words if he led them. The music was English, Scotch and Irish and was generally very risqué.

My friend James was very intelligent. When at work, he was deeply involved. He gave the impression he was a studious worker. His work seemed to be to gather information and try to develop a narrative around it. He would never confirm this or refer to his work. This gave him a profound sense of history and a mysterious persona. After all, at that time China, the Soviet Union and the future of Asia were highly questionable. This ignores the even greater question of what was to become of defeated Germany and Japan. The losers of WWII still had to be governed. The biggest question of all was that of the Soviet Union that swallowed all of Eastern Europe and was complicit in the fall of China to the Communists. It was a frightening time for millions of people and for those in many parts of the world. There was a 45-year period after WWII that heavy-handed and ruthless dictators such as Joseph Stalin ruled much of the world. These dictatorial regimes imposed closed societies.

Closed societies were able to place huge numbers of spies in the open societies and get unbelievable access to technical and all kinds of other information. In fact, a great deal of information is readily available in the open literature. Democracies hardly work if there is not a free press publishing all kinds of information. This goes hand in hand with investigative reporting whose role is to uncover secrets and publish them. In this case, secrets meant conspiracies, criminal activity and corruption. It is not to uncover national defense secrets that have now become fair game for any number of misguided individuals and peddlers of state secrets. They now have the ability with computer databases to steal massive amounts of information and peddle it across the world. This is a real problem in today's world since hardly anyone goes to prison and when they do, it is usually a slap on the wrist as a result of negotiating a deal. Someone is responsible for the defense of secrets or of facilities. The best way to protect them is to place a few of those responsible in hard labor prisons. This method concentrates the minds of all those responsible. Making deals does not radiate the message. Failure to prosecute just to protect evidence does not justify deals. We protect a few secrets while the perpetrator walks off with the farm. This does not work.

James worked in this murky world of human intelligence. He spoke a lot of Chinese and was generally a studious person. Yet, he had a wild side. When not at work, he flung himself into odd situations. He sang boisterously. Even in restaurants, he would talk loudly and joke with anyone. He burst into song for no good reason. Many liked this and thought it was fun; others thought otherwise.

Jackson liked James and they often got together for dinner. Then the fun began. This often ended in bars with girls around. Jackson liked fun times and he tried to make everyone share it.

Another friend was Alex. He was a co-worker and very close friend. Alex was also a technical consultant, like Jackson. Alex and Jackson were closer in their work than to James' so they saw each other more often than did James and Jackson. The three of them often made the rounds of the entertainment district of Taipei. The owners loved it since they brought business and the whole pub often rose and joined in song as beers were downed. Alex went along with the songfests but he was not totally into it as were Jackson and James. These were diversions anyway. They were all heavily dedicated to their work and remained serious about it.

Through this, Jackson became good friends with Madam Wu. She would sometime go with James, Alex and Jackson as they visited a few pubs. The madam was about 35-40 years old and she was adept at her business. Needless to say, she was well known and liked by the owners of the other bars. She would usually take one of her girls on the sojourn. Jackson favored a beautiful girl he always referred to as '*The Dragon Lady*'.

Jackson was a very good friend at work with Mister Wang Lin. Lin was a Chinese civilian that worked with Jackson on technical matters. He was game for every technical experiment and usually carried them out. Once the experimental phase was over, Lin was charged with building several units or replicating the design. When appropriate, several workers were diverted to him and his projects. He was an excellent technician with lots of experience. Jackson was lucky to have him. They thought alike and had little problem communicating. Because of their close technical relationship, they were often together and usually had some project going that required close attention.

Wang Lin was married and had two children. Yet, he was never bothered by family ties and availability. He always was eager to help and he was available when asked for.

Major Han Jing was an officer assigned to this little group. Major Han was a competent officer with a technical background. He spoke very good English and was always on top of whatever experiments Jackson and Lin were involved in. He also kept the manager-level Chinese officers informed whenever it was appropriate.

Lin worked down-island full time. He lived there and his family was there.

Major Han Jing spent much of his time down-island but he also spent about half his time at the Chinese Air Force headquarters in Taipei.

Dragon Lady

Jackson often discussed his tenure on Taiwan with me in considerable detail although we only got together infrequently. We kept in touch all that time although usually far distant from Jackson. Yet, we communicated through the mails, I visited Taiwan infrequently and we had many mutual friends. We also sometimes managed to meet somewhere for a few days or so and these were enjoyable times. That is how I heard the story of the Dragon Lady.

A cartoon strip of *Terry and the Pirates* was the first to introduce the *Dragon Lady*, as far as we know. The cartoon personality was developed over the years. It came to be applied to many different women, almost all applied to a Chinese woman that was strong, deceitful, domineering or mysterious. She became a female villain in the comic strip, a femme fatale. It usually was applied to powerful Asian women and to a number of film actresses. It was still also used to refer to any powerful but prickly woman, always in derogatory terms and fleshed out with pejoratives.

Madam Wu said she was a Manchu. As it turned out, Manchuria was experiencing a period of mass migration into that area by the Japanese, Han Chinese and Europeans. Immigration into Manchuria had not reached its later proportions. Manchus were very similar in appearance to American Indians. In fact, the migration of early people across the Alaskan land bridge would have been by Manchus. Many Manchurians have the high cheekbones, reddish complexion and a similarly tall stature of the American Indians.

Han Chinese are now almost universal in China or they are everywhere except the Xinjiang border territory with Russia and the other border regions of China. The Hans seemed to come from the many regions of China that were subject to invasions in the early days of empire. That is, they dated from about 2500 years ago. China found a huge repository of clay figures after WWII that became known as the Terra Cotta Army. We can deduce from the expressions on the soldiers' faces that they fit well with the Han Chinese appearances even 2500 years after the interment. This army was near the city of Xi'an.

Another famous occurrence at Xi'an was the house arrest of Zhang Xueliang, a famous warlord that stayed in the custody of Chiang Kai-shek for over 38 years. After Chiang's death, his house arrest under Chiang or his government lasted 56 years. He moved to Hawaii in 1993 and died there in 2001 when he was 101 years old. That was some house arrest!

The Dragon Lady was beautiful. She stood tall, much taller than the other girls. She made the Han Chinese girls look diminutive. Her body was shaped perfectly. She had large bosoms as opposed to the typical Han.

Her neck was long and shapely, reminiscent of Audrey Hepburn singing Henry Mancini's and Johnny Mercer's *Moon River* in *Breakfast at Tiffany's*.

The Dragon Lady's hair was straight and jet-black. It shone when light struck it. Her cheekbones were naturally high and she usually applied rouge that made them stand out more than naturally. Jackson never formed very close relationships with her but she made a wonderful showcase to take around and show. They fancied that she and I made a perfect pair. Jackson guessed that Madam Wu did not compete with the Dragon Lady since both were confident in themselves.

The Dragon Lady was astute and had looked through several sources to find references for the appellation she had been given. She soon recognized even the nuances of the character. She then took on many of the characteristics ascribed to her. She played a sultry Ida Lupino type. She sat on a barstool with her long jet-black hair falling around her arms and shoulders. She began to wear fashionable sunglasses that befit the character even in the dimly lit bar. She started to look like the Lady of the comic books. However, she always had a major dash of color. This could be a feathery plume of a hat, a painting of a colorful orchid on her lower dress or a brilliant vertical stripe. This stripe suggested what the NASCAR crowd referred to as 'racing stripes'. She was self-confident in her new appearance and worked at it before a full-length mirror. It was said that she had become more Dragon Lady than the comic book Dragon Lady herself. That is, she outdid herself compared to the comic books.

The *Terry and the Pirates* artists knew how to draw her in cartoons, showing her body in full blossom. They even had the luxury of overemphasizing certain aspects of her torso. Even so, the Dragon Lady was a strikeout beauty in the artist's imaginative drawings that could be unrestrained. This is seen for Roger Rabbit's wife in the movie, *Who Framed Roger Rabbit*. Further, she was a human flesh-and-blood strikeout in the beauty of her face and limbs and in her voluptuous body as she fashioned herself in reality. She was a knockout beauty.

This first group at the airport was made up of girls that worked in the bars. This was not so odd in Asia and it was not particularly condemned, certainly not in the same way as in Europe or America. The girls hustled drinks. What happened next was up to the individual girl or her boyfriend. Perhaps these could be called courtesans but the clientele here was somewhat short of the wealth usually associated with courtesans. Here, some wanted drinks, some wanted fun, some wanted a live-in mate and some wanted marriage. In this, perhaps the impetus of nature and its goals were not far different from those of most girls. Maybe the goals are almost universal.

The Dragon Lady was often the opposite of her reputation. She had happy times! Sun rays then gushed from her heart,

The kind saints had pity on Jackson and encouraged him for most of his life, and especially now. With the enthusiasm of youth, he knew he would always be so free. No curse would ever block his way or restrain him.

In truth, the opposite was Jackson's fate. He would never again be so free.

These were happy times for the Dragon Lady, for James and Alex and for others they met and enjoyed. Their work was important, critical they thought, and this made them important people and almost missionaries.
The Dragon Lady was beautiful, none could compare to her. She was poised in her movements and radiated a certain kind of charm. Her height indicated she was someone special. She spoke to you while she swallowed you into her deep pools for eyes. I swore, she projected light rays that seemed to come from her heart. She understood your story and sympathized with it. "I know, I know," she would say. "I see."

Then there were the respectable Chinese and Taiwanese in the second group. These were respected girls from good families. Some of the girls in this crowd were still in college. Alex, and some of our friends saw these girls often. These lived in Taipei. When good theater came to town, the guys often went with the girls. This included the classical music of the Boston Symphony, Jazz musicians such as Jack Teagarden, and others. Alex eventually returned to Boston, married one of these girls and had a family.

Tea Time

The Chinese Air Force and the Americans provided housing and transportation while Jackson was in Taiwan. He never knew who provided what. He was given a house in Taipei, two servants, a house-boy and a house-girl. He called for cars like a taxi service and one arrived with a driver. He also had American privileges like the Officer's Club and Post Exchange, or PX. He usually stayed in Taipei for weekends so that was a '*cushy*' job.

During the week, they rode down-island. The facilities there were less favorable in that the building they lived in was a dormitory or barracks. This had bedrooms, two workers to a room and a common dining room. The dining room also served as a recreation room where they watched movies and played games. Chinese boys in white jackets provided cooking and services here. Transportation was also provided here thc same as in Taipei. There was an engineering building that housed workspaces and analysis groups.

One anachronism in particular stands out while they were in Taipei for the weekend. By this time, they had met several girls on Taiwan.

Soon after becoming friends with these girls, there was a knock on Jackson's house gate in Taipei. This was about 11 a.m. on a Sunday morning. The houseboy answered the bell, then came and announced there were three girls to see Jackson. He went out to investigate. He had met them all. They were dressed in their fineries with hats and sun parasols. They made a colorful and thrilling group. Not knowing exactly what was going on, he greeted them the best he could. They came into the house as invited. Once seated and not knowing what to do, he asked the houseboy to bring tea. Serving tea is a proper ceremony in Taiwan as well as in most of the world. We drank the tea and chatted for half an hour or so. Then, they thanked Jackson and said their goodbyes.

It turned out they had watched enough movies to believe the English made tea calls on Sunday and they were doing what they thought was required of them. They had also made a similar call on Alex. They knew that they must dress in their best, carry a parasol and handbag and make a call for tea. This happened off and on for the several years he was in Taipei. It was a lovely experience. This only occurred with Taiwanese girls or those of the second group.

The third group consisted mostly of several co-workers and their spouses. These were not in costumes but were dressed appropriate for the occasion.

Cowboy Stunt

An elderly man named Frank Woodall was nominally in charge of the facilities and group down-island. Frank just had to tell the story of Jackson driving his car and sweeping a lady co-worker, Jean Garfield from St. Louis, off her feet. Jackson didn't like the story that resulted from this but there was nothing he could do. Frank and his wife had seen what they saw and Jackson had to endure the consequences of his rash actions. Actually, he had taken a small English sports car with him to Taiwan. It was an MG-TF. This little car was the epitome of the English sports car and it was beautiful. It was low-slung and had rakish horizontal lines. A running board completed the lines. It was a seemly horse for many of his episodes, for many cowboy stunts. These were often intentional but many were unintentional.

Jackson was sitting in the car waiting for a bill or something when he saw the lady co-worker walking across the wide concrete apron back of the garage area. He had watched enough movies to know the hero on his horse always swept the girl onto the horse as he rode past her. In this case, this amounted to catching her waist and pulling her against the convertible car door while her feet caught the running board. He traveled very slowly when he made this sweep. There was never much danger since he caught and held her body taut against the car door and the car body. It was a trick in that he gave the impression that there was a danger when he held her close to the car. She had a running board like stirrups to put her feet on and she was squeezed against the car like she was holding the saddle. At any rate, he later called this the '*Cowboy Stunt.*'

Nevertheless, Frank and his wife swung into the garage back-apron just in time to see the hero save the maiden. They assigned considerable danger to what Jackson had done. Frank continued to tell the tale every time there was an occasion. Naturally, he ballooned the danger every time he told it. That was all right. Jackson deserved it. Jackson really liked Frank and his wife regardless of this peculiarity.

At any rate, Frank loved telling of the cowboy trick he had seen.

How could Jackson leave the island without Frank and his wife sending him off?

Hoopla

The friends in each of the three groups stayed together and wandered around waiting for the PanAm passenger plane. Naturally, a large number of family and friends were also gathered to see their friends off. The members of each of my three groups clung together and seemed to have a joyous time.

Jackson had no choice but to wander from group to group. He did not reveal himself too readily since tales carry even if one is not there. He said pleasantries to each one there. After all, he owed them. They had taken the time and effort to dress for him and to come out to the airport. Everyone laughed and joked but it was a restrained performance. No one in a group referred to the other groups except through a brief nod of the head. After all, the social niceties still have an influence even if they do not prevail.

The Dragon Lady was there in her sultry best. She had on a dark blue frock whose length was all the way to her golden shoes. The dress had a large, blood red orchid on the hem. There was a pair of fashionable gold shoes with straps and bayonet heels. This presented a tall structure that rose above everyone else there. She also had on a hat that pointed upward and this added even a few more inches to her height. It was a fashionable presentation that one could hardly take one's eyes off.

Jackson approached Madam Wu. She said, "Well, you are finally going to leave me. I have had so much fun with you. You always treated me as a friend and I will always think of you that way. Please come back to Taiwan. We will all miss you. Go now and don't look back."

The Dragon Lady was standing beside Madam Wu. "Oh, Jackson," she said. "When will you be back. You have been so wonderful to me. Don't ever forget me. We will always miss you, especially me. You always treated me with respect and so well in everything. Come back soon."

They both reached out in a mighty bear hug. That was something!

He noticed a spot on their faces. Both of them had a tiny rivulet of light scrolling down their cheeks. As they moved their heads, the rivulets found tiny reflected suns. Bright spots tracked their tears.

Jackson was surprised. He accepted the general description that such girls were harsh and hard. He knew this was not true but it surprised him anyway.

Jackson's very best friend in Taiwan for most of his stay was Chen Bai, a Chinese girl. She was from an elitist family that had left the mainland in 1949 when Chiang fled the revolution to Taiwan. She worked for the Americans on Taiwan and had done so for some time. She was adept in all her undertakings. She acted somewhat like a chief organizer and implementer for the Chinese community that worked for the Americans. She lived and worked in Taipei. Her father was some sort of minor government bureaucrat for the Chinese.

She was a beautiful girl that was full of fun. She was game for every type of amusement, as long as it made sense and did not interfere with her work. Her face was always carrying a sweet smile and a wide grin. Every time you met her, you knew it was going to be a pleasant experience since her smile was so welcoming. This was probably why her work was so effective and she could calm both sides in any argument.

Chen Bai was there with the Taiwanese although she was Chinese. She gave Jackson a small present then pressed against him. However, it was brief and unnoticeable to everyone but to her and Jackson.

She wished Jackson god-speed and a quick return to Taiwan. "Please, Jackson?" she said. Please come back. I will always think of you and wish you well. Don't forget us. Don't make us *Madam Butterflies*."

Most of the people at the airport made similar comments. It was private in a sense although dozens of people surrounded them.

Jackson's friend, James, was there. Fortunately, he only sang one of his barroom English songs and even that was greatly subdued. It was actually whispered but understood by those who knew the song. The gods were with his friends on that score. I don't want to join the army

I don't want to go to war.
I just want to hang around
Picadilly underground
And live off the earnings
Of a high born lady

Call out me mother,
Me sister and me brother,
But for Gawd's sake don't call me.

So there you have it. Jackson ambled from one group to the other at the airport. It was uncomfortable but highly flattering. He was obliged to kiss each of the women on the cheeks, a veritable kissing machine moving through each crowd under their umbrellas.

Only the first and second group were in obvious costume. Their dresses were bright and they had all the accessories. The hats and parasols put them into a different time period but the whole costume was in this chosen period. Each group clung together and moved as a single group.

Finally, the airplane was loaded and they were ready to go.

They soared over the mountains of Formosa, the flowery island. The beauty of the island prompted the Portuguese on discovering it early on in the *discovery age*, to give it the name *Formosa.* That meant beautiful.

Soon, the island of Taiwan fell behind Jackson as he left the flowers and beauty of the island, its culture and its people. His multi-year adventure in Taiwan was over. Gone were the weekend drives to the fishing village of Keelung on the north coast. Gone were the Japanese preparations of freshly caught seafood, a remnant of the Japanese occupation. Gone were the wanderings from stall to stall for seafood and shellfish. The rice wine and warm Saki and even the beer would be missed. Many of them and their friends had made a ceremonial excursion to Keelung for many Sunday brunches. These always consisted of some exotic fish fare. It was a new and unrecognized delight at every stall.

CHAPTER 38

CRASH AND RETURN FROM TAIWAN

Jackson returned from Taiwan to Los Angeles in the last part of 1960. Many say he was shipped home because he had developed a mental condition. His management recognized this but few others did. This all resulted as a part of an over-flight mission he had participated in.

Of course, his boss, Glen Gable, knew everything about the incident and about his return to the U.S. Mr. Gable was the one calling his shots. He made the arrangements for Jackson to be in Taiwan and wherever else he went. There was a lot of travel so Glen kept busy.

What to do about Jackson — that was the question. There was no particular rule governing him. He was not a government employee nor was he a dedicated contractor employee. But he had to be taken care of. The best way was probably to get him on disability insurance and that would cover both short term and long-term requirements.

It is ironic that such a whimsical detail as disability insurance could cover their actions. Yet, there it was.

When the accident occurred, it required a lengthy hospital stay. Jackson accepted this. What choice did he have?

After his release, the lingering problems were not noticeable at first. After a lengthy period, he began to slowly slide into a mental condition that no one had expected.

Malinda sometimes bemoaned her loneliness.. She cried. She watched him deteriorate before her eyes but she was helpless to do anything about it. She formed a special bond with Bianca. "Everything seems so mad and at the same time, routine." Malinda confessed to Bianca. Their visits were often at first, but then they tapered off.

I don't think Malinda realized what she was signing up for. Jackson was erratic and that required constant monitoring to catch him before he harmed or embarrassed himself or others. Soon, his symptoms passed and he was normal again. This took its toll.

They played a little game for this.

When awakening in the morning, she would roll over and say, "Honey, what kind of day do you think this is."

"It is a wonderful day," he would respond. I love Wednesdays." If it really was a Wednesday, both he and she would chirp like birds.

They both dreaded it when the answer was wrong, it really was not Wednesday. He would then sink back in bed and try to hide from the world. They knew he was under some kind of spell. He, of course, assigned it to malevolent magic, a curse.

"It's the curse," Jackson would say. "It is the curse of the Zombie Woman."

He looked through the haze of morning and thought he saw the woman. To him, she was real enough. She was an apparition with spells of good or evil. Her curse could not be denied. Sometimes he saw the Chinese crew as they passed by and accused him with their bloodshot eyes. You have no right to do this, he would yell. I have paid the price.

He sometimes described her to me. "She is death reborn, a sort of living death. Her scalp has been torn off her face. She has long fingernails and they are purple. Her face is also kind of purplish. She has a ghoulish sheen and a horrible expression. Her clothes are wispy and torn. Her scalp is bloody."

He seems to discern what is real and what is unreal. He talks to her but he is fearful. She has a nightmarish form,

After a short time, the curse is gone. Jackson returns to his self again. Every day becomes Wednesday.

Bianca visited her often and they formed a special bond between them. Bianca was more emotional than Charlotte so she did not form that bond.

Malinda would discuss how lonely they really were. They would both cry as they revisited memories of the past. Malinda had a special loss of love never fulfilled. To Jackson, it was about Jackson. He had never really committed to Malinda. This was an injustice they both endured.

Bianca had continued to visit Buenos Aires so she had a strong emotional tie to several people and families there. Unfortunately, Malinda did not have this.

"Malinda," she asked, "What am I going to do?" Huge tears ran down her face. They also caused Bianca to shed similar tears. They expressed sympathetic loneliness.

There was no denying this. The trip had been a disaster for Jackson. It had been a disaster for the girls although not yet known by them. It had been a disaster for the crews' families. It had been a disaster for the entire project.

It was not too long before Jackson began to exhibit the result of psychological and physical breakdown. He was sent to Los Angeles as his usefulness no longer measured up. He then began a slow decline but one lasting a couple of years.

The metaphor of the Ancient Mariner then became more and more real to him and his associates. Both the Mariner and Jackson drifted into total madness.

PART 4

CHAPTER 39

SOURCE OF JACKSON'S MADNESS

A China over-flight was selected;
It was to dash across the North,
From South Korea, a flight projected,
On the mission, we set forth.
Intercepting data, along the way,
Avoiding detection, or hell-to-pay.

Flying nap-of-the-earth, to avoid radars,
Ditching, they died at sea, appropriately
They hit a tree; then died one-by-one.
See what that cursed bird hath done!

After going back to Los Angeles, Jackson functioned normally. However, when he had episodes of depression, they were severe. These episodes were frequent; they became more and more severe. After several months in Los Angeles, they became unbearably severe. This lasted through a year or so. He was never free of his health problems.

Jackson had flown with the Chinese crew in an over-flight into northern China or Manchuria. The flight resulted in a catastrophe with everyone dying but Jackson. He was then returned to Taiwan but he had problems that diminished his usefulness. Afterwards, he was sent home to Los Angeles. Malinda Lane became his caretaker and finally they found their true loves.

Aviation had passed into a mature industry in about 1960. After this, jet aircraft ruled the skies and these defined a new era in passenger transport and in cargo hauls, not to mention all other aviation segments.

A similar change occurred in penetration flights. Satellites became routine instruments for these missions. Although low altitude penetrations or atmospheric over-flights took most of the similar missions, many such missions remained. All penetrations challenge the sovereignty of a state. A height of about 100 miles is considered to be the limit of sovereignty since this coincides with the lower limit of autonomous satellite flight. At less than a 100 miles circular path, the orbiting satellite decays rapidly. Thus, a boundary of 12 miles offshore is usually declared on earth's surface while 100 miles is declared for the boundary altitude. The zone beyond this is defined as the zone of free navigation. That is equivalent to historical international waters for ocean navigation. Afterwards, satellites ruled the sky with diminishing dependence on aircraft penetrations. The new world for aircraft and satellites was thereby defined.

CHAPTER 40

AIRCRAFT DITCHING

Our plane is a good ole ship;
It gets us to and fro'.
We fly on many a trip,
Where no man should ever go.

It flies through the dark of night,
And through rockets red glare,
Collecting data on its flight,
With loads of secrets to share

The aircraft for this mission was a P2V, a hybrid design between propeller and jet. It was known to be a reliable aircraft with long range. These were required for this mission.

The P2V planes were put under the control of the Chinese Nationalist group according to Google and other search engines. They were taken from operational U.S. squadrons. The P2V was used for penetration trips into Mainland China. These had two piston-driven propeller engines and two jet engines mounted to the wings. The data in this section was much later described on the internet.

Two such aircraft were given to the Republic of China Nationalists Air Force. They became part of a black unit known as the Black Bat Squadron. This squadron included several types of aircraft. The mission was to conduct low-level penetration flights into Mainland China with Chinese operatives, to conduct Electronic Intelligence (ELINT) missions including mapping out China's air defense networks, to insert agents via airdrop, and to drop leaflets and supplies, and undertake other such tasks.

The Black Bat Squadron was operational over China from about 1957 until the early 1970's. Two such aircraft crashed in South Korea, three were shot down over China, often with all hands on board.

Jackson soon participated in a flight over Northern China. The crew were all Chinese except for him and he wore a Chinese uniform for obvious reasons. This flight proved to be disastrous for everyone on board.

The normal operations were to fly out of South Korea and return there. The mission was associated with Manchuria. The plane was to fly at treetop level. It had been painted black and no lights could be visible.

Most of the flight was without incident. His mission on this flight was to place a "black box" on the aircraft. He planted the box and antennas successfully. He was to pick it up after the flight and return it to Taiwan for analysis.

His presence on the flight was required due to the nature of the black box where he was the inventor of the box's interior and the only real expert on the data it produced. Many in the flying crew did not understand what the box was doing. They were not exactly afraid of it but they treated it with a great deal of respect. They joked that in case anything went wrong, it would explode, thereby denying its content and information from the enemy. No one went out of their way to dispel this conjecture since it may have served their secrecy interests.

CHAPTER 41

SPECIAL VULNERABILITY OF AIRCRAFT

All around, our compass confirmed;
Magnetic calibration, true without fail,
Radio direction-finder, affirmed
The needle tracked, o'er hill 'n dale.

A course is set, to a radio station;
But a chance jar, of a knob indentation,
Could change stations, and cause a ride
Into an intervening, mountainside.

There was a particular vulnerability on these and similar aircraft that was recognized but nothing was done about it for several aircraft design generations and for many types of aircraft. The Radio Direction Finder, RDF, was a unit that the pilot or copilot could tune to a radio frequency and a directional device pointed to that direction. This allowed one to tune to a particular radio station with music or news they favored. Then, the only requirement of the crew was to fly along the path of maximum signal strength. One was sure to find home this way or to pass on top of the radio station.

There was one problem in this. The control unit for the radio was a 6x2-inch panel with three or four buttons on it. This was located at a very convenient place since it was used so frequently. This was mounted on the flat portion of the console just to the right of the pilot. Unfortunately, that was also a convenient place for maps, note pads, sandwiches or coffee. Everything depended on the dials remaining clear. Otherwise, with the slightest jig of the dial, one may be homing on a station far away from the desired station. Oops! One could easily fly into an intervening mountain rather than going toward the expected homing station.

The cockpit between the two pilots is a busy place during flight. Other crew members crouch there while talking to the pilot, the mechanic often collaborates with the pilot, more eyes are needed to watch out the window or windscreen or to help monitor the instruments.

During this flight, the aircraft had intended to pass from South Korea to just north of Beijing heading toward Chifeng, then toward Harbin, then a loop back past Fushun to Zhuanghe on the Gulf of Liaodong, past North Korea and to the starting point. They had passed over Bo Hai Gulf outward and the Korea Bay inward. At least, this was the flight plan.

This was a winter month with very intense weather that was well known for the Gulf of Liaodong and its peninsula reaching southward to Dalian.

It was known that this winter was especially cruel. The jet stream wavered well off its normal path and that gave a dangerous aspect to all weather forecasts.

The crew had let their imagination drift and they had not been totally concentrated at the end of a long, stressful flight. Further, it took them a while to correct their navigation so they really knew where they were. It appeared that they had flown south from Fushan down along the Liaodong peninsula. They had checked the weather there before they left and were knowledgeable of that area.

In winter, rapidly moving cold fronts from north to south frequently pass the region causing ice formation and rapid changes in ice conditions. This they had been told. The Liaodong Gulf is normally ice-covered for three months in winter. Usually, the ice is formed in coastal waters and is driven southwards by the winds. The ice pack in the Bohai Sea has strong mobility due to strong tides and the relatively thin ice. The maximum mean tidal range or changes in depth due to tides is about three feet. The velocity range is about 2-3 knots.

Looking ahead, this approximates the weather patterns near the mouth of the Yalu where several small islands jut out into the Yellow Sea. Therefore one could expect unprecedented foul weather and ice in extreme conditions. The crew was aware of these general conditions in winter months.

Jackson was well aware of the vulnerable RDF control panel. He tried to be careful as he leaned over it to talk to the pilot as their flight was toward its end. He then returned to his station and someone else slid in next to the cockpit.

CHAPTER 42

DITCHING

The ice was here, the ice was there;
Lightening streaks were everywhere,
It cracked, groaned, roared and crashed
Yellow Sea noises as the tempest smashed

The wind and rain, were our bane,
Making perilous waves, across the sea:
While snow and ice made us insane,
As lightening cracked, warning us to flee.

Suddenly, the pilot screamed in Chinese, "God Damn! The frequency changed." Then, the pilot continued his scream in English, "What Son-of-a-Bitch changed the RDF frequency".

The plane had been flying only a few hundred feet above the hills. Suddenly it lurched upward. Yet, it was too low and sudden to make much of a change. There were reasonably smooth hills before us. Those in front of the plane were sparsely covered with trees. As the pilot pulled up, the right engine coughed several times and refused to answer the pilot's control for more altitude. They had hit a tree. Had it not been so dark, they could have seen a round semi-circle where the propeller bore a hole in the top of one of the trees. They then flew on. Both the jets had been running during the flight. Now they depended on the two small jets and only one main piston engine. The pilot now paid attention to the propeller engine, nursed it and prayed that everything would work out.

The weather was horrible. It was cold off the Gobi Desert and the plains going up to The Greater Khingan Range. Ice forms in the shallow Korean rivers for months with some sea ice locally for short periods. It changes from year to year. During our flight, we were continually using windshield wipers against the rain and snow and their de-icers.

Our flight continued. The engines held firm so we flew on 3 engines for several hundred miles. Finally, the engines were overburdened. They were incapable of holding us in the air longer. Ice had formed on the airframe beyond its limit. The ice was bothersome to the airfoils but mostly, the heavy weight of the ice passed the point of tolerance.

By this time, the pilot had figured out what was happening. He then knew that the frequency change had caused the problem. He did not know who changed it or how it happened; however, anyone in the cockpit after the last frequency change was a suspect. "God Damn him," they all agreed.

Jackson sighed. The data pointed to him. He was the prime suspect. "How could I have done such a stupid thing," he asked himself.

There was no time for recriminations now. The pilot ordered everyone to their ditching positions. No doubt, we had to land on the water. That is a terrible realization when it is snowing and raining so hard and the wind is practically a typhoon, or on the Atlantic this would be called a hurricane. Jackson had been in his ditching position for some time but he was probably reading a checklist for ditching in the water. He was folded up with his head between his knees. His arms held his legs as he waited for the first jolt. He expected the first to be a terrific chattering that was to be followed by a second that was less intense but stretched in time. He thought, the waves must be high with this wind. However, the pilot thought that the waves were moderate. He prayed we might experience a lessoning of the waves because the winds were attenuated or reduced by the rugged mountains in the area and by the cake ice that had broken into a million pieces.

They hit the water with a thundering crash. Then they popped back into the air. The plane sailed awkwardly while tumbling. One wing fell off with two engines. Bam! They hit the water at an odd angle that tore off the other wing and the tail section. The bow bent over and then folded alongside the main cabin, and then it tore off. This left thousands of wires, hydraulic lines and cables strung between the major pieces of what had been an airplane.

It was a miracle but the pilot bore only minor injuries. In one of those flukes of nature, Jackson walked out of the main deck onto one of the wing roots. He began to run and swim frantically, fearing the gas would explode. He was alone as an escaping crewman.

"Hold on," Jackson thought. "What about the others." He imagined they were all right like him. Unfortunately, that was far from the truth. Jackson went to each in turn. Only the pilot and copilot were alive; the others were dead or were soon to be.

Jackson saw the extremities they were in with blood flowing everywhere. Some looked at him with the frozen eyes of death. There was blood covering mangled organisms as body parts closed down. Their functions were ended. They were needed no more.

The pilot was in serious shape. His legs had been pinned beneath the control panel and appeared helplessly paralyzed. His speech was slurred. He was bleeding badly but the source was not found.

The copilot was in the best condition. He had what appeared to be a broken leg and several very serious cuts and lacerations. He hobbled and favored his right arm but he was mobile and helpful.

The aircraft had been rigged for ditching in icy conditions. That was so unexpected. A lanyard had held a rubber lifeboat with survival things. This ejected from above the wing roots just as it hit the water. There were two rafts, one on each side. Jackson and the copilot lashed the two together and put the pilot, the co-pilot and Jackson into the rafts. There was also a thermal suit. We were thankful for that. We could not survive in icy water for more than a few minutes without some kind of protection. We had tested these suits earlier by putting them on and getting into cold water. This suit is very thin and made of some kind of composite rubber. Yet, one had to be careful with this. The suit was one piece from the toes to the head. There was a pull-string cord around the neck that held the suit fast around the face. There was a tendency for water to leak underneath the tie string. If this happened, the buoyancy diminished and the water was cold. It was desirable for the suit to be watertight.

The copilot was maneuverable and essentially self-sufficient. This allowed Jackson to pull and wrestle the pilot onto the rubber raft as the storm continued to rage.

Both lifeboats had capsized before we could get control of things. In the melee, most of the items aboard were lost or made useless. We would soon be desperately short of food and water. The most desperate need was body heat and insulation so we wrapped ourselves with whatever fabric we could find. Even if the fabric were wet, it would help serve as insulation to keep our body heat from seeping away.

Jackson knew they had to abandon the dead crew except for us three. They had no way of converting the sea ice to fresh water so that would soon be a worry.

The pilot was in a sorry state. His legs were paralyzed and bloody. Gashes could be seen above and below the knees. He had very limited mobility. His eyes were continually glazed over as if he could see somewhere else, to another place far away.

The fog had been totally blanketing for all this time. The snow, ice and fog eliminated any chance of us being found on our small rubber raft. Days or weeks may intervene.

CHAPTER 43

STORM BLAST

The air was filled with fog and snow,
The waves were thunderous high;
Freezing rain swamped us and did grow
As lightening filled the darkened sky.

Day after day, we drifted away
The currents our only motion;
As if we were an aimless ship
Drifting on a giclee ocean.

By the second day, one recognized the pilot was far more injured than we thought. He was strung out and making all kinds of sounds and noises that made no sense. Things reached a climax. Jackson was tending to the copilot when he heard the pilot fumbling and pointing to the second raft. "Ugh, Ugh," was about all we heard. "By the time we looked around, the pilot had crawled overboard. Without a word he bobbled up and down a couple of times and then seemed to just give up. His arms were above the water. Then they slowly sank and did not come up."

Jackson jumped overboard the best he could and tried to see by dipping his head below the water. It was no use. The pilot never came up and he was not seen again. The pilot was gone.

In his imagination, Jackson thought the copilot assigned a little blame on him for not being able to save the pilot. It made no sense. But had Jackson been more responsive, surely he could have saved the pilot. He sat in my end of the lifeboat and brooded. It was bad enough to lose faith in yourself but even worse to think your mate held you responsible in some small way for the drowning. Remember, they were not so coherent, the wind and waves were killers and the crewmates were dead and mangled. It was a little bit of hell. How could he not have been off his game?

Although he was brooding, Jackson could not help but notice the copilot was slowing every day. After the forth or a number of days, he was sick and throwing up with coughing, chills, fevers and diarrhea. Jackson tried his best to help him for a very long time but he still faded. Afterwards, *the copilot didn't seem to care anymore.*

Jackson thought, "*Well, that's his problem. I can't do everything for everybody. And besides, do I not have chills and fevers? How about my diarrhea?*

The copilot did not seem to care anymore. Our faces were a mess with blistering and peelings. The sun was not doing this to us. It was the howling wind. It caused sores, worked on our insides and orifices. It was clear as clear could be. There was a curse on all of us. The gods disfavored what we had done. Or, perhaps, the gods disfavored their failure to succeed. Whatever it was, there was turmoil, and we were dying one by one.

There was little chance of help. The plane had flown at a low altitude to avoid radar or other sightings. Then, the major storm was continuing to sweep the South Korean coast. Snow, fog and ice flew through the sea and attacked all within their purview. We had lashed ourselves to the life rafts. The penetration into China of our flight may have been so successful that no one knew they were there. That would mean the North Koreans, Chinese, Russians or Japanese were unaware and could not help them.

After a number of days — was it days or weeks — both the copilot and Jackson were in sorry straits. Jackson watched the copilot try to do simple tasks but he could not. Finally, he gave up the struggle. Again, just like the pilot, he slid overboard with hardly a splash. No word nor breath came from his mouth. Life had become too much for him to bear. He silently slipped beneath the waves. The copilot was gone.

By this time, Jackson didn't much care. It was all he could do to hold his own. It was hell just to lie in the bottom of the rubber boat. His mind wandered. He saw the rungs of hell and it was just another ladder in Dante's Inferno.

A flash occurred to him. It was a scene of some movie, probably a cheap flick or a film noir as some call it. He remembered this scene from the movie. One imagined he was one of the Roman Gods looking down through a hole in the clouds. They were rating the Gods' performance and perception of what was happening. The imagined scenes did not hold together and soon roiled into a sky full of clouds. He lost the whole image and could not find any coherence. He sank into unconsciousness.

CHAPTER 44

THE ALBATROSS

A sea vulture came across our raft,
It flew over us, through the night;
Hovering o'er us, like a caring soul,
Had it come to change our plight?

God save me, and my crew, I cursed,
From the ills, that force us to flee,
Why accuse me so? With one sharp burst,
I choked, this vulture of the sea.

An Albatross had been following the raft for what seemed like days. It finally came close enough that Jackson could try to capture it.

He grabbed the Albatross, or was it a sea vulture, that insisted on circling the boat—nay, by this time, the bird was conjuring up the curse. Jackson's mind could conceive all sorts of conspiracies. Even the gods plotted against him. He was hungry. He thought back to his childhood. He had loved large birds. He watched them and dreamed with them. He knew a lot about birds.

As it turned out, he could not eat the bird. He stripped off the feathers and broke off a leg. Try as he may, it made him sick to taste it. Just the smell of raw flesh was overpowering. He told himself he had to eat since only death awaited the non-eater. He tried.

Sooner or later, another bird circled his little boat. Jackson was fortunate enough to grab him by the legs. He ate him like a savage. Apparently, the first bird carried great curses and baggage with him, like the Albatross. In his mind, the first bird was cursed. The second bird was not so cursed and was edible.

CHAPTER 45

THE CURSE

A ghastly thing, had I done,
And a curse would be my woe:
For all concurred, I had killed the bird
That kept our curse in tow,
And then I prayed, for the bird I slayed,
That held our curse in tow.

The ocean roared, the waves were high,
The wind screamed, through the night,
The storm seemed to intensify
And escalate our terrible plight.

"Give me water." Jackson had inhaled so much salt water by this time that his body wanted to reject any liquid; and food too. Jackson Lee's insides breathed powder and it was so dry. There was no moisture. His lips were running blood and were mighty swollen. He bit his tongue and it hurt so. He chewed it in his torturous sleep. It swelled and re-swelled. The skin was flaking off his face and head. Oh God, he moaned. Please give me some water. But it had to be salt-free. Somewhere he had read that the acid content of urine was such that one or two cycles through the body could be tolerated. He was mindful of this in his fevered state. He drank his own urine. It was revolting but it did moisten his system a bit. The urine composition was below the maximum that could be tolerated by the body. Thus, the second run-through could capture a small amount of water that could be processed by his organs. This would be even less for a third pass-through. The process would drive Jackson crazy. Even now, he was a little mad.

The process drove him even on the first pass to revulsion. He began over time to hallucinate. Reality and truth were just words, not even a process nor an idea.

Jackson rolled up like his womb experience. He pulled his knees up and wrapped his arms around them. He dug as deep as he could into a corner of the little rubber raft, and wished for death. He knew this could be fatal. His life didn't seem to matter.

CHAPTER 46

THE CREW KNOWS; A WEARY TIME

Looking westward, I espied
A something; coming fast,
A sail neared us, and I cried
T'is Zombie Woman, at the mast.
Is she and Death all the crew?
Can there be so few; in the crew?

The gossamer boat, came close up,
And the two, were casting die;
"The game is done! I've won! I've won!"
Her screaming voice did cry.

It was many, many days, or was it weeks, from the start. Jackson was beginning to see everything of his life differently. He was beginning to hallucinate. My God! Had he really jeopardized everyone in the crew by a careless detail? Was it just a careless trivia?

He stayed in a terrible state of mind for a long time. Why have we not been found? He was beginning to care less whether that happened or not. It really was a weary time.

A zombie appeared to Jackson. In fact, she was known as Zombie Death, a vulture of the sea. Zombies are un-dead creatures, typically known as mindless, re-animated human corpses. A zombie is a dead corpse re-animated by magic. She may be any gender and may be quite brilliant and relentless in discharging her mission.

As part of Jackson's hallucination, the crew was there. They were of their right minds but their minds did not favor him. Finally, they began to talk coherently and show their votes and preferences. This was devastating to Jackson since he was nowhere favored but was known as the man who had killed the Albatross.

Finally, the crew cursed Jackson. They shouted one by one. He did not know the pilot had told them all. Now they cursed and raised their finger to him. It was an awful lot for he had done his very best. They shoved and shouted. They cursed and called him names. Those were so foul and wretched that he took them to his grave.

But that was not the worst part. They then fell back to their zombie state. Their faces were torn off about their skull and blood flowed everywhere. In their zombie state they chased him and clutched for him as he ran. Their clothes were dirty and ragged. Their nails were long and ghoulish. They seemed half-men that lurched from the graves of the stone-strewn graveyard. It was like a movie, a very bad movie, a film noir, or a zombie movie, straight out.

In this instance, they really were as mad as Alice's mad hatter but these had ill intent. They had been robbed of life and their resentment was high. Their deaths had been so sudden; there was little time for analysis. Thus, they reacted as logically as possible and that was a form of madness.

CHAPTER 47

AM I DYING? EXTREMITY

Fresh water is our salvation,
We cannot do without,
Salt water; our temptation
And that was all about.

The ocean seemed to moan and groan.
How could it ever be?
Fiendish creatures, crawled about
And slime oozed from the sea.

Jackson was nearing exhaustion but from little or no work. He had lain in the bottom of the boat for days. Thank God for the fog and sleet, he thought. It hid us for the time being. The second bird had kept him alive, he thought. The birds must have provided some water since he seemed to lose many of his symptoms. Yet, there was a gnawing within him that could not be slackened. Way down somewhere, it growled and bit into his organs.

On the one hand he was free since all the crew was dead, and dead men carry no tales, it is said. Only one person knew and that was him. One of them had knocked the radio off frequency and caused the crash and dead flyers.

Jackson Lee did not know it then but he was as free as he would ever be. His accuser was himself, an implacable foe.

He thought that the tale died with the crew but it was not so. There was continuous communication, using their equipment, if the crew chose to use it. With something as important as the nipping of the tree, the pilot probably reported it immediately.

What about the suspicion about the cause of the crash? It is also probable that this would also have been reported. At any rate, it was later confirmed that the whole crew knew the cause of the crash, and further, many others in Taiwan knew it. Jackson could not contain the secret. He was probably responsible; there was no escape.

CHAPTER 48

THE CURSE OF DEATH

She won the curse, the souls flew by,
Each crewman's lot was bliss or woe!
And as each passed, with blood-shot eye,
He cursed me, his wrath to show.

The souls of the crew flew by me,
Each lashed out, with a sigh,
Each turned to me, as they did flee,
And cursed me, eye to eye.

Many fear the curse of death. It can be quick or it can be prolonged. With some, there is pain unbearable. To those prolonged, how merciful is death to take one in a moment? There is little pain or misery. One is taken in the night as the reaper makes his call. For those in misery, this can be a blessing. No one promised life forever. Three score and ten; that was the promise. We all must go, the sane and the mad. Yet, we cling. Our bodies reject the omen. Live on, live on, we understand. Our life is such a short window in the cycle. We must cling; we must follow our dictate to live on. Even in death, we are not the master. The dictate reigns. We suffer and suffer, but live on we must. Why are some lives cut short in an instant? These are far less than promised. Teens are cut short, their promise never answered.

It becomes a voodoo life, forever after. Magic controls us. At least, the rules of chance seem to hold us hostage. They seem to enslave the re-animated bodies, this simply can't be all there is. Is that all there is? We clutch at life; we'll take it in any form. Is it really Jackson Lee, or is it a voodoo doll? Is that all there is?

Jackson lay rolled up in a corner. The waves rocked his rubber boat in that Yellow Sea. The Albatross foretold the crew of miseries that were yet to be. Jackson would go mad.

CHAPTER 49

THE PROPHET IS MAD

Our window on life is short, as should be
It's three score and ten, don't you see?
That's time to do amazing things,
As dreams are the lift, 'neath our wings.

Peace and love, are our expected return,
The universal dreams of our ambition,
This is what, we are sent here to learn,
The reason for us, and our earthly mission.

Jackson Lee remained in his womb position for days. Or was it weeks? Finally, the weather broke. The surface ice had broken up. The wind became calmed. The waves calmed themselves. Now was a dangerous time but he hardly cared. Was he in North or South Korea? That made all the difference in the world but he cared not.

Finally, a South Korean Coast Guard boat pulled alongside the rubber rafts. They were partially deflated and lying low in the water. The smell was terrible, even with the periodic submersion due to weather. The South Koreans seemed to know who he was but were surprised there was only the one survivor. They did not question him too much. They promised that would occur when they got back to base.

Jackson was in a terrible state. He was deathly sick. His skin was turning a yellowish-green. He could barely talk. He sounded almost incoherent. His words did not fit the circumstances. The Coast Guard wrapped him in warm blankets and tried to get water into him. He just spewed out the vomit. There was precious little to worry about. He shook volcanically and kept having chills and fevers.

The boat headed for shore. In this case, it was a small island on the northwest corner of South Korea. The run to shore had taken several hours.

When they arrived, there were ambulances and helicopters waiting. A different group took over and started to call the shots. Soon, the South Korea sailors left and Jackson was in the hands of these new people. Clearly, the new people were part of a black program. Even some of them were civilian clothes. Soon, Jackson was put on a stretcher in the ambulance. It was only a short ride then to a private jet aircraft where he was bundled aboard. The plane flew for an hour or so. There was a large contingency of people and officials when they landed and taxied to the apron of a hangar. The doors of the hangar were open and the plane taxied inside. He was back in the fold, near the fold he belonged to.

There were many Americans in this group at the airport as well as Chinese and South Koreans. They hustled him inside the offices and tried to question him. They soon recognized that this was futile now, he was incoherent and declining fast. Apparently, they recognized this to the extent that arrangements were made to keep him in the hospital here for at least a week. Naturally, the Chinese on Taiwan were anxious to get him back.

He wallowed in his bedding; half conscious from his fray. The world was against him, he thought. He knew he could not return. For some reason he was sent here and surely there was some mission. But these encompassing thoughts were beyond him. He had been cursed by fate under the name of Zombie Death. He was sure that he would never be free from this curse. Ah, woe is me. The good times are over. His stay was a burden and a curse on anyone befriending him. Mad as a hatter was he, a frail and dying creature with a curse hung round his neck. The Albatross passed on the curse; he would never be free.

Jackson, however, was sane enough to recognize some of the conclusions being passed down. He was not totally lost in what was happening, just selective in what he could understand. He did hear the gist of the proceedings. He then held forth in soliloquy. He recognized Zombie Death, Death, the Albatross, himself and others. The exercise had not been in vain.

Jackson was slowly passing into insanity. Never again would he be free.

CHAPTER 50

JACKSON'S RETURN TO CALIFORNIA

Life is the ultimate creation;
Sweet love, the Godly gift to all,
Joy, laughter, jubilation
For all there is, a heavenly call.

First we crawl, and then we walk;
At last we walk, and then we crawl,
Birth, childhood, maturity, and death
T'is the cycle of life, applied to us all

After weeks in the South Korean hospital, Jackson Lee was finally released. The American had made provisions for his return to Taiwan. It was a joyous day for many, all his friends.

Finally, it had become clear to all that he could not carry out tasks assigned to him. He had to be replaced and returned to Los Angeles. He could carry on with some of the tasks assigned to him.

Meanwhile, Malinda tended to him and kept him productive the best she could. In the end, it was clear that he could not continue. The true Jackson did not return from Taiwan to Los Angeles.

He became a thorn in the side of the project. He was unable to carry on the tasks assigned to him. Finally, it became clear to all that he had to be replaced. This was soon done.

The true Jackson did not return from Taiwan to Los Angeles. He was almost the antithesis of the Jackson that flew to the Yellow Sea. Gone were the carefree days. Gone was the fun-loving youth. He now appeared as an old man. His hair had even become powdered; he had a touch of white. He was cantankerous and unyielding in any discussion. He often struck out into an argument that did not relate to the conversation. Then, he would stop in mid-sentence as if held by the throat. He often retreated into his own world. His eyes looked skyward, what did he see? Many of his friends talked to him about this, counseled him, and tried to be his friend. He would have none of it; he remained prickly and did irrational things. He started throwing things when he could not have his way. He demanded pain killer drugs. He became addicted. He fell deeper and deeper into this addiction, into his despair. It appeared that his brain had been rewired. Some of the signals went the right way but not all. Much of his brain was not really available to him.

He became a manic-depressive. He would burst out laughing even when there was no reason. He laughed uproariously; looking where only his eyes could see.

Afterwards, he would begin to cry. There were monster tears. His face would be awash. It broke one's heart to hear that wailing. He beat his breast like a lost child.

All agreed. He had become a lost soul. He was finished as far as his usefulness on the project. He must be institutionalized.

Yet, he had moments of clarity, even sometimes for days and weeks. He recognized his own condition. He bemoaned it and put his things in order. He certainly would not last. Everyone expected something to happen to him. He sought dark corners and could see no sunlight. He was a lost soul that had paid the price.

Jackson slowly seemed to withdraw from his friends and society in general. He had long conversations with himself and was surprised to some extent of what he had to say. He felt like he was being persecuted and that the world was against him. Others were taking advantage of him.

This was nonsense, of course. His mind was playing tricks on him.

There were times that he was perfectly lucid. In others, he was bad and deteriorating.

There were times he did not want to eat. He also sometimes wanted to sleep all day. Even that did not satisfy him. He really wanted to sleep all the time. His schedules were all adrift.

His friends tried to talk to him and reason with him but this was a lost cause.

There was one overpowering emotion that kept haunting him. He could not explain this. It was a feeling of impending doom. This was not the ordinary depression and blackness one often feels when they are down. It is an ultimate doom.

"We try to reason with him and change his attitude." Eliot was talking to Malinda. She was a consoling influence.

After Jackson left for the orient, she kept flying as an airline stewardess. She had been wounded, seriously wounded, in the airline crash in Palm Springs. Yet, she carried on.

Malinda had always been an empathetic and caring person. She was a mothering-type; she cared for everyone. Even strangers received a kind word from her. She felt sorry for animals and fed even the wayward puppy or kitten that came her way.

Perhaps, the best thing that could happen to both of them was their friendship. This was rekindled when Jackson returned to Los Angeles. Malinda ignored her ills as she continued to recoup her strength from her wounds.

She took him in as if he were a wounded puppy. Their friendship had developed into love on her part before he left for Taiwan. It was rekindled when he returned. She tried so hard to reach him but she could not. He was having his demons and that took precedence.

Jackson carried the burden of the aircraft crew that he had unwittingly cursed to death. He remembered the pilot and silently mourned him. He also had met the pilots' families. This all weighed heavily on Jackson.

It was not only that burden but there was the burden of the whole crew. And one cannot limit the grief there. Each of the crew had a family. They also had to be mourned. He often imagined his work family. He loved his sister Charlotte. He liked his brother Vic. Bianca Bruno was a shining light for him. And Malinda? She was his ultimate love. He even liked Charlie. We had all gone through so much. But I can't stand this life of misery, he admitted.

Jackson could not explain or would not explain any of this to his friends. He became sullen and morose.

Malinda tried to console him, bring him out of his quandary. But she could not.

Jackson became suicidal. He was reaching beyond normal relations with Malinda and with others that had been his best friends. Finally, Jackson could bear it no longer. He became irrational and beyond this world.

Mostly, he continued to sense impending doom.

This all foreshadowed what was about to happen.

CHAPTER 51

CURSE AND REMORSE

I swam, and I swam some more,
Beyond the point of no return;
Peace, let me have peace, I prayed
For that I do solemnly yearn.

But I say farewell, farewell,
And this I tell, in truth to you;
This curse has made, my life a hell
So I must bid, farewell and adieu.

The End

www.ingramcontent.com/pod-product-compliance
Lightning Source LLC
Chambersburg PA
CBHW070643310726
48982CB00001B/388
9781604149470